LANA LEA

Atomic Goddess: Isis Reborn

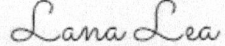

First edition

ISBN: 978-0-6482479-3-7

This book was professionally typeset on Reedsy. Find out more at reedsy.com

This is for everyone who has supported my journey as an author – the teachers, the librarians, the fellow-writers and artists, the friends, the family. And most of all, for the friends and family that are my writing group. You guys rocken roll!

And also my two beautiful purr-kids, Mojo and Arwen, and my husband Paul, who kept the coffee coming. (Yup, some things about me are that predictable)

"You've always had the power, my dear. You just had to learn it for yourself."

Glinda, The Wizard of Oz

Contents

1

Something In The Air

1. Wednesday, 15th October, 1969 – Jacksonville, Florida

So the whole thing started when Gabriel Serapis – love of my life and tall, dark and handsome to my short, dark and average – got himself shot and left for dead right before my eyes...

Yeek, enough of the melodramatics already.

It was early evening in downtown Jacksonville. We'd just been to Tallahassee, at the moratorium to end the Vietnam war – us being such everlovin' peacenik doves – and had driven home high on hope and optimism, singing Give Peace A Chance, Get Together, People Gotta Be Free, and every other relevant song we could think of. It was already dark when we arrived, so we ate a takeout dinner amongst the rainbow of neon lights, then chilled at our favourite bar.

We must've made everyone so sick, holding hands and gazing into each other's eyes while 'Girl from Ipanema' drifted languidly through the smoky air. For once, I didn't care. I was with my favourite person in the whole world. Someone who laughed at my wise cracks and accepted me just as I was, who's melting brown eyes I could get lost in so easily.

We finished our Mai Tais and Gabe went to the bar for another round. That's when the trouble started, with a loud southern drawl.

"Hey! You pushin' in, raghead?"

I looked up to see Gabe stumbling backwards out of the crush around the bar. A great bear of a man wearing a cowboy shirt, blue jeans and fancy western boots loomed nearby, thrusting a ruddy face and sandy moustache at him. I couldn't hear Gabe's reply, but knowing him, it was most likely something oh-so polite and, of course, completely useless.

I leapt up and hurried towards them. If this good ol' boy was going to cause trouble, he'd have to cause it for both of us.

"What you say? You wanna drink? Ain't they got none back in ol' Araby?"

The guy laughed heartily. Gabe faltered, wearing that uptight smile he resorted

to when nervous. As I reached him, he tried to steer me away.

"Yeah, go back where you came from, camel jockey!" the man sneered.

I was incensed.

"What the hell's his hang up?"

"He's spoiling for a fight, I guess. Let's just split, okay?"

"No way! That's not cool!"

"Yeah, I know. I'm a real flake, aren't I Ange?"

"So just hang tough and tune him out."

"But he's enormous! And he's fixing to trash me, in case you hadn't noticed."

I glanced at the guy. He'd leaned back against the bar, crushing a massive fist into his other hand as he eyeballed us. I had to concede that Gabe had a point.

"Well, call the fuzz!"

"Now who's uncool? Look, let's just cut out and find somewhere else to hang, okay?"

My face burned. I should've just chilled out, but I was so hacked off I couldn't resist a parting shot. As Gabe turned for the door, I narrowed my eyes on the man and flipped him the bird.

"Eat dirt, you sheet-wearing redneck scuzz!"

The smirk slid off his face as it flushed a darker shade of beetroot. He huffed indignantly, then came at us bellowing like a wounded bull. Man, we bailed out of there big time – well, Gabe bailed, dragging me along with him. I was plenty ticked off that he chose to run instead of putting his muscles to good use. And I ached to have another go at the guy.

Until I noticed he had friends. Three other checked-shirt-blue-jean-boot-wearing hicks with identical expressions and bad attitudes were right on his heels. So you know what? If I'd had any idea a Convention of Racist Rednecks had convened in Jacksonville that week, I sure would've suggested we did our drinking at home.

We hurtled through the door to the parking lot. Our pursuers were momentarily held up as the door swung shut in their faces, giving us enough time to get into Gabe's flame-red Pontiac Firebird, which he'd jokingly dubbed The Phoenix. As he fumbled to get the key into the ignition, the four men burst from the building and strode towards us.

"Far out!" Gabe said, groping around on the floor.

"What?"

"Keys went south…"

He stiffened as the Chief Redneck strutted up to the car with something black and metallic in his hand. He used it to smash the driver's side window, sending chips and shards of glass everywhere.

"Have you flipped your wig?" Gabe cried, shielding his face with his arms. "Just cool it, already!"

"Got you now, raghead! And your foul-mouthed bitch!"

He hawked and spat, and time stood still as Gabe and I stared down the barrel of the revolver he levelled at us.

"In the name of Jesus Christ," he intoned, "I'm gonna put you back in your place, you filthy ape!"

"No!" I shrieked.

Noise exploded through the car, echoing thunderously in my skull. Blood spattered everywhere as the bullet smashed into Gabe's head. In the confusion of the moment, explosions seemed to go off all around us. My lungs were sucked dry of air, and I fought to gasp a breath and scream.

Drawing another ragged breath, I tore my seatbelt off so I could try to help Gabe. I'd be damned if I was going to just sit there screaming like some chick in a horror flick while the only real love I'd ever known bled to death.

As I leaned over him, he rasped in a shallow breath, his black hair slick with blood, his eyes pleading. I glanced at the bozo. The man stared back in horrified astonishment. The revolver was now a smoking, twisted wreck, its barrel peeled apart like a banana skin. His fingers still grasped the grip of the gun, but they were blackened and charred, like the flesh had been burned right off them.

One of his cohorts, a short, wizened-looking old fellow with a face like a gnome, whistled to him before disappearing into the shadows at the edge of the parking lot. The other two followed, the injured bozo stumbling after them, clutching his burnt hand.

"Hey!" I called out. "Don't let those guys get away!"

But the couple of bystanders who appeared once it was safe were more concerned about helping me with Gabe than following the men. One ran to ring for an ambulance and the police, whilst another helped me to make Gabe more comfortable and staunch the flow of blood. He'd lost consciousness, and I was desperate to help him.

The rest was a blur – flashing lights, sirens, Gabe being lifted onto a gurney and put in an ambulance. Uniformed officers who picked their way across shattered glass from the shop fronts. A nearby hydrant erupted masses of water into the air, causing fire fighters to struggle as they wrestled it off. Babbling onlookers crowded around, and had to be moved along.

It was so unreal, like I'd been suddenly plucked up and thrust into the Twilight Zone. I barely took it in, and answered the police officer's questions obediently, numbly. They were confused by the large amount of damage to the area, but I knew only of what had happened inside the car. Then I was whisked off to the nearest hospital, checked over, and left to sit and wait for the next storm to break.

2.

"Miss Jones?"

I raised my head. It throbbed with the mother of all headaches. I tried to not move it any more than necessary as I met the doctor's eyes through the dark bangs of my bobbed hair.

"Our top surgeon, Doctor Jay Scott, is operating on Mr Serapis. Has his family been informed?"

"Yes," I croaked, thinking back to a call I'd made once I'd hunted down the payphone in the hospital's foyer. "They're chartering a flight down from New York. They should be here very soon."

"It's a really difficult situation," he said. "I'm afraid it could still go either way. Doctor Scott will be able to give you a better idea once he's finished."

I was grateful for the man's compassion. As he walked away, I found I ached for that compassion, for a human touch, anyone's. The feeling hurt inside my ribs, and my eyes burned as tears finally came. A torrent burst out, from a place deep inside that I usually denied existence to.

When I could cry no more, I went back to the payphone to ring my mother. Predictably enough, she wasn't home. So I rang my older sister, Karen, who lived in L.A. with her husband and young son.

Karen and I were tight. We'd been military brats, dragged to various bases around the U.S. by our patriotic elders. Karen made heaps of friends during our fragmented childhood, and kept a list of pen pals from all over the States. I didn't. Playing nice with a different set of children every couple of years did zilch for my self-esteem and sense of stability, and I'd kept mostly to myself.

Not much had changed. Karen had always been the anchor in my messy life – part bigger sister, part mother, and best buddy. Everyone, everywhere we went, loved her. I could've been real jealous and torn-up over that, but I loved her too.

Karen answered the phone on the third ring. I nearly teared

up again when I heard her voice. Then I told her the news.

"Oh no!" she gasped. "Is he – is he..."

"They're operating now to get the bullet out," I quavered, fighting to keep control. "I'm so scared, Karen! I don't wanna lose him!"

"Oh Ange... Do you want me to fly over?"

A little flame of hope leapt up in my heart. Karen was the one person who could truly soothe me, who I could talk to about anything. But I knew she was going through a bad patch with her husband, Eric, so it seemed best to swallow down that flame of hope and be practical.

"Gee, I'd love that. But don't worry – I'm gonna ask Mama. Besides, I wouldn't want to cause any problems between you and Eric."

"No, it's okay. We're doing great, honestly."

I bit my tongue. What I thought of Eric had long ago crossed the border from simple dislike to plain contempt based on certain truths about his character. However, I couldn't bear to hurt Karen by making her the meat in a hostile sandwich. And I was truly concerned that her marriage wouldn't last a weekend of them being on opposite sides of L.A., let alone a week or more on opposite sides of the continent.

"Right, no biggie, then. And I'm sorry to get all heavy on you. I'll be fine once Mama gets here."

"If you're sure. But if anything else happens, you don't get a say. Newt and I will be over there on the first flight."

I couldn't help but grin. When Karen and Eric named their son Newton, I'd coined the shorter version of his name. Karen thought it was cute. Eric didn't.

"Okay," I conceded. "Karen... you're the best sis ever!"

I returned to the waiting room and sat down, trying not

to look at the spots of blood on my jeans and shirt. Gabe's blood. I'd already visited the hospital bathroom and washed my hands and arms, but I still longed to scrub myself clean under a steaming hot shower with tonnes of medicated soap and a stiff brush.

Doubts bombarded me as I thought back over the night's events. Was all of this mess my fault? If I'd just left like Gabe wanted to instead of getting tee'd off and hurling insults at the bozo, would we now be blissfully asleep in our bed? Or had the guy been determined to make trouble for us no matter what?

I wished I'd told Karen my thoughts. But I was scared. Voicing my doubts would make them more real, and then I'd have to face them openly. And without Karen actually by my side, I wasn't sure I could handle where that might take me.

"Angela?"

A tearful voice echoed down the corridor, and I looked up. I'd never liked my full first name, and normally encouraged people to just call me Ange. On pain of death. But I figured this was an exception I had to make.

Gabe's family moved towards me as if in a dream. His parents, originally from Egypt but now citizens of the United States, his sister and brother, all wore the same haunted, half-dazed expression.

This was going to be a serious downer.

"Mrs Serapis," I replied, and stood up.

Zahra Serapis took my hands, fresh tears running down her face. Usually the trimmest and best-dressed of women, her tailored beige pant suit was crinkled from the flight, something as out-of-place as her current lack of make-up and jewellery.

"Tell us everything," she pleaded as we sank onto the chairs lining the corridor.

Her husband, Abasi, daughter Sagira and eldest son, Adio, also sat. I hesitated as I got a closer look at them all.

Abasi looked bone weary, like he hadn't slept in days instead of the three hours since my phone call. Adio's face was a mixture of concern and anger, and, I thought as I met his dark eyes, barely concealed fear. Sagira's eyes were red and swollen from crying, but otherwise she looked like a fashion model in her short designer Rajah dress and flipped bob.

"Gabe and I were out having a drink," I started.

"Alcohol," Adio muttered with distaste.

"Hey, cool it, okay? It was just a couple of little drinks to relax. Well, this guy started making trouble for Gabe, so we left. He followed us out to the car park and – shot Gabe in the head."

Zahra and Sagira cried out.

"But why?" Abasi croaked.

I hated to tell them it was an act of racism. I never was the most tactful person. I tried to put it delicately.

"He thought Gabe wasn't – well, American enough to share a bar with him."

Zahra fell against her husband, sobbing loudly. Yup, that's me, delicate to the end. I sighed, and noticed the mutinous look on Adio's face.

"Yeah, crazy isn't it?" I said. "I'd never even seen that guy around here before. I sure hope the police caught up with him."

Adio looked away. Tears slid down Abasi's face as he held Zahra. Sagira sobbed against her father's shoulder. I felt terrible.

"The surgeon should be here soon to tell us how the operation went," I said, hoping that would help.

The only change was that Adio got up to pace the corridor. *Too proud to cry*, I thought, trying to admire his strength. But I couldn't quite pull it off. There was something about Adio that left me cold.

No one felt like small talk after that. We sat in silence, waiting for news in the kind of stunned shock that I remembered happening after President Kennedy was assassinated. As we waited, I couldn't help but think about the relationship that meant most to me in my life.

Gabe and I had met just over a year before, when I started work at the Jacksonville Veterinary Clinic as an animal nurse. Gabe had been there for a year, after studying and working as a junior vet in California. As soon as we laid eyes on each other, I felt an incredible spark of attraction. And he felt it too, 'cos we'd enjoyed every moment of each other's company since.

With our complimentary career paths, it felt like we were fated to meet. I'd made the decision before finishing Junior High that I wanted to work with animals rather than with people. By then I'd reached the conclusion that most humans had rather less to recommend them than the average cat or dog.

And by the time I started work at the clinic, I was already keen to return to college to study ethology, the field of animal behaviour. I started to get a reputation as a bit of an animal psychologist...

Don't laugh.

There are so many sweet, innocent animals who've been

totally screwed up by their owners. I informed the more ignorant of them that overfeeding Poopsy is not good for her physical or mental well-being, or that locking great big Growler in a tiny yard all day with no mental stimulation or exercise makes him aggressive, or that Fluffy pees on your cushions because she doesn't like your current squeeze.

Come to think of it, I often don't either. Animals are so smart.

I found myself touching my pendant as I thought about Gabe. Besides our careers, we shared an interest in Egypt, as we both had Egyptian heritage. On our recent one year anniversary, we'd bought each other gifts that signified our bond. I'd given Gabe a golden ankh, which symbolises life, and wasn't radically different to the little gold cross he'd worn when we first met. The pendant he gave me was a red jasper tyet, which looks similar to an ankh but with the arms folded down.

"It's also called the knot of Isis," he'd said as he fastened the leather cord around my neck. "So I couldn't think of anything more appropriate..."

He turned me around and kissed my forehead.

"...because you are my goddess..."

It all seemed so sappy and overly romantic now, in the light of what had just happened. I closed my eyes to pray – to I don't know what god or goddess – that Gabe would make it through the operation alive.

3.

"Ange?"

I awoke as Sagira touched my shoulder. She looked impossibly fresh, her shiny dark flipped bob brushed and her dress neat. I marvelled at her and wondered briefly what sort of mess I looked like in my blood-spotted jeans and knit tee-shirt.

Doctor Scott approached, accompanied by another surgeon who had assisted him. The dark circles under his eyes gave him the air of a man who had just spent the evening engaged in making life-and-death decisions instead of sleeping.

"It may be touch and go for a while," he said wearily, brushing a hand over the grey haze of stubble on his chin. "Luckily, the bullet didn't penetrate very far because of the shallow angle of entry. But Gabriel fell into a coma while we worked on him, and we can't say when he'll regain consciousness. Hopefully while he sleeps, his brain will be busy repairing itself."

"So he'll recover?" Abasi asked hopefully.

Doctor Scott paused.

"The surgery itself went well," he said, "but Gabe has some damage that only time can heal. He'll likely remain stable while he's in a coma, but I think you should prepare yourselves for the possibility that he may not wake up, or that there may be permanent damage when he does."

Zahra sobbed against Abasi's chest, and he held her tightly as he stared at the surgeon in horror. Sagira hugged them both, her tears flowing freely, and I found myself continuously swallowing a stubborn lump in my throat. Adio alone had no reaction, beyond a tightening of his jaw.

Strangely enough, I didn't feel grief any more, although I was aware of it lurking close to the surface. Oh no. What I felt more than anything at this news was anger – pure, red-hot, totally righteous anger. Like, how could this freakin' happen?

How could someone just walk up to another person and shoot to kill, based on nothing more than skin colour! What was wrong with the world? This was America, God damn it! Things like this simply shouldn't happen.

But they did. All the time. The news headlines constantly screamed at us that there were more murders in Jacksonville than anywhere else in Florida. Not to mention all the violence that had sprouted from student protests, civil right's extremists, and pretty much anyone with a militant attitude and an axe to grind, despite the example set by people like Doctor King. But then, look what had happened to him. It was enough to make you wonder if maybe the hippies were onto something after all.

Thoughts tumbled through my head as I comforted Sagira. Was religion to blame? The guy had cited Jesus as he aimed the gun at Gabe. Such an irony – if only he'd asked, he would have found that Gabe, named for one of the most famous angels, had been brought up in a Christian household.

Or perhaps he only used religion as an excuse to air his prejudices, and a convenient cover to conceal his real beliefs. Plenty of people did, especially in the south. Maybe he wasn't a Christian at all. My brain was scrambled just thinking about it, but I had to understand.

I compared it to animal behaviour. If you mistreat a dog or cat for long enough, eventually it will bite. Maybe not you, the abuser, but some innocent party. So perhaps this loser had been raised in a household where he was abused, or had witnessed his family abusing others and getting away with it. But that still wasn't a reason to gun an innocent person down!

These thoughts swirled around my head long after Doctor Scott had left. He'd reassured us that Gabe's prognosis looked hopeful, and that he was receiving the best care available.

The police found me again, though it was close to midnight by then, and asked some more questions, hoping I'd seen something to explain the shattered glass and exploding fire hydrant. I told them I hadn't, and they eventually left, promising, like General MacArthur, that they would return.

After a while we were allowed into Gabe's private room for a few minutes, to watch his chest rise and fall with the pumping of the ventilator as he slept. His head was heavily bandaged, his usually tanned complexion a sickly grey.

The nurse suggested we go home and try to get some sleep, saying we would be notified if there was any change. But the thought of leaving Gabe was unbearable, so we trooped out and silently took up residence in the nearest waiting room.

4.

I managed to get hold of Mama on the phone around midday on Thursday.

"What do you mean Gabe's hurt?" she drawled in the annoying southern-belle accent she affected to impress her lady friends and church group. "You need to be a little more explicit, darlin'. I'm not a mind-reader, you know."

I took a deep breath, determined not to let her silly mannerisms get to me.

"Mama, Gabe was shot last night. He's in hospital."

"Shot? You mean with a gun?"

"Yes, he was shot in the head. He's had surgery, but now he's in a coma and we don't know what's going to happen."

She gasped. I felt a mean little stab of gratification that she was at last truly concerned.

"Oh darlin, how dreadful! It's just the worse timing imaginable!"

"Timing?"

"Yes, darlin'. You were driving over for the fund-raising ball Friday night, remember? You were both going to stay here, at Niceville, for the weekend."

"Gabe's in a coma and you're worried about us missing some stupid ball? Mama, he could die!"

"Alright, darlin', I get it's serious. You always were so melodramatic, that's all."

"Gee, thanks."

"Well, it's not just any little ol' ball, you know. It's the first time I've been entrusted with such an important function for the S.P.D.A.D.P., and you did promise that you and Gabe would come to support me..."

I sighed. Frankly, I could care less about the wretched ball. Or the even more wretched S.P.D.A.D.P. – supposedly the Society for the Prevention of Discrimination Against Displaced Persons, which provided Mama and her churchy friends ample opportunity to play at being model citizens and mix with people that impressed them – businessmen, politicians, doctors, lawyers – and their wives. Et cetera.

Needless to say, my own charitable instincts differed significantly to Mama's.

"Angela? Are you alright? Have Gabe's parents come down?"

"Yes – his whole family's here. And I need mine."

"Of course darlin'. You must be devastated. I can't come straight away – as you know, I'm the hostess for the ball, and they simply can't do without me. But after that I'll be right over there quicker than you can wink, I promise."

"That's great," I said, unable to muster much enthusiasm. "Okay, let me know what time you'll get here."

"Of course, darlin'. I will."

Somehow the thought of my mother coming didn't provide the comfort I'd hoped for. But then, she'd never exactly generated stability.

My mother – Patsy – was a total ditz. She existed purely for shopping, trips to the hairdresser to maintain her Marilyn Monroe look-a-like bob, her churchy lady friends, and her stupid 'charity'. She'd had a haphazard way of rearing children, and she seemed eternally surprised upon entering our house to find two young girls expecting her to perform magical, motherly duties of which she only seemed to have a vague idea.

Our father, Ronald, had managed to fulfil some of the functions that were so out of Mama's realm of experience, like making pancakes for breakfast on weekends and reading us bedtime stories when we were little. But he wasn't always there because of his work for the air force, and we'd often had to fend for ourselves.

Darkly good looking (and I mean like Omar Sharif) with Egyptian and Welsh heritage, dad had always been steady and reliable – until he came home from 'Nam in '66 after taking a Vietcong bullet in his chest. I didn't even get a chance to see him after he got back. As soon as his wound healed, he took off up north with some free-lovin', flower power chick half his age. We hadn't really talked since.

I was so glad that Gabe had a nice family and stable parents. I respected Zahra Serapis, and was comfortable with the thought of her as my mother-in-law.

We eventually got taxis back to my apartment, stopping on

the way to grab a takeaway Indian banquet for dinner. After eating, I took to the bathroom to wash properly, and spent ages scrubbing myself all over. I finally emerged, tingling and fresh, but still hankering to go back in and scour everything again.

I let Gabe's parents have my double bed — a little luxury I'd invested in on finding myself with a serious boyfriend. I was sure they'd speculate about the things Gabe and I had done there, but I was too tired to care. So we'd had sex. Big deal. (Well, it actually was to me. He was the best thing I could imagine in or out of bed. They could think what they liked.)

Sagira and I squeezed onto the two vintage chaise lounges in my lounge room that I'd inherited from my grandmother. Although they looked super cool with their patterned chintz and gleaming woodwork, they sure were hell to sleep on.

But I suspect we were more comfortable than Adio, who tossed and turned on a nest made up of every cushion I owned, arranged on the loungeroom floor. I'm totally surprised he stuck with us for the whole night instead of finding a comfy room in a motel somewhere.

Friday crawled by. Eating, sleeping, sitting with Gabe, sitting at home. Again, I had to convince the cops — who'd impounded Gabe's car and gone over it with a fine-toothed forensic comb, to no avail — that I knew nothing about the excess damage at the crime scene. I even had to dodge a reporter or two! The Serapis family moved to an up-market motel nearer to the hospital, and we visited Gabe morning and evening.

We sat and talked, and read to him from the daily paper, despite that he seemed oblivious to everything. The doctors had told us to talk to him, as it might stimulate his brain. We tried to sound happy and normal to encourage him to heal, despite the strain we felt. Sometimes Zahra burst into tears, sobbing quietly into her handkerchief. Abasi sat silently and stared into space, and Adio paced, looking sullen. I wondered if he was thinking of revenge. I certainly had.

Sagira and I just tried to relax and be ourselves. It was probably easier for us, as we found hope in doing little things for him. But it wasn't easy to see the rest of his family suffering.

Mama arrived at the Jacksonville International Airport on Saturday morning, complete with a ridiculously huge suitcase. I'm sure I nearly ruptured something as I carried it out to the car and hoisted it into the boot. I imagined it was crammed with a dozen pairs of stilettos, enough clothes to fit out a fashion parade, and a hundred scarves – her latest fad.

As I started the car, the radio bounced to life, screaming out Crosstown Traffic by Jimi Hendrix. Mama immediately switched the channel to find something more mundane. Cue the song I hated more than any other in the whole history of music.

"Oh listen!" Mama said, delighted. "It's your song."

I groaned. 'Angela Jones' by some cat called Johnny Ferguson had come out only a couple of months before my sixteenth birthday. Hearing it made me want to barf. Of course, some people seemed quite happy when a song came out that had their name in it. I was not one of those people. Not just because it used the full version of my first name that I already despised by the time I was two. But to then pair it with my surname seemed a cruel joke. One that some people wouldn't let me forget.

Once home, I related the whole horrible story of Gabe's

shooting again.

"Sweetheart," Mama crooned, swamping me in the stench of her latest designer perfume as she embraced me. "What a terrible thing to happen! I'm so sorry!"

This was an uncharacteristic display of sympathy. She really wasn't the huggy, motherly type, after all. But at that moment it didn't matter. I hugged her too, and found myself holding back tears.

"Thanks Mama. I'm really glad you're here."

"Darlin', why don't you go and wash your face and put on some fresh clothes, and we'll go out shoe shopping. How does that sound?"

I declined. I appreciated that she was making an enormous effort to be sympathetic and cheer me up, but shoe shopping was the last thing I felt like doing. And I had a rotten track record of finding anything I liked, especially in the types of stores that my mother frequented. So she left to 'run some errands', which likely involved the boutique district. I lay down with a throbbing headache and tried not to think.

I was unsuccessful.

A new thought crystallised in my mind. I'd suffered the guilt, grief, and anger, and they still lurked close to the surface. But now I also felt a cold, hard resolve to put things right. There was too much evil in the world. The peaceful neo-pagan spiritual beliefs I'd fostered didn't console me. But they gave me one heck of an idea.

If our supposedly great God was just going to sit by and let people rape, pillage, kill, and steal (and let's face it, we've been doing it for millennia without learning from our mistakes), then maybe it was time to join the counter-culture, give it the boot, and find a new ideal that would support world peace and harmony.

Well, why not? After all, conventional petitioning for divine intervention didn't appear to help, considering the amount of disaster we humans suffered. Granted, we generated much of that disaster ourselves. But what if some other force could be found to bring enlightenment and peace to earth? To act on our behalf and kick some immortal cosmic ass to get things working better?

Considering the countless numbers of gods, goddesses, and god-its worshipped since humankind's origin, my mind boggled over which deity or deities to ask, let alone how to convince them to help us. From what I knew, many had considered humans to be playthings for their amusement. And then there was the creeping question of the karmic consequences for messing with the grand scheme of things on that scale...

I'd just about exhausted my options for this crazy idea and dismissed it when something happened that put it right back before my eyes in glowing neon letters a hundred feet high.

2

She's a Rainbow

1. Saturday 18th October 1969 – Jacksonville, Florida

I'd rung the veterinary clinic the day after the shooting and talked to the owner, who was also the head veterinary surgeon. He kindly allowed me a month's leave, the situation being so traumatic. But as I nursed my throbbing head, he rang to ask if I'd come in and sign some forms. With nothing better to do, I drove to the clinic. And yeah, I switched back to my favourite radio station on the way.

As I left through the waiting room, the scent of patchouli made me look around. I noticed a friend of mine sitting nearby. To be honest, she was difficult not to notice, in faded purple jeans, tie-dyed t-shirt, tonnes of beads and bangles, and a rainbow-coloured scarf holding back a wild tumble of black hair from her golden brown face. It was Amy Zamora, who I'd had natural and spiritual therapies with – until being distracted by Gabe.

I smiled and nodded towards the door. She got up and followed me out to the parking lot.

"Amy!" I said, giving her a hug.

"Ange, honey," she replied, her familiar husky voice sending waves of comfort through me. "Long time no see. How are you?"

"I've been better."

She gazed at me with piercing eyes.

"You've had a tragedy," she said. "Just recently."

"Holy moley! I almost forgot how good you are at that," I said with a laugh.

She flashed a grin.

"You've hardly been to see me in the last year. What's going on with you, girl?"

I sighed.

"It's a long story. Can I come over and tell you some time?"

"Sure, honey. I'm free Wednesday morning, if that suits you."

"That's fine. I'll call before I come."

"You still got my number? Here..."

She took a small stack of cheaply printed handbills from her beaded bag and gave me one.

"Thanks Amy. I'm glad I ran into you. And here of all places!"

"Yeah, my neighbour's cat had kittens and I gave her a lift so the vet could check them out. They should be done any minute."

"Okay, then. See you Wednesday."

We parted company, Amy re-entering the clinic as I got in my car. I felt a lot happier as I eased out into the traffic, especially when Incense & Peppermints came on the radio. The upbeat song lifted my spirits even more – until I got home and returned to my dreary existence of apartment to hospital,

hospital to apartment.

Over the next couple of days, Mama continued her attempt to cheer me up in her ditzy, careless way, taking me out to lunch and shopping, a movie, and for drives in my caddy – really hers and dad's old car, a classic black 1959 Cadillac Eldorado Bairritz convertible they'd passed on to me when I left home. I loved it. In a world where cars were getting more and more compact, it was big, bold, and kind of bad-ass. I thought myself extremely lucky. They'd almost bought an Edsel instead.

Of course, we silently battled over which radio station to listen to every time we got in the car, and I tried not to get too upset when I found myself suffering Frank Sinatra or Bing Crosby. She meant well, but I so wished that Karen was there to really sympathise and give me her support and strength.

And now I had another option. The meeting with Amy played on my mind, especially the super timing of it. She was exactly the person I needed to talk to, and she'd magically, mystically turned up exactly when I needed her.

I read her handbill over and over. Amy taught meditation, and used crystals, tarot, palmistry and herbal medicines. She also gave readings and located missing objects and people. I'd come across others making such claims, but most of them were crazies or outright shuckers. Amy, I knew, was the real McCoy.

Gabe's condition remained the same, and Mama made her excuses and left on Tuesday. I hardly minded, as I was now freed up to visit Amy, and have a good talk with someone I knew would be able to help me straighten out the mess in my head.

Tuesday night I visited the hospital as usual. I hadn't

planned to tell Gabe's family about Amy – what with them being devout Christians, I was sure they'd flip out. But I'd grown close enough to Sagira to wonder how genuine her faith was, as she seemed dismissive of religion.

"So, have you guys found a church to go to here?" I asked as we took the elevator down to the hospital cafeteria for a coffee break.

"We're going to an orthodox church a couple of blocks away," she answered. "It's deadly dull, but it's what my parents and Adio like."

"Not you?"

"I have trouble believing in all that stuff," she said quietly. "They'd be horrified to hear me say that, but it just doesn't ring true to me. The teachings of Jesus – yes, I can accept those, but the rest of it – and the way they preach. It just feels all wrong."

"Hey, me too," I said. "And my parents were only Sunday Christians at best."

"I just don't think you need to go to a church to worship," Sagira continued. "And there's so much they don't talk about – like people with psychic gifts, and nature spirits and auras and stuff. Like they don't exist, or if they do, it's something evil."

"I'm going to see a friend who's a psychic tomorrow. Wanna come?"

Sagira's eyes lit up.

"Yes, I'd love to! But don't say a word to my parents or Adio – they'd kill me!"

2. Wednesday 22nd October, 1969

I picked up Sagira the next morning and drove to Amy's place. It was in a poorer part of town, but the house was well-kept with garden beds and trees around it. Tie-dyed curtains in rainbow colours hung at the windows, and wind chimes swayed and tinkled in the trees. Amy answered at my knock, smiling warmly when she saw me.

"Amy, this is Sagira," I said. "Do you mind if she sits in?"

"That's fine, honey," Amy said, showing us in. "Would you like something to drink?"

The fragrant scent of patchouli followed Amy as she bustled about, getting us glasses of home-made iced herbal tea, and then seating us around a small oval table in her consulting room at the front of the house. I told her about Gabe and the shooting. I told her about the hydrant erupting, the windows shattering, the chaos and confusion, the police, the ambulance, the hospital. I told her about Gabe's family and my mother's visit. And I told her about the crazy thoughts I'd had.

"Hey, you didn't tell me that," Sagira said when I stopped.

"Well, how cracked does it sound?" I asked.

A wry smile crossed Amy's face.

"Hmmm, I always thought there was more to you than meets the eye. I have some suspicions, but I'll need to ask some questions to confirm them."

"Shoot," I said, then groaned at my poor choice of word.

"Okay. But firstly, the stuff that happened when Gabe was shot? I believe that was your psychic awakening, although you didn't know it at the time. Your conscious mind was in shock, but inside, you knew exactly what to do to save yourself and Gabe."

"So why did it go Looney Tunes on me? I only needed to

stop the gun from firing, not turn the place into a demolition site."

"Perhaps you'd never consciously accessed these powers before. You probably had little control over what was happening."

"If I did, I sure would've trashed that guy who shot Gabe."

"Depends on your focus. You were looking straight at the gun, weren't you? So your subconscious mind said 'stop the gun', not 'stop the guy'. And because you didn't know how to control the power yet, you sent out much more than was needed. Has anything like that ever happened to you before? In your childhood, maybe?"

"Sort of," I said. "I always kind of knew when bad weather was coming, or who was about to ring or knock on the door. I used to joke about it with my sister and dad, but not in front of Mama because it kind of freaked her out. I never talked about it at school either, in case the other kids thought I was some kind of freaky weirdo."

"So you felt you had to suppress it much of the time?" Amy asked.

"Yeah, it was a bummer. Then when I hit thirteen, my dad got transferred to the Eglin Air Force Base, and we moved to Niceville, over in the pan handle. God, can you believe that – an actual town actually called Niceville?"

"Sounds... nice," Amy said.

"More like Squaresville," I said with a groan. "It's always the way with these military towns."

"But you must have been proud of him," Sagira said.

"Oh yeah," I said with a mock salute. "Giving selflessly of himself – and his family – to make America a better place."

Sagira giggled, and Amy smiled.

"Anyway," I continued, "at school there I made friends with Jody. We were both outsiders, so we got on really well. We'd huddle between classes and make plans to explore the abandoned house at the edge of town, or decide what we were going to do for Halloween. We had so much fun, until..."

I swallowed. The memories that flooded my mind were not pleasant.

"What happened?" Amy prompted.

"Jody was raped and left for dead. She survived, but... She was never the same again. It was like she turned inwards, and left only a shadow of herself to deal with the outside world."

Pity filled Sagira's eyes as she squeezed my arm.

"Go on," said Amy.

"I was horrified. Sad. Angry. Disgusted. I swore if I ever found the scum who did it, I'd kick his sorry ass to Albuquerque and back and dump his broken body right in Choctawhatchee Bay. Actually, I took a kind of grim delight in imagining myself doing just that."

"I can imagine," said Sagira.

"Yeah, but then a body *was* found, floating in Choctawhatchee Bay right near where we lived. They never identified it – he was pretty beat up and starting to decompose. But I was completely certain that he was the guy. After what I'd imagined doing, I was really freaked out."

"Ah," said Amy, nodding. "That's interesting. Is there anything else?"

"Yeah, that's when I started having those nightmares you helped me with."

"Poor you," said Sagira sympathetically. "What kind of nightmares?"

"Well," I said reluctantly, "I'd be in the dark, looking for

27

someone. When I first had the dreams it was Jody, but later on it switched to Karen. I'd call and call, and finally I'd see her, tied up and screaming for help. I'd go to rescue her, but then I'd be attacked by these shadowy creatures that were controlled by a monster with a weird animal head. I could fight them off for a while, but they always got me in the end."

I shuddered. It'd been a long time since I'd thought about any of this.

"That sounds horrible!" Sagira said with a shudder. "How did you cope?"

"Ha!" I laughed humourlessly. "I just tried to pretend it wasn't happening. Which didn't help. I was getting no sleep, I was upset and snappy with people, and weird stuff happened around me. Like if I was angry a pane of glass would crack, or the plants near me would blacken and shrivel. I didn't understand it, and I didn't like it, but I didn't have a clue what to do about it."

"What did your family make of it all?" Sagira asked.

"Mama thought I was crazy. Sent me to a shrink. Kids at school called me 'the prophet of doom', 'cos I always seemed to know when bad news was coming. And after the body was found, there were rumours I'd somehow been involved in his death. I was shocked anyone would think that, but I didn't bother to disillusion them."

"Unreal!" said Sagira. "That must have been the pits!"

"Yeah," I replied. "It was. But I didn't just sit around, getting unglued. I quit gymnastics and took self-defence lessons. I guess I felt I had a lot to prove. Everyone at school avoided me like the plague and people in town literally crossed the street when they saw me coming. I told myself I didn't care, that I was being realistic and making sure I could protect myself so I'd never become a victim like Jody."

"So how did you cope with all this?" Amy asked.

"Well, I'd always been a tomboy. As soon as we moved to some new town, I'd go out exploring on my bike, and I'd find all the trees that were worth climbing. I was lucky at Niceville – there's a great big old sycamore right in the front yard. So I'd climb up there to get away from everyone, and spend hours just reading."

I chuckled to myself.

"Karen always thought I climbed up too high. She'd order me down, but I'd pull faces at her from way up in the branches, and there was nothing she could do about it. But... after what happened to Jody I'd just hear her out and then skulk off somewhere else to be alone. It's incredible she still loved me after all that."

"That's what sisters are for," Sagira said, squeezing my arm.

"I know, but she had so much to put up with because of me. Like when people said horrid things to her because she was my sister. And when I scared off her boyfriend because I didn't like him. And then when I wished all the other contestants in the local beauty queen pageant would fall ill so Karen could win... Well, I hadn't expected it to really work!"

Sagira laughed, and Amy smiled.

"But you know what? After that I kind of learned my lesson. I didn't meddle in anyone's life and expected no one to meddle in mine. I stopped going to the shrink Mama sent me to, and I started learning about meditation. Then when I moved to Jacksonville, I decided to find someone who could teach me properly, and that was a big help. The nightmares eventually went away, and I got on with life."

"Glad to hear it," Amy said. "So nothing out of the ordinary has happened since you moved to Jacksonville?"

"Well, one thing," I said with a self-conscious grin. "I met Gabe."

"And then this incident took place?" Amy said.

"Yeah," I answered, my brief moment of happiness gone. "Actually, it's kind of strange I didn't see it coming. Considering everything else."

I shuddered as I recalled that night once more, but found, to my relief, that the memories didn't hurt quite as much now. I felt that talking it all out had clarified a lot for me. Many things now made more sense, including what happened to the guy I believed was Jody's rapist.

"From what you've told me," said Amy, "I think I understand what happened. You've unknowingly accessed those powers in the past, so when you needed them this time, they were there. Remember learning in your science class at school that energy cannot be created or destroyed, only transferred from one form to another?"

"Sure."

"Well, that excess energy had to go somewhere. So it grounded itself harmlessly in the surrounding environment."

"Harmlessly, huh? How am I going to tell the cops that?"

"Well, gee," Amy said with a smile. "I guess they'll have to write it off as an unsolved mystery. So how about we do a reading, see if we can get some information that can help you?"

3.

Amy lit a dark blue candle at one side of the table, then studied me through half-closed eyes. Finally she handed me a deck of tarot cards.

"Give them a shuffle," she said. "Then cut them and we'll see what they reveal."

I did so, and she gathered the deck up and dealt three rows of three cards. I'd played with a friend's tarot cards a couple of times, but knew little of their meanings and subtleties. However, when I saw which card had come up first, I couldn't help but smile. It was the Knight of Cups – Gabe for sure.

"Ah, a romantic partner – perhaps a soul mate," Amy said, then tapped the next card, the Tower. "And a sudden, unexpected event in your lives."

I swallowed hard as I saw Gabe laying in his hospital bed.

"This," she said, pointing to the Nine of Swords, "tells me that this event was very distressing, traumatic even. And there's something else..."

Amy gazed at me piercingly.

"Guilt? You feel responsible in some way?"

"I think I might have – well, provoked the guy."

Sagira gasped, the colour draining from her face. I was kind of shocked myself. How could the cards be so accurate? Amy tilted her head, as if listening to someone speaking from beyond our dimension.

"Yes, a nasty business. Something not quite right there."

She turned back to me.

"Ange," she said, "I'm getting a strong sense of predestina- tion. I think it would have unfolded the same way no matter what you did or didn't do."

I frowned as she studied the next row – Justice reversed, the Fool, the Ace of Wands.

"New beginnings," Amy said, almost to herself. "This event

31

was certainly a great injustice, but it happened to spur action and changes. Not always easy to deal with, but necessary for your life purpose."

I stared at her, bemused and puzzled. She was dead right about the injustice, and that it'd sparked in me a desire to do something. I just hoped it included seeing the son of a bitch who'd shot Gabe getting the maximum penalty for it.

"Five of wands. Confusion, struggles – internal and external, if I'm reading this right. And again, drop the guilt, honey. Strength. Yes, you will need great strength of character and willpower to keep moving forward with your life's purpose. And the Chariot is also about having the internal fortitude to overcome adversity."

She took the deck up again and dealt another three rows over the first three. Sagira shivered. We'd both spied the Death card in the last row.

"A man," Amy intoned, gazing solemnly at the Knight of Swords reversed. "Not someone you want to be near. See the cards around him? The Devil and the seven of swords? He's not good news. In fact, I wouldn't trust him as far as I could spit."

I searched Amy's face for further enlightenment, but it eluded me. Perhaps it eluded her too, as she jabbed at another card.

"The High Priestess – you must learn to trust your intuition. And she sits right over Justice – you must rely on your strong sense of what is right. Your intuition will help you stay on track."

"Okay," I said meekly.

"Eight of Cups – right on top of the Fool. Your quest in life will take you far away from everything familiar. You'll be leaving behind more than just your friends and family. This suggests you'll be discovering new things about yourself and leaving your old self behind."

"Like a journey of self-discovery?" Sagira asked.

I jumped. I'd almost forgotten she was there.

"Yes, and maybe more," Amy said. "Temperance, sitting above the Ace of Wands. Patience and adaptation are her message. She will bring powerful changes in your life, if you let her. Next row, Death, on top of the five of wands."

I shuddered.

"Don't fear this card," Amy said. "It nearly never means a literal, physical death. It simply indicates the end of a cycle in your life, a chance at regeneration and rebirth. Internal transformation. Your whole life will be completely changed by discovery and pursuit of your life's purpose, or quest."

I didn't know what to think. My fanciful noodlings of the previous days came back to mind. Could they have something to do with this mysterious quest?

"Judgement on Strength. Again, powerful cards. There'll be some sort of big awakening; truth being exposed to plain view. And the World over the Chariot. The fulfilment of destiny, the eventual completion of your quest, whatever it may be."

Amy nodded as she met my eyes.

"You're bound for interesting times, Ange. There's no room for doubt. Too many Major Arcana cards – a phenomenal amount for one reading. They tell us what is destined, things that can't be changed. You're going to be very busy, by the looks of it."

I waited for her to elaborate, but instead she shuffled the cards back together, then fanned them out before me, face down.

"Ask the spirit realm what it is you most need to know about your life purpose," Amy instructed, "and then take a card at random."

I did so, and flipped the card over onto the table.

"Two of Cups," Amy said. "Partnership. It looks like you won't be alone on your quest."

"That's good to know," I said with a nervous laugh. "But who on earth who would be crazy enough to help me... do whatever it is I'm meant to do?"

"Probably someone you're very close to, like a family member or soul mate. Someone who would gladly give up everything to help you, and go to the ends of the earth with you if necessary, so close that you're like two halves of a whole."

"Well, that kind of limits the choices," I said.

"You must find out who this person is, and work with them for the higher good. Your mission can't succeed unless you are both in complete accord."

"Really? I guess Gabe would do that... but how can he when he's in a coma?"

My dismay must've been plain. Amy gazed off into space for a moment, then turned back to me.

"My spirit guide tells me that Gabe has an important role to play in your quest. Which I assume he won't be able to do while he's laying in a hospital bed..."

"You mean he's going to wake up?" Sagira asked, her eyes wide.

"My guide says that Gabe will transcend his current situation in order to take his rightful place..."

"Then he'll recover!" I cried, dizzy with relief. "Will it be soon?"

"I don't know. But as the cards say, someone you're close to will be instrumental in helping you with your life purpose..."

"It must be him!" I said, finally swallowing that awful lump I'd had in my throat since the shooting. "He's gonna be okay!"

Sagira and I laughed in relief. Neither of us questioned Amy's words – it just felt right. And, of course, we both wanted Gabe to get well more than anything.

"Thanks so much," Sagira said, wiping tears away. "That's the best news."

Amy smiled.

"The human spirit has an enormous capacity for survival," she continued. "And Ange, you may have to draw on that capacity a great deal in the coming days."

I felt my eyebrows raise involuntarily. Her words were surprising and not entirely comforting. But not nearly as surprising and discomforting as her next words.

"There may be dangers you've never even dreamed of if you choose to continue on your current course. You alone must decide if the possible outcome is worth it."

"Dangers?" I gulped. "What kind of dangers?"

"I don't know enough to tell you anything concrete. It's just a sense, a feeling that I have..."

"There must be something you can tell me!"

Amy gazed at me, then took my hands and turned them palms up. She studied them for a few moments, then leaned back in her chair.

"I'm picking up very strong vibrations – you seem to radiate a great deal more energy than most people. The emotions I sense are both negative and positive. There's anger – a great deal of righteous anger. Fuelled by what happened to Gabe, no doubt."

I had to nod agreement. There were a few bozo rednecks that

needed their heads busted, as well as plenty of other issues I considered not forgotten.

"And there are also many dark shadows looming ahead for you," Amy said. "How about we do a past life regression? I have a strong feeling that the key to your future lies buried somewhere in your past."

"Well, sure," I said. "If it will give you more information. And I'm curious about past lives too. Do you want to stay, Sagira?"

"Of course! I'd love to know who you were in the past – maybe someone really cool, like Cleopatra."

I smiled despite myself, and my pulse quickened.

"I've really looked forward to doing a past life regression with you," Amy said, lighting some incense and placing it opposite the candle. "There's something important to reveal – so my guide keeps telling me. I think he's just as excited as I am!"

A thrill raced down my spine as I looked about. I knew I wouldn't be able to see her spirit guide, but I couldn't help it. Sunlight slanted through the tie-dyed curtains in shafts of purple and orange, green and yellow, and the spicy aroma of frankincense filled the room as the incense wafted through the air in thin tendrils.

We started with a deep breathing exercise. When I was totally relaxed, Amy's low-pitched, husky voice took me further from the here-and-now, back into the mists of the past. I felt myself sinking deeper into a soft, cloudy mire where there was no light or sound, and when I opened my inner eye, I was nearly blinded.

4.

Gradually I made out shapes, colours. The air shimmered in a heat haze over barren, rocky hills that stretched into the distance. To my right flowed a river – a wide, slow-moving crescent of startling blue. On either side of it lay lush, fertile lands, green with crops. The body I now occupied turned, and I realised she wasn't alone. Her companion came fully into view, and my heart leapt. Gabe!

"Ese, my very life and breath, your loveliness outshines the stars in the heavens," he said, holding out a golden, jewel-encrusted goblet. "I will miss you dearly while I am gone."

A delicate female hand took the goblet and lifted it. As my avatar sipped from it, I found that the liquid was cool, sweet, and refreshing, somewhere between apricot nectar and liquid sunlight. It was like nothing I'd ever tasted – ambrosia, the nectar of the gods.

My companion sipped from his own goblet, and I gazed into his loving eyes. His name hovered at the edge of my consciousness, but I hesitated to acknowledge it. This was not my boyfriend as I knew him, and his name here wasn't Gabe. My mind stretched out as I examined my new body's thoughts and memories. I couldn't find anything to tell me who or what she was, as she was so focussed on the handsome vision before her.

"Usir, my love," I heard Ese say. "Usir, the sun in my life and that of our people. I will await your return, my heart filled with longing."

I wanted nothing more than to stay with him in that sun-drenched land, to spend eternity lost in his soft brown eyes. But Amy's voice broke in, dragging me back to the present. I gazed down at Usir as I floated into the mist, then I sank into my own body and consciousness.

37

"And as you come back to this reality, just take a moment to breath slowly and deeply to ground your body and mind," Amy's voice droned on. "Let feelings of peace and contentment wash over you until you're ready to open your eyes again."

My eyes flew open and I nearly hyperventilated as I blurted out what I'd seen. Words tumbled out, scattered thoughts and the smells and tastes and the presence – his presence. I nearly screamed in frustration that I couldn't tell it all at once, and took a deep, shuddering breath to stop my heart from racing.

"It was him – Gabe!"

Sagira gasped, and I paused, trying to order my thoughts anew. Amy smiled.

"You may not have been aware, but I was asking you questions while you were regressed. You described a desert land, which doesn't seem unusual with your heritage. It could be that you had a forebear in Egypt that you went back to."

"That makes sense."

"You also said the name Usir. Was that your name in that life?"

"No, it was Gabe's," I answered. "He called me something else – Ese. It didn't ring any bells, though."

Amy frowned.

"I feel like those names are ringing bells for me," she said. "Let me get one of my books..."

Amy left the room, returning a moment later with an enormous old book about Egyptian mythology. She flicked through pages, stopped and read. A few moments later she leaned back in her chair, staring at me.

"The name Usir," she said, "is the ancient Egyptian name for Osiris, one of their chief gods. We know him as Osiris today because that's how his name was expressed when translated into Greek."

"Oh," I said, wondering what Amy was getting at.

"On it's own, it might not mean anything much," she continued. "Many people in ancient times would have been named for popular gods and goddesses. But teamed up with Ese – well, it is suggestive."

"Of what?"

"You can't guess? You might have heard of Ese by her better known Greek name – the goddess Isis."

3

Season of the Witch

1. Wednesday 22nd October, 1969 – Jacksonville, Florida

"I'm pretty sure none of my ancestors were gods or goddesses," I said with a laugh. "Nor were Gabe's, unless there's something he hasn't told me."

My grin faded as I turned to Sagira. Her skin had paled, and her eyes were wide.

"Heavens to Murgatroyd! How could I have a past life as a goddess and not be one now? Gods and goddesses are supposed to be immortal. It doesn't make sense!"

"Doesn't it?" Amy asked. "Deities have manifested in human form in many myths – and in certain religions. What makes you so sure it's impossible?"

"Well, wouldn't I *know* if I was a goddess?"

"Maybe," Amy said with a shrug. "Maybe not. But why else would you regress to ancient Egypt and have the name Ese, and find yourself with someone called Usir?"

I found my hand was enclosed around my pendant again, and its significance hit me. The Knot of Isis – the very symbol of Isis herself! I realised I'd been fiddling with it, and lowered my hand. Amy pushed the book over in front of me, so I leaned forward and started to read out loud.

"'Isis (Greek pronunciation; Egyptian: Eeset, Ahset, Eesay) was an important deity of Ancient Egypt who's worship eventually spread throughout the Roman Empire. With her siblings, Osiris, Set, and Nephthys, parents Geb and Nut, grandparents Shu and Tefnut, and the Creator god, Atum, made up the group of nine deities known as the Ennead of Heliopolis.

'Isis was a goddess of magic, healing and funerary rites, a protector and idealised as the perfect wife and mother. She married her brother Osiris, who ruled Kemet (Egypt). Isis and Osiris were wise and much loved rulers...'"

I skipped ahead, and saw that the section about Isis went for several pages.

"Would you like to borrow that?" Amy asked. "It'll tell you much more about Isis than I can."

"Okay, thanks. I will."

I drove Sagira back to the motel where her family were staying, and she invited me in for lunch, as her parents and Adio were out. We made sandwiches, poured ourselves some juice, and took it all out on the balcony.

"This whole thing is nuts," I said, my head still swirling.

"I guess so," Sagira replied. "But it is kind of fascinating, don't you think?"

"Sure. I just can't see how I could've had a past life as a goddess and not know a thing about it now."

"Anything's possible," Sagira said. "Maybe you've been so caught up in your current life that you forgot about it."

"And Gabe too? Do you honestly believe that your own

brother is a god in disguise – and has no idea of it himself?"

Sagira laughed.

"No, I guess not. But how else do you explain everything that's happened?"

I wondered about all the kooky events of my childhood, all the times I'd predicted stuff, even the wish-fulfilment of Jody's rapist being punished the way he was. Had I really accessed long-repressed Goddess powers to bring those things about? And if I had, could I do it again, with intent?

Or was it all a pipe dream?

"Nah, there must be some other explanation. It's too far out there..."

"Did you say that Isis was a healer?" Sagira piped up.

"Yeah, it's in the book. Magic, healing, and... something else. I dunno. Is it important?"

Sagira sat up, excitement lighting her eyes.

"Imagine if you are Isis. You could heal Gabe! Maybe it will take Isis healing him for him to be able to take part in the quest..."

"Do you know what you're saying? You might be able to believe a thing like that with zero proof, but I don't think I can..."

A door quietly opened and closed in the suite behind us. I turned and peered through the glass, but it was too dark inside to see anything.

"Ange?" Sagira said. "What if it's true? Really, truly true? What if you are Isis?"

I noted her hopeful eyes, her pleading tone, and decided to humour her a little.

"Okay. Am I Isis? I don't know. Do I want to be Isis? Sure. It'd be fantastic – of course I'd heal Gabe, for starters. And punish the jerks who hurt him. I'd change the bad things about the world and make it right, wipe out evil corporations and governments and poverty and disease – Isis could do a whole lot of good."

"See, you have all the best intentions!"

"But what if it's not true, if Amy made some sort of mistake? Anyway, the world's such a mess, I'm not even sure Isis could put it all right."

Sagira looked momentarily deflated, but then she noticed my pendant.

"Well, what about Gabe? What if all you could do was just heal Gabe? Wouldn't it be worth finding out just for that?"

"Of course. But he's not the only person in the world who needs healing."

"That's true," Sagira said, pinning me with a direct gaze.

"What?"

"Just saying."

Sagira's observation made me uncomfortable. I hadn't been thinking of myself when I spoke. I fell silent as I contemplated what needed fixing in my own life. But it all seemed such a big, sticky mess that I could hardly bear to look at it. Later. I'd tackle stuff like that later. I finished my juice and turned to Sagira.

"I'll go and see Amy again. Maybe she can help me find out if I really am Isis – and if I really have her powers."

"Cool," Sagira said with a smile. "I'm sure it's worth a try."

"Against my better judgement," I warned her. "It could be a total waste of time."

If I'd only listened to my own counsel then, I'd have stayed put, Gabe may eventually have healed by himself, and the world would still be one great big rotten apple the way it always had been since civilisation began.

But no, that would've been too easy, right? And I was curious about the quest Amy said I had to fulfil. I didn't know why the heck anything of any magnitude would become my responsibility. Still, if there *was* a chance I could change the world for the better, I had to try. Considering it was the world Gabe and I wanted to bring children into some day, that was a powerful incentive.

Sagira excused herself to go to the bathroom. I heard quiet voices inside. A moment later I felt more than heard something behind me. I turned quickly. Adio stood at the balcony's glass sliding door, staring at me with an intensity I found disconcerting.

"Hey," I said, wondering how much of the conversation he'd overheard.

"Hey," he muttered, frowning, and pinned me down with that intense look again. "Did I hear the name Isis?"

I stared back coolly, making him squirm.

"I didn't listen in on purpose," he said. "I heard someone talking out here."

"You heard more than me," I said, standing and shouldering my handbag. "I didn't even know you were there."

He flushed.

"Sorry. It's just that I know plenty about old pagan Goddesses like Isis."

"Well, that's a surprise," I quipped.

"Being a Christian doesn't make me ignorant of my heritage. I have Egyptian blood too, and I studied paganism and other false religions in theology class at uni."

"Paganism and other false religions? Which, if I remember my own studies correctly, long predate Christianity."

He shrugged and stepped back to let me through the door. But I knew the gleam in his eyes meant trouble.

"The God of Abraham predates all false religions."

"Is that so? Can you prove He was around before the Gods of Ancient Egypt and the Middle East?"

"It's all in the bible."

"That's your book of worship, not mine. Do you have any real evidence?"

"Faith provides the answers that science can't."

"Well, little kids have faith that the tooth fairy, Santa Claus and the Easter bunny exist," I replied. "Sorry, but that doesn't cut it with me."

I turned for the door. Sagira came out of the bathroom as I crossed the suite.

"I'd better be going," I said. "Thanks for lunch. See you at the hospital later."

I took the elevator down, still prickling, and tried to shake the feeling as I drove home. I needn't have left, but I didn't want to be anywhere near Adio. He brought out my antagonistic side, which I had trouble controlling at the best of times.

The Devil card in my reading came to mind, then Amy's words echoed in my head – 'He's not good news; in fact, I wouldn't trust him as far as I could spit.' I couldn't help but wonder if it referred to Adio.

As soon as I got back to my apartment, I read the rest of the entry about Isis in Amy's book. Then I read the entries about Osiris, Nephthys, and Set. I began to see my relationships anew and reset as these ancient personalities. And it made sense that if Gabe was Osiris, then his own brother and sister had to be Set and Nephthys.

What cemented it was that despite the goodness of the other three, the intense hatred and rivalry borne by Set towards his siblings caused chaos and cataclysm in the lives of his family and the people of Kemet. He was one mean cat. Gabe had seldom spoken of Adio, but I knew they weren't exactly on good terms, which echoed the myth.

I rang Amy and asked if I could return to talk about it some more. She agreed. Then I called Sagira to see if she wanted to accompany me again, but she'd already promised to go shopping with her mother that afternoon. However, she said they would drop around for a coffee afterwards. I got in my caddy and started towards Amy's place.

And a cacophony of warning bells started to ring in my head!

2.

I noticed a blue Buick sedan behind me, keeping a respectable distance two or three cars back. I was unnerved at how closely it followed my own route. Curious, I doubled back towards the centre of town. The car followed. I drove a couple more blocks, then turned into a lane half-hidden by a removal van.

The sedan braked and edged towards the lane, but had to stop as the van pulled out to straighten before it backed up. I turned onto the next street going back towards Amy's, still feeling jittery. I felt I'd lost the tail for now, but something told me it wouldn't the last time I'd be followed by the mysterious driver.

I parked around the corner from Amy's house and hurried back, keeping a sharp lookout. Amy greeted me at the door and I scrambled to get over the threshold in case my tail went cruising past and saw me there.

"My, you're eager," Amy said, shutting the door.

"Sorry. I didn't mean to be rude. But I'm pretty sure I was being followed."

"Followed?"

"There was a car tailing me. I managed to lose it in town, but I don't think I've seen the last of it."

Amy frowned.

"Yeah, I'm getting a sense of him now. Do you want me to try and get more?"

"Hell yeah. I don't like being hunted like that."

Amy closed her eyes and her lips moved silently. I figured she was talking to her spirit guide, and went to sit in the front room to give her some space. She came in a moment later, shaking her head.

"It's gone, I'm afraid. How about we do another regression, and put this behind you for the moment?"

I agreed. Amy lowered the window shades, lit the candle and fresh incense, and sat opposite me. We did the deep breathing exercise, and Amy guided me into the meditation, her voice droning softly. My eyes felt glued shut as I drifted into a trance. Again I sank through the fog that separated my conscious self from that of Isis.

Then I was back in her world, under the blazing sun. Isis was climbing the last few steps towards a small granite temple on a rocky hilltop. She paused at the entrance, and turned as she heard someone else scrabbling up the uneven path towards her. To the west stretched barren, rock-strewn plains, then the great sand dunes of the desert.

A figure came into sight, climbing the hill. One that filled me with horror. I'd read the description of Set in Amy's book, but nothing prepared me for coming face to face with him.

Like Osiris, he was tall, with the same slim, tanned body. But his head was that of a strange beast – a drooping, elongated snout, tall, upright ears that were cropped flat at the top, and a mane of vibrant red hair that fell to his shoulders. I saw a cruel gleam in his eyes as he planted his *was* sceptre in the ground right at Isis' feet.

With an even bigger shock, I realised I'd seen this monstrous visage before – in my nightmares.

"My lady Ese."

"Sutekh."

The word slithered through Isis' lips, like a serpent.

"My Lady, have you news of our dear brother?"

"He returns today. The sun will not set before he joins me on my barque."

I had no idea Isis possessed a barque, and yet, when she looked to the east, towards the river, there it was. A great vessel of gleaming black ivory, white linen canopies and sails. Very striking. I was starting to think Isis had killer taste.

"I have an invitation for him, my Lady," Set said, and licked his lips subtly. "One I prefer to deliver personally."

"An invitation? Our beloved Usir will welcome you, I am sure."

"And do you welcome me, oh Lady of Ten Thousand Names?"

I was sure I heard a sneer, however slight, in his polite tones. His eyes had narrowed, and I began to suspect his intent. So it was war, was it?

Something tore at me, sucking me back to my present life. I couldn't fight it, and I floated away, back through the clouds to the chair in Amy's room. I opened my eyes, still feeling dazed.

"...don't think he likes me," I muttered, trying to focus on Amy.

"Take it easy and breath," she advised. "You were gone longer this time, and you seemed too busy to talk to me."

"Sorry, Isis was dealing with Set," I said. "He turned up just after I got there."

"Did you interact with him?"

"You might say that. He was ever so polite, but inside I think he wanted to spit."

"Sounds charming. Did you pick up any other impressions?"

"Isis has a nice barque."

We both burst into laughter.

"So guess what?" I said. "I realised that Set was the horrible creature in my nightmares all those years ago. Go figure. And I read that in the myth, he killed Osiris and made darned sure he couldn't be brought back to life. That's some pretty serious sibling rivalry. It just feels so freaky weird..."

"The myth reflecting real life?" Amy guessed.

"Yeah," I said with a nod. "Neither brother likes me – Set there, Adio here. One hell of a coincidence."

"It may be a pattern you're all fated to repeat to release karma," Amy said. "After all, Gabe befell an attempt on his life just recently."

"Yeah, but Adio wasn't tied up in that... Was he?"

"It depends how closely you're all following the karmic pattern," Amy said. "We know that you're Isis, and Gabe is Osiris, so Adio may well be Set. But it's also possible that if Karen is Nephthys, her husband might be Set."

I chewed over this for a moment, but shook my head.

"Eric has no reason to hurt Gabe. He doesn't even know

him."

"That may not matter," Amy said. "With reincarnation, you may be someone's child this time around, and their parent next time, or a sister, brother, or a marriage partner or soul mate. Personally, I think that such close relationships as those between Isis and her siblings are bound to be preserved in some way. They may very well be exactly who you think they are."

"Perhaps if I found out who Nephthys is in this life time, it might help. I thought it might be Sagira, but maybe it *is* Karen..."

"We can do another regression next time you visit, and try to find out."

We talked some more about the legends of Isis and Osiris before I left. The visit had been a mostly pleasant diversion after the disturbing scene with Adio (was I doomed not to get along with people's brothers?) and then being followed. I glanced about as I walked to my car, but the streets were deserted.

On the way home I bought milk and some TV dinners, and also fell victim to the temptation of the chocolate display. Not long after I got back to my apartment, Sagira and Zahra arrived. They had a modest haul to show for their afternoon out. Mrs Serapis had bought a couple of new shirts for her husband, and silk scarves for herself and Sagira. Sagira had only one package, a small, gift-wrapped box that she passed to me.

"Open it, it's for you," she said. "I couldn't resist it – as soon as I saw it, I thought of you."

I opened the box. Inside I found a gleaming golden bangle that coiled several times before ending in the diamond-shaped head of a snake with glittering green eyes.

"Gee willikers!" I said, slipping it on. "You shouldn't have – it looks expensive."

"Don't worry, it wasn't," Sagira said. "It's only costume jewellery."

"Thanks for thinking of me."

I had stacks to tell Sagira, but not with Zahra there. We talked for a while over coffees, then I offered to fix dinner before we left to visit Gabe, and popped some TV meals in the oven.

"Angela," said Zahra, shaking her head, "Surely you and Gabe haven't been living on these?"

"No," I answered truthfully. "We eat out two or three times a week."

"But don't you cook properly? This isn't very healthy, you know."

I bit my lip. I'd learned a little about cooking from my Gran, and Karen had taught me what she could when Mama wasn't there to interfere and suggest easier options. I guess I'd got lazy since moving out of home. Zahra smiled understandingly.

"Maybe Sagira and I can teach you to cook properly sometime? I'm surprised Gabriel didn't – he can cook up a storm when he puts his mind to it."

I remembered a couple of times when Gabe had impressed me by cooking proper meals. I was grateful for Zahra's support, and also felt a pang at what I'd missed out on with my own mother.

We left for the hospital afterwards, and joined Adio and Mr Serapis there. Gabe looked the same as he did every morning and evening. His colour had gradually returned as he slept and recovered, but that was the only obvious improvement.

We sat, and engaged in our usual light-hearted chatter, including Gabe as though he was fully conscious and could answer whenever he wanted to. After about an hour, Zahra and Abasi went down to the hospital cafeteria for some coffee. Tension built in the room. Sagira fell quiet. Adio glanced at me furtively, his eyes boring into me whenever he thought I wasn't looking. Finally, I couldn't stand it any more.

"Hey Gabe, you should see the bangle Sagira got me," I said, casting around for something new to talk about. "It's shaped like a coiling golden snake, and it has little peridot crystals for eyes..."

I suddenly had the sinking feeling that I'd said something I shouldn't have. And that the consequences could be extremely unpleasant!

3.

Adio gazed at me with distaste.

"Let's see."

I could tell the casual tone was forced. I glanced at Sagira, then pushed the sleeve of my jacket up, exposing the bangle. Adio eyed it suspiciously.

"You're not worried about the symbolism of that?" he asked.

I raised a questioning eyebrow.

"You know, Eve and the serpent, and all that," he continued. "Sagira certainly should have."

"It only means that if you believe it does," I replied. "Snakes were actually a respected symbol of wisdom and healing before Christianity came along. And still are."

I recalled my dealings at the clinic with people who kept

snakes as pets. To them, the creatures were very special, despite their odd undesirable behaviours like trying to join their owners in the bathtub (snakes can and do swim in the wild) or eating the family dog (I advised them to get something bigger than a Chihuahua next time). Some were great escape artists, and devoured the kid's hamster, chicken eggs, golf balls and other strange items before being returned to their enclosures.

Adio snorted. He obviously didn't pay that.

"Well, you're interested in snakes as well as Isis. That makes me wonder what you believe in."

"What I believe in?" I said incredulously.

"You do know Gabe's a Christian, don't you?"

"What? Are you saying I have to be a Christian to be with Gabe?"

"Yes!" he said, his face flushing. "Gabe should marry another Christian. He's never been strong in his faith, and since he left home, he's drifted from the church. How's a partner who's into ancient pagan worship and snakes going to help him with his journey towards God? His very soul would be in danger because of you!"

I was taken back at the vehemence in Adio's voice, but I drew a deep breath and tried to reason it out calmly.

"So who says he has to be a Christian, or that he has to be with one? Isn't that his decision?"

"He was brought up a good Christian, like Sagira and I," Adio hissed, springing up. "You're tempting him into evil ways, the ways of Satan..."

"Hey, watch who you're calling evil! And I don't even believe in Satan. Besides, if Gabe had been a full-on Christian when we met, we'd never have started dating. If he isn't one now, it's nothing to do with me. He was already off the boil."

Adio stared at me as if I'd laid some deadly curse on his family. His right eye twitched as he fought to control his anger. Finally he sighed, and sank onto his chair.

"You're probably right," he conceded. "I remember when he visited us at Christmas a couple of years back, after he'd finished uni in California. I became worried then because he was completely dismissive of our festivities."

"Well, you can't blame anyone for getting discouraged at all the hype," Sagira pointed out. "Christmas has become an enormous sales spree."

"Yes, I understand that," Adio said, rubbing his temples. "But he wasn't even interested in the traditional ways we celebrated, like lighting candles and singing carols and stuff."

"Look," I said. "I think each of us is on our own spiritual journey. You can't force someone to believe what you do, Adio. They might pretend to go along with it to please you, but that's not belief, is it? Gabe needs the time and freedom to explore his own spiritual path, not yours, not your parent's, not mine either. It's his choice."

"What choice is there to make, when there's only one choice that's right for your own salvation at the end of time?"

I couldn't believe he wanted to continue this argument. I needed to put a stop to it for Gabe's sake, and for Sagira, who now looked desperate.

"That's your belief," I said firmly. "You'll have to accept that Gabe doesn't choose Christianity for himself."

"If he's not a Christian any more, what is he?"

"He's exploring other options. Christianity no longer fulfils his spiritual needs."

"It fulfils all spiritual needs! There are no other options for spiritual fulfilment. God makes that quite clear in the bible..."

"The bible is just one spiritual book among many," I said, gritting my teeth again. "And Christianity is just one religion among many."

"And which belief does Gabe now follow? Which belief do you follow?"

"That's my own private business," I replied, barely holding my anger in. "And Gabe's spiritual belief is his. We just so happen to share similar beliefs, that's all."

"Why are you so ashamed of them that you won't tell me what they are?" Adio asked. "Are you embarrassed by them? Are you scared of ridicule?"

"No. Not ashamed, not embarrassed. Not afraid of anything you can say or do. Just disgusted by your attempt to control your brother."

"I don't wish to control anyone," Adio spat. "But I do have concern for my brother's well-being."

"Why – are you your brother's keeper?" I asked. "No? Well, you'll just have to trust that he's making the right choice for himself."

"How can I, when no one even has the guts to tell me what his choice is?"

That stung. I knew that telling Adio the truth would cause cataclysmic reactions within his family, but I was starting to see that it had to come out sooner or later, as he would never let it rest.

"Fine. Gabe has given patriarchal religions the boot for good and become a neopagan, like me."

"And I'm seriously considering it myself," Sagira burst out, her eyes defiant.

4.

Adio looked like he'd just witnessed Satan himself dance a jig naked on Gabe's bed. I was proud of Sagira for helping me stick up for our chosen beliefs. But as I thought, trouble had just landed, with a great big capital T.

"Holy mother of God," Adio choked out, probably the closest he'd ever come to blaspheming. "Sagira! You and Gabe – neo*pagans*?"

Adio sounded incredulous; scandalised. He closed his eyes, inhaled deeply, and refocused himself.

"Okay, nature worship. Who do you think created nature in the first place?"

"Why does it have to be a 'who'?" I countered. "It could've just evolved. You know what? Creation is in the past. It's so long ago that no one knows for sure what happened, so what does it matter?"

"It matters that we were fashioned by a loving creator," Adio said, "to whom we should be eternally grateful for our lives on earth and the redemption that follows."

"But I am grateful for my life. Just not to your god, that's all. Yours is just one amongst thousands of gods that have been worshipped since civilisation began. And He's hardly got a good track record. I mean, look at all the divisions within Christianity, about how to believe in God and do His will. What a nightmare!"

"The same could be said of neopaganism," he bit back. "What about stuff like voodoo, witchcraft and Satanism? Why should I take your beliefs seriously, knowing how misguided you are?"

I almost lost my cool, but Sagira jumped up to stand between us. I swallowed the blind fury I'd nearly given vent to while Sagira stared her brother down.

"Adio, I'm ashamed of you. Our parents brought us up to be better than all this sniping about spiritual beliefs. Didn't they always say that if our heart wasn't in our religion, then we should find one we could put our hearts into?"

"I didn't think they meant we should turn to the extreme opposite," he replied, his voice husky. "What you say you believe in now, you don't know how dangerous it is, how close you are to temptation into evil ways."

"If that's what you think, you know nothing about it at all," she snapped, her eyes flashing.

I followed the exchange with interest. I'd never seen Sagira angry before.

"It's a peaceful belief system," she continued. "Christians are only too happy to march off to war, whereas neopagans object to violence and killing. Have you forgotten what it says in the bible about murder?"

"No, but..."

"And what about capitalism? With all the wealthy Christians in the world, why is there so much poverty? And why are so many people with physical or mental disorders not given what they need to improve their health, when a little charity might make all the difference to their life?"

Adio seemed to subside in on himself.

"I didn't say it was perfect," he mumbled. "People always mess up the good stuff God gives them. But I know He's there. He made all of us and He loves us. And I will not abandon Him."

"No one's asking you to," Sagira said. "But Gabe and I need you to accept that we have our own lives to live, with our own beliefs. Just because we're no longer practising Christians doesn't mean we reject our family. Just the opposite, actually. We probably love you guys more now than we ever did."

Adio looked all kinds of confused. Sagira returned to her seat by the head of the bed, and I sank onto the chair I'd occupied before the row. Silence fell, an intense silence through which I heard the rhythms of life continuing all around us – nurses swishing along the corridor, cars honking on the street below, the beating of my heart. Somewhere nearby, a tap dripped.

Finally Adio rose, went over to the little basin in the corner of the room, and turned it off. I looked at Sagira, and she at me. I hoped Adio would leave and give us some time with Gabe. I wanted so badly to tell him all that had happened lately, even if he couldn't respond to it. As if he sensed my thoughts, Adio abruptly left the room.

"Yeah, it's been real," I muttered.

Sagira smiled wistfully.

"I'm sorry about Adio. He can be really difficult at times, especially if you question his beliefs. He's a very devout Christian."

Rabid was the word that came to my mind, but I let it go and sat on the edge of Gabe's bed. The ventilator rose and fell evenly, just as it had on that first night when I wondered if he was going to live or die, and whether I would live or die without him. A lot had happened since then, and this was my first chance to tell him about it.

"Gabe," I said. "I have news – lots of news."

Sagira smiled as she settled more comfortably in her chair. We each took one of Gabe's hands, free now to focus all our attention on him.

"Guess what?" I said. "I ran into my old friend, Amy.

Remember I told you about her? She's psychic. She took one look at my aura and wanted do a tarot reading and a regression with me."

I could imagine how Gabe would react if he were awake. He would raise his eyebrows and say, 'Really? See, I told you there was something special about you. Your aura must be incredible!' But he couldn't speak, he couldn't move. He could only lie there and listen, if he could even do that.

"It was super! You'll never believe the life I went back to."

Sagira leaned forward.

"I'll say! It blew our minds!"

It was my turn to smile.

"I was in Egypt. Guess that figures. And I was the Goddess Isis!"

"Only about the greatest Goddess ever," Sagira added.

"Yeah," I said with a laugh. "But you know what was really amazing? You were there too. You were Osiris. Usir."

Gabe's breath caught and the muscles around his eyes twitched faintly.

"Sagira!" I cried, jumping to my feet. "He's coming to! Quick, get a nurse!"

5.

Sagira fled the room while I stroked Gabe's hand and face. His breathing settled back into its usual pattern and the twitching muscles relaxed.

"Please wake up, Gabe," I whispered.

Footsteps approached, and Sagira re-entered with a nurse on her heels. The nurse checked Gabe's vital signs, then went out to page Dr Scott. As if the gods of perfect timing were on our side, Gabe's parents returned from the cafeteria, and they cried in joy at the news. Adio, who came in after them, went down on his knees to thank God. Dr Scott soon joined us and gave Gabe a thorough check over. We all held our breath.

"This is good," he finally said. "He's not conscious yet, but to see a response to stimulus like you've described means that the brain is repairing itself. I can't tell you when he'll wake up, but I'm confident this is a good sign."

After he left, the room buzzed with our excitement.

"Do you think he actually heard us talking to him?" Sagira asked.

"The doctor said it would stimulate his brain," said Zahra.

"Well, I guess it must be working," Adio said huskily.

"What did you say to him?" Abasi asked. "What was it that he responded to?"

Sagira and I looked at each other.

"It was – I don't know," Sagira said. "Nothing special. Was it, Ange?"

"Er. I don't even remember," I answered, playing along. "I forgot in all the excitement."

Gabe's parents looked puzzled.

"Would you please try to remember?" Zahra said. "It's important – if we keep talking about whatever it was, he might respond again and wake up."

Sagira looked guilty. I knew she was going to tell.

"It could've been anything," I blurted. "We held his hands. Maybe that was it?"

"All of us have done that," Adio said, annoyed. "For goodness sake, what were you talking about?"

"We were telling him about Ange's past life regressions," Sagira replied, "where she visited her lifetime as Isis."

Silence fell. Her parents gazed at her open-mouthed, as if she'd announced she had just been to the moon and back. Adio looked poisonous again. I remained still, wondering how we were going to patch this one up.

"So that might have triggered some memories for him too," Sagira continued bravely. "Maybe he remembered being Osiris."

I grimaced, dropping my eyes to the floor. I really didn't want to see how the others would react. Adio exploded.

"Her life as Isis? What's that supposed to mean? That you silly girls think Ange is a goddess – a pagan goddess? Do you know how ridiculous that is?"

"No!" Sagira cried. "That's not really what I meant! Just that Ange was Isis in a past life..."

"You're kidding me, right? You actually believe this stuff, Sagira?"

He turned to their parents.

"You see what's been going on here? This one," he turned and pointed at me, "calls herself a neopagan, and she's dragged Gabe and Sagira into sin with her!"

"That's not true," I said, my voice shaking. "Gabe and Sagira were already following their own paths before they met me."

"Well, you didn't exactly discourage them," Adio shouted.

"Why should I? They've the right to choose their own beliefs..."

"What – that you were a goddess in a former life? Is that what that disreputable psychic told you?"

I froze.

"That *was* you following me today, wasn't it?"

"Adio?" said Abasi, turning to his son. "What does she

mean by that?"

"I had to do something, dad! I feared for Gabe's soul, and Sagira's, and for all of us. I couldn't just let her elbow into our family and tear it apart with her false beliefs!"

I felt winded. I turned to Mr and Mrs Serapis.

"Does Adio own a blue Buick sedan?"

"No," Abasi said tiredly, shaking his head.

"What about any friends he might have here? Colleagues? Someone in an organisation he's part of? Anyone at all?"

Again Mr Serapis shook his head, but this time he was frowning.

"Is it true, Adio? Did you really follow Angela today?"

Adio looked mutinously at Zahra, as if expecting her to bail him out. She didn't.

"Alright, I hired a car, just to see what she gets up to when no one's keeping an eye on her. I feel totally justified – she visits some woman who claims to be a psychic."

He brandished Amy's flyer in his parent's faces.

"Hey," I cried. "How did you get that?"

"It was on the balcony," Adio said. "It must have fallen out of your bag."

He read from the flyer, each word loaded with venom.

"Past life regression, tarot, palmistry, scrying, psychometry, divining... Of all the rot!"

"Amy is a true psychic," Sagira said. "I was there – I saw Ange's reading."

"See?" Adio pleaded with his parents. "See what has become of your daughter? And Gabe heading down the same path too. Tell me I'm not justified!"

"You broke the law!" I said. "I could have you arrested!"

"Adio, how could you?" Sagira cried.

The agony in her voice was devastating. Her dark eyes pleaded with her brother's, begging him to stop. But Adio wasn't finished.

"Sister, what has happened to you? Has this witch cast a spell on you that you can't see your own true God beckoning? Have you lost your senses?"

"Adio, please," Mr Serapis rasped, his breathing ragged.

Sagira quickly poured him a glass of water. Tears stung my eyes as I saw how fragile the family was. And here we all were, arguing in front of Gabe. He could probably hear everything.

"This isn't doing Gabe any good," I said. "He needs peace and quiet to recover."

"Then you should leave," Adio said, his eyes full of malice. "Leave my family and take your hideous beliefs elsewhere. None of this would be happening if you weren't here."

"I've just as much right to be here as you," I stated.

"You do not! You're not family and you don't belong here."

"This is ridiculous! I'm Gabe's steady girlfriend. We're planning to get married. *He* wants me here, and I'm staying!"

"Angela," said Mrs Serapis sympathetically. "My dear, we have all suffered, you as much as us. After all, you were with him when it happened. You saw him get shot. I cannot pretend that wouldn't affect you."

I could hear a big 'but' coming up.

"But there seems to be such aggravation between yourself and Adio, and no one gets any peace when you're in the same room. Maybe it would be better if you visited at a different time to the rest of us..."

"Mother!" Sagira protested. "That's not fair! It's Adio who picks the fights!"

"I know. But Adio has a point. He's family, and blood should stick by blood."

"Adio's actions were not honourable," Abasi said. "And he is often informed more by passion and righteousness than a true desire to do God's will. But his wish to protect his family is correct and commendable, even if his methods are not."

I held my breath. I knew the final decision as far as the family was concerned would lay with Mr Serapis, and that they would abide by it, even if I disagreed.

"I'm sorry to say this, Angela, but our son is right about the spiritual damage you could be causing his siblings. Even if they were drifting from their faith before they met you, knowing you has only encouraged them to leave behind completely the true beliefs that we taught them as children, that they once believed whole-heartedly."

It seemed to be a difficult speech for him. I hadn't become terribly close to Gabe's parents, but they had seemed to accept me. That was now changing.

"I knew when we met that you weren't a Christian," he said wearily. "But I had no idea where your beliefs lay until now, thanks to Adio. Although we tried to give our children the freedom to explore different spiritual choices as they grew, I really can't approve of such beliefs as yours being encouraged in them.

"I think it would be best if you stayed away, at least until you've thought it all through very carefully. After all, we believe in our faith with the very best of intentions, to bring the light of God's love and His wisdom to those around us."

I felt like mentioning that old adage about the road to hell being paved with good intentions, but I knew it would sound facetious. I looked at Sagira, my last port of comfort in this storm. She seemed heart-broken, but I sensed she wouldn't speak against her father. I swallowed, and found my throat incredibly dry. There was nothing I could say anyway, and Sagira seemed to have lost the will to speak.

"Well, are you leaving?" Adio said coldly. "Don't you know when you're beaten, witch? Out, and leave my family alone!"

4

Good Morning, Starshine

1. Wednesday 22nd October 1969 – Jacksonville, Florida

"Ange," Sagira choked out, tears in her eyes. "Just for now. It'll be okay. You know they can't keep you and Gabe apart forever."

"Gabe," I whispered to the still form on the bed.

I wanted to say I was sorry – sorry I hadn't been able to stand up for us, sorry I'd let Adio get the better of me, sorry I wasn't strong enough to keep fighting, even though I knew it was right. And sorry that I hadn't had the opportunity to learn enough about Isis to try to heal him. There was only one thing I could say that mattered.

"I love you, Gabe. I'll wait for you."

They all stared at me, Adio triumphantly, Gabe's parents wearily, and Sagira tragically. But I only had eyes for Gabe. I silently sent my message of love to him, then I turned and walked from the room. Tears nearly blinded me as I hurried down the corridor and banged the button for the elevator.

Once inside, I slumped against the wall, totally bummed out. It was so unfair. And yet hope kindled even as I wallowed in self-pity. Gabe would live. He'd recover, and he'd come and find me once he was well, perhaps with Sagira's help.

Rain pelted down hard outside, so I pulled my jacket up over my head and ran to my car. I slammed the door on the rain and stopped to think. If I went home, I'd brood. I'd eat all that chocolate I'd bought. I wouldn't be able to sleep. I didn't want that. I went back in to the hospital foyer and used the phone there to ring Amy. The dial tone seemed to go on forever, but finally she answered, breathing hard.

"Hi, it's me, Ange," I said. "Look, I know it's late. I'm sorry if I've interrupted something, but I really need to talk to you."

"I don't mind at all. I was just out in the garden covering some new seedlings so the rain doesn't pound them to smithereens. It sure is one heck of a downpour. So, how can I help, honey?"

I smiled. It was good to hear Amy's voice.

"Okay," I said. "the good news is that Gabe started responding to our voices. He's still unconscious, but the doctor was certain it meant he'd be alright."

"That's wonderful," Amy said. "And I assume there's other news as well?"

I paused. It was so much easier to tell someone something nice than something awful. Unless you're a real sadist, and I didn't have it in me just then.

"Yeah. Adio's been trying to estrange me from his parents. And it worked."

"Oh no, that's terrible. Are you saying they're not going to welcome you into their family now, after all you and Gabe have been through?"

"That about sums it up. Adio overheard me talking about Isis. And it was him following me today. He's hell-bent on keeping non-Christians out of his family. And his parents listened to him. I know Gabe and Sagira won't just meekly give in, but they can't really do much until Gabe's recovered. However long that takes."

"So what do you want to do?" Amy asked. "Hey, how about you come and spend the night here, and we can do girl stuff, if you like. I have a spare bed."

"Gee, thanks! I knew you'd understand. As long as you're sure it won't be any trouble? I know it's getting late…"

"Honey, you just get your sweet little self over here, and I'll get a cup of hot cocoa going, okay?"

I smiled. It nearly cracked my face after all the scowling I'd done that evening, but it made me feel surprisingly good inside.

"Heck, yeah. I'll pop back home and grab a couple of things, then I'll be right over. Say, half an hour?"

"I'll be looking out for you," Amy promised.

I drove home slowly in the heavy rain, not wanting to have an accident and end up back at the hospital. It would be so humiliating to be wheeled in on a gurney just as Gabe's family were leaving. I could imagine how smug Adio would look.

Several younger tenants from my apartment block were standing about in the foyer, waiting for the rain to ease off so they could go to the discotheque without getting their fancy duds wet. I ploughed through them, showering droplets everywhere, and took the elevator up.

It felt strange and unreal to walk into the dark quiet of my apartment after all the noise and fury I'd been through. I snapped on a couple of lights, then I grabbed my pyjamas and overnight bag, and a change of clothes for the next day.

I locked up, returned to my car, and drove to Amy's. My car radio treated me to Rhythm Of The Falling Rain, then switched to Halloween mode and churned out an old number from my teenage years, Spooksville by the Nu-Trends. The downpour had really settled in, and I cursed my stupidity in not bringing an umbrella or my waterproof poncho. I gathered up my things and made a dash for the front door.

"Well, look what the rain brought," Amy joked as she shut the door behind me.

"Yeah, great weather for frogs," I said, shaking water out of my hair.

I followed Amy to the small kitchen at the back of her house. Bunches of herbs hung from a coat peg, drying, and jars of herbs, spices and pastes occupied the counter. The room was infused with a delicious, spicy baking smell, along with Amy's favourite patchouli scent. A chorus of frogs croaked from somewhere outside, barely audible above the rain that belted on the roof. I broke out in goose bumps of excitement, recalling how, as kids, Karen and I used to hide under the bed telling ghost stories during thunder storms. Well, I told the ghost stories. Karen stuck to fairy tales.

While Amy poured the cocoa, I flicked through a book about mythical creatures I found on the table. Amy leaned over to see what I was reading.

"Unicorns, eh? You have to be a virgin to catch one of those."

"Aw, too late," I sighed.

I'd always been fond of horses. It made my blood boil to deal with people who treated them badly, even from ignorance. During my childhood, we'd sometimes lived where I could go riding with the local pony clubs. Karen never came. For some reason beyond my understanding, she was scared stiff of horses, even the gentlest pony. But unicorns had always fascinated both of us. I gazed at a picture of the famous Medieval tapestry that showed a maiden trapping a unicorn.

"They're beautiful, but they're just another myth, aren't they? I mean, like dragons and stuff."

"Well, that depends on a lot of things, like when you lived, and your religion. People thought dragons and unicorns were real because they were mentioned in the bible. And even in times before that, such creatures were truly thought to exist."

I wondered with a wry smile what Adio would make of the subject. Would he believe in such things because they were written into his precious book?

"It's almost a shame it isn't true," I said.

"Ah," said Amy, smiling. "But who says it isn't?"

I raised questioning eyebrows, and she continued.

"Have you ever considered the possibility that these creatures might exist on another plane of existence? A different dimension to us?"

"I guess anything's possible. But if that's so, how did people know about them?"

"Perhaps through dreams and trances, or astral travel. Some people may have the ability to pass between dimensions, people like shaman and high priests and priestesses. There may even be portals where people can slip between dimensions and see things that are invisible to this realm."

"So what about things like vampires, and werewolves, and stuff? People say they exist in our realm."

"The Hidden Ones? Yeah, they're real too. I guess I know plenty about them. More than I ever would've wished. And trust me, the knowledge is a burden."

"What can you tell me about them?" I asked.

"Well, they're not completely of this world, nor of the spirit realm. They keep themselves hidden away in the shadows most of the time, waiting for the next victim to come along. Just waiting. And watching."

I shivered.

"I think I need to know about them, just in case."

Amy half-smiled as she gave me an appraising look.

"Oh yes, you need to know about them, alright. And I'll tell you. But I'm warning you, it ain't pleasant."

2.

"I can't afford to worry about that," I said. "Tell me now."

Amy shrugged.

"Sure. For starters, they're very dangerous. They're cunning and unnaturally strong, and can make you into one of them – if you live beyond an encounter."

"So how do you know if someone's a vampire?"

"Firstly," Amy said, "don't believe all the myths about them. Like they can't go out in the sun? Garbage. They can and they do. It's true their eyes are sensitive to bright light, but they go out on cloudy days, or wear dark sunglasses. They look pale, but then, so do lots of young people these days."

"Well, I can't go around suspecting everyone who wears sunnies and hasn't got a tan," I commented. "How else can I recognise them?"

"Their auras, for one. They have very dark, unhealthy-looking auras."

"Oh. I'm not really good at seeing stuff like that."

"That's okay. I'll teach you how to view auras. You'll also sense there's something not right about them. If you meet someone you just don't trust, or who seems invisible to others, check out their aura. Some will try to mask their auras if they sense they're in danger of being discovered, but you'll just know."

"Okay. Can I block them from seeing my aura, too?"

"Depends. In a crowd, it's best not to draw attention to yourself. Let your aura shine, just like everyone around you, so it blends in. But if you're alone, they'll know there's something different about you, which might tempt them to check you out. Then it's safer to shield yourself. Besides, you'll likely need spirit help to deal with them, so you'll be shielding yourself anyway to stop any unwelcome spirits getting at you."

"Boy, it sure sounds like a lot of work," I said. "I wonder if I'll start seeing them everywhere I go, once I'm aware of them?"

"Yeah, probably," Amy said with a nod. "There aren't as many of them as there are everyday people, but you'll see them. And they'll certainly see you."

I shuddered. If this was true, someone like me might make tempting prey.

"I'll show you the spare room," Amy said when we'd finished our cocoa. "It's just through here."

I followed her, carrying my overnight things. A single bed divided the room, the head under the window. Wardrobes lined one wall, and ceiling-high bookcases the other. A small desk stood by the door.

"It ain't anything special," Amy said, tidying a shelf as she spoke. "But the bed's comfy, and I'm sure you'll find plenty to interest you if you can't sleep."

I scanned her shelves. The books were mostly about spiritual practices, tarot, palmistry, meditation, the paranormal, and mythology, along with some dealing with native Indian customs, natural remedies, gardening, and herbs.

"This is cool," I said. "And thanks heaps for having me."

"That's okay, honey, any time. How about I show you the bathroom? Feel free to have a soak in the tub, if you like. That should help you to feel better."

I grabbed my overnight bag and pyjamas, and Amy led me back through the kitchen. Through a door to the right I entered a small, lime-green coloured bathroom, and I gave myself up to the pleasures of a steaming hot bath.

The rain still drummed down as I dressed, brushed my teeth, and repacked my overnight bag. As I brushed my hair before the mirror, I noticed an area of shadow forming behind me. I whipped around and found myself confronted by a pillow-sized patch of darkness that hovered at head height.

I stared at it. Then I blew at it. It didn't move. I walked around it. Yep, just a big old patch of Dark, hovering there. To my horror, it moved after me, and I suddenly felt icy cold. I backed to the door and felt for the knob with shaky hands, then fled into the kitchen. The Darkness stopped at the doorway. I felt like it was observing me, waiting for my next move.

"Amy?" I called, my voice cracking. "Can you please come here?"

With my eyes locked on the Dark patch, I listened for Amy's footsteps. A moment later, I heard the soft thump of her slippers and glanced around. But another apparition hovered at the kitchen doorway, one in a billowing white gown, its face pale under what looked like a white turban – a real, live

– well, dead – ghost!

3.

I screamed. The apparition blinked, then started to laugh. I felt like an idiot.

"Sorry. Last time I looked, you weren't all kitted out as the Lady in White."

"No honey, I'm sorry. I didn't think how I must look, in my nightie, with herbal face cream plastered all over me and my hair up in a towel to dry."

I turned back to the Dark patch. It was gone.

"Ah, phooey!" I said. "Is there something haunting your bathroom?"

"My bathroom?" Amy echoed, surprised. "What sort of something?"

"It looked like a blob of shadow," I explained. "Just floating in the air."

I checked in the bathroom again, but saw nothing. Amy looked thoughtful.

"Nothing dark here, so far as I know," she said. "That's one reason I liked this house – no bad vibes, no negative energies, no paranormal history. There are fairies in the garden, though."

I burst into laughter. Amy smiled.

"For real. There are some lovely nature spirits out there. That's probably why I have so much success with my herbs. Not all of them are native to this region, or even this continent. If I didn't have help, a lot of them would fail."

"Oh," I said. "Sorry I doubted you. So what do you think this dark thing was?"

Amy frowned, making her gooey face cream wrinkle on her forehead.

"I don't know. Let's see if my books can tell us anything."

We did just that. Nearly an hour passed before Amy remembered her face cream had to be washed off. I flipped through a volume on supernatural entities. Not ghosts – we'd quickly dismissed those. Amy felt this was more like a manifestation of spirit, or ungrounded energy. I looked up as I heard the distant splash of water in the bathroom basin, and came face to face with the Dark patch again.

Its coldness engulfed me, and I had the impression of an inquiring mind tugging at my thoughts. I shrank back, but then I decided to talk to it, just to see what happened.

"Hello? Are you trying to tell me something?"

A barrage of random sounds and images assaulted my inner eye, a dizzying array of stimuli I could barely process.

"Whoa," I said, holding my hands up. "Slow down. I can't understand all this."

The swirl of images slowed. There were people and places I recognised, and many I didn't, and all sorts of events, mostly disasters. I watched, fascinated, until the progression of images blinked out, leaving only one. I focused on it, wondering who the man before me was.

He was darkly good-looking, with angled brows above sparkling blue eyes, trim sideburns and goatee, and a careless, debonair grace. He wore a stylish black leather jacket, black jeans and black leather boots. A pair of very dark sunglasses were hooked into his jeans pocket. He looked straight into my eyes and switched on the charm.

"Well, hello," he said, smiling wolfishly. "I thought it was about time we met, Cheri. To tell you the truth, I

75

couldn't resist having a peek before – hope you can forgive me, darling."

I didn't know what to think. He looked as fine as wine, but his manner and roundabout way of introducing himself set off my weird alert.

"Oh, sorry," he apologised, and slapped his own hand. "I haven't introduced myself – how rude."

The water stopped splashing in the bathroom. Amy would be back in seconds, and I didn't know if this cheeky fellow would show himself to her.

"Who are you?"

"Call me Lou," he said, winking conspiratorially. "Can't stay, I'm afraid. So much to do, so little time. Eternity is so limiting! But I'll be back, my dear. Oh yes, I'll be back to get to know you better. Toodle-oo!"

He raised his hand up near his face and wiggled his fingers in a wave goodbye. Then he vanished, and I found myself looking straight into Amy's questioning eyes.

"You're not going to believe this," I said.

I described what I'd just experienced. When I finished, Amy turned and scanned her shelves. She picked out a book and flicked through it, then pulled out a couple more and sat down on the bed to look through them. I wondered what angle she was investigating. Finally she shut the books, frustrated.

"I'm sure it's not a normal haunting. They tend to be somewhat regular in their appearances, and I've never seen anything ghostlike in this house. It could be a wandering spirit, which would make more sense as its chosen only you to show itself to, but again, the method of revelation is rather strange. You said it called itself 'Lou'?"

"Yep. I suppose that could be short for Louis or something.

But Louis who?"

"Your guess is as good as mine, honey. It could be anyone, from any time. Usually spirits appear in whatever form they think you'll be most receptive to for the transmission of their message."

"He was keen to talk to me. Perhaps it's something to do with my life purpose?"

Amy looked at me levelly, her dark eyes serious.

"He doesn't sound like the sort to pass on helpful messages. I'm warning you to be extremely careful. He might try to mess with you, and it can be hard to defend yourself against that sort of messing."

"Well, if he's gonna chase me around your house and flirt with me, I might need some lessons in self-defence."

"I'll teach you the basic skill now, just in case he comes back, and in the morning we'll work on it some more."

First Amy showed me how to ground myself and stay centred. Then came the real thing, visualising a protective white shield around myself to repel psychic attack. I practiced it under Amy's supervision, then she tested me by trying to view my aura while my shield was up. To my surprise, she sat there, frowning.

"Very good. I couldn't get a foot in anywhere. You're very adept at this."

"Thanks. What do you see when the shield is up?"

"A white mist," Amy replied. "As you gain skills and grow stronger, it will get lighter, until you can put up a really strong wall of pure white light."

It was late, so Amy went to bed while I sat up to look through her books. I found one about angels and demons, and snuggled down under the covers to read. I tried to stay alert in case the strange patch of Darkness and attendant weirdo returned, but soon I started to yawn and nod. I put the book face down on the floor by the bed so I didn't lose my page, switched off the light, and fell asleep.

I can't remember whether I dreamed or not. I awoke to a knock on the door, and Amy entered with two steaming mugs of coffee. Light rain still tapped on the roof, and I got that delicious feeling that rainy days always gave me as a kid. I sat up and gratefully accepted my drink.

"Did you sleep okay?" Amy asked, sitting on the bed.

"Must have," I mumbled through a yawn. "Don't remember a thing."

"Ready to get to work?"

"Work? I only just woke up, you slave-driver."

Amy smiled.

"You have a lot to learn," she said, picking up the book I'd left on the floor. "Ah. Interested in angels and demons?"

"Yeah, there's so much I don't know about them."

Amy frowned and turned the book towards me.

"Well, you sure went for the heavyweights to read about."

"That's not where I left it open," I said, suddenly wide awake. "I was reading about Archangel Michael before I went to sleep."

The pages before me were about Satan – the devil himself, accompanied by a gruesome medieval woodcut print and list of all the names he was commonly known by.

"Lucifer," I whispered, gazing at Amy. "Lou..."

She stared right back, and exhaled sharply.

"If you're right, I'm going to have to teach you some real advanced stuff. He's not good news, in case you hadn't heard."

4.

We practiced building the white wall of protection again, then we ate breakfast. As we munched through a pile of toast, Amy related some of her experiences with dark entities. Her stories made my flesh crawl. The psychic battles she'd fought made my argument with Adio seem like a stroll down Jacksonville beach. In spring. With a nice little breeze at my back.

"So," she said, noting the dismayed look on my face, "you still going to go through with whatever quest lays ahead of you?"

"Um," I answered. "Do you think I could just gracefully decline?"

"Ah, if only it were that easy," Amy said with a laugh. "Trouble is, if you avoid it in this lifetime, it will just come up again in your next life. So I'd get it over and done with, if I were you."

"I don't even know where to start!" I said helplessly.

"How about a quick reading? I might be able to find out more for you to go on."

We went to the front room and I shuffled the tarot deck. The first card I turned over was the Devil.

"Great," I said. "I guess he's just making sure I don't forget him."

The next card was the five of wands again.

"You also got this one yesterday," Amy reminded me. "Upheavals in life, fighting battles..."

"Great," I said. "Especially if it means I have to fight battles with powerful, invisible thingies floating in the air."

"Relax," Amy said, as I flicked over one last card. "I'm sure you'll know what to do when the time is right. And look – the

Chariot again. I think that's suggestive, don't you?"

"What – you mean I've got to drive somewhere to fulfil my quest?"

"The cards are rarely that literal, though it could be meant that way."

"Hey, what if Mr Dark Patch shows up while I'm driving?"

"I doubt he will. He's far more likely to appear when you're receptive, not when you're actively doing something that needs your concentration."

"Do you think he'll come back while I'm with you?"

"He doesn't seem too keen on company. For the spirit world to appear to you, a number of conditions must be met, and if one of his conditions is that you be alone, then it's unlikely he's going to drop in while I'm around."

"Great. So I've got to handle him on my own?"

"Honey, you're never alone in the spirit realm," Amy said.

"And what about in the real-life, day-to-day realm?"

"What I meant was, even though you're going about your business, day in, day out, in the real world, you can call on help from the spirit realm any time you need it. Remember Archangel Michael? He's one strong entity you can call on in times of trouble. And there are tonnes of others. So you're quite literally never alone."

I digested this, wondering if there happened to be spirits floating about, peering over my shoulder at that very moment. Apparently, there were.

"I'm looking at your aura," Amy said. "There's a lovely patch of green by your left side which isn't a part of your own energy. There's a departed soul who loves you very much, who looks out for you and keeps you safe. It feels motherly – perhaps a grandmother who has passed?"

"Yes," I said, blinking away sudden tears. "Dad's mother died when I was sixteen. Karen and I always loved staying with her on vacations. We were very close. I'm really glad she's with me now. It makes sense if there's a spirit around me, it would be her. I just hope she isn't too shocked at some of the things I've done."

Amy smiled gently.

"Honey, by the time you reach old age you've experienced so much that nothing really shocks you any more. Especially after you pass and regain the memories of all the other lives you've had. There's very little that can shock your grandmother now."

I was glad to hear it. Sex before marriage had been frowned on when Gran was young, and probably some of the other things I'd done. But I knew Amy was right, and I felt my grandmother's love wash over me.

"So," I continued. "How are Gran and I going to handle Lou?"

"Well, firstly I wouldn't make jokes about him. Dealing with Lucifer is like playing with fire. This is a serious business, so best to get that straight from the get go."

I nodded.

"Secondly, you need to call on spirits of light, like Archangel Michael, entities that will help to restore the balance between good and evil."

"Wouldn't it be better to wipe out evil altogether?" I asked.

"Honey," Amy said with a sigh, "that's a nice sentiment, but ultimately a fool's dream. There is bad in the world. It's necessary. We can't get away from it, ever. We have free-will, and while people can choose evil, or justify evil actions, we'll never be rid of it. And believe me, people are so easily

81

tempted."

I had to agree.

"Besides," Amy said, "without evil, how would we recognise good? Good and bad aren't as black and white as they're made out to be. A lot comes down to individual perception. When one person kills another, it's murder. In our country, the law mandates the death sentence for murderers. So it becomes acceptable for God-fearing, law abiding people who believe they live by the Ten Commandments to wish death upon another, because that other has murdered."

"An eye for an eye," I said.

"Yes. And whether the law upholds it or not, that attitude is still very much a part of the human condition. Everyone knows right from wrong in their heart. But not everyone chooses to listen to their conscience. Those people are easy prey for Lucifer. Think of him as a predator, like a lion or a shark. He'll attack the weak and vulnerable. They're easier to lead astray. Putting up a big fight makes it harder work for him."

Amy looked around conspiratorially.

"That's where he's subtle. He won't let you go, just because you're strong and protected. No, he'll go and fed on easier souls while he rallies his resources, then he'll sneak in some way you never expected. You might think you have all the entrances to your soul locked up tight and guarded, but that's nearly impossible. He'll find a weakness to exploit and try to gradually turn you against yourself."

Alarm must have shown on my face. Amy put a reassuring hand on my arm.

"I know it sounds like a fight you can't win, but believe me, you must try. He might win some of the battles, but you must win the war."

"But... Isn't Lucifer kinda in the realm of Christianity?" I asked, hoping for a loophole. "Like, don't you have to be a Christian to believe in him?"

Amy pursed her lips thoughtfully.

"Not necessarily. There are millions of people worldwide who believe he exists. All that belief has to count for something, doesn't it?"

"So you're saying that belief in Lucifer is what makes him real?"

"It helps. There have always been dark spirits – in all the religions of the world, there are plenty of evil entities. And when an evil one gets very powerful, he can influence the minds and spirits of those he comes into contact with and feed off the power of their fear, as well as their belief in his existence."

"Until in time he becomes the most powerful evil dude around?"

"Yes."

My insides churned. It seemed Lucifer could slip in and out of my mind whenever he chose, and do whatever damage he wanted to. I wasn't about to put up with that without one heck of a fight.

"Great. So, what can I do when he tries to get in?"

"Ground yourself," Amy said, ticking off the points on her fingers. "Don't believe what he says. Call on spirits of light and love to help you. Visualise. Learn charms of protection. Wear amulets of power. That one you've got on is a good start."

I repeated the list out loud, my fingers grazing over the tyet I wore.

"It's a lot to learn," Amy said earnestly, shaking her head.

"There's only so much I can help. The rest is up to you."

"Huh, right. Can I please wake up from this dream now? It can't be real."

Amy leaned forward.

"Oh, it's real alright. Many people mightn't think so, but that's one thing I can assure you of. And it's deadly serious – literally, a battle for the soul."

5.

"So my life purpose?" I asked. "This mission? What've I got to do, exactly?"

"Part of your spiritual mission will be to discover your own strengths and weaknesses," Amy said. "You will learn best from your own inner journey, otherwise your mission will be undermined."

I groaned, thinking how difficult it had all become.

"Wouldn't it be so much easier if you just told me what I have to do?"

"I can't do that," Amy said. "I don't know what you have to do. I can only see what is necessary to pass on to you, not things you have to find out for yourself. Even my spirit guide can't tell me more than you strictly need to know."

"So how do I get one of these spirit guides?"

Amy smiled.

"Honey, everyone has spirit guides. Apparently, there's a very strong guide on the way for you. Until then, you have your grandmother. But you have to learn how to tune in and listen to her. Ready for another lesson?"

Boy, was I ever. With all this other-worldly stuff going on about my sweetly oblivious ears, I really needed to get in touch with someone I could trust in the spirit realm. And who better than my Gran?

Amy showed me how to meditate to open a channel for communication, and I soon felt a familiar presence by my side. I swear I smelt my grandmother's favourite perfume, though very faintly.

"I love you, Gran," I whispered, smiling with all my heart and soul.

Her presence grew stronger, and I smelt another aroma. Gran had been one mean baker, and always whipped up trays of cookies and muffins when Karen and I visited. Our favourite had been a Halloween treat we called 'skulls'. She'd bake balls of stiff cookie batter, cover them with white icing, and stick liquorice in the right places for eye sockets, nasal cavity and mouth.

The memory was so strong I almost felt like I was back there in her open, sunny kitchen, with Karen making perfect skulls by my side. Mine were always wonky and lopsided, but Gran said that was how they should be, because everyone's skull is different. I laughed inwardly, and I knew she was laughing with me.

"I know you're here," I said. "I need you, Gran. I need your help."

I felt a slight tugging in my head, and Gran's voice echoed between my ears.

"My little Ange," she crooned. "My sparrow. Look at you now. You're all grown up, but you're still so little. And I don't like the things you have to face."

"Oh Gran," I whispered back. "I've missed you so much."

A wave of memories and feelings washed over me. I couldn't help but smile, because they were happy memories, good feelings. She'd always called me her sparrow, as I was small and skinny. Karen had womanly curves at fourteen, but mine only developed in my late teens. And they didn't bother to develop much. At least my years of gym training had upgraded my physique from thin to athletic.

"I've always been with you and Karen," Gran assured me. "Though more with you. I knew Karen would get on in the world with her bright, blessed spirit. You were always a loner, Ange. You seemed so lost, so filled with hurt that I tried to help you with. But you clung to it, didn't you? You wore your frustration and anger like a cloak, to protect yourself and keep others out. Did you know that?"

I was taken aback by her words, but saw the truth in them. I'd always felt like an outsider, even in my own family, and I'd been angry at Mama for being so ditzy and shallow. I realised a lot of things in that moment, and with an inward sigh, I started to let go.

"That's right, my sparrow. Get the shovel and start pitching out all that trash you've accumulated over the years. Clean it out, all that hurt you've clung to. I can tell there's a beautiful, shining you under all that garbage. Let's get at it."

Tears stung my eyes again as I thought about all the defensive walls I'd built around myself since childhood. I'd hurt lots of people in defending myself, and hurt myself worst of all by not being more open and trusting. I nodded as I examined my true feelings. They'd been buried for so long that they'd become almost numb.

I realised I'd battled against the world needlessly, always trying to make it conform to what I thought it should be, when in reality all I was doing was building ever higher walls around myself. The trouble with these walls was that they were built on very weak foundations of fear, and they'd always been shaky at best.

"I'm so sorry," I cried. "I've been so horrible, and hurt people and shut them out. I didn't realise what I was doing. How could Gabe ever have fallen in love with someone like me? I don't deserve him..."

"There, there," Gran said. "It's only natural to feel this grief, once you realise how self-destructive you've been. Some people go through their whole lives – even many lives – and never realise it, so you're doing well.

"And don't fret about your young man. He fell in love with the good in you, the good he knew you could be – the good you will be once you've done some work on building yourself up again. And the most important part of that is to forgive yourself."

I sniffled and dried my tears. I wasn't sure how I was supposed to do that, but I knew I had to try. I looked to Amy, who had only heard my side of the conversation.

"I'm supposed to forgive myself," I said. "How do I do that?"

"It's not easy," she said. "It's one of the hardest things for anyone to do. It's so hard that most people spend a lifetime running away from it. Will you run, Ange? Or will you face it?"

I weighed up how hard I thought it could be compared to battling evil spirits and Lucifer himself to make the world a better place, and suddenly self-forgiveness didn't seem quite so difficult.

"Okay. How do I start?"

"Well," Amy said, "first you must acknowledge your mistakes, and you're doing that. You own those mistakes – you've made them yourself, and now you're learning from them. So they're not all bad, really."

"Oh. I hadn't thought of that."

"Then you need to acknowledge that everyone makes mistakes, loads of them in every life time, and that you have a right to make mistakes too. It's perfectly normal. It's part of human experience, and how we best learn.

"Lastly, you need to release any bad feelings you have about your mistakes. You can't go back and undo them, so you must accept them and move on. Leave them in the past, where they belong. But if you ever have the chance to make amends, do so. Karma always comes back to you, whether you do bad or good. So when you patch up an old argument with someone, or apologise for an old hurt you've caused, it gets the karma cycle rolling in the right direction, bringing good stuff into your life instead of bad."

I liked the sound of that.

"I couldn't have put it better myself," Gran's voice echoed in my head. "You've got a very wise friend there."

"And I've got a very wise Gran," I replied.

She chuckled in my head. It felt like champagne bubbles rising through my soul. I couldn't help but laugh along with her. Amy picked up our long-empty mugs and walked towards the door.

"How about some lunch? I think we need to relax and think about something else for a while."

I was about to get up and follow her out, but something held me back. I still felt my grandmother's presence near me, but someone – or something – else was now present. I looked about, and spotted it floating across the room, straight at me.

"Oh, here we go," came Gran's voice.

"That's for sure," I thought back, and launched into shielding myself.

"Oh Cheri," Lou said. "You know, that can't keep me out forever. In fact, it can't even keep me out for a second."

5

Everybody's Been Burned

1. Thursday 23rd October 1969 – Jacksonville, Florida

I ignored him and concentrated on building a wall of pure, white light around myself. At first I thought it was working, but Lou stepped through my wall as though it was nothing but mist. His black leather jacket shimmered with moisture, and he made a show of brushing it off his sleeves.

I was so disappointed that I nearly let my shield crumble, but I sighed inwardly and worked on maintaining what I had. Patience and practice were the keys to learning, Amy had said. Gran was suddenly short on both.

"Hey, you!" she cried. "You leave her alone! She's just a little girl!"

Lou smirked.

"Yes, a little girl who should know better than to play with dangerous toys."

His eyes never left mine, and I swear I could see fire dancing in them.

"Gran, you're reacting instead of helping to ground me."

"I know honey, but I can't help it. I'm not going to watch evil personified walk up to my granddaughter and not fight."

"We need to fight together, as one," I said, concentrating harder.

"Oh bravo," Lou said, clapping. "You want to fight the good fight. So commendable."

"Back off, you vulture," Gran said. "You're nothing but filth dressed up. You're completely abhorrent and despicable. You have no redeeming features whatsoever."

Lou pretended to look hurt.

"Oh, you cut me to the bone," he said snidely, one hand over his heart.

Well, where his heart would be if he had one, which struck me as unlikely.

"Gran!" I hissed. "Please help me concentrate. He's not worth it."

"You're right, Ange. He's so low he's beneath my contempt."

From then on, I felt a force greater than my own sweeping in, stabilising and grounding me, strengthening my wall until it was more than just mist. It shone with a pearly radiance, now that I had confidence in the technique. Lou's image wavered before me, like static on a TV screen. He didn't seem to like it.

"Oh, very well," he huffed. "We'll play the game your way for now. But I'll be back, you tasty little morsel. You can't be on guard all the time."

With that, he faded away. Gran let out a victory whoop, and I opened my eyes, grinning. Amy appeared in the doorway, a frown on her face.

"He doesn't muck about," I said. "As soon as you left, he had a go at me."

"We really need to work on your protection, then," she said. "And we'd better stick together so you have a chance to develop your skills before heading out alone."

I followed her to the kitchen, where we made sandwiches and ate at the table. Amy went through a checklist of does and don'ts she thought would help me.

"Stay alert and keep in touch with your grandmother as much as possible. If you get in trouble, she can help."

I thought of how she'd reacted to Lou's presence, and hoped she was listening.

"No alcohol or drugs. They'll slow your reaction time and mess up your thinking, giving attackers an immediate advantage."

"No problem there," I said. "I like a drink, but I can live without it. And I tried one of dad's cigarettes once, when he wasn't looking. Nearly barfed up my lungs. That put me off any kind of smoking for life."

"And other substances?"

"Well, Gabe brought acid around a couple of times, but I always had a bad reaction to it, so we decided not to experiment with drugs any more."

"That's good. Remember, people out there could be anything. Some may be guardians watching over you. Some may be evil spirits disguising themselves so you don't see them for what they are. And you need to be alert to pick 'em. On meeting someone new, take a peek at their aura. That should tell you all you need to know."

I'd tried to see people's auras before, but never had much success. Now I realised it was probably because I couldn't see through my own dark aura. I cleared my mind, softened my focus, and just made out a glowing outline of energy around

Amy, which became stronger as I gazed. A radiant light pulsed around her, interspersed with patches of bright colours. I blinked and grinned.

"You did it!" Amy said. "I could feel you reaching out, probing and exploring. Mind you, I've experienced that before, from people who were mostly up to no good. But you need to learn this skill, so I'm okay with it. Wow, you're really coming along!"

"Thanks," I said, beaming. "But I guess I still have lots to learn."

"When you have questions, you can always ask spirit."

"But how do I know I can trust the answers? What if someone gives me the wrong information?"

"Only talk to entities you know," Amy said. "And when a new one comes along who claims to have information for you, test them out. Don't trust them until you're sure of them. If they're really there for your highest good, they won't mind."

"So when did you first meet your guide?" I asked.

"I was thirteen when he made his presence known. It took me years to really trust him, but once I did, my spiritual growth was rapid."

"Is he here right now? Can he tell me what I need to know?"

"If it's in divine order. Go ahead and ask your questions, and I'll give you his answers. But be prepared – you mightn't like what you hear."

Amy closed her eyes and breathed in deeply several times. When she opened them again, I got a shock. It was like someone else was looking out of them.

"Whoa, that's – freaky," I said. "Are you being possessed?"

A deep, gravelly voice issued from Amy's mouth.

"Amy Zamora has volunteered to become a physical vehicle

for spirit. In this way, your questions may be answered."

It took a moment for me to adjust. It wasn't at all what I'd expected.

"Okay. So, what can you tell me about my life purpose – my quest?"

"Nothing."

I blinked. I'd sort of hoped for something better.

"Why not?"

"You have much to learn yet. Your spirit guide will help you."

"So, when do I meet my spirit guide?"

"When you are ready."

"And when will I be ready?"

"When you have mastered certain lessons."

"Which lessons?"

"Those that come to you along your path."

"You're not being very helpful."

"You do not ask the right questions."

I sucked a cheek in, frustrated.

"I just want to know about my future."

"You wish to have it made easy for you. That is counter-productive. It is for you to choose your future, to be active in selecting an outcome."

To my irritation, I realised he was right. Time for a different approach.

"So just how much can you see of the future?" I asked.

"We in the spirit realm see many possibilities, but cannot influence them outside of divine order. However, when there is a mass, heartfelt petition by many souls, an opportunity opens for change. Wherever the greatest benefit lies, is what will happen."

"So people *can* influence events?"

"Yes. Your thoughts create your reality, and so does karma. You must be aware of your thoughts and the consequences of them. It is simple cause and effect."

"And prayers?"

"The Great Spirit and its helpers are willing to listen and to act on petitions. But prayers must be made with strong, heartfelt intent, and be in line with the best outcome for all involved."

"Is that why so many prayers go unanswered?"

"Often. People poison their thoughts and intentions with wrong beliefs, beliefs that they aren't good enough, that they don't deserve, that others don't deserve, that prayers don't really work, that no one really listens. They unconsciously poison themselves, and the prayers are thus poisoned too. But when the petitioner is completely focussed, has only the best intentions at heart, and it is within divine order, the prayers will be heard and answered."

"What about spirit guides and angels? How do they fit in?"

"Guides help many souls during their physical journeys. The angels, archangels and ascended masters help an infinite number. The further one has progressed on their spiritual journey in life, the more souls one can help when in spirit."

"And karma?" I asked, eager to know more. "The more good you do in life, the higher up the karmic cycle you get?"

"If one follows their Universal Duty, then yes. That's also the threefold law. Whatever you do, whether good or evil, will come back to you times three."

"Gee, that's sure an incentive to lead a good life. Only so few people realise it."

"Young souls have long journeys ahead of them. Many resist

their path from fear, choosing instead to be victims. It may be many lifetimes before a soul is ready to take this journey, let alone deal with all the struggles on the way."

"And that's where I am," I said, my heart sinking. "Still right at the beginning."

2.

"That perception is inaccurate. You are already well on your way on the path."

"Glad to hear it," I said, without much enthusiasm.

Amy closed her eyes again and took some deep breaths. When she next looked at me, I could see she was back to normal.

"That was a bit freaky," I said.

"Was it helpful?" she asked.

"Some of it was. I found out some interesting things, but not what I really wanted to know. Still, it's a start."

"You've done well, honey. I think a celebration is in order."

"Celebration? To celebrate what?"

"A milestone. You've made a lot of progress in a very short time. I think we should acknowledge your new skills with a ceremony to thank the spirit realm for all the help you've received."

I was aware of the concept of thanking spirits for the help they gave, but I'd always felt awkward, not knowing whether they'd actually helped me or not. Now that I understood more about the process, it seemed the right thing to do.

Amy spread a purple tablecloth on the table in the front room, lit some candles and incense, and placed a number of gemstones around the surface. The room became ambient, like it was a channel for some sort of mystic energy. Of course, the good vibes couldn't last.

"What's that smell?" I asked, wrinkling my nose.

Amy sniffed the air.

"All I can smell is the incense. Why? Is it making you ill?"

I shook my head, perplexed.

"No, it's not the incense. Don't worry about it. Let's get started."

"If you're sure," Amy said, looking troubled. "But if it gets any worse, tell me."

She began a message of thanksgiving to our spirit guides, including my grandmother. But as soon as I started to speak, the stench worsened, filling my nostrils with the smell of rotten meat. I also heard flies buzzing, a couple at first, then dozens. I swayed in my chair, wondering what was going on.

Startled, I looked at Amy, and she began probing. I did too, and what I saw horrified me. In my inner mind festered a macabre image, the carcass of some small animal, possibly a cat or dog – it was hard to tell – rotting. Flies and maggots crawled over the exposed entrails and dried blood on the ground around it, and the stench became even more putrid, threatening to overwhelm me completely.

I nearly gagged. I was certain I knew who'd planted this foul thing in my head. I wanted to jump up and shout at him to get out, but I stopped myself. As satisfying as the action and words might feel, they would only increase his hold on me.

By a massive effort, I refocused and breathed deeply. My wall had been defective the first time around, but I knew I could only improve on that with practice. I concentrated on building it up again, and felt my grandmother adding her powers to mine. I could also hear her.

"Dirty, rotten, stinking coward," she mumbled. "Picking on a little girl like that. Disgusting asshole."

I almost giggled. I'd never imagined her saying such things. Amy's presence was also noticeable, along with two other spirit entities. Between all of us, my wall grew strong and gleaming white, and the putrid smell and sound of flies faded away. But the image in my head took longer to disappear. After ten more minutes of telling it to go back where it came from, it started to fade.

And so did I. Totally exhausted, I slumped back in my chair. Amy came around beside me and took my hand, and I could feel Gran at my other side. The other spirits were still nearby.

"That was... interesting," I said.

"Was that you-know-who?" Amy asked.

"Didn't see him, but I'm sure it was."

"I'm guessing whatever you smelt was a part of it?"

I nodded and drew another deep, energising breath. I never thought air could taste so good.

"It was disgusting – a rotting carcass covered with flies."

"That figures," Amy said, nodding. "The Lord of the Flies."

"I thought that was some book," I said.

"It is, but the name's been around a long, long time, in connection with Lucifer's main henchman, Beelzebub. This will be a friendly reminder of what he's capable of."

"We got rid of it."

"Yes we did, with some very powerful help from the other side – my own guide, and Lucifer's old adversary, Michael."

"You mean Archangel Michael?"

I was awestruck when Amy nodded. But a frown creased her face.

"Look, he didn't attack you willy-nilly. He waited until your defences were right down so he could test how strong you are and how quickly you can defend yourself. He'll probably keep testing you like that for a bit, and then he'll get serious."

"You mean that wasn't?"

Amy looked me in the eyes. She, for one, was deadly serious.

"Honey, that was barely a taster for what may yet come. Like I said, he doesn't like people to put up a fight. He'll be back for more, you can bet your sweet life on it."

So much for good news. I took a few minutes to gather my strength, and when I could stand again, Amy helped me to the spare room to lay down.

"So this is good, right?" I said. "I'm learning to face my fears, work through them, and come out stronger. And fight off demons. I might just take a nap now."

"Okay," she said. "I'll do some research and try to get some answers for you. Your grandmother is here, and so is my guide, and I'll ask for Archangel Michael's continued help, so you'll be well guarded."

I wondered about that. This was the first time he'd tried anything in Amy's presence, and it had taken five of us to repel him. What would happen if he waited until I was alone when he next chose to attack me?

3.

Despite my worries, I drifted off to sleep, and awoke in the late afternoon when some knucklehead cruised past the house playing Monster Mash far too loud on his car radio . Amy brought me a cup of herbal tea and sat on the end of the bed.

"So," she said, "are you ready to learn some more?"

"Sure," I replied. "I'm curious about these Hidden ones. Like werewolves."

"Okay. They have animal instincts and are adept at staying hidden. But you'll know them by their auras. I've had personal experience with werewolves myself."

"What happened?" I asked. "If you don't mind telling me?"

Amy drew in a deep breath, and her eyes took on a haunted look.

"Okay. I've just... never told anyone before. Well, I grew up in a little town in Louisiana. I was fourteen and my kid brother, Jesse, was ten, when his classmates dared him to spend the night in a swamp near our town. He was a brave little soul who thought nothing of camping out under the stars, so he accepted the dare. He told our parents he was sleeping over at a friend's place, and no one bothered to check.

"When he didn't turn up the next day, I came clean. I led the search party to the swamp, and we found signs of a struggle, and blood. Not a lot. Just a few little spatters."

I felt horrified for the teenaged Amy who'd made this gruesome discovery.

"His tent was ripped – great rips like a bear might make. So everyone thought a bear got him. But I knew it wasn't. The vibes there were very disturbing. I was sent home, and the adults kept looking. But they never found anything.

"I'd been exploring my psychic gifts in secret, so people wouldn't make fun of me or call me a liar. I went back out there the next weekend, and opened myself right up. I was drawn to the woods. It was dark in there, and I should've high-tailed it out. But the trail was strong; I sensed I was real close. And there was a terrible smell..."

I recoiled. I knew plenty about terrible smells after that

day's attack.

"I crept through the bushes, and... a horrible sight. A man laying there, dead. Naked. All covered in scratches and bruises. His leg was caught in a bear trap – one of those heavy steel-jawed things – crushed to a pulp, covered in dried blood..."

"Oh Amy! And your brother?"

"He was alive. Squatting nearby, all scratched and bruised. He just hunched there, staring at me like some kind of wild animal. I went closer, but he scuttled away. I asked why he hadn't gone to the searchers or come home. He growled and whined, tried to talk. I barely understood – it sounded like, 'hairy man came. Hairy man dead'."

"Hairy man?"

"That's what I think he said. He must've meant the dead guy, but I didn't see why, 'cause he wasn't very hairy. Then I saw a bite mark on Jesse's arm. I begged him to come home to have it tended to, but he just hunkered down and wouldn't budge. I was afraid to go near him again in case he ran away and I lost him for good, so I sat there with him for hours, with the dead guy behind us. It was creepy as hell.

"Near sunset, I decided to go home and bring Pa back the next day. As I got up, Jesse leapt at me, clawing and biting. I pushed him away and ran home, and tried to tell my parents. But they were furious I'd gone into the woods alone, and were too angry to listen. I kept at them, and finally Pa and a couple of other men went to look. When they came back, they hit the liquor. They must've seen the man's body, but they never said. And they swore they never saw hide nor hair of my brother.

"Well, I was too scared to go look for Jesse again. Then one night several weeks later our dog, Mickey, kept barking like mad. Pa looked around outside, but he didn't see anything.

Later that night, something woke me. At first I thought it was just Mickey snuffling around outside. Then someone climbed through the window into my room."

I gasped. I hadn't thought it could get any worse.

"I was attacked in my bed. I fought back, screaming and hollering, and Ma and Pa came running. When they turned on the light, Jesse up and leapt out the window. They couldn't believe their eyes. What we saw that night wasn't my brother... more like a wild beast. He was hairy all over, even his face. His eyes were wild. He had claws, and he scratched me up pretty bad, I can tell you. And you know what else? It was a full moon that night.

"Next day, we found what was left of Mickey outside. We didn't tell a soul about it, and we hoped we'd seen the last of Jesse. But a month later – next full moon – he came back. And the month after. Those nights, he snuffled around, scratching and trying to get in. Broke Ma's heart and near sent her crazy. So we sold up and moved to San Francisco. I finished school, went to college, tried to get on with life. We never spoke of Jesse again.

"I was nineteen when he found us. I was out with my boyfriend, Lester, at the flicks that night. I'll never forget – it was 'A Place in the Sun'. Montgomery Clift and Elizabeth Taylor. When Lester took me home afterwards, we found a horrible mess. It looked like burglars had ripped through the house, turning everything over."

Amy drew in a long, deep breath, sadness in her eyes.

"My parents... were in their bedroom, so badly scratched and bitten they were unrecognisable. I lost it, and Lester had to carry me out of there. He called the cops, they came around, and I was put under sedation and taken to hospital."

I was shocked. I hadn't imagined anything so awful when Amy started her tale.

"I couldn't talk about it at first, I was such a mess. When I could, I tried to tell them about Jesse. He was down as missing, possible foul play. The police thought he was dead, and even if he wasn't, they saw no motive for him to attack us. So that was that. When I left the hospital, I moved in with Lester. We buried my parents, the house was cleaned up and sold, and I started over fresh.

"I was terrified Jesse would find me again, so Lester and I dropped out of college and went travelling. It was the best thing we could have done. We hiked all over Britain and Europe, working and studying. We met people who helped us develop our psychic skills and spiritual practice. We also learnt about dark creatures like my brother. We so loved travelling that we continued on to Egypt, the Middle East, India."

"Wow," I said. "Sounds like a dream journey!"

"Yeah, it was pretty wow," Amy said. "We learnt heaps, and we were totally in tune with spirit, and with each other. It was our own special place in the sun for those few years. Then we came home. It'd been wonderful, but we wanted to settle down and have kids, and kids need stability and a steady income."

She sat lost in thought, her eyes far away. I wondered what had happened to change her life course – I'd seen no evidence in her house of her being married or having children. Amy suggested coffee, and we moved to the kitchen.

"Of course, we wondered if Jesse was still around, but there was no way of knowing. So we moved up to Portland, Oregon. Life settled down and we were happy. A year went by and everything was peachy. Then our spirit guides indicated a life-changing event was coming. We hoped it meant a baby..."

Amy sighed and poured boiling water into our mugs. The aroma of the coffee hit, anchoring me in the reality of the kitchen.

"Then Jesse found us. So every full moon, we secured everything and stayed up all night. I felt his presence moving around and around the house, looking for a way in."

A shiver crept down my spine.

"Then one full moon we heard an explosion. A café two blocks down was on fire. Sirens, flashing lights – yeah, we were well and truly distracted. I heard glass breaking, and I turned to see Jesse climbing through a window. He was all shaggy and matted and wild-looking. He ran at me and Lester leapt between us..."

"He didn't – Jesse didn't kill Lester, did he?"

"No. Lester was a pacifist, but he wasn't a fool. He knew self-defence and he kept fit. But death might have been better after all. Jesse bit Lester's arm and wouldn't let go. I was so desperate to stop him, I grabbed some scissors and – stabbed Jesse in the throat. It's the most horrible thing I've ever done. But I had to do something."

Amy shuddered. So did I. She finished her coffee in one long gulp.

"When Jesse finally let go, I didn't know what to do – I'd hurt him pretty bad, and there was blood everywhere. I shoved him down the hall, ran back in the bedroom and locked the door. I washed and bound Lester's arm, and prayed he'd be okay. But I knew Lester was doomed to become a werewolf too."

"Oh Amy!" I said, and she sighed and patted my hand across

the table.

"Yes, it was horrible, but we knew what to expect. It broke our hearts, but we knew Lester had to go make a life for himself somewhere he couldn't hurt anyone. At sunrise we went out to see what'd become of Jesse. Blood was smeared on the floor where he'd crawled to the back door. It was wide open, and he was gone."

"For good?"

"We sure hoped so. We cleaned up the house, and then Lester prepared to leave. He planned to hike up through Washington State into the forests, far from civilisation. He phoned his folks and told them, as it was something he'd always said he wanted to do. It was his way of saying goodbye to them, though they didn't know it."

Tears sparkled in Amy's eyes, and she blinked them away.

"At the end of the week, we said goodbye to each other. I sat tight for a month before reporting him missing. His family flew up, but there was nothing they could do."

I sipped my coffee, now lukewarm, made a face, and quickly swallowed the rest.

"The police found no trace of him, of course. They thought he'd got lost in the wilderness and fell off a cliff or something. He called me a few times from pay phones, to check I was okay. The last time was two weeks after I reported him missing. It was the middle of the night and he was using a phone outside some isolated garage."

Tears slid down Amy's face and dripped off her chin.

"He missed me so bad. He just wanted to let me know he loved me and that he'd keep me in his heart forever. Then he said a car was coming and he had to hide. That was the last I ever heard from him."

Amy brushed her tears away. I felt so sad for her. What she'd gone through was terrible, and then years of not knowing what had happened to her soul mate – I was sure I could never have handled that.

"So I waited another couple of weeks, then I quit my job and had a garage sale to get rid of everything I didn't need. I moved to Florida to start over, and here I am."

4.

I got up and hugged Amy.

"I'm so sorry all those awful things happened to you."

"Thanks, honey," she said, hugging me back. "But remember, I had lots of good times too. I found my soul mate and travelled the world with him."

"And you don't know what happened to Jesse?"

Amy shrugged.

"Maybe he died. I don't know. I've lived here for thirteen years now, and I don't plan on moving again. If he finds me, he finds me. I only hope I'm well prepared if he does. But I think he would have found me long ago if he'd been able to."

"Geez, kind of makes my life seem pretty normal."

Amy laughed.

"Really? You're the Goddess Isis, incarnate. And your boyfriend is Osiris. Not to mention that your sister may very well be Nephthys. You think that's normal?"

I smiled, in spite of myself.

"Is it possible to know for sure if Karen is Nephthys? You said a regression might help me find out."

"I'm not sure you'll be up to a regression after what you've been through today. How about I try to find out what I can?

Just give me a moment."

Amy closed her eyes and sat very still. It seemed as if the air around her moved and shifted, faint patterns and colours swirling about her. I watched in fascination until she opened her eyes again.

"I'm not one hundred percent sure, but yes, I think Nephthys has incarnated as Karen. Her powers are latent, buried so deep inside her that she has no idea they exist. But I feel sure enough..."

Amy was silent for another moment, looking inward. She nodded, and smiled.

"Actually, Karen's doubly lucky. She was born to lead a charmed life. To dark spirits, she's practically invisible, so she's the perfect person for you to be with whilst you pursue your life mission."

"But wouldn't I bring the dark spirits with me if I went to her?"

"Honey, her aura's so bright it will help shield you. They won't find you if you stick close to her. You're very lucky to have someone like that."

I considered. It explained why Karen had never got in trouble or hurt herself when we were growing up, and why just about everyone liked her. Goddam. And I had to be born the exact opposite. Lucky to the last. I smiled bitterly.

"But how long would it be safe for me to use her as a shield? It doesn't sound very fair, when I have nothing to give back to her."

"Oh, but you do," Amy said. "You have more than you know. You share a sacred bond, more than just as sisters. I can't quite put it into words just now, but you need to be together, to learn together, to grow together..."

A frown crossed her face.

"What's wrong?" I asked, my voice trembling.

"You need to go to her soon. Before the end of the year – no, the end of the month... Halloween..."

"Why? Is something bad going to happen?"

"I'm... not sure. Do you have a photo of your sister with you?"

"Er, yeah."

I grabbed my handbag and riffled through it. In my address book, I kept several snapshots – one of my parents, before dad got sent to Vietnam, one of Karen and I, and one of Gabe. I extracted the photo with Karen and handed it to Amy. She stared at it hard for a moment, her brows drawn in concentration. Finally she raised her eyes to meet mine.

"Honey, I'm not real sure what it is... Some kind of danger..."

"But you just said Karen had a charmed life! What's going to happen to her?"

"I don't know. But she's going to need you with her, real soon. That's the message I'm getting right now – not so much what, but when. You need to be with her by Halloween."

A shudder ran through me. I felt seriously spooked.

"But that's only a week away! Why Halloween?"

"Because... that's when the veil between the human and spirit realms is thinnest. If something nasty is going to come through, that's when it will happen."

"Something *nasty*? Like what?"

Amy studied the photo of Karen again, then sighed and handed it back to me.

"I'm not getting that information. Just that there is some threat to her safety. Something that feels supernatural. And you need to be there to protect her, because no one else can."

My head reeled as I tried to process her words. The thought that Karen might come to some sort of harm was unbearable. I would have to go to her. But how on earth would I be able to explain my decision to travel to the other side of the country while my beloved Gabe lay in a coma in hospital?

5.

I decided to return to my apartment for the night. I needed some alone time to absorb all I'd learnt and do some thinking. Amy invited me to stay with her again after that, and I accepted. It would be good to pick her brains and learn as much as I could from her before going anywhere. And although I hated to admit it, she would help fill the gap left by Gabe.

I straightened Amy's spare room and dithered over which of her books to borrow overnight. Amy smiled at my indecision.

"Take 'em all, honey, I don't mind," she said with a laugh. "Variety's good."

I took her at her word – I really couldn't narrow it down to only one when I had so much to learn. I chose about seven books and put them in a carry-all Amy gave me, then I went out to my car.

I hoped I was safe with my newly-acquired skills and ghostly grandmother. I sensed her with me as I slipped behind the steering wheel, and smiled in gratitude. I knew I'd turned a major corner in my life, and my heart swelled with happiness. For the first time I could remember, I basked in positivity.

It was short-lived. Just down the street, a hobo staggered out in front of my car. I nearly had a heart attack as I swerved to avoid him. He shambled off into the gathering dusk, and

I heaved a deep breath of relief at the near miss. Time to concentrate rather than bask.

Back at my home plate, I showered, ate an early dinner, and packed a few things to take with me to Amy's the next day. Then, over several delicious hours, I read more about spiritual subjects, the light of the waxing moon casting its magic glow through my window. I switched my bedside lamp off, and gazed out at it for several minutes before dropping off to sleep, hoping that now humans had managed to get up there and walk on it, they wouldn't completely trash it like we were doing to the earth.

In the morning, I woke up completely refreshed and happy. Nothing nasty had happened, and no bad dreams had bothered me. Not even a sniff of Mr Dark Patch. I counted myself lucky. I lay in bed awhile and savoured the feeling of normality that had been so absent lately. Gran's presence was strong beside me.

"Gran," I whispered. "Thanks for being here for me."

"Ah, my sparrow," she said wistfully. "Gather your strength, child. You're going to need it."

"Is there something I should know? Is You-Know-Who coming back?"

"He's never far away," she said enigmatically. "Especially at this time."

"Damn. How long do I have to prepare?"

"Oh, not long now."

"Gran?"

I waited, but she stayed silent. Figuring she'd warn me if I was in any immediate danger, I got up, dressed, and ate breakfast. Somehow the nice feeling I'd woken up with had slipped away, replaced by an uneasiness I couldn't explain.

Perhaps Gran's words had spooked me, but it felt like more than that. A sense of danger hung in the air.

I finished my coffee and lugged my duffle bag and the carry-all of books down to the car. I felt a bit strange and woozy by then, almost physically sick, and I wondered if I should even risk driving. An eerie prickling down my back urged me on, and I started the caddy.

The trip was uneventful until I neared Amy's suburb. A grey pall of low-level cloud hung over the area, and people and cars clogged the street as I came up to her block. My feeling of uneasiness intensified as I saw police weaving through the slow-moving traffic, waving people on.

Then the horror met my eyes, and I nearly gagged. Amy's little house, so full of colour and spirit and life, was nothing more than a charred frame. Fire had consumed everything, leaving an empty, blackened shell in its wake.

6

Over, Under, Sideways, Down

1. Friday 24rd October, 1969 – Jacksonville, Florida

I parked in the first available space and walked shakily towards what was left of Amy's house. A newspaper journalist and his photographer were just leaving. Vultures. I stalked past them and headed for the nearest police officer.

"Excuse me," I said, my voice a croak.

"You need to move on, Ma'am," the man said. "There's nothing to see here..."

"Please," I begged. "My friend lives here. Amy Zamora. Can you tell me what happened to her?"

"You knew the occupant of this house?" he asked.

I nodded, unable to speak another word. The officer put a hand on my arm.

"Was she a close friend of yours?"

I nodded again, tears springing to my eyes. He shook his head sympathetically.

"I'm afraid Miss Zamora was trapped inside her house, along with an unidentified person. We think the circumstances are suspicious. I'm very sorry."

Tears trickled down my cheeks. No wonder Gran had told me to be strong. I stared at the charred remains, picking out details – pale wisps of smoke curling into the air, pools of water on the lawn from the fire-fighter's hoses, the acrid smell that hung thick as the cloud above.

"Are you alright, Ma'am?" the police officer asked. "Why don't you sit down here on the curb while I move the rest of these people along? I can get you some water if you feel faint."

"No thanks," I croaked. "I'll... I'll be alright."

I walked slowly back to my car, and slumped behind the steering wheel. My heart ached and my mind was a swelter of wild thoughts.

"Poor Amy," I said. "I can't believe she's gone. She didn't deserve this. And I needed her so much – who's going to help me now? Oh yeah – I've got you, Gran. Where are you? Why won't you speak to me? I need you, Gran. I need you!"

She didn't speak, but I could feel her presence, and thought I could detect the faint pressure of an invisible arm about my shoulders. I understood. There was nothing she could say to comfort me at a time like this.

"Gran, is Amy in the spirit world now? Can you contact her? Can her spirit come and help me, just like you?"

I knew these requests sounded selfish, but I was suddenly afraid. Now would be the perfect time for Lou to attack, while I was weak and disoriented with grief. I needed Amy more than ever, and I didn't know what I would do if she didn't come.

Finally I wiped away my tears, took a deep breath and drove off. I figured a good, strong coffee would help, and I looked out for somewhere, anywhere, that sold it. A few minutes later

I spotted a diner, parked, and went in. It was empty, which suited me just fine. I ordered a coffee and, desperate for some comfort food, a slice of chocolate cake. Then I found a booth at the rear and slid onto the seat with a heavy sigh.

"Ah, Cheri. The weight of the world is on your shoulders, is it not?"

My head snapped up. Lou lounged on the seat opposite, his blue eyes twinkling.

"What the heck do you want?" I hissed.

"And greetings to you, my dear. And after I've been up all night, so busy."

I started, glaring at Lou.

"Such a shame about your friend," he continued, snapping his fingers.

A stylish black mug monogrammed with a shiny silver 'L' appeared on the table before him, filled with steaming dark liquid. He sipped from it delicately and made an approving sound.

"I am so good at coffee."

The waitress brought my coffee and cake, not appearing to notice Lou. I waited for her to disappear behind the counter before speaking again.

"Listen, you scuzz," I said, leaning forward. "Did you have anything to do with Amy's house burning down? 'Cause if you did..."

"Oh, listen to you, darling," he said, rolling his eyes. "Saying that as if it made any difference."

"Crap! If you did... Huh! Who am I kidding? Of course you did."

"Oh," he said, "I can think of one or two others who might have had an interest."

"Like who?"

"Not telling," he pouted, and giggled when I glared at him even harder.

I would've given anything to go ape, but I knew it wouldn't do any good to lose my cool. It was just what he wanted. It would give him all the ammunition he needed, and more again. And I didn't want to provoke him into another attack on me.

Besides, my usually sharp tongue felt a little blunt.

"Yeah, you must really enjoy your work," I said darkly, and sipped my coffee.

I saw Lou's eyes travel across to my cake, so I shovelled some into my mouth.

"Oh darling, your manners are quite deplorable," he said. "Besides, I'd never eat the stuff they serve here. I know what's in it."

On that note, he Vanished.

"Yeah, like I care," I mumbled.

I stabbed my fork into the cake again, but didn't feel like eating any more. I swilled the remaining coffee – it had a burnt flavour reminiscent of Amy's destroyed house – and stomped out to my car. My mood wasn't improved when the radio blared to life in the middle of Purple People Eater, and I snapped it off furiously.

Back at my apartment, I tried to ring Karen but got no answer. I considered calling Sagira, but it wouldn't be safe to contact her at this time of day – there was too much risk of her parents or Adio discovering we were in touch. I felt like I'd explode if I didn't get everything off my chest, but who could I possibly tell?

I flopped on my bed, fuming. Had Lou been involved in the burning of Amy's house? I certainly thought so. But he was too subtle to have started the fire himself. Oh no, he'd use someone else, someone whose soul was easy prey. Someone unquestioning of the influences being woven around them. But who?

Maybe Adio? Adio had it in for me, so why not Amy? He'd know all the verses in the bible condemning people who talked to spirits and practiced magic of any kind. It was just the sort of thing he'd be fond of quoting – 'suffer not a witch to live'. I hadn't thought he'd stoop to murder, though. A horrible feeling of guilt stabbed through me at the thought that I'd led Adio to Amy – was I responsible now for this second attack?

Though if I was right, Adio had died in the fire as well. I was torn between relief for myself, guilt about Amy, and sadness for the Serapis family. I wondered if I should ring Sagira and test the waters, but I decided to wait until she contacted me. After all, I could be mistaken. In the myths, Set didn't die – Osiris did. And was restored to life by Isis. Only Gabe hadn't died. It was all so confusing. What was going on?

2.

I decided to visit Isis again, and see what I could find out about her siblings. I focussed myself with deep breaths, and cleared my mind of thoughts, worries... Amy's words hovered in the ether before me, the very ones she used to take me back to that desert world, back to Isis...

"My love," came Osiris' soft voice.

The body I occupied lay in a darkened room. Oil lamps glowed around us, and I felt the slight shift that told me we were on a boat. Isis' barque. Ebony furniture stood about the room, stark against the walls of paler timber.

Osiris and Isis lay on an enormous bed covered with silk sheets the colour of lapis lazuli and matched cushions with gold tassels. Both were naked. Her eyes travelled over his athletic, lightly muscled form. The body I was in – that of the goddess Isis – felt sensuous and silky, with a sheen that suggested she'd been anointed and rubbed with scented oils.

"Usir," Isis said, sounding utterly contented.

"Every time we make love, Ese, the heavens roar and the earth moves," he said, gazing lovingly into her eyes – my eyes. "It is never less than perfect."

She smiled, and I felt her joy. A girl sure could get used to this.

"Shall I have refreshments brought?" he continued.

"I do thirst, my love," Isis answered languorously. "Though you fill me up over and over, my cup overflows with desire."

"It is done," he said.

He sat up and clapped. A hand maiden swathed in blue linen entered, bringing a tray with a pitcher and goblets. She deposited it on a side table and left. Osiris filled the goblets and brought them over to the bed. The cool ambrosia was delicious, and Isis drank deeply. Osiris drained his goblet and lay back to gaze at her once more. She returned his gaze, and I was saturated by the embrace in his dark eyes. Then a disturbance broke out on the deck.

"No, you cannot enter," cried the chief handmaiden.

A gruff laugh followed, and Isis sighed. Set. She rose, slipped on a robe of deep blue silk, and turned to meet the unwelcome guest. Osiris eyed the door with irritation, but didn't get up or cover his nakedness. I wondered if he meant to provoke Set's jealousy. I didn't have to wait long to find out.

Set burst in without so much as a knock, already half-drunk on ambrosia, and banged the end of his *was* sceptre on the floor.

"My Royal brother," he mocked, bowing low. "Queen Ese. What a shame you started the celebrations without me."

"Sutekh!" Osiris' voice thundered. "You are drunk!"

Set's eyes wandered over Osiris' form.

"Brother, you are naked. Shouldn't you take better care of your – uh – tools? Anyone could just walk in and – covet them."

He looked back out the door, trying to catch the eye of one of the hand maidens, but none were there. Isis smiled at his provocative manners, knowing that her maids would not be tempted, even by a God. Thwarted, he scowled back at Osiris.

"Doesn't seem much of a party without any wenches," he muttered, "unlike the one I'm throwing tonight. There'll be plenty of everything at mine – especially for you, my dear brother."

"Sutekh," Osiris sighed. "Must you provoke me so? Why would I attend such a rabble as would gather to you?"

"Because you are to be my guest of honour! A feast in celebration of your safe return from travelling Kemet and the lands beyond!"

"And are you to be sober for this grand celebration?" Isis asked.

Set glared at her and helped himself to the pitcher of ambrosia without the benefit of a goblet. Thick streams of the nectar flowed down his snout and over his chest, puddling on the floor around his feet. I felt Isis' irritation grow to anger, not because of the mess, but because of his lack of respect for Osiris and herself.

"It would seem not," she said icily. "When you have finished, perhaps you would care for a swim in the Nile to wash that muck off yourself."

He lowered the jug and leered at her, one cropped ear flopping crookedly.

"Only if you come too," he said suggestively. "Such a shame I got landed with the wrong sister..."

"Indeed!" Isis said. "Will Nebet-het attend your celebrations tonight?"

"I did not invite her. In any case, she will be too busy caring for that squalling brat of hers."

"He's your child too!" Isis cried. "Your son!"

"Mine, is he?" Set said with a gruff laugh. "No, dear sister, I think we all know who's son Anpu really is..."

Osiris leapt to his feet, enraged.

"That's enough, Sutekh," he ordered. "You act abominably, and haven't the grace or humility to realise it while your belly and veins are full of ambrosia. Have the sense to leave of your own accord, brother, or I'll make you food for crocodiles!"

Set swayed where he stood, both forks of his tail drooping.

"Can I assume you will not attend my feast tonight? Will the most honourable Usir snub his own brother?"

"I will come if I must," Osiris snapped. "But I'm warning you, Sutekh, I'm rapidly losing patience with your antics."

"Well, who got out on the wrong side of bed?" Set sneered, his snout wrinkling. "Perhaps as Queen Ese is so perfect, one should only get out of her bed on her side." "Sutekh!" Osiris roared again.

"Fine, I'll go," Set said sulkily, his other ear flopping as well. "Perhaps your celebrations are only for intimates of the Queen."

He looked pointedly at his brother's exposed loins, turned, and staggered out the door. Osiris followed, Isis at his elbow, draping his robe about his shoulders.

"Don't provoke him any further," she said. "He may just leave if we let him."

"He has insulted you beyond tolerance," Osiris replied as we reached the deck. "He deserves at least a dunking for the trouble he's caused, and it might just serve to cool his passions and repel his drunkenness as well."

"Then let me," Isis whispered back. "He insulted my own beloved, and for that I would be the one to cause his baptism of sobriety."

Osiris smiled and nodded. Set approached the edge of the barque, making to climb down the rope ladder to the row boat below. Isis exerted her power, pushing it with her mind until it reached out and caused Set's foot to slip. He fell, hanging onto the ladder by one arm. Another prod of her powers, and his grip on the rope was gone. He back-flopped into the Nile, his scream cut off as its waters filled his mouth, and Osiris and Isis smiled together.

Set resurfaced, coughing up water, and waded to the shore. He stood on the bank, his forked tail swishing back and forth in fury, glowering as he wrung his robes out. Then he turned and vanished into a swirling sand storm that appeared on his command. The satisfaction of that moment washed over me as I came back to my conscious self again, and I lay back to think.

3.

"When I regress, I can learn skills to bring back with me," I said out loud.

A warm presence by my side chuckled.

"That might be a start, sparrow," Gran said. "I feel your power growing after each visit. So what did you learn today?"

I smiled, wondering just how much would be polite to reveal.

"Isis repelled an unwanted visitor," I said. "I felt the power forming inside her, and the way she channelled it to do as she wanted."

"Do you think you could do it too?" Gran asked.

"I don't know," I said. "But I'd like to try."

"Well, what are you waiting for?"

"I don't really know what to do."

"Well, she must have started somewhere," Gran said. "Try to remember exactly how she did it."

"I need something to focus on," I said. "How about I move that pillow?"

"Sure. I guess you should start small. Although you're hardly going to win a battle against the Lord of Darkness by chucking a pillow at him."

I closed my eyes and focussed on one of the pillows on my bed. However, thinking about moving the pillow wasn't the same as moving it, and I struggled for a couple of minutes before giving up.

"This is hard," I said.

I glared at the pillow, which had exactly zero impact on it. Then I detected a new presence, and heard a familiar, deep male voice in my head.

"Form the intent in your mind, draw the emotional power from your heart, channel the power through your fingertips and aim it at the object of your thought."

I hesitated, still unsure of the new spirit. Gran hadn't said anything in warning, and he seemed kind of familiar, so I accepted him.

I tried to follow his instructions – focussing on my task, then searching deep inside for the power I needed. I imagined that it was very important to move the pillow, and the satisfaction I would get from moving it, and then I aimed my fingers at it. Nothing happened, so I closed my eyes and concentrated harder.

"You try too hard," the new voice said. "If you persist, you will only succeed in wearing yourself out."

"Well, what?" I cried, desperate to get it right. "Can you help me out here?"

"You are too tense. Imagine that you are completely safe, relaxed, and happy, and that moving the pillow is your right, your path to continued freedom to feel this way. You command the pillow..."

I stifled my laughter and straightened my face.

"You command the pillow," the voice repeated "to do your bidding. And you must have faith that it will happen. Doubt will negate everything."

'So, sure I can move the pillow,' I thought, squinting at it as I focussed. 'There's energy in my body, just like everyone has. If psychics can control that energy and make it do stuff, then I can control it too. So move, pillow. Move!'

4.

"That's my girl," Gran crowed.

I un-squinted one eye, then the other. The pillow hovered a few inches above the bed. In my mind, I flipped it, and slowly, like it didn't really want to, the pillow turned over. I made it come to me, and was surprised at how easy it was, now that I believed I could do it.

"Faith can move mountains," the male voice said.

With the pillow in my hands, I turned to look for the newcomer. I could discern Gran's wavery, greyish presence, but I had to look hard for the other one. He was barely a shimmer in the air.

"Thanks for your help," I said. "Do I know you? Are you... Michael?"

Silence. I wondered if I'd breached some spirit protocol by asking. Then the shimmer became more solid, and I could see vague outlines of a figure.

"In life, I was known as Vaiveahtoish. It is Cheyenne, and means 'Alights upon a cloud'. You may call me Vaivea if it is easier for you. I guided the one you knew as Amy Zamora."

"You were Amy's spirit guide?" I asked in awe.

The presence bowed its head, and I fought back sudden tears at the memory of Amy working with him to answer my questions during my visit with her.

"Thanks for coming, Vaivea. Can you tell me – is Amy alright? Is she... has she passed into the spirit realm now?"

"She is in spirit, and completely unharmed by her physical experience of death."

I was glad of that, but still had to wipe tears away before speaking again.

"That's good to know. But what happened? Was it... was it Adio?"

I waited, holding my breath in anticipation. After a moment, I decided it would be better if I breathed. And also if I clarified my question.

"I mean, did Adio have anything to do with the fire that

killed Amy? Am I to blame – you know, for involving her in my problems and leading him right to her?"

"The one of whom you speak was not involved in Amy's transition."

I breathed out in a gush. If Adio hadn't been there, then he was still alive, and I was off the hook. I wondered who the mystery corpse was that had been found in Amy's house, but I had other questions to ask.

"So, does this mean you're my spirit guide now? Do I get to choose? I'm putting it badly, I know, but you were with Amy for years, and she was so wise and all."

"I am not to be your permanent guide," he answered. "But I have been directed to fulfil that function temporarily."

"So, am I any closer to getting my own spirit guide?" I asked.

"Soon. I and the one you knew as your grandmother will watch over you until the time is right for your guide to be revealed."

"Can you tell me more about my guide?" I asked. "Like, is it an angel or a spiritual master? Or a relative or friend who's passed over?"

I gasped, my mind running away with me.

"Perhaps it's Amy! Can you tell me? Is Amy coming to be my guide now?"

"I cannot say. You will know only when the time is right, and not before".

"Don't worry," Gran said. "I promise, you will never be alone."

"That's what Amy said," I murmured.

I still felt devastated at her sudden death. I was also filled with smoking hot righteous anger once more. There was something seriously wrong with the world for things like that to happen. Bad things, supernatural things, things like werewolves and vampires and Lucifer himself, sitting back and pulling all their strings. And the supposedly benevolent, loving creator who allowed it all to happen.

Not saying I thought bad stuff shouldn't happen. I could think of plenty of people I was quite happy for bad stuff to happen to. But I believed the karma you create in a lifetime should come back to you within that lifetime.

"And it's true," Gran said. "There are lots of spirits around you, all watching you live and learn and grow, and helping you along your way if you ask them to."

I shuddered. She made it sound like pervert central. Still, if I could call on good spirits to combat the bad, maybe I wouldn't have such a difficult time after all.

"So," I said, "is the time right yet to ask about this 'quest' of mine?"

Vaivea started to fade.

"The answers lie within yourself," he said, then he Disappeared altogether.

"Huh. I sure wish spirits would stick around and tell you what you need to know."

"You think he didn't?" Gran said.

I thought about that. *The answers lay within me.* Well, of course they did. I'd been thinking about this stuff all along, and now I knew it was my destiny I was thinking about. That's why I'd accessed Isis through my regressions – because it was time for me to learn how to use her powers so I could fulfil my life's purpose.

It was up to *me* to make the difference; it was up to *me* to heal Gabe and protect Karen from whatever threat loomed in her life; it was up to me to change the world for the better, and only *I* could do it, because I was Isis. But again, I came up against the brick wall of not knowing how to be Isis and use her powers. Healing Gabe, protecting Karen, and saving the world was a far cry from simply moving a pillow, after all.

"Okay, so here's the thing," I said to Gran. "I know I'm Isis. I know Isis has incredible magical and healing powers. What I don't know is how to get good at accessing and using those powers quickly so I can get on with things."

"Trouble is, you're impatient," Gran replied. "You want to know it all straight away, without putting in the time and effort necessary for true learning and understanding of what you're doing..."

"Hey, I'd love to take all the time in the world to learn about this stuff. But in case you'd forgotten, I don't exactly have all the time in the world. Neither does Karen — and neither does Gabe. I want to heal him as soon as possible, so I don't have to face doing all this quest stuff on my own. And before anything... happens to him."

The thought that Gabe might not recover without my intervention worried me immensely. Of course, I wanted to believe that Doctor Scott was right about Gabe — and also what Amy had passed on from Vaivea about him 'transcending his current situation'. But a small seed of doubt lingered, and I didn't like leaving it up to chance.

"So," Gran said, "what you're really saying is that you're afraid. That you don't trust things to turn out for the best without your helping them along."

"Of course I'm afraid. He could still die! That's why I want to know how to heal him, so I'm sure he'll recover."

Gran sighed and shook her grey head.

"How can there be a good outcome when your biggest motivation is fear? You must learn to trust in the higher good, or you'll taint all you do with negative emotions."

"Well, in my experience, trusting the 'higher good' usually turned out pretty darned rotten..."

I realised as I said it that the reason things had often turned out rotten was precisely because I *hadn't* trusted, because I'd tried so hard to control everything about my life without trusting anything or anyone outside of myself.

"I'm sorry, Gran. You're right, of course. Old habits die hard, I guess. It's just that I've never been that good at hoping for the best and trusting fate."

"Did I say anything about hoping for the best? Or fate? It's true that some things are fated to be, but most things can be influenced, depending on what kind of energy you put into them. All I'm saying is that when you are driven by fear, the results will reflect that. Look forward to your learning experiences and embrace them, whether you end up enjoying them or not, and don't try to hurry them."

I sighed. It seemed like nothing was destined to be easy – or fast. It was all so contradictory and confusing. On the one hand, Gabe was supposed to recover soon, and I was supposed to be involved. On the other, I had no idea yet how to go about healing him, and it looked like that knowledge would be a long time in coming.

Not to mention the danger to Karen that Amy had picked up on. It seemed incredible to me that I needed to be in L.A. to protect my sister, yet I was bound to stay in Jacksonville to be on hand should Gabe's condition change. Just as I contemplated this conundrum, the phone shrilled, making me jump.

"Ange?" came my sister's scared voice before I could speak. "Something really freaky's going on here, and I don't know what to do!"

7

Going Up The Country

1. Friday 24th October, 1969 – Jacksonville, Florida

"Whoa, slow down there," I said. "Karen, what's wrong?"

I heard her take a deep breath on the other end of the line.

"I'm sorry, I know it's going to sound crazy, but... I *saw* something! Something really weird... and I can't explain it."

"Well, try," I urged her. "I've seen plenty of weird stuff myself, so I'm sure anything you've seen won't be that strange."

"Oh yeah? Well, this was, I assure you. I was putting some washing away in the wardrobe this morning, and I felt like... oh God, this sounds demented! Well, I felt like I was being *watched*!"

"You mean, there was no one else there? No one could have been in your apartment without you knowing?"

"No. Eric was at work, of course, and Newt was down having a nap. It felt like someone was right there in the room with me – but no one *was* there! I went to the kitchen, and the feeling went away. But just now, I felt it again. And then I saw it.

You know that lovely old full-length mirror I inherited from Gran? I turned quickly, to see if maybe someone had climbed up to our bedroom window and was peeking in... and I caught a movement in the mirror, and... God, it was horrible..."

"What?" I asked. "Karen, what did you see?"

"I don't know, exactly. It looked like some sort of weird animal with reddish fur, just staring at me through the mirror. It disappeared before I could get a good look at it."

"An animal? What kind of animal? Was it big, or small? Hairy? Did it look like it wanted to attack you?"

"Well, it was large, like a bear – though it looked more dog-like, now that I think about it. Like a big wolf, but red. It didn't look vicious, exactly, more a kind of hungry look. God, this must sound crazy!"

"Karen," I said soothingly. "It's alright. And no, it's not crazy. It may be something supernatural, something from the spirit dimension. I know it must've been scary, but I'm sure it can't harm you."

"How can you know that? You didn't see it. It wasn't natural – it had a forked tail, for Pete's sake! Doesn't that usually mean something demonic?"

"Not necessarily. I'm guessing you haven't told anyone else?"

"I couldn't imagine who else to tell, except you," she answered. "I'm so scared. Either I'm going crazy, or something evil is stalking me. And there were all these awful murders in L.A. a couple of months back, as well as that serial killer up in San Fran... What am I going to do? What if it hurts Newt? Oh my God..."

"Karen, you said it was looking at you through the mirror. So maybe it's in another dimension. It may not be able to pass through to ours..."

"But what if it can? What if I'm in mortal danger, right now, as we speak?"

"Hold on, I'll think of something," I blurted. "Even if I have to come over there myself. Okay?"

"Okay. You know, I don't expect you to do that. I know how you hate flying. And besides, what about Gabe?"

"Yeah, well, this sounds like an emergency," I said. "Just leave it to me, okay?"

After the call, I paced up and down for a few minutes, trying to work out what to do to help Karen. Finally I threw my hands up in the air and faced Gran.

"I'm going to have to go to her. It's the only way I can be sure she's safe."

"That's the way," Gran said. "Though it took you long enough to decide."

"What should I pack?" I asked, sweeping my wardrobe door open. "I don't know how long I'll be gone or anything..."

"Don't worry about that. You know in the bible, where it says, 'ask and you shall receive'? Well, that works in every belief system, and in the spirit realm as well."

"Great," I said, hauling out a suitcase and a canvas duffel bag. "Can I please get a plane ticket to L. A. – actually, how about my own personal jet – yes, one of those brand new Concordes should do. Very 'now'. It can just land on Venice Beach, only minutes from Karen's. Much as I hate flying. At least it would be quick..."

"You're being sarcastic," Gran said as I pulled out some clothes. "And I know it can be hard to believe that things work like that. But it's true."

I pondered as I sorted, folded and stacked. I needed to get

to L. A., fast. What did I need to achieve that? It would be quickest to fly, despite that air travel always made me gut-wrenchingly ill. I surely couldn't drive that distance; it would be impractical, and take close to a week.

I picked up my jacket to fold and add to the pile, and felt something hard in one of the pockets. I felt inside, and drew out the silk bag containing Amy's tarot deck.

"How did this get here?" I asked, taking the cards out of the bag.

"You asked for help, didn't you?" Gran said.

My hands shook as I shuffled the deck. A card flew out, landing on my bed. The Chariot. I picked it up. It showed an armoured man standing in a chariot pulled by a pair of Sphinx, one black, one white. The chariot's canopy was spangled with stars. The man within looked strong and determined, standing firm like a captain at the helm of a warship, ready to overcome any opposition. He held no reins to guide the Sphinxes, and I understood that he controlled them through his will alone.

Into my mind came an image, a vision. A lonely desert highway. A small highway marker sign, the number sixty six within a shield. A black Cadillac convertible, the soft-top down. A young woman at the wheel, black hair whipping about her head, sun glinting off her dark glasses. One hand on the steering wheel, the other tapping along with the music blaring from the speakers.

I blinked in surprise and the vision disappeared.

"I do have to take the caddy," I said. "I've gotta drive to L. A."

I shook my head. It was madness. But there was no mistaking the car in my vision, or the woman driving it. Especially the woman driving it. Unless I had a mysterious twin out there somewhere also with a black Cadillac convertible and the same love of music...

I reconsidered what I needed to get to L. A. as I resumed packing my clothes. A full tank of petrol, and money for refills, food and accommodation. A good supply of water, as I'd be travelling through desert areas. I decided to stop at Niceville and fill some bottles at Mama's place...

"Do you plan to wear more than one set of clothes at a time?" Gran asked. "I suggest you take only what you need. The rest will be provided."

I sighed and dragged out the clothes I'd packed.

"And dump the suitcase," she added. "What you need will fit in that duffel bag. Believe me, you'll thank me for this later."

I eyed the canvas bag. It was spacious, but how I would fit in all I needed for a car trip to L.A. for who knew how long, was a mystery. I tried to be methodical. I packed a pair of jeans and a shirt, a sweater and pyjamas. Underwear and socks. My overnight bag was already packed. I added it to my stash, along with my hairbrush, Amy's tarot cards, and my brand new Polaroid Swinger camera that Gabe had bought me before we went to Tallahassee.

I sat and wrote a letter to my bank to arrange payment of my rent and utilities. I had plenty of money in my account. I'd saved ever since I moved to Jacksonville, not so much because I had a goal in mind for the money, but because I was already pretty frugal in my spending habits. I didn't buy much, but when I did, it was quality.

Then I rang Sagira to update her, and Mama, to let her know I was coming. I rummaged through my fridge and pantry, shoved anything that might spoil into the freezer, ate lunch, and packed a stash of snacks for my trip.

Finally I locked the door behind me, went down to the caddy, stowed the canvas bag in the boot, and slid behind the wheel. It had seemed so urgent to be gone while I was packing and making arrangements that I felt an absurd sense of unreality when I started the car. I wiped unexpected tears from my eyes as I drove away from the apartment complex, and snapped the radio on to cheer myself up. I chuckled as the cool vibes of Get Back oozed from the speakers.

"I will be back," I vowed to myself. "I have to come back, to heal Gabe. Just as soon as I know how to."

I stopped at the nearest post office and mailed the letter to my bank, then set out for the Florida Panhandle. As I left Jacksonville behind, the soft-top down, the wind in my hair and the radio on, I wondered what lay ahead. There was nothing to faze me on the way to Niceville – I'd done the trip many times by car and was confident I would arrive just before nightfall, all going well.

It was after that, striking out across the vastness of the United States, that worried me. I'd have to sit down with my roadmap and spy out the best route to take. But for now the going was easy. The sun shone, the fields were green and yellow with late crops, and the air was fresh and clean.

As I drove, Stevie Wonder's soulful voice crooned out My Cheri Amour. I reached over to the passenger seat for a box of Cheez-Its to keep me going until dinner, and felt a leg there. A smoothly-trousered leg with muscle and definition. It certainly didn't belong there, and I glanced to see who or what now occupied that seat.

2.

"Oh, Cheri," Lou echoed the song. "I didn't know you cared."

I sighed and put my hand back on the steering wheel. This was one devil I just didn't want to dice with.

"Ah, and I thought we had something special," he said, his voice laden with sweet reminiscences.

"Don't make me puke," I said. "Haven't you got anything better to do than bug me?"

"Darling, what could be better to do than bug you?"

I glanced again, and he wriggled his eyebrows over the top of his sunnies. I turned my attention back to the road, and mimed puking.

"Ah, we do have something special," he said. "And to prove it, I'm going to keep 'bugging' you, as you so charmingly put it, until you give in and beg for more."

"In your dreams."

"Maybe. Would you like to be in my dreams? I could be in yours too – oh so romantic!"

"Jesus," I swore under my breath.

"A threesome? Mmmm..."

"You foul bastard," I heard Gran say from somewhere behind me.

She'd been so quiet I'd forgotten she was there. I glanced in the rear view mirror and just made out her shimmery form on the back seat. Now that I was aware of spirits, I could see them a lot better. Gran was still pretty grey and nebulous, like a smudge in the air, but I could make out facial expressions and hand gestures.

"Climb it, Tarzan," I said, flipping Lou the bird. "What do you want, anyway?"

He made a show of thinking.

"Well, you could give up this ridiculous chase across the U.S.A. and wherever else it takes you," he mused.

"Yeah, that would suit you just fine, wouldn't it?"

"No, actually, it wouldn't."

I looked his way again. He gazed back at me, dead serious. He'd removed his sunnies, and his eyes were a bright, piercing blue that kind of looked straight through me. I turned away, my heart racing, and reminded myself of just who he was.

"What do you mean?" Gran snapped.

"Just what I said," he replied earnestly. "I know where you're going, and why, and what you intend to do."

"Well, you know more than I do," I muttered, concentrating as I came up behind a loaded semi-truck.

"You need only look inside yourself to know you aren't satisfied with this world and want to do something about it. And you know who's to blame for the rotten way things have turned out."

"Yes!" Gran harangued from the back seat. "You!"

I smiled. Lucifer was not going to get it all his own way.

"That's not quite right," he said patiently. "If anything, I've tried to – shall we say 'ease' suffering, helping humans towards self-fulfilment through the more pleasant diversions available."

"Leading them towards sin, in other words," Gran shot back.

"What is sin but a perception perpetuated by religion?" he replied. "Why are we even having a theological debate when I'm here simply to offer my services?"

"What services?" I yelled as we plunged past the big rig.

Lou waited until we had raced ahead of the vehicle before

he answered.

"I could smooth your way. Make it easier for you to reach your goals."

"And why would you do that? Why would you help me? More to the point, what would you want in return?"

I expected him to say, 'I want your soul to burn in the fiery pits of hell forevermore', or something equally Mephistophelian. But no, apparently not.

"I just want you to succeed in your quest."

"Why?" Gran asked.

I felt waves of anger coming from behind me, her aura casting a faint red glow.

"Cool it, Gran," I called over my shoulder. "I don't need the fuzz pulling me over to investigate the fire in the back seat."

She dimmed her aura, and I returned my attention to Lou.

"Right. You tell me why you want me to succeed, and what you get out of it."

"The world isn't a nice place," he said. "You want to change that, make it better. A better world means happier people. Happy people have less to pray for, less reason to believe in God. Which makes my work so much easier."

I considered his words. They had a certain twisted logic, but still didn't tally with my idea of how the devil operated.

"I thought you existed to make people unhappy, to destroy their souls and torture them. What do you get out of people being happy, exactly?"

He sighed.

"Who do you think caused the world to be such an unhappy place? Who gave his children a beautiful planet to live on, then broke their backs with so many laws and taboos that life isn't worth living? Who has controlled the systems of law and religion over most of the earth for thousands of years? Who is responsible? God!"

I glanced at him, thunderstruck, even though I'd been thinking something similar myself.

"Yes, God," Lou continued. "I know you think so too. He's the one who made everyone's life so miserable. Every human I tempt away from his inexorable laws and rules is a kick in the guts to him. Every soul who finds joy in life from things other than belief in him twists the knife in his back."

"Gee, you really hate him," I observed as I overtook a battered old Chevy Nomad full of rowdy young people.

"Ah, does my heart good," he sighed, watching their laughing faces as we passed. "They're having such fun."

"Won't be if they crash," I said, pulling in front of them. "They're probably fuelled up on alcohol or dope. Car's probably stolen too. Parents at home without a clue where their kids are."

"Killjoy," Lou murmured.

"No," I replied. "Just being realistic."

"Yes, but they're living life, not stifling to death from constraining religious beliefs. So what if they crash? At least they'll have enjoyed themselves."

"And that makes it alright, doesn't it? Oh yeah, forget the grieving parents, forget the friends and family they leave behind, the plans for careers and marriage and having their own kids and stuff like that. Not important at all, in the long run."

I'd meant it sarcastically, but Lou waved a nonchalant hand.

"Exactly! Think of all the billions of people who have lived, facing the question of whether to experience life to the full, or to die believing God would allow them the fun they forwent on earth in the afterlife he promised. Well, if you think religious communities on earth are straight-jacketed, you should see heaven!"

I shot him a side-long glance.

"What do you mean?"

"Just that heaven's empty. There's no one there but God. Everyone else is down here, endlessly going through life after life, pursuing the ideal existence on earth before they can actually ascend. And those in the spirit realm are busy helping them, not lounging around in some mythological paradise in the sky."

He looked at me piercingly again.

"There is no heaven, no hell. Both are here on earth."

Then he disappeared.

3.

I turned the radio down so I could think. It was a serious under-statement to say I had rather a lot to think about. Lucifer, the devil himself, helping *me* for the sake of humanity? The idea would be anathema to anyone who was even mildly religious. Everything I'd ever heard about him firmly described him as pure evil, but it sure was tempting to imagine the rest of my trip going smoothly. Trouble was, I knew there'd be one hell of a price to pay for it.

The carload of teens hung close on my tailpipe. I glanced in the rear view mirror and saw Lou lounging casually on the roof of the vehicle. I was sure he had something devastating in mind for them – car crash, fiery inferno, no survivors. You know the sort of thing – it's in the news all the time.

Finally they took the turn-off to the next town, and I cruised on. There was a period when I couldn't sense Gran's presence. I guessed she dropped in on Karen when she wasn't with me, and I wondered if my sister could sense her too. But I was aware of Vaivea nearby, so I relaxed.

"You like music, Vaivea?" I asked out loud.

"Music is good," he answered. "It liberates the soul."

"Er – yes," I agreed. "Well, I feel like listening to some tunes..."

"I will sing the songs of my tribe," he offered. "This is the song of the hunted beasts..."

Before I could blink, Vaivea had launched into a vigorous chant, which lasted a good fifteen minutes. He next announced the song of the raging river, but I'd had my fill of Indian chants for the moment and intervened.

"My turn. Do you like rock 'n' roll?"

"Rocken roll? Like the song of a landslide on a great mountain?"

"Er, no. I meant rock music, like the Rolling Stones."

"Rolling Stones? The song of a landslide on a great mountain?"

"Er, no. It's way cool music. Makes you want to dance."

"Like a war dance? Yes, play your rocken music."

I turned the radio's volume up, and settled back to my driving as My Generation pulsed from the speakers. I couldn't tell what Vaivea thought – if he thought anything at all. He just shimmered in the passenger seat, looking serene, if rather vaporous. Gran joined us a little further on. I saw her wavery outlines in the rear view mirror as she leaned forward on the back seat.

"About time you put the music back on," she said.

"Oh yeah, baby!" came a gravelly voice over the radio. "And

that was My Generation by who? You know who – that *was* The Who, right here with Wolfman Jack. Ah-whooooaaa!"

I cracked a grin at Wolfman Jack's crazy jive. He was such a gas. Vaivea faded away. Not a fan, obviously.

"Now, stay tuned for more tunes, as we switch across the ditch for their Satanic Majesties – The Rolling Stones!"

As the opening words of Sympathy for the Devil came on, Gran stopped bopping and leaned forward again.

"Uh oh," she said. "Quick, turn it off or you-know-who will be back..."

"Oh, too late," came a familiar voice from beside me.

"Darn, I should've moved up front," Gran grumbled.

"Charmed, I'm sure."

"Okay, you two," I said before it could escalate. "What do you want, slime-o?"

He ignored the insult and smiled at me, white teeth dazzling.

"Have you thought about what I said earlier?"

Truth be known, I'd thought about little else. In fact, I'd turned the radio back up to distract me from thinking about it.

"Oh sure," I said breezily. "As I recall, you were offering your support in my ventures. You neglected to say what that would cost me."

Lou waved his hands.

"Cost you? As if I were a business and you my client? Oh Cheri, where did I go wrong?"

"Well, getting kicked out of heaven might have been the start," I said snidely.

"Hah!" Lou retorted. "Boring place. Nothing to do but be good and play harps and sing. And God always sang bass, the stinker. Jesus had a nice falsetto, though."

He sniggered rudely.

"Got sick of preening my feathers anyway – do you know what a pain wings are when you have to clean them all the time?"

"You're stalling," Gran said. "Answer her goddam question!"

"Alright. You want to know what I want in return for supporting your mission? Nothing. Absolutely nothing. One hundred percent free of cost. Can't get a better deal than that."

I had to wonder.

"So you're saying you'll smooth my way, help me and run interference with anyone who wants to, oh, eat me or decapitate me or possess me or otherwise monkey with me, all for nothing in return? Are you having me on?"

Lou smiled and smirked at me over the top of his sunnies.

"Darling, I'd love to have you on!"

"Hey!" Gran interjected.

"Okay! I'm not having you on. I'm serious. I mean it. No cost to you at all. No earthly treasure would be enough to pay for my services anyway."

"I wasn't thinking of earthly treasure," I said. "More like the future of my soul once this life time is over – or would you even wait until I'd passed on? Probably not."

"I assure you, my dear, there is nothing desirable about possessing people's souls. It suits my purposes better to let them be. They do much more damage that way."

"So Faustus was wrong?" I asked, grinning on the side of my face he couldn't see.

"Oh, the abominable man! Yes, it was a smear campaign worthy of Him up there," he said, and motioned rudely towards the sky with a single raised finger. "Dante too. Total misrepresentation."

I raised my eyebrows.

"So you don't want money, you don't want my soul. There must be some catch."

"You can bet on it, sweetheart," Gran said from the back seat.

Lou sighed and massaged his forehead.

"I suppose I can't blame you for being suspicious. What with all the bad press I've had, mainly thanks to Him upstairs. But seriously, I don't require payment of any kind. All I want is the satisfaction of helping Him towards His downfall."

I thought about that before I said any more. Would my quest cause the downfall of God? Seriously? Sure, I wanted to kick some spiritual ass, and what Lou had said about God being responsible for so many of the world's ills resonated with me, but to actually cause His downfall? I wasn't sure if that was even possible.

Besides, dealing with Lucifer was trouble itself. If God was brought down, the devil would be free to wreak even more havoc on earth, and who knew where he'd stop – or if he'd stop.

"I guess I see where you're coming from," I said. "You've got some pretty serious issues with God. But I think you should fight your own battles. I don't want to be used by you, with who knows what ulterior motives and at goodness knows what cost to myself. Even if you ask for nothing in return, you'll still be bringing issues into it that aren't on my agenda, and it's just too messy, too complicated."

"You're turning me down?"

He sounded utterly astonished, as if he'd never been refused anything in his whole existence.

"I don't know. I need more time to think about it."

"Don't take too long," he said softly, and disappeared again.

"Jumping Jehoshaphat!" I swore. "I'm never going to get used to people popping in and out like that."

"Yes you will," Gran assured me. "And he's not people. He's dirt. Filth with a capital F. Don't let him talk you into anything. You don't need him. Don't trust him."

"I won't," I answered. "And I don't. Trust him, that is. You know what they say – don't trust anyone over thirty. Well, except your Gran, of course."

4.

It was a golden afternoon. The drive was uneventful, though clouds built on the horizon after I passed through Tallahassee. My thoughts were scattered, so I tuned out by tuning in to the radio. Wolfman Jack's gravelly tones and smart-ass inuendo spilled out buoyantly between songs, lifting my spirits. With only a week until Halloween, lots of golden oldies featured, like The Blob by The Five Blobs, and Rockin' In The Graveyard by Jackie Morningstar – you know, the kind of songs that are only dragged out at that time of year.

At four o'clock I switched stations for the hourly news and weather report. I jumped in my seat as the radio issued a cacophony of screams and rattling chains. Then I realised it was just an advert for some Halloween shenanigans. The lead-in music for the news followed.

My relief soon vanished. The opening news item was about a horrific car crash in a little town back up the highway. The first thought that entered my mind was the carload of teenagers I'd passed earlier on my trip.

But I was wrong. A young mother driving with her two small children had swerved to avoid hitting another car and crashed into a power pole. My heart ached for them, and for the wretchedness the husband and other members of their family would be going through. Not to mention the anger I felt at the way something that I thought should be as private as death was splashed all over the news, like some kind of grisly entertainment.

"This is so, so wrong," I said, and switched back to the music station.

"I know, darling, I know," said Gran. "But it's the way of the world, and the truly sad thing is that most people are immune to it, until it happens to them."

I gritted my teeth. If I was going to make changes, I'd better get on with it. I put my foot down, determined to make it to Niceville before dark. The weather changed to match my mood. Rain clouds scudded across the sinking sun and plunged the world into an early twilight. The radio also chimed in with I'll Do My Crying In The Rain.

Rain pounded down on the car's soft-top as I continued west on the Florida Twenty, which followed the shoreline of Choctawhatchee Bay. Misty lights shone on the water, where pleasure cruisers were safely moored to ride out the rough weather.

Soon I turned into Niceville, my windshield wipers working overtime in the sheets of rain. Finally I approached the two story brick house I'd spent my teenage years in. It was no more than a murky outline in the downpour. I pulled up in the driveway and waited, hoping the rain would ease off so I could get to the house without being soaked.

A moment later Mama came out the front door, half hidden

under a bubble umbrella covered with a bright floral pattern. Yep, she liked loud. I slid out of the caddy and under the scanty shelter of the umbrella.

"I totally forgot you were coming," she said, her voice strained.

"That's okay," I said. "I thought you would."

We huddled under the umbrella as I retrieved my baggage, then we hurried for the front door. Here I got the surprise of my life.

8

King Midas In Reverse

1. Friday 24th October 1969 – Niceville, Florida

"Dad!"

He was the last person I expected to see, but that didn't stop me from giving him the biggest hug ever. His hair was ruffled and stubble smudged his chin – the first time I'd seen him look uncared for in my life. I stepped into the loungeroom and then looked again. Deep lines creased his face, and I was sure I could smell whisky.

"Something's happened?"

My parents shared uneasy glances, then my father shrugged.

"She's an adult. I think she should know."

A look of distaste crossed Mama's face, and she stretched an artificial smile over her features to hide it.

"I'll go make us some coffee," she said, and whisked from the room.

I looked around as I sat down. Nothing much had changed – expensive olive green Danish sofas, Italian glass and ceramic picture frames housing members of the family, pale green wallpaper and curtains with gold floral accents, shag carpet in gold and brown geometric patterns. A new orange lava lamp bubbled away on a teak coffee table. I looked at dad again, and my heart went out to him.

"Jenny and I have broken up," he said.

I nodded. I guessed everyone would have said 'I told you so' already, and he didn't need to hear it again. I was just surprised it had lasted as long as it did.

"She went off and joined a commune," he added, and shrugged.

"More the fool she," I said bleakly.

Dad smiled. He looked like he hadn't done a lot of that lately.

"You win some, you lose some," I continued, and at his hurt look, added, "If she was worth winning, she'd still be with you."

"I know. It's just a bit hard to adjust, after three years together."

I leaned forward, keeping my voice down in case my mother could hear.

"It's okay, dad. We all go through stuff like this. Mama has. And so have I."

He looked at me in surprise.

"What – don't tell me you've lost your nice young man? Jake?"

"Gabe. Not permanently, thank goodness. But we're laying low for a while – I've fallen foul of his family."

"Oh."

Coffee arrived in sunflower-print mugs on a decorative copper tray, Mama beaming proudly.

"I've just about mastered the new coffee maker," she said,

handing mugs out. "Lola showed me how to use it yesterday and I think I've got it quite good now."

I paused, the mug halfway to my lips, hoping I wasn't about to be poisoned. Thankfully, the coffee was drinkable, and I savoured it as I leaned back on the sofa.

"Did I hear you say something about Gabe?" Mama asked as she settled on the opposite sofa next to dad. "Is he any better?"

"No," I said with a sigh, "still in the coma. And his brother Adio made trouble for me until his parents decided it was better if I left them alone."

"What? Coma?" dad said stupidly.

I'd somehow forgotten he didn't know all the details of my recent life. Strange, seeing how he had been so absent for the past three years. I brought him up to date on the attack on Gabe and the vigil by his bedside. However, I left out anything to do with Amy, Isis and other related topics, with my mother present.

I totally believe you should follow your heart and choose the spirituality that feels right to you, and not be ashamed of it, but sometimes it's truly best to minimise the impact of your beliefs on those you love. Trust me, in Mama's case, it was necessary.

"So basically it's religious differences?" dad asked, finishing up his coffee.

I nodded, wanting to keep it simple. Mama couldn't, though. Heaven forbid.

"Wasn't there something to do with paganism?" she asked with a little frown. "Nature worship or something weird? I can't remember what they believed."

"No, they're Christians," I said. "And I'm not."

"Ah," my father said, understanding crossing his face.

I was sure he'd figured out what my spiritual leanings were years ago, and that he was okay with them. Mama, however, would have pink fits all over the place if she suspected my true path for even a second. And I didn't need that.

2.

I gathered the mugs and took them to the kitchen, where I found Gran.

"You could've told me dad was here," I whispered as I rinsed the mugs at the sink. "Do you think he'll stay and patch things up, now he's sowed his wild oats?"

Gran chuckled.

"I think so. He always loved Patsy, and I'm sure he hated hurting her by what he did. But what happened to him over in Vietnam must have shaken him up a lot. When he went over there, and saw what was going on, and nearly got killed, it changed him and made him question everything about his life, including your mother."

That made sense. I raided the fridge for something quick to eat, then returned to the lounge room. My parents were speaking in hushed tones, and didn't stop as I re-joined them.

"I could just sleep on the sofa," dad said. "Save you making up a bed for me."

"Nonsense," Mama replied. "What's the point of having a great big house full of spare bedrooms if no one uses them?"

She spoke casually, but I heard a brittle note in her voice. The years without dad had affected her more than she let on, and I was sure she wanted him to stay. I felt terribly sorry for both of them, for the hurt and pain they'd caused each other, and decided to leave them to their plans.

"I'm falling asleep on my feet," I said, "so I'll go up to bed now. My old room still there, or has it been converted into an art studio?"

My father chuckled, a low, gravely laugh that signalled the return of his usual good spirits. Mama had always regretted letting me have the east-facing bedroom upstairs when we moved into the house, and had threatened many times to chuck my stuff out and put her art things in there. Not that she really used them. She dabbled, but I think she just did it so she could say she did.

"Your room is intact," she answered. "Be thankful I haven't expanded my art practices to the point of needing the extra space yet."

"Just give me a week's notice if you do need to move from the broom closet," I said, and kissed my parents goodnight.

"Wicked child," Mama chided as I gathered my bags.

I found my room unchanged. I'd pounced on it when we'd moved in, claiming it solely for the dark purple plush pile carpet and lavender-painted walls. I'd added curtains, knotted rug, lampshade, alarm clock, bedspread, candles – if it came in a shade of purple, it found a home in my room. As a teenager, I'd called it my purple palace. Turkish bazaar, Mama said in disapproval at every purple thing I added.

I unpacked my pyjamas and toiletries, looking forward to a soak in the bathtub. Gran hovered on the chair at my writing desk, and sighed tiredly.

"You absolute fraud," I said. "You can't tell me spirits need sleep and relaxation like people do."

"Who says we don't need to relax?" she asked. "That was one – no, two – taxing battles of wits we had with that fellow on the way here. I need to recoup my resources before anything else crops up."

I laughed, and picked up an old copy of my university magazine that I'd found in the drawer. I tossed it towards my writing desk, and it sailed through Gran's middle, making her groan.

"Have a read. That'll get your wits together."

"Hah!"

I tried to ring Karen from the upstairs extension in the hall, but there was no answer. Gran appeared to doze on the chair, and I couldn't help but tip-toe past her nebulous form to grab my pyjamas and overnight bag and then head for the bathroom. With the taps running, I squeezed in some lavender bath foam. The water steamed gently as I sank into the warmness, sighing inwardly and out.

I lay back amongst the drifts of bubbles with only my head poking out, day-dreaming about what Isis and Osiris had been getting up to before Set arrived in my last regression. My eyes slipped shut, and I deeply inhaled the herbal fragrance of the bath foam as I relaxed even more.

Suddenly the room dimmed, and I opened my eyes to find it transformed. The light was off and red candles of all shapes and sizes occupied every surface. The sensuous aromas of rose and musk hit my nostrils, and crimson rose petals floated down from the ceiling.

"Do you like, Cheri?"

I wanted to reply, but I was lost for words. Yeah, I knew it was the devil. I knew he was evil incarnate. I knew he couldn't be trusted. But at that moment, I just didn't have words to say anything.

"Of course, I could have whisked you off to Venice, or Rome, or Paris," he said, emerging from the shadows by the basin. "But I didn't want to shock you too much."

"No, no shock at all."

I was glad to find that my tongue still worked. Ditto my sarcasm.

"Champagne?"

He Conjured a crystal champagne flute full of bubbling golden liquid out of thin air and handed it to me, then produced another for himself. I sniffed at it suspiciously, but decided he was hardly likely to poison me now, after all the opportunity he'd already had to crash my car or asphyxiate me with imagined smells.

I sipped the champagne, and it tasted good. Lou sat on the edge of the bath, and I slipped further under the bubbles, suddenly feeling vulnerable. He tilted his head, gazing at me speculatively.

"I've considered your reluctance to accept my offer," he said. "It seems you're so sure I'll ask for something in return that I've decided I will ask for something."

"Ah," I said, and sipped some more champagne.

"There is something you can give me," he said, "that won't hurt you or anyone else, and is yours to give freely. Something you have that is very desirable, as your dear boyfriend knows well."

My hackles rose. Whatever he meant to imply, I already didn't like it. At my sudden glare, he hurried on.

"I mean, I don't see why you wouldn't. Gabe is miles away and can't see what you're doing. He need never know. Unless you choose to tell him, of course..."

"Let me get this straight," I interrupted. "Are you saying you want me to... to do the wild thing with you? Is that what you want in return for your 'help'?"

"Now don't take it the wrong way," he said quickly, holding a hand up before him as though I might toss the contents of my glass in his face.

In fact, I very nearly did. I so wanted to show exactly how repulsed I was at his suggestion. But I breathed deeply, gripping the stem of the champagne flute, and kept my cool somehow.

"Does the mention of a monogamous relationship give you some indication of my feelings?"

"Darling," he crooned, his eyes twinkling. "I'd love that, but you have a boyfriend and I have several, and also girl-friends, demon friends, spirit friends, animal friends..."

"Ewww!"

I splashed some bathwater on him in frustration, and he tut-tutted as he wiped the bubbles off his leather jacket.

"Now I might just need to spank you for that," he said sternly.

3.

"Oops!"

I cringed as far as I could into the foamy bubbles. After all, he was the devil, and I was sure he could do me some serious damage at the slightest whim. But he smiled indulgently and trailed a finger in the water.

"You know, it's a shame your bath doesn't have spa jets. However, I can provide."

Suddenly streams of bubbles started to rise from the bottom of the tub, bursting all around me and making the bath foam froth up even more.

"Whoa – we'll be flooded!" I cried.

"So? What are a few bubbles between friends?"

Lou sipped his champagne, eyeing me wolfishly. Well, what he could see of me amongst the now towering drifts of bubbles. Don't get me wrong – I was glad, for modesty's sake, that they covered me up. The trouble was that I felt in imminent danger of suffocation beneath the foamy, uprising mass, and that once it had accomplished its first murder, it would continue to fill the room and then the entire house, and drown my parents as well...

"Okay, stop with the bubbles already. And as for the part about being friends, do you think we could just keep it as a business thing? After all, you are the devil."

"Oh, you bet I am," Lou purred, snapping his fingers.

The bubbles stopped, and I breathed a little easier.

"I mean, you seriously expect me to trust you," I stated, looking him straight in the eyes.

I did a double take. Previously, his eyes had been blue. But now they were a glittering, gleaming jade green.

"You like?" he asked, seeing I'd noticed them. "I change the colour every now and then. I like to project an image of being adventurous, trying new things..."

He waggled his eyebrows suggestively, and I sighed. He just never gave up!

"My Gran is here, you know."

"Er, no. She might have been a little while ago, but she isn't now. I believe she's visiting your sister – again. That charming man she married has a few vices. Takes some sorting out. You know."

"What, Eric? What vices?"

I'd never liked Eric. Karen knew it. Eric knew it. But I

thought *they* were coping, even if things were a bit rocky for them. I realised we hadn't been in touch that much lately, as my relationship with Gabe had taken priority in my life. All of a sudden it was four years since their wedding, and there could be heaps wrong that I didn't know about.

"Do you really want to know?" Lou asked. "I could tell you, but then I think you'd kill him, which wouldn't be a good idea. Don't worry. Your do-good grandmother is busy placing spirit helpers around them. She's going to be awfully busy, by the way. What she can do, I can undo."

"How about you leave my sister alone?" I snapped. "She was perfectly happy until you started meddling."

"Is that what you think?" Lou said eagerly. "You should see the rows..."

"If you don't mind, Mister Tattletale, I'll find out about my sister's marriage properly, by asking her. And if she considers it my business, she'll tell me."

"But you'll only be getting one side of it," Lou complained. "I feel kinda sorry for the guy. For starters, how would you like to be lumped with a name like Eric Erickson? What were his parents thinking? Did they lack creative drive? Or were they just plain lazy? Actually, I should know. I probably had something to do with it."

I huffed in annoyance.

"Look, can we cut the crap? Just leave Karen and her family alone! And as for that other matter... Can you actually offer some sort of guarantee that your help is non-conditional, that I won't owe you anything?"

"Like I said, all I want is the pleasure of seeing you-know-who toppled off His throne. The axe I've had to grind is nice and sharp, and I just need Him to come down low enough for me to swing at Him, a chance He's made sure I've never had."

"So if I take you at your word, you help me, I get my chance to – adjust – the hierarchy, and you leave me alone?"

"Yes," Lou said, nodding. "Unless you don't want me to leave you alone? I can be quite – adventurous."

"What does it take to get it through to you that I'm not interested?"

In the split second it took to blink my eyes, he was gone, the candles and the rose petals were gone, and the light was back on. My voice echoed around the empty bathroom, and I found the only thing he'd left was the champagne flute in my hand. At least it was full again.

I sipped and lay back in the tub, thinking over this latest encounter. I wondered if I should try to get hold of a real, proper chastity belt to wear under my pyjamas at night. It seemed my virtue would be constantly under attack while Lou considered us business partners. I shuddered. Let's say business associates.

After my bath, I found Gran slumped at my desk, snoring. Well, to L. A. and back was a long trip, I supposed, even for a spirit. I grabbed the book on angels and demons and slipped into bed. I caught Gran peeking at me as I settled in.

"Thanks for leaving me alone with you-know-Lou," I said. "He's great company, especially when he's got his mojo going."

"Goddam," Gran swore, sitting up. "He just won't leave you alone, will he? I'm sorry, sweetheart. I thought you'd be okay while I was gone. We can only be grateful he hasn't really harmed you."

"Maybe not yet," I said. "But what about the future?"

"Sweetheart, I'm real sorry. I'll stay with you as much as I can, I promise."

Lou's words about Karen and Eric came back to me.

"How is Karen really? Is she okay? Eric had better be treating her right."

"Listen," Gran said. "They've had their little ups and downs, just like everyone, but I'm helping them out. Karen knows when I'm there and she's real glad of it. I'm sorry I've had to split my time between you, but I have to do what I have to do."

"That's okay, Gran," I said. "Thanks for looking after her. It means a lot to me."

I settled down to read, searching out whatever I could find on Lucifer, Satan, the devil, demons, anything related. Information wasn't hard to come by. I discovered that all mythologies and religions had an evil figure, sometimes several, whether gods or spirit entities or demons. And that they were all cunning, conniving, and very tricky to deal with.

I was still reading when I heard my parents come upstairs to bed. I listened for two doors to click shut – Mama's, and one of the spare bedroom doors. I listened in vain. Only one door shut, and I grinned as I realised they were going to bed together. I guessed they must have patched it up pretty good. I looked over at Gran's shimmering grey form, and could have sworn she was smiling.

I read a bit longer, then decided to do a regression. I lit a purple candle on my dresser, turned off the lights, lay down and meditated to a relaxed state.

I was falling, rushing through the darkness, only it didn't end this time. I struggled, but something held my body down. Something wet and all encompassing, with a strong current. Isis kicked and came up for air, and the night sky exploded over her head, filled with stars.

Isis felt desperate, but I didn't know why, apart from the fact that she was caught in a raging river. But then I realised the river wasn't raging. It just flowed with its usual, slow currents, and Isis struck out for the shore.

Several women waited there, holding linen drying cloths. As Isis climbed the bank, two of them stepped forward to dry her. Another draped sapphire blue robes around her shoulders, and I realised she had been naked.

She was also crying. It seemed she was going through some trauma at the time I had regressed to, but I had no idea what it was.

"My Lady?" one of the handmaidens said dolefully, and Isis shook her head.

"He is not there," she answered, and it all became clear in a flash.

Osiris was missing. He'd attended Set's celebration, without Isis. He hadn't been seen again. Being a God, he could have willed himself anywhere in the world, but Isis would still be aware of his Ka — his energy, his essence. Which meant someone had taken his essence from him, made him no more. In effect, he was dead.

4.

"No!" Isis cried, loud and long.

Her wail carried on the stiff breeze, and her hand-maidens also wailed and beat their chests. Isis was devastated. Desolate. And frightened. I couldn't remember ever feeling so utterly alone as she did then.

I felt a tugging, and, lost in grief, gave in to it completely.

Suddenly I was back in my bed, in my own room, with my mother and father bending over me on either side. My face felt cold and wet; the tears I'd cried were real.

"Hey there," dad said softly as I drew deep breaths of lavender scented air. "It's okay. We're here. Just keep breathing."

"Angela?" Mama said from my other side. "I thought you'd got over all of this."

She meant the dreams I used to have as a teenager. But that was years ago, and what I'd just experienced was completely different. Unfortunately, I couldn't tell my parents that.

"It's okay," I said as I sat up.

My voice was a squeak. Dad rushed to the bathroom to get me a glass of water.

"I am over those old dreams," I said. "It wasn't one of those. It was..."

I couldn't say anything. It was too painful. I sipped the water, trying to calm myself, but still I shuddered at the memory of that regression.

"What was it, sweetheart?" my father asked gently.

"He was dead," I croaked. "I dreamed he was gone and I couldn't find him. But somehow I knew he was dead."

"Who?" Mama asked, her brows drawn down in a frown. "Gabe?"

"Her boyfriend?" my father asked across the bed, and at her nod, he turned back to me. "No wonder you're upset. But it was only a dream, honey. Just a dream. I'm sure nothing's happened to your young man. He's safe in hospital. Nothing bad can happen to him there."

I nodded. Best to let them think that. I swallowed my fears temporarily and smiled as I lay back in my bed.

"Yeah, of course he's okay. It was just a stupid dream. I'm alright now."

"You sure?" Mama asked. "I can leave the night light on if you like."

"Mama! I'm twenty five, for goodness sake. I'm okay, really."

They went back to their room – again I listened for the single click of a door shutting – then I sat up.

"Gran!" I whispered into the semi-darkness.

The candle still burned. There was just enough light for me to make out the comforting surrounds of my room. Gran's shimmering outline moved to the bed and settled on the edge. Vaivea was also present.

"So, my sparrow," Gran said, "what did you see?"

I took a moment to think back and get it all clear in my mind.

"Isis was diving in the Nile River," I said. "She was searching for Osiris' body – she knew he was dead. When she couldn't find him, she cried out, and all her hand maidens started wailing and beating their chests. It was weird. And scary."

"He was murdered," Vaivea said matter-of-factly.

"Yes, by his brother Set," I said, gasping. "Set killed him!"

"Yes?" Gran prompted.

"Osiris is Gabe in this life," I pointed out. "And I'm sure Adio is Set. What if Adio's done something to Gabe? What if he's really killed him?"

Overcome by the need to find out if Gabe was okay, I fumbled my way out to the hall phone, dragged it into my room, and rang the motel where the Serapis family were staying. When it connected, I asked to be put through to the extension in Sagira's room. I hoped she wouldn't mind me ringing so late.

After what seemed like ages, her sleepy voice answered.

"Sagira, it's me, Ange," I said. "Please don't be mad at me. I need to know how Gabe is. When did you last see him?"

"Just tonight," Sagira answered. "He seemed okay, but he hasn't woken from the coma yet."

"And he was alright when you left him?"

"Yes, he was fine. What's going on?"

"I just did a regression, and in it, Osiris was dead," I said, my chest tense. "Where's Adio right now?"

"He's in the loungeroom, watching TV. I can hear it through the wall."

"Are you sure he's there?"

"I can make an excuse to go check, if you like. Just a minute."

A couple of minutes passed in silence. By the time Sagira returned, I was just about eating the grapes off the wallpaper.

"Ange? He's there. I told him he had the telly up so loud I couldn't sleep. I'm sure he hasn't left the suite since we got back."

"Maybe I should ring the hospital," I said.

"You can if you want to, but I'm sure Gabe's okay. If anything happened to him, the night staff would ring us straight away."

"You're right," I conceded, feeling the tension ease. "Sorry for all the fuss. It just seemed so real."

"It's alright," Sagira said. "Just be careful, okay?"

"Sure. Thanks for everything. And I'm sorry for waking you up."

"That's okay. I'd only just gone to bed. And I feel better knowing what's going on with you. Then I can tell Gabe, when we're alone."

"Thanks heaps, Sagira," I said. "That means a lot to me."

I returned the phone to its place and went back to bed. If events in my regressions reflected real life, why hadn't Adio made his move on Gabe? But perhaps he already had...

"Gran?" I said. "Can you tell me if Adio had anything to do with that redneck who shot Gabe?"

"It's possible," Gran answered. "Christians kill just like anyone else. And some have probably killed their own brothers for having different beliefs."

"And sisters!" I whispered, suddenly afraid. "Sagira may be in danger too!"

"Adio will not harm her," Vaivea intoned. "You are the one in most danger. He wishes to carry on the ancient feud, to stop you from fulfilling your quest."

That took my breath away. I wanted to ask more questions, but Vaivea faded, leaving me alone with Gran.

"Go to sleep," she said. "He won't be back for a while, and you need to rest up."

"I thought you guys could just flit straight where you wanted to at will," I said, snuggling under the covers. "In the blink of an eye."

"We can," Gran said solemnly. "But he'll be checking the lay of the land, searching out possible menaces. Now try and sleep, my sparrow. Think about Gabe. That should bring you happy dreams."

I closed my eyes, and images danced on the backs of my eyelids. Gabe and I playing tug-of-war with a pillow in my apartment. Walking down Jacksonville Beach on the weekends. Sipping coffee at a cafe after work.

And Isis and Osiris – standing at the prow of her barque as they drifted down the Nile, watching the stunning desert sunset. Strolling through crowds of adoring worshippers, dispensing wisdom and healing. And some activities that would be X-rated to most people.

I drifted off to sleep with a smile on my face. My dreams of Gabe were blissful, especially one where we were making love. I breathed in his scent, delighted in the sheen of candle-light on his olive skin, lost myself in his marvellous, melting brown eyes, his gentle, loving smile...

But as I gazed, his smile grew into a wolfish grin that was most unlike Gabe. I stared for a moment, confused, and I could swear his eyes flickered with jade green fire.

9

Strange Days

1. Saturday, 25th October, 1969 – Niceville, Florida

I woke late the next morning to dads voice drifting up from the kitchen as he sang Delilah along with the radio. I grimaced. It was too early in the day for Tom Jones or his imitators. I dressed and hurried to join my parents for breakfast.

"Did you sleep okay after all that disruption?" Mama asked.

"How do you feel?" my father added.

"Fine, I'm fine," I said. "I went to sleep and had some nice dreams."

"So what are your plans?" dad asked, dumping a spoonful of sugar in his coffee.

"I'm gonna rest up today; get some supplies together. Then I'm driving over to visit Karen."

My parents gaped at me in surprise. Both of them. Scary.

"Well, its ages since I've seen her. I miss her."

"But what about your job?" Mama said. "You can't just up and leave like that!"

"My boss gave me a month's leave."

"And Gabe?" she asked, looking scandalised. "How could you leave him at a time like this?"

"I don't like leaving him. Honestly. But his family is there all the time, and they're too uptight about me hanging around. The doctor said Gabe would likely be okay, but he just don't know when he'll wake up. I'm keeping in touch with Gabe's sister, so she'll tell me if anything changes."

The dark look on Mama's face told me only too clearly what she thought about it all. But I wasn't about to ruin the morning arguing with her, and neither was dad.

"Whatever's best for you, sweetheart," he said.

Dad changed the subject by quizzing Mama about the various activities she and her group of friends had planned. I helped clean up after breakfast, then I went into the garage and got out my old bike. The tyres needed to be pumped up, and, eager to make himself useful, dad inflated them in no time flat.

"So where are you off to?" he asked.

"Just around town," I answered. "I might hit one of the parks – maybe check out that new one at Rocky Bayou. Or look at the shops. Dunno yet."

"I'd love to come with you," he said wistfully. "But I guess you don't want your ol' pa hanging around."

"What's this 'ol' pa' stuff?" I said. "I'd love to spend time with you, dad. How about we drive down to Destin later and have lunch on the beach?"

"Sure," he said with a grin, and suddenly looked ten years younger. "Is your mother invited?"

"Didn't she say she'd be at her sewing circle this afternoon? Knitting baby moccasins for the homeless or something. Just you and me, okay?"

He ruffled my hair and puttered about with some old tools he found in the garage while I wheeled my bike out to the drive.

"Watch out for the rain," he yelled after me, and I waved back.

The sky was still dark with mutinous grey clouds. I didn't care if it rained on me – I'd always loved wet weather. But I didn't want to look at Niceville's rather limited collection of shops – they probably still had the same old stuff on the shelves as when I left anyway.

Besides, I didn't fancy the thought of running into any old school mates. I'd had few friends amongst them, and didn't care to talk shop with the catty bimbos and brain-dead jocks who'd considered themselves too cool to talk to the likes of me.

Instead, I rode through town, where people were busy festooning everything in Jack-o-lanterns, broomsticks, black cats, and other Halloween decorations. I crossed the bridge to the Rocky Bayou State Park, turned in at the entrance, and rode until the bayou came into sight. It was still and dark, reflecting the grey sky.

The park was eerily deserted. I leaned my bike against a bench under a tree, sat down, and sipped from a thermos of coffee I'd brought, listening to the calls of the swamp birds hidden in their bowers in the bayous. Gran appeared next to me.

"I don't like it, you know," she said, as though continuing a discussion we'd been engaged in. "It's an ill-omen to have weather like this over Halloween. Something terrible is sure to happen."

"Do you believe in fate, Gran?" I asked.

"Que Sera Sera," her scratchy old voice sang, sending shivers down my spine. "Sweetheart, we have the power to influence future events, but some things that are meant to be will happen in one form or another, like it or not."

"Do you know what's going to happen to me in the future?"

Silence. I slipped a sideways look at Gran. Her eyes seemed far away.

"Would it change the things you'd do if I could tell you?" she asked.

"Might do," I said with a shrug. "If something bad was going to happen, I might be able to stop it. I could try, anyway."

"If only it were that easy," she said. "Say you'd been able to warn people not to sail on the Titanic. Would it have stopped the tragedy from happening?"

"No. But saving lives would've been more important than saving the ship."

"Your heart's in the right place," Gran said. "It always has been. Your circumstances made you choose to withdraw from people. But it's the grit those circumstances bring out in you that will get you through what you have to do."

"Meaning the bad stuff in my life made me strong enough to do the good stuff?"

"Yes, my sparrow. Now I must go."

"Why?" I said, alarmed. "Is it Karen? What's happened?"

But Gran faded away. I shuddered. It unsettled me to be alone, even though I was right out in the open where I could see trouble coming.

"Vaivea? Are you there?"

"I am present," he said from behind me.

"I'm afraid of being alone," I said.

The words sounded strange in my ears. I don't think I'd ever admitted to being afraid to anyone before, even myself. Vaivea moved in front of me, and my eyes adjusted to his energy field. I was able to make out arms, legs, his buckskin clothing, the feather dangling beside his face, and I felt better at having this sight.

"You are right to be afraid. It takes fear to bring out true courage."

"So my courage will be tested?"

"Inevitably."

"Did you find out if Adio was involved with the attack on Gabe?"

"Adio is surrounded by a darkness that is difficult to penetrate. But he is indeed acquainted with one of those who attacked Gabriel."

"No way!"

A heady mix of emotions swept through me – rage and repulsion, sadness and confusion that Gabe could be so betrayed by his own brother. And fear. Fear that Adio wouldn't stop there.

"You assume much," Vaivea said calmly. "You also assume the identity of those involved is important. It is not. Karma will exact its price in time."

"And meanwhile Adio goes on attacking people. Just like Set."

"You confuse Adio for his earlier incarnation."

"It makes sense, doesn't it? Set killed Osiris. And now he's having another go in this lifetime!"

"Others were involved," Vaivea said. "All were simply the tools of destiny."

"What? Adio could've killed Gabe!"

"Adio is not yet fully aware of his connection with Set. Therefore, many of his actions are not consciously chosen. You must learn what Isis knew – that forgiveness is everything."

My sense of justice was outraged.

"Forgive Adio? I'm sorry, Vaivea, but that's asking the impossible."

"You must, for your soul to progress to its most powerful state. Forgiveness will truly free you."

"Huh, I've heard that before. Next you'll tell me to forgive you-know-who."

"Lucifer has already tempted you."

I pursed my lips, angry at myself for mentioning Lou.

"That'll never happen."

"Hmmm."

"What are you saying? You think I'll give in to him?"

"I see many possible futures. Only you can choose the one you think best."

"Can't you just tell me the best way to get where I'm going? That'd be easier."

"Spirit cannot influence your decisions, unless it is to save you from harm in an emergency. And on such an occasion, it's the angels or your guide who will act."

"Ah, the mystery guide. And you won't even give me a hint as to who that is?"

"I cannot. I can offer you guidance, but the choices remain yours. You may choose to listen or to ignore me, just as you might listen to or ignore your own conscience. I cannot interfere with your free will."

"What harm is there in telling me who my guide is?" I probed. "Is it Amy?"

"It would not be ethical to reveal that which it is not in your best interests to know at this time. But it will be someone who has your best interests at heart, for your progress and their own."

I nodded and smiled. It had to be Amy – it made sense. And I truly was grateful for all the other information. Vaivea was rarely so talkative, and I welcomed the opportunity to pick his brains. Even if they were nothing but ectoplasm.

"Beware," Vaivea said. "Someone unclean approaches."

2.

"Huh?" I said, looking around.

A young couple strolled nearby. They were clearly in love, with their arms about each other and gooey looks on their faces. As they came near, I took a peek at their auras. The girl's aura was mostly pinks and greens – love, love, love. But the boy's was a swelter of murky dark tones banded with sickly, dull colours. The pair strolled past, engrossed in each other. Then the boy glanced back at me.

What I saw made me gasp. His face was no longer that of a moonstruck teenager. His eyes had turned a rusty red, his smile a warning grimace that showed off incisors longer than were humanly possible, and he seemed suddenly to move with the grace of a wild animal. The impression was gone a second later, as he turned back to his sweetheart.

"What is he?" I whispered.

The pair were well past by now, but I still had the heebie jeebies. I couldn't take my eyes off them.

"He is infected with the vampire curse," Vaivea answered.

"Jeez," I said, my voice cracking. "Shouldn't I do something to help the girl?"

"You cannot save her."

"I can't just sit back and let him infect her!"

"She is already partially infected. It is too dangerous for you to interfere. You would be putting yourself at risk unnecessarily."

Frustrated, I watched the couple disappear between the trees. What was the point of having the powers of Isis if I couldn't use them? The sooner I learned about accessing her magic, the better. And the best way to do that was to do another regression. In any case, I needed to know what happened next in her world, however bad it was. I took myself into the necessary state and slipped back through time.

Isis paced along the bank of the Nile, where the sun beat down with a fierce intensity. I felt it burn her skin, but it seemed of little importance. She had wandered for weeks, searching for her love. Time had no meaning. Nothing had meaning except that she locate his remains. She peered long and hard at every inch of the opposite shore, waded through the mud to shake out clumps of papyrus, scanned every wave, every ripple in the great river. And yet there was no sign of him.

A little way ahead, a grove of date palms loaned the shoreline their scanty shade. Underneath squatted a cluster of adobe huts, before which sat several women who ground corn into meal. A group of children played noisily beneath the date palms, screaming and giggling with the wild abandon of their game.

As Isis approached, the children fell still and stared in awe. The women by the huts were too busy gossiping and grinding to notice her presence. She knelt in the shade and held her hands out to the children, and they came to her.

"Pray, little ones," Isis said, "have any of you seen Lord Usir hereabouts?"

Eagerly they crowded closer, grinning shyly and reaching to touch her robes.

"Lord Usir I have not seen," said one boy.

"Nor I," said another.

"Then have you seen anything unusual?" Isis asked.

"Lady Ese," said a sweet-faced girl, "I saw a box floating in the river."

"Yes, yes, a box," several others joined in.

"A most wondrous box," the girl said, "with gold and silver and jewels set in it."

"I need to find that box."

"It went that way," chorused the children, pointing.

"Thankyou, little ones," Isis said. "And bless you, bless you all. Forever more, children just like you will speak with wisdom, if only adults will have the ears to hear."

She got up and trudged on along the river's bank in the direction the children had pointed out. Ahead, a lone figure approached. My gorge rose when I saw the upright, cropped ears, the mane of red hair, the forked tail. Set strode towards Isis warily, and in his eyes burned a coldness that almost made her quail.

"Why do you come here, brother?" Isis demanded. "Did you think I would welcome you with open arms?"

Set eyed her icily. The hostility in his features was not the only emotion to be read there.

"Your consort is dead, sister. I am sure you will soon take another."

His arrogance made me prickle, but Isis didn't have the will to sustain anger.

"You imagine I would take my lover's murderer to my bosom? Oh no, Sutekh. I love you as my brother, and though it kills me inside to do so, I forgive you as my brother. Any more is asking too much."

Set's eyes narrowed, but he held her gaze steadily.

"Usir is dead. I am alive."

"Are you?" Isis asked pointedly. "You lack pity and compassion, and cause nothing but misery. Do you think I could ever find pleasure in your presence?"

"It has nothing to do with your pleasure," Set snapped. "Kemet has lost a ruler, and I am next in line. We could rule together, sister..."

"You are mistaken," Isis said. "Leave me now, Sutekh. I no longer wish to endure your presence."

What emotion crossed Set's strange animal face, I couldn't make out. It may have been hatred. It may have been pleasure. It may have been both. It struck me that he might be enjoying the confrontation, finding arousal at Isis' anger. I felt sick to the stomach. His footsteps crunched on the sand as he strode off, but Isis turned so she could no longer see him.

The insult he'd just offered was unbearable. I understood only too well why he'd disposed of Osiris, though no admission of guilt had yet passed his lips. And then to come back and wave his sin in Isis' face like a red flag to a bull – if he expected her to fall into his arms, he had another thing coming!

3.

Isis sank to the ground, rocking back and forth with her sobs. The swirl of emotions darkened her mind, and I was suddenly jerked back through thousands of years to the bench at the park. I blinked and calmed my breathing. While I was still alone – barring Vaivea and a chorus of frogs that had started up somewhere nearby – I wanted to examine my latest regression.

True to the legend, Isis had pinpointed Set as the murderer of Osiris. Set had disposed of the body, and so far Isis had been unable to find it. I knew she would continue to search – Isis wasn't the type to let setbacks stop her from getting what she wanted. Heck, with Osiris' body missing, I'd want it back too.

I hadn't anticipated that Set would approach Isis with the intent to replace Osiris as her consort. Fat chance he stood. The thought of getting it on with your lover's murderer was utterly repugnant. There was no doubt of his guilt, even if he wouldn't admit it to Isis. He'd been dead jealous of his brother, and desired everything Osiris had for himself.

A distant rumble of thunder reached my ears, heralding another storm. I got on my bike just as the first jagged streaks of lightning flashed over the coast near Destin, and cruised through the spitting drops, savouring the cool and delicious wetness in the air. Halfway home, I was forced to take cover for nearly an hour as the storm raged over Niceville, dropping hail as well as heavy rain.

An eerie prickle went up and down my spine as I finally steered onto the driveway at home. Something felt different, though I couldn't put my finger on what it was. I found the front door locked. I hadn't taken a key with me, as I'd expected someone would be home when I returned. I knocked a couple of times, then I hammered on the door and called out. Nothing.

I was so surprised that I didn't know what to think or do.

Neither of my parents had said anything about going out that morning. And I had a sinking feeling that they hadn't simply popped out to grab groceries. A massive peal of thunder shook the ground as the storm swung back over the town. '*Great*,' I thought as I turned for the back yard. '*It never rains but it pours!*'

I ran around the side of the house, where a hedge of native firebush along the fence shielded me from the worst of the rain. However, I got soaked as I skirted the raised deck behind the house and nearly slipped over on the wet grass. I skidded onto the garden path and turned for the stairs up to the deck.

Flanking the stairs were a pair of white marble statues of Grecian ladies carrying urns, one of Mama's frivolous additions. In the misty rain, they looked startlingly like angels – the type often seen in cemeteries. By now my nerves were shot, and I bolted past them and flung myself at the back door in a panic. To my eternal relief, I found it unlocked, and bolted into the house.

"Mama?" I called out, checking the kitchen, the dining room, the loungeroom. "Dad? Where are you?"

There was no answer. I ran upstairs and looked in every room, but they weren't to be found. I couldn't even find a note, or any explanation for their absence. By now I was sure something terrible had happened.

"Gran? Vaivea? Where are my parents? Where'd they go? Why didn't they leave a message for me? Talk to me, damn it!"

All I heard was the pounding of the rain. I couldn't believe my guides would abandon me when I needed them so badly. It didn't seem right after what I'd been told about never being alone in the spirit realm.

"Vaivea? Come on, man," I wheedled. "I'm kind of freaking out here!"

"You must calm yourself," said Vaivea. "The time has come for clear thought."

"How can I think straight when I don't have a clue what's going on?"

"Be patient. The answers you seek will come to you at the appropriate time. Being in a state of panic will not make them appear any sooner."

"Oh yeah? Well, you could help me out here, instead of leaving me hanging in suspense. Surely you can tell me something?"

"What is it that you really need to know? Remove yourself from this moment of perceived stress and try to act as Isis would..."

"How?" I wailed. "I don't even know how to act like Isis, let alone use her powers. If I could, do you think I'd be upset like this?"

"You are overwrought..."

"No freakin' joke! I'd like some information or advice, if you don't mind. Isn't that what you're here for?"

"I advise calmness and caution. The outcome may mean life or death."

I felt pretty spooked at his words. I looked around again, hoping to find some clue that explained where my parents had gone so suddenly. I saw the internal door into the garage, and went to look. As I expected, Mama's 1962 Ford Fairlane wasn't there. Everything looked as tidy as usual, with no indication of where they'd gone or why.

I heard a sound from the driveway, and hurried to open the garage door. Mama drove in and parked, then hurried to help dad out of the passenger seat. I gasped in shock when I saw that his chest was thickly bandaged under his bloodied shirt.

10

Suspicious Minds

1. Saturday 25th October 1969 – Niceville, Florida

"Dad! Shit, what happened?"

"I got bitten by a big old dog," he said sheepishly. "Nothing to worry about."

"A dog? When? Where? Are you okay?"

"Yes, I'm fine. It was when the storm came over earlier."

"I told you not to go out in it," Mama scolded, and slammed the car door.

"Well, someone had to get that big branch off the road," dad said. "Came right off that sycamore over there."

He pointed at the front of our yard, to the very tree I'd often climbed as a teenager. A chunk was gone from it, and there were signs of something heavy having been dragged onto the lawn.

"Where is it now?" I asked.

"I called old Sol next door," Mama said, fiddling with the garage door's remote. "He came and cleared it away. Damn, why won't this blessed thing work?"

"Give it here."

My father took it from her and pressed a button, and the door obediently slid down. I turned to hide a smile as Mama huffed in exasperation.

"I meant, where's the dog? And how the heck did it bite you on the chest?"

"I don't know. I was moving that branch, I heard snarling behind me, I turned around, and it leapt at me and bit me, through my shirt and everything."

"Must have been big," I said. "I sure hope you'll be okay."

He smiled as I hugged him, then he and Mama went inside. I fetched my bike in, wiped it down, and put it away, then stood at the garage door and watched the steady downpour of rain, thinking about what had happened to dad. Whatever had attacked him, it didn't sound natural. With a shudder that had nothing to do with the weather, I closed the garage and went inside.

The lounge-room was empty. My mother came out of the kitchen carrying a steaming bowl and started towards the stairs.

"What's happened? Where's dad?"

"He came over faint and had to lie down. A bit of peace and quiet will do him good. And some chicken soup."

I wandered into the kitchen to make myself some lunch. A saucepan of freshly heated tinned soup sat on the stovetop, so I grabbed a mug and helped myself.

"I see Ronald has gotten himself into trouble," said a voice at my side.

I nearly dropped my soup. Gran shimmered beside me.

"Freakin' heck!" I said, trying to keep the soup from slopping out of the mug. "Yeah, he got bitten by a dog.

Must've been one mean mother."

"A dog, eh?"

Gran's voice sounded sceptical. I scrutinised her closely. It felt like she had information she was bursting to share with me. And not the good kind, either.

"So what really happened?" I asked. "Was it a dog, or was it... something else?"

"I don't know," she replied. "But his aura's changed. You take a look – something murky's crept in, and it's getting murkier by the minute!"

"What?" I choked out, feeling very unsettled..

"And while you're at it, look at your mother's."

I shivered, not liking where the conversation was going. I heard Mama's voice from the stairs, so I tried to compose myself. It mustn't have worked, because she stopped two steps into the kitchen and frowned.

"What's wrong now? Are you worried about your father? They gave him a rabies shot, you know. He'll be fine."

I sighed and put my soup down.

"I know. Everything's already been a mess and a half lately, and now this..."

"I suppose it is a good idea to go see Karen. Get the wind in your hair and blow away all the cobwebs, do girl stuff together... Is that what you were planning?"

"More or less," I said with a shrug.

I had no intention of letting her in on any of the spiritual stuff I was going through. Mama considered herself a good Christian, which meant she turned up at church every Sunday, if she got out of bed early enough, or if there was something interesting happening, like a christening or a funeral. She called it taking an interest in her community; I called it hypocrisy.

Remembering Gran's words, I peeked at her aura, and was surprised to see the muted and dull colours that moved sluggishly around her. She frowned and went into the loungeroom. I picked up my mug of soup and found it was at just the right temperature to sip.

"I don't know about any of this," Gran said, shaking her head.

"Should I go and check out dad? If something's not right, maybe I can do something about it."

"He has needs beyond physical healing," Gran said.

I didn't know if she was being mysterious on purpose, and waited for her to elaborate. She didn't, so I went upstairs. Dad lay in the master bedroom in a clean change of clothes, looking kind of grey. He smiled as I sat next to him.

"Hey, kiddo," he said weakly. "Don't know what came over me – I just felt so tired all of a sudden. Now don't you go getting worried. I'll be fine."

There was a moment, as he lay there breathing softly and looking up at me, where I felt like our roles were reversed, like he was the trusting child and I was the parent whose job it was to kiss his injury and make things all better. I fleetingly wondered if I could heal him, as I felt his forehead to check his temperature. His skin was cold and clammy, although he was perspiring.

"Maybe you're having some sort of reaction to the vaccine," I said. "That can happen, you know."

"Could be. The doctor warned me there might be side effects."

"Well, you just take it easy and relax," I said. "I'll stay and do whatever I can to make you feel better. Maybe you'll feel well enough tomorrow for us to have that picnic down at Destin."

"Sure thing, honey," he said with a grin.

He yawned and closed his eyes. I softened my focus to look at his aura, and saw what Gran had meant. Amongst the vibrant yellows and oranges that usually accompanied naturally cheerful, confident people were dark and murky smudges. He snored softly, and then Mama came in with a glass of water and some pills.

"How is he?" she asked.

"He's asleep," I said, standing up. "He looked a bit sick, but hopefully it's just a reaction to the vaccine."

"Hopefully," she said, and shut the door after me as I left.

I felt restless after that, and took to my own bedroom. I wanted to ask Mama how things were between her and dad, but I didn't know how. Was it even polite to inquire – to broach the subject of marital relations between your parents to their faces? Still, I thought Karen and I had a right to know what was going on.

Thinking of Karen reminded me I'd meant to ring her, so I tiptoed out to the hall extension, dialled her number, and leaned against the wall.

"Hi big sis," I said.

"Hey there," Karen said eagerly. "I'm glad you called. I feel like I'll go crazy if I don't talk to someone about what's happening here."

"I tried to call last night, but no one answered. Has it happened again?"

"I haven't seen that – thing – again, but I've felt it watching me a few times. I'm hoping it will just go away if I pretend not to notice it. Anyway, I've been wondering what happened with Gabe – any news?"

"Yeah," I said. "Is there ever."

I told her about being cut off from Gabe and his family, and my trip home to Niceville. Again I didn't mention the spirit stuff – I wanted to save that until we were face to face. She didn't say much, but exclaimed over our father's incident, and when I finished, she was silent. I could hear her breathing on the other end of the line, and guessed it was a lot to absorb.

"He's okay," I said. "He's just resting. If he's up to it, we're going to Destin for a day out tomorrow."

"Ange, I don't know what to think," Karen said. "Are you sure he'll be alright? Should I fly over?"

"No," I said, "I'm coming to you. I'm gonna drive the caddy over."

"Is that wise?"

I actually stopped to think about that. For all of two seconds.

"Yeah, I'll be fine. And so will dad. You know how worry-prone Mama is. If dad gets worse, she'll have him at the hospital quicker than you can blink."

"But she might need some help nursing him," Karen said. "After all, she's not exactly Florence Nightingale."

"Don't worry," I said with a laugh. "I'm keeping an eye on things. If he recovers quickly, I'll leave day after tomorrow, otherwise I'll postpone the trip. Okay?"

"Okay," Karen said. "Keep me up to date, alright?"

I promised, and hung up. Back in my room, Gran shimmered softly by my desk.

"I hope Karen understands when I tell her about the spirit stuff," I said. "I'm still getting used to it myself – it's all been so sudden."

"You'll be alright, sweetheart," Gran said. "As long as

184

you're careful – stay alert to danger, read and learn more, practice your skills..."

"Yeah, I will," I said. "I wish I could've taken more of Amy's books with me. What a waste. I really wish I could have saved her, too. If only I'd known..."

"You have everything you need," Gran said. "The resources open to you from the spirit world are endless. All you've got to do is learn to ask!"

2.

I read for a few hours, then Mama called out that dinner was ready. I slouched down to the kitchen. She'd simply heated some TV dinners in the oven, but she did take the trouble to make up a couple of gin and tonics.

She took dad's dinner upstairs, then we sat in front of the telly to eat, watching Hee-Haw and not laughing. To give it its dues, it had lots of jokes and gags, but they were so damned corny. Besides, the canned laughter always ruined it for me. How bad must the material be if you needed to be told when to laugh?

"So, Miss, what are you going to do now?" Mama asked as she levelled the remote at the TV and jabbed it several times before it switched off.

"What, as in right now, or my plans for the future?"

"You know what I mean," she said ominously. "You left a good job and went racing off, not knowing where it'll all end. I just can't understand why."

I had the sudden impression she'd drunk rather more than the one cocktail we'd had with dinner. I gazed at her, weighing up whether it was worth the risk of saying what I really wanted to say.

"I mean, look at you," she continued.

"Look at me what?" I said.

"For goodness sake, you must know what I mean. You've always been different. You've never been able to settle down. Got too much of your father in you, I guess."

Mama drained her glass and looked at me with pity in her eyes.

"You poor, silly little girl," she said, shaking her head. "One thing goes wrong in your life, and poof! You throw everything out the window."

I sat completely still, not knowing how to react to this unexpected appraisal. Mama had never said anything like it before – at least, not in my hearing. I wondered if that was secretly how she'd always viewed me. Whether it was her own honest opinion or the drink talking, I started to feel uneasy.

"Your clothes," she continued, "your hair, the way you do things. Slinking around like a cat with burnt feet. You've never been open and honest like Karen. Everyone likes her. No one ever liked you much. I'm not sure I like you much. But you're my daughter, and I suppose that has to count for something."

"Mama, have you been drinking?"

"There you go, suspecting the worst. You always think the worst of everyone. No wonder people don't like you."

"Mama, life isn't a popularity contest," I said, not really wanting to get drawn into the argument but unable to help it. "I don't care who doesn't like me – I just believe in being true to myself. And there are lots of people out there who aren't nice, who just want to hurt and use other people. Why should I be worried about what they think?"

Mama gazed at me unsteadily.

"Look," I said, standing up. "I'm sorry if I don't live up to your expectations. No one can get through life without disappointing someone – even Karen. I love and respect you, Mama, but I'm a totally different person to you, and I expect to be left alone to live the way I think is best for me."

Her mouth fell open as I left the room. I kind of felt sorry for her, because she'd always had such a limited view of life and expected others to be the same. Just because she was happy that way – or pretended to be happy – she couldn't, or wouldn't, understand anyone who was different. Maybe now she realised she couldn't maintain the illusion, and she didn't like coming to terms with it. Whatever it was, I hoped she would be okay, for her sake and dad's. Perhaps it was a good thing he was back.

I brushed my teeth and got ready for bed, although it was earlier than my usual bedtime. The rain had eased off after dark, but the sky was still shrouded with clouds. I sank into bed with a book, determined to find out everything I could about werewolves and vampires. I found myself re-reading a lot of stuff I already knew, but I didn't want to miss anything.

After a while my mind wandered. I thought about dad again, and what had bitten him. He'd said it was a big dog, making the obvious supernatural suspect a werewolf. But I wasn't so sure. The full moon was still a couple of nights away...

"Gran, can vampires disguise themselves?"

"They can project an illusion around themselves for camouflage," she said. "I think I've seen one or two of them do it, although it's hard to be sure. Their auras stay the same, though. I'm certain I've seen some bats flying about with really dark auras. Could've been vampires."

"But that means they can fly," I said. "In their disguise, I mean. They can't normally fly, can they?"

I figured if I came up against a foe that could get a height advantage like that, I was done for. Gran sighed.

"I can't really say. Perhaps you should try and talk to Amy. She's seen a lot more of this dark stuff than I have."

"Yes – I'd love to talk to her. How can I do that?"

"You meditate, and send out a call to the universe inviting Amy to come to you. Then you sit back and wait, and if she's not doing something important, and it's in the highest good, she'll come."

"What, that's it?"

It sounded rather hit and miss to me.

"You can't call us like you call for a dog. Spirits don't just sit around playing cards all day, waiting for people to call on them. They work actively with people, sometimes with many people at once, trying to guide them to live better lives and fulfil their life's purpose. You'll just have to be patient."

"Okay. So I ask her to come to me. That's all I have to do?"

"Yes, but remember, she may not be able to come right away."

With those words in my ears, I turned off the lights and settled down to meditate. Before I even got comfortable, something else came to mind.

"Can dark energies and spirits intercept messages sent through the ether?"

"It happens all the time," Gran said. "People send out calls for help, for instruction, for reaching loved ones. Evil spirits can and do attach themselves to these pleas, and come for the easy pickings, like sharks to a feeding frenzy."

I didn't care for Gran's analogy, but I got the message loud and clear.

"So that's how Lou tracked me down?"

"Possibly. But remember who you are. There's plenty of interest in the spirit realm in following fallen gods and goddesses."

That took me aback. I hadn't quite thought of myself in those terms, and wondered if I was under surveillance right then by dozens of nefarious spirits all intent on bringing me down. Lou sure had it easy with so many willing minions to spy on me for him.

"Okay, so I put up some protection while I'm meditating and sending messages," I said. "Easy."

"Don't expect it to be too easy," Gran warned me. "They'll be interested to find out what you're so keen to protect. Remember, phones can be tapped in both worlds."

"Gee, so much for privacy," I huffed, and settled back to meditate.

When I'd completely relaxed and focussed on the target of my message, I let the words flow from me, out into the universe.

"Amy, please come to me when you're able to. I need to know more. I've got so much to learn. Please help me."

I sent it again and again, like a mantra, radiating out in all directions. My protective wall didn't seem to impede the progress of my message, so I hoped it was safe and that I wouldn't get buzzed in the night by Lou or any of his cronies.

After I'd concentrated on it for some minutes, I allowed my mind to drift back to my normal meditation. I was curious to know what happened next in Isis's world, but I was wary after today's visit. It had drained me in a lot of ways, and I decided the best thing to do was to get a good night's sleep.

"Goodnight Gran," I said, and drifted off.

A noise jerked me back awake. I looked over at the alarm clock on my bedside table, but it was too dark to see. I picked the clock up and drew my curtain open just enough to read it in the patchy moonlight. One fifty AM. It took a moment to realise I'd been asleep for several hours.

More noise. It sounded like it was just down the hall. I tiptoed to the door and put my eye to the keyhole. The hallway light was on, but I couldn't see anything out of the ordinary. I wondered if I should go look when a crash came from downstairs.

3.

I tore the door open and ran to the staircase. No lights were on downstairs, so I descended carefully and felt for the lounge room light switch. Nothing out of place there. I tiptoed to the kitchen, dreading what I might find, but it was only dad rummaging around in the fridge. I noticed a chair by the dining table had been knocked over, the cause of the crash.

My father sensed my presence, and sprang to face me with a packet of steak in his hand.

"Midnight snack?" I teased.

"What? Oh yeah. I need something to eat. That TV dinner wasn't very filling."

"You gonna cook up that steak?"

He smiled sheepishly at the paper-wrapped bundle, and replaced it in the fridge.

"Naw, I just thought there might be something behind it. Ham maybe – ham and cheese toasted sandwiches. Mmmm..."

"Sounds good. I think there's a packet of ham on the bottom shelf. Look, you've dripped blood from that steak all over the place."

"So I have," dad mused, looking at his red-stained fingers.

He turned away from me, towards the sink, but I could tell he was examining his hand. Then I heard him sniffing.

"Dad?" I said.

I placed a hand on his arm. He looked at me strangely, like he was stoned or something, then he glanced at his fingers and shook his head.

"Oh, I'd better clean this up," he said.

While he washed his hands at the sink, I wiped up the blood from the floor. Then we made ham and cheese toasted sandwiches together, and I had one with him. I was surprised Mama hadn't come down with all the noise, and said so.

"She's sleeping the sleep of the dead," my father joked, taking the last sandwich.

I stared at him in shock, then realised it was just a manner of speech and he'd only meant that she was fast asleep. I wondered if he knew she'd been hitting the bottle.

"I think she had a bit to drink this evening," I said. "That's probably what zonked her out."

My father's smile drooped.

"She's been drinking too much for years," he said, licking crumbs off his fingers. "You probably had no idea. That's why I volunteered for 'Nam, you know. I was sick to Christ of dealing with it; thought doing something drastic like that might wake her up."

I gasped.

"What? She was drinking back then?"

"She was drinking for years before that, even. You know all

those dinners and parties and galas we went to? She'd have several glasses of wine or champagne, then come home and drink some more. She drank before dinner, she drank during dinner, she drank after dinner. Then she'd have a nightcap or two before coming to bed."

I sat dumbfounded whilst dad took our plates to the sink and rinsed them.

"It got even worse when she discovered gin," he said. "Gin and tonic, gin and soda, gin and lemon, gin on the rocks. I'm sure she could've drunk Dean Martin under the table."

I was speechless.

"I guess you never knew," dad said. "Karen did. She tried to get Patsy to dry out, make her sign up for Alcoholics Anonymous. Never worked, though. She never would admit she had a problem."

"Heck. I had no idea."

Dad shrugged.

"I'd hoped she'd eased off now she's getting older, but it doesn't look like it. She's drinking as much as ever."

"Maybe that's why she's been so up and down while I've been here."

"Yeah – she has been pretty moody. I thought it was because of me turning up out of the blue just before you arrived..."

"We have to do something about it, dad. We can't just let her keep doing this to herself. It could kill her – her liver's probably toast by now..."

"I know, sweetheart. But she's not going to be easy to convince. I tried for years, and that was before her drinking got serious."

I was stunned all over again. My mother had been a closet alco for ages, and I'd never guessed it.

"When did she start?"

"She got hit with depression pretty bad after you were born. She hardly drank at all before that."

4.

That was like a clout to the head. And the heart. And wherever else it might hurt. And it explained why she'd always held me at a distance. We certainly never had what I'd call a good mother-daughter relationship.

"So she only started drinking after *I* was born," I said.

"Oh now honey," my father said, giving me a big hug. "It's not like that. You know we both love you. It wasn't your fault she couldn't handle the depression. And she got over it eventually."

I lay my head against his chest, wanting to feel comforted the way I had as a child. I breathed in the scent of him, the manly smell of strength and protection, and then I jumped backwards. His scent was different – sweat and blood mingled with something less definable. I tried to hide my disgust, but it was too late.

"Sorry, dad. I didn't mean to jump like that, but you smell gross, like you've been rolling in the garbage or something."

My father lifted an arm and sniffed.

"Oh yeah. Sorry about that, hon. I've been sweating heaps all wrapped up like this. I'll give myself a sponge bath before I go back to bed. Can't disturb the bandages, you know."

"Hey, it's cool. You must be feeling better. Good to see."

"Yeah, I am. See you in the morning, okay?"

"Sure, dad. We've got a date, remember?"

I left dad in the kitchen, and went back to bed. The things

I'd found out were horrible, and it felt like they'd turned to stone in my stomach. I tried to convince myself that a little baby isn't responsible for the actions of its parents, but that didn't help. And then there was the hurt and betrayal I felt that no one had told me about Mama's drinking problem. I needed to talk to Karen again, as soon as possible.

I lay down, convinced I'd never get back to sleep, but somehow I did. When I awoke, dawn had sent its first golden rays over Niceville. My thick purple curtains kept most of the light out, so it was still fairly dark in my room. Gran was nearby, watching over me.

"Boy, I feel like I haven't slept at all," I said through a yawn.

"You didn't look like you were sleeping well. You found out some disturbing things last night. I'm sorry I couldn't warn you, but you had to find out for yourself."

Reminded forcibly of all the twists and turns my life had taken recently, I sat up in a huff.

"What, that my mother's a closet alco and has been for years? That I was the only one who didn't know? That my father may be turning into something dreadful right before my eyes and I don't know what to do about it?"

I ticked off the points on my fingers, my voice rising with each one.

"Mama hates me for causing her depression, which started her drinking in the first place. My boyfriend's in a coma. Something horrible's threatening my sister. I'm being constantly bugged by the devil. And I'm a goddess who doesn't know the first thing about *being* a goddess. Holey Moley – disturbing doesn't *begin* to cover it."

Gran just sighed.

"Don't get me wrong," I said. "I'm not mad at you guys for

having secrets. I'm not leaden down with feelings of guilt and despair. I'm not even sorry about Mama not liking me. But I am angry that things have turned out like this."

"My poor little sparrow. I wish you could have been spared this heartache."

"Gran, I know you couldn't tell me. I know how it all works. I gotta make my own mistakes and learn stuff by myself to get anywhere. But I really have a bone to pick with whoever set it up this way."

"Sweetheart, would you make war on those who shaped the way the world works? There's no one entity to blame – they've all had a hand, even Isis. Would you be so willing to attack yourself?"

Okay, I had to admit that pulled me up a bit. But there was one presence I couldn't help but feel was to blame more than any other.

"And who's been in charge for the last couple of thousand years?" I said. "Who's the most powerful god, the one who might have done something to better our lot on earth, the one who, if I remember rightly, tried to destroy humankind once or twice, and allowed His only son to die horribly?"

"There's more to it than that. Just because He's been the most powerful god for some time doesn't mean that He always was or will be, or that He's free to go changing things at the drop of a hat. He's bound by certain constraints, just like we all are..."

"You're telling me that God can't choose to make our lives better? Isis could – she helped people and gave them the knowledge to help themselves. She walked amongst them and saw their suffering, and did something about it. You're telling me that the most powerful god in existence today can't do that?"

Gran sighed again, but I was too riled up to care.

"He ignores us. He lets us suffer. He says to love thy neighbour on the one hand and then promotes exclusionism and intolerance on the other! Hello!"

"Sweetheart, that's just the way the world interprets God, despite His best intentions. Believe me, he's not the enemy here. And you've got to remember, even His power is limited, as are the powers of all such entities."

"God's power is *limited*?" I said disbelievingly.

"Yes. The God of Abraham is only one small cog in a greater wheel, the cosmic wheel of life, death and rebirth that is common to all cultures and religions. And even having that power doesn't allow Him to change everything. It works this way, because this is how we best learn our lessons in our lives."

"But is it fair to make us suffer quite so much?"

"Angela?" came Mama's voice through the closed door. "Are you alright? Who're you talking to?"

"It's okay, it's just my radio," I called back.

The lie didn't bother me. Even at that time of day, I sometimes liked to have some noise going. I waited to be sure Mama had left, then I turned back to Gran. Only she wasn't there.

"Hello Cheri, long time no see."

I nearly blurted out, 'Jesus' again, but recalling Lou's previous comments regarding the Son of God, I refrained.

"Gee willikers!" I said instead. "Where's my grandmother? What've you done with her?"

Lou blinked, the picture of innocence.

"Who, me? What have I done with her? Moi? Oh what

a treacherous girl you are, always thinking the worst of people…"

"Can it. I'm sick of that crap about my motives. And you can talk. Like you're squeaky clean."

"My dear, you have got up on the wrong side of the bed, haven't you?"

"No I haven't – I haven't got up at all yet!"

"As I can very well see," said Lou, raising his eyebrows suggestively.

"Forget it. You're a fallen angel, and I've just read that angels aren't supposed to have genders."

"Wanna see for yourself?"

"No."

"Darling, I can give you the best sexual experience of your life. Of many lives, even. Just say the word…"

"The word is no. I'm practically engaged. I'm no cheat."

"Oh yes, the guy in the hospital," Lou said. "The one whose family told you to take a hike."

"Yeah, the one whose family told me to take a hike," I said. "But *he* didn't, and we're still together. We'll always be together, heart and soul."

"Oh how dreary," Lou said with a yawn. "I often reflect on how the word monogamous is so like the word monotonous."

"You must have less to do with your time than I thought."

"Ooh, you stab me to the heart," he said. "But the offer still stands. You look like a girl who'd enjoy some adventure."

"I will be soon. Just me and my caddy, across the U.S.A."

"That sounds rather dull. All those miles and miles of desert and dead lands. I thought you'd want a little… more."

"You can't always pick 'em," I said with a smirk. "And I won't be alone, as you well know."

"Ah, the grandmother."

"Yes, the grandmother."

"And the Indian shaman."

"Yes, the... Vaivea was a shaman?"

"My dear, there's so much I could teach you."

"What could you teach me that's worth knowing? How to hurt and use and abuse people?"

"How to indulge in your sweetest fantasies and make them real..."

"Or give in to temptation and find it isn't all it was cracked up to be?"

"How to enjoy life, free from guilt and self-reproach..."

"And throw away everything good to become the scum of the earth?"

"How to reach the highest of highs and then get higher..."

We'd leaned close to each other, our eyes deadlocked. My breaths came short and fast, and despite my best efforts, I couldn't tear my gaze away. His eyes were a soft, melting brown, which really did something to me. He suddenly seemed incredibly alluring and seductive. And I felt myself irresistibly drawn to him, despite the bad ending I knew would be in store.

11

Magic Carpet Ride

1. Sunday 26th October, 1969 – Niceville, Florida

I reached out with my mind, determined to break the spell.

'Gran? Are you there? Can you help me?'

"Your grandmother is visiting Karen," Lou whispered. "And I tangled Vaivea up with some mischievous little spirits I found in Rocky Bayou. We're alone."

"My parents are just down the corridor," I said, feeling hot all over.

"Your father sleeps like a rock, and your mother is outside, gardening. We are alone."

That snapped me back to myself.

"Gardening? At this time of day? That's a pretty dumb lie, even for you."

"Well, okay, she's downstairs, chatting to one of her friends on the phone. What does it matter? I can make it so your screams of ecstasy don't leave this room. No one need ever know..."

"I'll know."

"I can arrange for you to forget. Then we can do it all again, and it will be just like the first time for you. Every time."

"You've messed with my mind enough already," I said, narrowing my eyes at him. "No way I'm letting you lay a trip on me again, ever. And for the millionth time, I don't want to have sex with you!"

"Uh, uh, uh," Lou said, wagging a finger at me. "I've been counting, and I can assure you it isn't anywhere near the millionth time you've rejected me."

"Just bag it already. I mean, how plainly do I have to put it?"

"Darling, it doesn't matter how you put it. I don't give up that easily."

"Apparently."

"I know you're tempted."

"You think so?"

"I know so."

"So why are you trying to talk me into it? You've got powers. Why don't you just take me by force?"

I knew that was reckless talk, but you know how we all have a little angel on one shoulder and a little devil on the other? I think by that point my devil had bound and gagged my angel, and had him on the railway tracks, just waiting for the Florida Special to run him over.

"Well, I could," Lou said. "But that wouldn't be half as much fun as you coming to me willingly. You're closer than you think."

I screwed my eyes up tight in an attempt to break contact.

"Never."

"Oh darling, you think you can shut me out as easily as that? Remember that little – test – I tried on you back in Amy's house?"

My eyes flew open.

"So you finally admit it? I knew that was you!"

"Yes, and I can do it again. But I'd much rather do it the easy way."

"Well I wouldn't!" I snapped, glaring at him.

He sniggered like a naughty little boy. I glared at him some more, and he laughed some more. Damn him.

"I like a challenge," he said, wiping tears from his eyes. "It makes me want you even more."

"Why?" I demanded. "Why do you want me? What's so special about me?"

"Why, you're a goddess, my dear. You just don't realise it yet."

Boy was I dumb.

"You mean, I'm more than just a human incarnation of Isis? I'm Isis in the here and now?"

"I can't believe you still doubt it. Let me show you."

Before I could protest, Lou reached over and took my hands. We lifted off the bed, floating up through the ceiling, over the rooftops of Niceville. I felt kind of exposed, being clad in no more than my short pyjamas. I was about to say something about it, but then we took off at light speed. Streaks of glowing brilliance like falling stars flashed by, my hair whipped back from my face, and a fresh, dewy aroma filled my nostrils.

We stopped just as suddenly as we'd started. I blinked and pushed strands of hair back behind my ears.

"Okay, that was kind of awesome," I said, not wanting to sound *too* impressed.

"We took a short cut through the spirit dimension," Lou said. "Now behold, thy kingdom on earth."

2.

I looked down and saw we were on an island in a lake, deep blue water stretching out around us towards a distant rocky shoreline. We stood atop part of an enormous gateway of carved granite blocks, below which opened a central court-yard with a tiled floor. Elaborately carved, brightly painted colonnades stood solid on either side. The sky stretched huge and blue above us.

"I have a feeling we're not in Kansas any more," I said wryly.

"This is one of the centres of your worship. Here's a hint. We're in Egypt."

I must've looked confused, because Lou slapped his fore-head and groaned.

"Philae! The Island of Philae! The major centre of Isis' worship!"

"Okay!" I said. "So this doesn't look like modern times. When are we?"

"About one hundred BC. Give or take a year or two. And all those people down there are your adoring subjects."

I looked down upon a solemn procession making its way into the building via an entrance below. A line of men and women shuffled along, singing softly in a language that seemed somehow familiar, although I was sure I'd never heard it before. In this lifetime, at least. As I listened, I found myself starting to make sense of their words.

"Can they see us up here?" I asked.

"They can if you wish it."

I didn't feel particularly comfortable with the idea of people bowing down and worshipping me. Especially in my short pyjamas.

"Er... not today. I'm not really dressed for the occasion. So what am I supposed to be looking at here?"

"Step this way."

We floated across the courtyard and sank through the roof of the temple itself into a large room on the ground level. Here stood a great altar with candles and incense burning atop it, being tended by priestesses in blue gossamer robes. On the wall behind the altar was a larger-than-life image that I recognised immediately. There knelt Isis, her wings painted brightly with sapphire blues, ruby reds, and emerald greens, and so much gold ornamentation that she shone like the sun.

As they entered, the priests and priestesses chanted a list of names that I recognised from somewhere deep in my past – the many names of Isis.

"Oh Queen of Heaven; Mother of the Gods," they intoned in a low harmony, "The One Who is All; The Lady of Green Crops..."

The sound awakened a distant memory in the back of my mind. I chased and tried to grasp it, but it proved elusive.

"The Brilliant One in the Sky; The Star of the Sea; The Great Lady of Magic; Mistress of the House of Life..."

The chanting affected me strangely. I felt as though I was seconds away from being struck by lightning, but couldn't move. I took some deep breaths to ground myself again.

"She Who Knows how to make the Right Use of the Heart..."

The feeling slowly left me, and my skin tingled all over.

"Light-Giver of Heaven; Lady of the Words of Power..."

I rubbed my hands up and down my arms, trying to force myself to feel normal.

"This is all very nice," I said to Lou. "But is there something I'm not getting?"

"You will very soon. Just relax, let the chanting flow through you. You were nearly there a moment ago."

I was sick of not getting answers, and turned to face him.

"No. I want to know why you brought me here. What's a temple on an island in ancient Egypt got to do with me being Isis in my own time?"

"Just want to demonstrate your... appeal."

"Yeah, but things've changed a whole lot by the nineteen sixties."

"That's where you're wrong. Allow me."

We rose into the air and took off at the speed of light again, coming to rest in the bell-tower of a little white-washed church. Leafy suburbs stretched all around, full of weatherboard and brick houses all decorated for Halloween. Cars drove on the streets, and people in modern clothing walked and cycled on the sidewalks and in a nearby park awash with bright autumn colour. The aroma of fresh-baked pumpkin pie, full of sweet spices, wafted up to us.

"Speaking of Kansas," Lou said, sniffing the scented air deeply. "Ah, the great mid-west..."

"Your point being?"

"Believe it or not, there are little spots like this all over the world, where, underneath the veneer of Christian convention and respectability, lies a seething cesspool of discontent. Behold, thy kingdom on earth."

I let my eyes wander over the townscape again, and shrugged.

"I don't get it. I have no believers here."

"Okay, let's zoom in."

Holding my hands, he floated us down towards a nearby house. It looked as normal and conventional as you could get, with a mother pruning rosebushes, a father mowing the lawn, and a little girl playing dollies on the porch.

We floated through the roof and dropped into an upstairs bedroom, where several girls sat in a circle on the floor. A candle burned on a saucer between them, and one of the girls recited a passage from a thick old book on her lap.

"Isis, who gives birth to the heaven and the earth, hear our prayers..."

I jumped in shock. What was going on here? The first girl passed the book on to the next, who continued the prayer.

"Isis, who knows the orphans, hear our prayers..."

Somewhere deep inside me, that strange feeling started to bubble up again. The second girl passed the book to the third.

"Isis, who knows the widow spider – ugh, why do I have to get the bit about spiders? Gross!"

"Sophie!" the second girl said. "You'll ruin the prayer. We'll never achieve world peace if we don't take it seriously."

"But spiders are so groady!"

"Just say it," the first girl said. "Spiders are good luck, you know."

"Oh, alright," said Sophie. "Isis who knows the widow spider, hear our prayers."

She passed the book back to the first girl.

"Isis, who seeks justice for the poor people, hear our prayers..." The strange feeling welled up through my torso and throat. I tried to breathe deeply again to maintain control, but it didn't work this time.

"Isis," the second girl intoned, "who seeks shelter for the weak people, hear our prayers..."

Waves of dizzying electricity raced all over me, engulfing me. I felt like I was about to pass out.

"Isis," the third girl said, "Queen of Heaven and Mother of the Gods, hear our prayers..."

My breath caught in my throat. Suddenly the strangeness was gone. For the first time, I felt like the Isis I visited in my regressions. The girl's petitions opened up something inside me – a long-forgotten, hidden well of powers and emotions.

"Isis of ten thousand names, hear our prayers..."

Tears flooded my eyes, welled out over my cheeks, and the final vestiges of the electricity I'd felt surge through me crackled out of my fingertips. Then I realised the strangeness hadn't gone at all. It was still there. It was normal. This was how it felt to be a Goddess!

Lou smirked at my side.

"Told you so."

I wanted to say something cutting, but my throat was all choked up. Lou took my hands and floated us back to the bell-tower, where the breeze felt cool on my wet face. I expected him to have plenty to say now that he'd proved his point, but he was strangely quiet. I turned to find him looking in the opposite direction, and was touched by his apparent sensitivity.

"All that world out there to enjoy," he murmured. "We could enjoy it together, ma cheri. It's been so long..."

All sorts of rebuffs came to mind, but I couldn't voice any of them. Suddenly I was in his world. A world where the greater powers gave and took at a whim without regret. A world where illusion and supernatural powers were normal, and physical life and death didn't matter. I'd tasted it briefly in my regressions, but it hadn't made much of an impact on me.

Now I was a part of it, and it was a part of me, and nothing would ever, ever be the same again. A profound realisation jolted me.

"If I'm truly Isis, then Gabe is truly Osiris. He's a god, just like me!"

Lou's wistful smile turned into a woebegone pout.

"Aw, always him. Him, him, him. Never me."

"Ugh, hang it up!" I said. "You're such a darned phony."

He pouted some more, on purpose, I thought.

"You know," he said, "I could just leave you here. Leave you to find your own way home without any help from me. In fact, I think I will."

3.

My first thought was to plead with him to take me home. In my mind, I was still a mortal girl who couldn't quite get her head around the idea that she was a goddess, and able to go wherever she wanted. When I realised this, I smiled, closed my eyes, and Wished myself home.

I found myself sitting in my bed, just as I was when Lou had whisked me away. I felt dazed and my ears hummed. This would take some getting used to.

"Breakfast's up," came dad's voice from down the hall. "I'm making pancakes."

I bolted out of bed, dressed in no time flat and raced down to the kitchen. Dad stood by the stovetop, tossing pancakes into the air with that knack he had that Mama had never mastered, and plumping them down on a serving dish with a flourish. His colour had returned, and he obviously felt a lot better after having a good night's sleep.

Mama kissed me absent-mindedly on the cheek and handed

me a glass of juice. She seemed to have forgotten all about our disagreement. I couldn't help feeling a bit weird, knowing about her alcoholism. I had to talk to Karen about that. And soon.

After we'd eaten a mountain of pancakes with maple syrup, dad and I washed up and put everything away. While he was still in the mood for cooking, he showed me how to make pizza dough – something he'd learned from Jenny – and we put it in the fridge to rise for use that night. When we were finished, we packed a picnic lunch to take with us to Destin.

"I'll drive," I offered, dangling my car keys in front of him.

He looked at me warily, then burst out laughing.

"Heck, you probably drive better than I do. Let's go."

Dad and I piled into the caddy. So did Gran and Vaivea, though dad was unaware of them. We sang along with the radio as I drove south through Fort Walton Beach, crossed to Okaloosa Island and whizzed past the Gulfarium. The morning sun sparkled on the emerald green water and crystalline sand as we drove over the bridge into Destin. We continued past the town – not much more than a picturesque fishing village – and pulled over alongside the long, curving beach.

Dad and I laid a picnic rug down on the sugary white sand, then we strolled a good way along the beach, looking for sea shells. When we returned to our spot, he collapsed in mock fatigue, dropping his meagre collection beside him.

"I'm too old for this."

"Dad, you're doing pretty well for someone who got chomped up by a dog and had to have a rabies shot."

"Oh yeah – funny, but I forgot about that."

I took a swig of coffee from my thermos and handed it to him.

"How do you feel?"

"Not bad. Still a bit tender."

I smiled as I got our lunch out.

"You're still pretty fit, though, right? Sandwich?"

"Thanks. Actually, I haven't been in good shape at all lately. I hit the burger joints pretty bad when Jen left – and the booze, I'm ashamed to say."

I watched him as he bit into his sandwich. His eyes were far-away, as if seeking something on the distant blue horizon. The shadows of his recent grief clung to his body and his aura. I sighed.

"I know what you mean. I haven't really eaten healthy in ages, and I sure haven't felt like exercising."

We ate our sandwiches in silence, watching the blue/green waves roll in and out, the seagulls scrabbling and squabbling over the crusts we threw them. I cherished this time with my father, just being close and breathing the same salt-scented air, side by side in quietude. I had an odd feeling that after today, it might never be like this again.

The sun grew warmer overhead, so we walked back to the car and headed for the main street at Fort Walton Beach. We got soft drinks and spent an hour strolling up and down, looking at the shop windows, all decorated for Halloween. Whilst Dad visited a rest room, I spied a little esoteric shop I hadn't seen before, and peered in at the window. A young woman in beads and a kaftan dress beckoned to me from behind the counter, and, surprised to find any shop open on a Sunday, I went in.

Trails of smoke from burning incense wafted lazily towards the ceiling, and nearly knocked me back out the door. It smelt like she was burning several of each kind.

"The incense is half price today," the woman said dreamily.

"And there's a special on the jewellery."

I considered backing out and regaining regions with fresh air. Instead I decided to get a present for Karen, and headed for the jewellery. I was instantly drawn to a necklace with a moonstone pendant. The gem was set amidst a fine swirl of silver filigree that made up the head and mane of a unicorn. I knew Karen would love it. She'd always liked unicorns, despite being afraid of horses.

I also looked at the books, and found several to add to my collection. One was about vampires. Another explored myth and religion, and the third, supernatural subjects. When I left, dad was looking at a nearby shop window. I hurried over.

"Sorry, I didn't mean to be long," I said.

"You weren't, sweetheart. Ready to go?"

"I've never seen that shop before," I added as we back-tracked to the car. "It must be new. I got a present for Karen, a moonstone pendant set in silver."

"That sounds nice," dad said. "What else did you get?"

"Oh, just some books," I answered as we reached the car.

"Let's see."

I gave him the package and slid behind the wheel, and dad got in beside me. I pulled out into the traffic and turned for home, the radio turned up loud. I smiled when the next song started – David Seville's The Witchdoctor.

"Hey dad, remember how we all used to sing along with this one?" I asked.

"Mmm."

I glanced over to find dad flicking through the book on vampires. My heart lurched. I couldn't help but wonder if he was merely curious, or if he had some mysterious, deeper interest in the subject. What if he really had been bitten by a vampire disguised as a wolf, and was now turning into one himself? It seemed quite a leap to believe that humans – even ones who were vampires – could transform into other creatures. But if not, what were werewolves?

I looked again. My father was engrossed. To my knowledge, he'd never been interested in anything supernatural before, so it rattled me big time to see him scrutinising that book so closely. I continued to sing along with the radio, but deep inside, my uneasiness grew. In an uncanny twist, the next song to come on was He's a Vampire by Archie King. I switched stations to one playing Strange Brew.

When we got home, I hurried upstairs to put my purchases away. I hid the books in the carryall with Amy's, and put the pendant in my duffel bag. Then I went out to the hall phone and tried to ring Karen, but got no answer. I tried once more, with no luck, and banged the phone down in frustration.

I frowned as I re-entered my room. Something tugged at my mind, a feeling of insecurity, of not being safe. I looked around. Gran floated in her usual spot at my writing desk. Everything seemed normal enough – a cool, shaded, purple haven. And yet I felt strong vibes that something wasn't right.

"Gran, I don't know how much you can tell me," I said in a low voice. "But I sense something. I feel like it's not safe here."

"My sparrow, the catalyst of evil has long been in this house," she said mysteriously. "But you must discover the source for yourself."

I frowned again, reaching out to explore the vibes. I thought I could smell something. It didn't smell good, either. I tried harder. It was elusive.

"Is that smell something to do with it?" I asked.

"Does evil have a smell?"

"It might," I said, remembering Lou's little trick at Amy's house.

I heard footsteps in the hallway, and the smell got stronger. It was sickly sour, like rotting meat, and my gut clenched.

"Maybe it's Lou again," I said, to reassure myself.

"You think?"

"Perhaps I should just leave now. I was going to go tomorrow anyway."

"If you go now, you'll lose something you cherish and regret it for the rest of your life," Gran said.

I looked at her. My instincts told me that although she wanted to protect me, whatever was going to happen was something I had to go through, to learn from. It was for my own good, perhaps to propel me on the next stage of my journey. I sighed and tugged my fingers through my hair. It was so frustrating. I couldn't just stand about speculating, not if I wasn't going to be given any clues. I would have to ride it out, whatever it was.

More footsteps sounded in the hallway. Both my parents had gone up to their room now. I wondered if my father was dangerous, if he would turn into something evil that very night and attack us all. Eerie shivers ran down my spine as I imagined him holding me down, sinking his fangs into me, blood spurting...

4.

I returned to my stash of books, dug out the new one about vampires, and read up until sunset. The older lore said that victims had to be bitten seven times to be fully transformed into a vampire. I wondered if he'd already started on Mama

– I couldn't recall seeing any wounds or puncture marks on her, but as I continued reading, I discovered that traditionally, vampires bit people on the chest to feed, so the marks might not be seen.

Just like dad! I snapped the book shut. If Mama was in danger, I had to save her. He might already have fed from her many times since being bitten himself. Perhaps she was so drunk half the time she didn't even know. In any case, I couldn't just let him keep feeding from her and turn her into a vampire as well. I had to stop him, and the book was quite clear on how to do that. I sighed a long, shaky sigh, and put it away.

"Will I have to kill him?" I asked, hoping Gran wouldn't answer.

"You will know the right thing to do when the time comes."

"Geez, this sucks."

Gran groaned, and I realised what I'd said.

"Sorry, Gran. No vampire puns intended."

I slumped down to the kitchen, where dad was busy shaping the pizza dough.

"Do you want to get the toppings ready?" he asked.

"Sure, dad," I said, and shuffled over to rummage in the fridge.

"I'm not hungry," Mama said. "You go ahead and put whatever you like on it."

I got out tomato paste, pepperoni, olives, an onion, some cheese, and a pepper. But as hard as I looked, I couldn't find any garlic anywhere. That seemed odd. I briefly wondered if dad had thrown it out because of his... condition. I sighed deeply.

"So what's made you so glum?" dad asked.

"Nothing."

"Come on, out with it. You look as gloomy as midnight. Is it this road trip you're planning?"

"No," I said, perking up. "I've been looking forward to it, honestly. And I can't wait to see Karen again, and Newt."

"Why not just fly?"

"I hate flying. Have you forgotten how sick it always makes me? Anyway, remember when Karen and I were kids, you used to talk about driving Route Sixty Six some day? I guess you inspired me. It'll be a real adventure. Besides, I need my car so I'm not a burden on Karen and Eric once I'm there."

"I suppose you're right," he said. "I'd love to come with you."

My heart leapt. Maybe that would solve everything – it would get him away from Mama and then I'd be able to get rid of him somewhere along the way. After all, Route Sixty Six went through Arizona and New Mexico – plenty of places to hide a body. I shuddered at what I was contemplating.

"Why don't you, dad? It'll be fun."

"No, I really don't feel up to it just now. Best to stay put. Maybe we can do it properly when I'm better – you, me, your mother, Karen, Eric and Newton, go up to Chicago and drive it all the way. A real family holiday."

I nodded. Whatever was going down, it was going tonight. No way around it.

When the pizza was ready, we ate in the lounge room, while Laugh In dumped excess noise around our ears. Dad seemed to get the lame jokes, and laughed heartily. Mama looked tired, slumped on the sofa next to him with a gin and tonic in her hand.

My heart went out to her, and I offered her a slice of pizza.

She nibbled at it and sat back with a sigh, while my father laughed longer and louder than was warranted. I felt that weird tension build up, like something was about to explode at any moment.

But it didn't. I went up to brush my teeth and go to bed, and heard my parents move about as they washed and got ready for bed themselves. Weird vibes hovered in the air, an almost tangible barrier between me and... I wasn't sure what.

I knew I wasn't going to sleep well, so I sat up in bed, reading more about vampires. Soon I heard noises from down the hallway. It sounded like my parents were – well, you know. Too gross. I tried to ignore the sounds, but then something in the nature of them changed.

I got up and padded to the door. The noises I heard now just weren't associated with sex, at least in my mind. There were desperate thumps and a drawn-out gurgling sound. This was serious.

I burst from my room and stopped outside my parent's bedroom door. I only hesitated for a second, but the gurgling sound became ragged and raspy, as though someone was being strangled. Whatever he was doing to her, it sounded like it would kill her. I wrenched the door open and reached for the light switch. White brilliance flooded the room, and silence fell.

12

Wild Thing

1. Sunday 26th October 1969 – Niceville, Florida

It was my father who lay across the bed, with Mama astride him in her pink nylon nightie, holding him down with her hands and knees. His pyjama shirt had been torn open, revealing a bloody mess underneath where his wounds had reopened.

Blood covered Mama's lips, dripped down her chin, lay in smears across her cheeks. Her hazel eyes flashed with a wild and fierce fire, so unlike her usual ditzy expression that I stood for some seconds in shock. But then the truth of the situation sank in, making me bold.

"So this is what you get up to when I'm not looking?" I asked. "Mama dear, look what a mess you've made of my dad."

Mama hissed at me, a savage, scared-animal sound. She lowered herself against my father's chest like a wild cat protecting its kill from a scavenger, and licked her lips. Her gaze never left my face.

"Are you okay, dad?"

He nodded weakly. The blood that had pooled in the cavity below his neck ran down over his shoulders. I turned back to my mother. A look of intense cunning filled her eyes.

"What am I going to do with you?" I asked her. "You know I can't let you keep sucking dad's blood, don't you? I'm not going to lose both of you this way."

he watched me steadily. My father closed his eyes, as if it was all too much for him. I wondered how to get her to move without harming myself or dad, and silently prayed for help from Vaivea, Archangel Michael, God, anyone who could hear me.

"All this time you've rubbished the spirit realm," I contin-ued, "and yet here you've been, open to dark powers, using them on your victims. How long have you been infected, Mama?"

She drew her lips back from her teeth in a silent snarl, and tensed her arm and leg muscles, as though to leap. However, she stayed crouched over my father, and I despaired of getting her off him.

"You can't stay there forever," I said. "Sooner or later you'll have to move. May as well get it over with."

Harsh sounds came from her throat.

"What was that, Mama?"

"You – talk – too – much."

Her muscles tensed again and she sprang from dad's limp body, right at me. I ducked away, and she landed on her feet exactly where I'd been standing. The look in her eyes was still feral and cunning. I'd have to trick her away from the room for my father to have any chance.

But would I then be able to escape? I felt that if she attacked me, she wouldn't let me live. I remembered Amy's story about her brother, Jesse. As a werewolf, he'd wished death on his family, even though they'd been close beforehand.

"Mama," I said softly, hoping to lull her into a passive state of mind. "It's me, your daughter Angela."

I hated saying my whole name, but it was worth a try. She blinked a couple of times, but maintained her stance.

"You – no daughter of mine," she choked out, battling with something inside.

"I am, and I love you. Please calm down so we can talk."

"Liar," Mama spat, her eyes growing hostile again. "You never loved me. You loved him."

She tilted her head in dad's direction. I wanted to look at him, to see how he was, but I knew it was a trick. If I took my eyes off Mama, she would attack me. I kept eye contact, my mind working furiously.

"Mama," I said, trying to sound sympathetic. "You're infected. You're sick. I can try to heal you if you'd just let me..."

"Lies!" Patsy cried, stamping a foot. "You lie. You always lie. You hate me. You wish me dead. I will kill you!"

So that was that. Mama would never allow me to attempt to heal her. Her fate was sealed. Which meant it would be a true kindness to put her out of her misery. But how? I sent my consciousness out to the spirit realm. Gran huddled by my father's head, doing what she could to calm him and ease his discomfort. Vaivea stood at my side, strong and dependable as a mountain, but also as silent.

Mama looked confused. She could sense the spirit presences too, but didn't know what to do about them. I used this break in her attention to gather my thoughts. I knew that to kill a vampire for certain involved beheading it, but I had no weapon at hand, and wasn't sure I could kill my own mother anyway. But I had to do something.

I took a deep breath, and tried to remember how to access the powers of Isis, how to manifest something from magic alone. I visualised a sword, but making one appear was quite different to simply moving something that already existed. And now that Mama had realised that no one was making a move to stop her, I found her glare upon me again.

I fell back on the one thing I knew I could do for sure. Without taking my eyes off her, I pointed a finger towards the bed and summoned one of the pillows, then whipped my hand across to point at Mama's head.

"Ouff!"

She beat the pillow to the floor, and turned back to me, snarling in rage.

"Oh shit," I breathed.

I frantically flicked my awareness around the room, looking for something else to throw before she lost it and went apeshit – something hard, something that might knock her out. There wasn't a lot to choose from. In sheer desperation, I summoned a barrage of cosmetics, perfume bottles and hair styling items from her dresser, which bounced or shattered on the cupboards behind her as she ducked out of their way.

Gran shook her head in disbelief, and Vaivea frowned in utter confusion. Great. Even my spirit guides had lost faith in me. I tried to think of something else – anything – to use as a weapon. But there was nothing.

"Well," I said under my breath, "I guess this means I'm dead meat!"

2.

At that moment, the room filled with radiant golden white light.

"Allow me," said a low voice.

Lou stepped forward, brandishing a gleaming sword that looked like it was made of pure light. Mama hissed and backed away as he hefted the weapon. I almost pitied her for the terrified look on her twisted face, but it wasn't the time to be sentimental. This creature wasn't my mother any more. She was a dangerous, evil, blood-sucking monstrosity that would only be at peace when dead.

Lou glanced at me, and I gave the nod. I got the impression he relished what he was about to do as he turned eagerly towards my mother again. By now she'd backed into a corner, hissing and snarling. Lou advanced, swiftly raised the sword, and slashed.

Mama's head lifted from her shoulders and blood sprayed across the room. I flinched as I felt the warm, sticky liquid splatter across my face and torso. When I opened my eyes again, the room was a mess.

Blood had spattered on everything. Mama's body lay crumpled on the floor, a great pool of the dark liquid soaking slowly into the carpet around her neck. Her head had landed several feet away, issuing its own, smaller pool of blood. The walls, bed, curtains and cupboards all bore streaks, spots, and specks of gory red.

I heard soft sobbing from the bed, and saw that my father was crying. I went to him, covered in blood as I was, and hugged him. He hugged me back fiercely, despite that his chest still oozed. I looked around for Lou, and my heart nearly stopped beating.

He stood bathed in golden light, his sword still held aloft, pure white wings folded down his back. There wasn't a speck of blood on him or the sword – both were as clean and shining as if they'd just walked through a spring shower and into the morning sunlight. His skin was translucent – even his clothes had turned from black leather to pearly white robes. He shone, bright as the morning star for which he was named, and I knew things would never be the same between us again.

"I must say, red becomes you," he said to me, licking his lips.

Yep. I might have known he'd still be the same old Lou underneath.

"And white becomes you," I replied snidely.

He smiled, a gorgeous, gleaming smile that sent rays of light across the room and set off his golden irises. I had to close my eyes and breathe deeply to get myself together again.

"Who is that?" my father whispered in awe, gazing at Lou.

If ever there was a moment when I felt like cursing, it was then. I hadn't realised that dad could see Lou, and I was darned if I was going to tell him he was looking upon the devil himself at a moment like this.

"It's an angel, dad," I whispered back.

It wasn't quite a lie – after all, Lucifer *was* an angel. A fallen angel, to be sure, but dad didn't need to know that right then.

"An – angel?" my father said. "Is it the Archangel Michael?"

I almost laughed at the expression on Lou's face. I cleared my throat to cover my mirth.

"I don't think so, dad. There are lots of avenging angels. This one came to save us from the vampire curse."

My father struggled off the bed, then dropped to his knees before Lou.

"Oh merciful angel," he cried. "Please accept my heartfelt gratitude for your actions! Without you we'd be lost!"

I grimaced and tried to get dad to rise, but he wouldn't. Tears streamed down his face as he beheld Lou, and a strange light gleamed in his eyes.

"It is not I you should thank," Lou said to him. "There is one far greater than I, one who made all things as they are and should be. That is the one to thank for your deliverance."

I couldn't believe my ears. Had Lucifer just told my father to worship God – his own enemy? I puzzled over this for all of two seconds, until I was distracted by my father's fresh outbursts.

"Oh God, I have strayed from your path of righteousness. I am sorry, Father in heaven. Forgive me, oh God, help me to live in accordance with your laws..."

I was so stunned, I didn't know which way to turn. My father continued on for some minutes, whilst Lou stood basking in adoration. I narrowed my eyes at him, but he ignored me. I was sure he enjoyed every second of my discomfort. He really knew how to hit low.

Fine, if he wouldn't talk to me, I'd talk to him. I cleared my mind of distractions and projected my inner voice at him.

"Right, you, how about an explanation?"

He gazed steadily upwards, as though in rapture of God himself.

"Hey!" I shouted in my mind. "You there with the sword! I want to talk to you!"

Lou threw me a lame look, like I'd interrupted something really important.

"Are you talking to me, by any chance?" he spoke in my mind.

"You darn-well know I am," I thought back. "What's all this with my father? Why did you do that?"

Lou sighed.

"You wouldn't believe me if I told you."

"Try me."

"Oh really, Cheri, it's so tedious. Can't you just enjoy the moment, like your father is? He's really getting into it now."

I looked down at dad's kneeling form. His hands were clenched together, his eyes shut, and he babbled feverishly.

"Oh Lord, heal me from this affliction. Cure this cursed bite, so I'm clean and fit to do your work. Please God, oh please, save me from being one of the undead. Let me fulfil your sacred duties on earth. I'll never fail you again, I promise."

A golden white spark blazed through his torso, growing until his entire body and aura was filled with white light. I was paralysed with fear. What the heck was happening now?

3.

In a flash, the light was gone, and my father took a deep breath before starting his praise of God anew.

I was utterly dumbstruck. Perhaps stranger things had happened, but I couldn't for the life of me think of them. Afraid the neighbours would hear my father's cries, I tried to calm him. Gran stooped at his other side, whispering comfort into his ear. He eventually got to his feet and onto the bed, where he lay back, looking as stunned as the proverbial mullet that Niceville was so famous for.

"Welcome to the twilight zone!" I mumbled, and sank onto

a chair by the dressing table. "How can this be happening?"

I looked over at Lou, but he was gone. The fallen cosmetics, hair products, and broken perfume bottles were gone, and so was all the blood, except for traces on Mama's body and head, and what was on me. Vaivea still stood where he'd been through the whole drama.

"Vaivea," I thought, "what just happened?"

"Illumination on your road to destiny," he answered darkly.

I turned to Gran, wondering what he meant.

"I don't know," she thought back. "Who the heck would want to be illuminated by the devil?"

She snorted in disgust. I turned to my father and looked for the bite wound on his chest, but it had been completely erased. Not only that, his aura was free of all traces of the darkness I'd seen earlier. He gazed at me serenely for a moment, blinked tiredly, then fell asleep. "He's been healed," I whispered to myself. "Gran, how did that happen?"

"I guess God must have listened to his prayers," she said. "Sometimes happens, you know. I told you he's not the enemy."

I gave her a sharp look, but she appeared to be serious. Not knowing what else to do, I had a hot shower and scrubbed every inch of my body. Twice. Now that the emergency had ended, I could barely handle the thought that I'd had my mother's blood all over me. Vampire blood, to boot.

"Have I missed anything?" I asked Gran, when I finally got back to my room.

"No, it's been peaceful here."

"Well, that's a mercy."

I looked at my wall clock, and was amazed to find it was only a few minutes after eleven. I sat on my bed to brush my hair, and went back over the unreal events of the evening.

"So, what do I do with her body?" I asked. "Can't just bury it in the back yard, can I?"

"You must burn her to ashes to ensure she never bothers anyone again."

"Yeah, I guess so," I said, realising I would have to perform this gruesome job all by myself. "I don't know how I'm going to do that. And all without leaving any traces of what happened to her."

"You must," Gran said.

My mind worked quickly, a feat it's not usually known for at bedtime.

"We could tell everyone she decided to come to L. A. with me."

"Could do, could do," Gran said. "Trouble is, how would you explain her not being with you when you got there?"

"So something needs to happen to her on the way. Well, there's plenty can go wrong on a long car trip..."

"Sure," Gran said, "but there would still be questions. You can't just turn up in L. A. without her and not have a good explanation."

"Hmmm, maybe she could accidentally fall into the Grand Canyon... No, I know! She could be abducted by aliens in flying saucer..."

"You don't seem to be taking this very seriously. If anything happened along the way, you would be expected to stop and report it to the police, and they'd have plenty of questions. And that could hold you up significantly."

"Okay, so we need something that won't arouse any suspicion. That may be a little difficult."

"Well, there's always New Orleans," Gran said.

"What about New Orleans? That it's a good place to disappear?"

"Exactly."

I thought about it. New Orleans was a mysterious city, where people sometimes got swallowed up without trace. If Mama 'disappeared' there, who would suspect anything but that she was abducted or mugged? Happened all the time, right?

"Okay, but I'll still have to report her missing and get held up by cops," I said.

"Not if she had gone to visit someone there."

"I hardly think that's likely," I said, then paused. "Actually, she *was* planning to go straight on to New Orleans after she visited me at Jacksonville. I only knew because the plane ticket fell out of her handbag. She didn't seem to want to talk about it."

"Aha!" Gran crowed.

"So the story is that I drive her to New Orleans to visit with someone she knows, and somewhere between leaving me and arriving at her friend's house, she disappears. I don't report it because I don't even know she's missing. Perfect."

"Perfect," Gran echoed.

"It would be if I was sure she did know someone there," I replied. "Wait – maybe she kept some letters or something."

I crept into my parent's room, past the bed where dad slept peacefully, and knelt before Mama's dresser. I quietly riffled through the drawers until I found an untidy bundle of cards and letters, and carried them back to my room.

Sitting on my bed, I started sorting them. The first few were from Karen in L. A. Then there were some from various members of her family in Pennsylvania and Maryland. I kept looking and hit pay dirt. The return address on the last few envelopes was just what I needed – Ursulines Avenue, French Quarter, New Orleans.

I opened one of the letters and scanned the contents. The woman's name was Patrice Moreau, and I gathered from the letter, dated only a month ago, that Mama had planned to visit her for her eightieth birthday.

"So who is this woman?" I asked Gran. "How is she connected to Mama?"

"That's for you to find out," she said.

"So I go through New Orleans, to make it seem like Mama's gone to visit her. Okay, I can do that. Might even stop and see some of the sights while I'm there."

"You'll have to be careful, you know," Gran warned me.

"Of course I'll be careful," I said, rolling my eyes. "I'm only going to look. What could possibly go wrong?"

4.

I got up, packed my bags for the road trip, and carried them out to the car. A chilly night breeze whipped my hair back and stung my eyes as I loaded my stuff into the boot and shut it as quietly as I could. The nearly full moon sailed high overhead, illuminating the street and houses with their Halloween decorations in monotone.

I went back inside and tiptoed into my parent's room again. Dad still slept calmly, so I addressed myself to the problem of removing Mama's remains. I still didn't know how or where to do what was needed to ensure she wouldn't come back to life and start sucking people's blood again. But I didn't want my father to see what was left of her when he woke up.

I started by picking up her head. It was light, and, providing

I didn't look at it, easy to carry. The body was a different story. Mama had been a bit taller and heavier than me. She was no longer taller, but she was still heavier. I didn't know how I was going to move her, but then I remembered my Goddess powers. I still wasn't used to having magical powers, so I didn't always think of a magical alternative.

I focussed on the thought of her body lifting into the air, so I could simply float it along. It gave a shudder, but wouldn't rise. I pointed an index finger at it, to concentrate my powers, and finally it levitated about a foot in the air. I guided it along before me down the stairs, her hands dragging and thudding gruesomely on each step, and into the lounge room.

"Really, darling, there are so many easier ways to do that."

I lost my concentration and the body flopped to the floor, some bits of it wobbling rudely. I turned on Lou, who lounged on the nearest sofa, back in his usual black leather.

"You could help, you know!"

"Well, I'm here now. Better late than never, Cheri."

"You know, that Cheri stuff is really starting to bug me. Can't you call me by my name?"

"Of course, darling Angela. I just thought Cheri would appeal to your French side."

"I don't have a French side, and just call me Ange, for goodness sake."

"Oh, I never do anything for the sake of goodness."

I was so mad I nearly flung Mama's head at him. But there were more pressing matters.

"So what am I supposed to do now? I know I've got to burn her body, but where am I supposed to take her to do that without anyone seeing?"

"My dear, you can do that right here."

"What? Right here in the house?"

I looked at the richly coloured shag carpet, the modern sofas, the stylish coffee table. I really didn't want to destroy the house along with my mother, but that seemed to be what Lou had suggested. I looked at him blankly, hoping for a better option.

"Like this," he said, waving a finger in her direction. "Zap, and she's gone."

Of course. I placed Mama's head by her feet, as instructed by my books, took a couple of steps back, and concentrated again. This time I pictured intense flames in my mind's eye, consuming everything in their path. I pointed a finger at Mama's remains, and they were no more. A shadow of fine ashes showed where she had been.

Then I pictured a shiny black urn, and her ashes lifting up and pouring into it, and it was done. Not a trace of her was left, apart from a singe mark on the carpet in roughly her size and shape. I Wished a snugly-fitting lid onto the urn and put it on the coffee table, then I turned to Lou.

"Look, what you did tonight," I said awkwardly. "There's no way I could've done that. I feel I should thank you for helping out, but I've got to know whether it's going to cost me anything or not."

"Ever mistrustful," Lou sighed, gazing up at me from the sofa.

I saw his eyes were now purple, an exotic shade of violet. Before I allowed myself to be mesmerised, I snapped my head up.

"Because if I owe you anything, I'll find some other way to pay it. What I said about the subject still stands."

"Ah, the biggest disappointment of my existence. But no,

dear Ange, I won't ask a price for tonight's service. It was my pleasure."

"I kinda thought so," I said. "And by the way, I want to know why you told my father to turn to God... Damn you!"

5.

He'd vanished again. I stamped a foot in frustration, and stubbed my toe on the solid teak leg of the coffee table. I hopped about in furious silence for a moment, biting my lip to keep from making a noise that might wake my father, then I limped back upstairs – cursing Lou in my mind only – and fell onto my bed in exhaustion.

From what I remembered later, my dreams that night involved a lot of travel. In one sequence, Isis appeared to be high in the Swiss Alps, looking out over lush green valleys and crystalline streams. In another, she trekked through boggy marshes, and in yet another, she sailed down a broad, slow-flowing river surrounded on either side by thick jungle. The places that would become India, China, Siberia, and other countries – here she sought out word of Osiris, with no result.

Noises floated into my room from the hallway, waking me, then I heard the shower going. I looked drowsily at my alarm clock. Six forty. Dad must be feeling a whole lot better if he was able to get up and wash at this hour.

I wondered if now would be a good time to ring Karen. She'd be home, for sure. But then, so would Eric, and in any case, what was I supposed to say? 'Hi sis, just wanted to let you know that our alcoholic mother – yeah, thanks a heap for telling me about that – turned into a slavering vampire and tried to turn dad into one too, so I had to get the devil to behead her?' I'd obviously have to give it more thought.

"Gran?" I said, searching out her shimmering form by my desk. "I wish you'd woken me up earlier..."

"You needed your sleep," she said. "In fact, you'll need all your strength today."

I looked at her sharply as I got out of bed.

"Why?" I asked, wriggling out of my pyjamas. "Is there danger?"

"Just be prepared. Today's events could change your perspective dramatically."

I stared at her – through her – in surprise. I really hoped that whatever it was would explain how Mama became a vampire, how long she had been infected, by whom, and give me a chance to stop them. Permanently. But going by previous experience, I figured that would be too much to ask.

I finished getting dressed and went downstairs to make breakfast. By the time dad came down, I had a plateful of hot buttered toast ready. I poured us both coffee as he entered the kitchen, and he looked at me sheepishly as I handed him a mug.

"I – I'm not really sure what all that was about last night," he said as he sat, his eyes on the swirling brown liquid.

"Dad, some serious stuff has been going down. I don't know where to begin, either, but we need to talk about it."

He glanced at me, then resumed contemplation of his coffee.

"Look, dad, I guess you know the thing that attacked you wasn't a normal dog?"

He nodded slowly.

"Dad, the thing that bit you was a vampire. They can change themselves to look like bats or wolves. And we both know who that vampire was."

He sat silently, eyes down.

"Dad? I know this all sounds crazy, but it's real. It happened."

"What happened," he finally said, "was that I got attacked – yes, I agree it was by something supernatural, and yes, it was evil. Satan has many forms, and many ways of seducing us. The evil spirits he sent to attack me prove it."

"You call them evil spirits, I know them as vampires," I said. "Whatever name you give them, they're out there and they're dangerous."

I couldn't tell what he was thinking. His eyes were locked on his mug, as if the answers were swirling around in his coffee.

"Dad, I'm worried about you," I said.

Now he looked at me properly. There was sorrow in his eyes, but the rest of his face conveyed strength and determination.

"Sweetheart, I've just walked through the Valley of the Shadow of Death, and came out alive. Nothing can ever turn me to sin again."

"I'm not talking about that. Everyone makes mistakes. That's okay, as long as we learn from them. But I'm worried about how you're coping with all this stuff that's happened. I love you, dad."

"I love you too, sweetheart."

He returned to his coffee.

"Your mother," he finally said. "I suppose she's... dead now."

"Yes, she is."

"Where's her – her body?"

"It kind of combusted. There's nothing left but a pile of ashes. They're in the urn on the coffee table."

Dad sighed sadly.

"Honey, I sensed something wasn't right about your mother. But I was so hung up on the guilt of my own sins that I wasn't about to go picking fault with anyone else. I can see now I should've been even more vigilant. I should've been watching out for the sake of all my family."

"It was too late, dad. By the time you came home, she was already – one of them. A vampire."

"It's never too late," dad stated. "While there's life, there's hope. I'm a living example that God can work miracles, and from now on I'm going to do His will and spread the good word to save others like her."

"It's a noble intention, dad," I said. "I hope you do help lots of people. Heaven knows, we need it with all the evil in this world. You know, we have the same goals. Just different ways of going about them."

He looked at me sadly.

"Sweetheart, surely you must know in your heart of hearts that without the true grace of God's love, you'll never really succeed?"

"No, dad..."

"Ange, only God can give us the real hope of defeating the enemy. Until you accept that in your heart, and ask God into your life, it's all meaningless."

"Dad, that's not the way I see the truth. There's more to what's going on than simply believing in God and asking for his help."

"Sweetheart, I hope for your sake you come to know differently. God created you, and He loves you. The only way to truly succeed is through Him."

I sighed in exasperation. He drank his coffee and pretended to examine the tabletop, running a finger over the pale yellow

Formica. Sadness washed over me. If this was how it was going to be with my father, we'd be at a stalemate forever. I washed my mug and packed some snacks for my trip. Nuts. Dried fruit. A box of Cheez-its. A packet of Twinkies.

"Aw, you could leave the Twinkies," dad said.

I put them back and deposited my bag of goodies on the coffee table next to the urn. Finally, I rang Karen, and hastily explained that Mama had decided to accompany me to New Orleans to visit a friend there. I hated having to deceive her, but I didn't want to leave it up to dad. I ended the call, and turned to face my father, who was frowning at the singe mark on the lounge-room carpet.

"You might want to buy a rug to cover that up," I said, and gestured towards the urn. "So, uh, do you wanna keep this?"

Dad looked blankly at the coffee table, then it dawned on him what I was asking.

"Oh! Her... uh, remains? No, I don't want anything to do with them. Take them with you, if you want. Karen might be sentimental enough to hang on to them."

"Yeah, I was kinda thinking that. Okay, I'll take them with me."

I nestled the urn into the crook of my arm, picked up the bag of snacks, and headed for the front door.

"Give Karen a big hug from me," dad said. "And take some photos for me along Route Sixty Six if you can."

"I'm not going to follow it absolutely," I said, stashing the urn in the boot, and my snacks and camera within reach on the passenger side seat. "I won't even be on it until I get to Oklahoma City."

"Have a safe trip, honey," he said. "Be careful going through Mississippi. I heard there's still a lot of damage and debris about from Hurricane Camille. I'd feel better if you'd give me a call when you can, just so I know you're okay."

"Sure, dad," I agreed. "I need to know you're alright too. I'll ring you as soon as I get to New Orleans, okay? And it's probably a good idea to spread word that I've taken Mama there with me, so her disappearance isn't so newsworthy."

"That's not very honest, is it?"

"You think?" I asked. "After what really happened?"

He nodded half-heartedly and gave me one last goodbye hug.

"I love you, dad."

"I know, sweetheart. Love you too. Look after yourself."

"I will. And you look after yourself too. No more getting bitten by nasties."

"You bet. I'll get the house blessed, get to know the local churchmen. Join a prayer group, too. I'll be well protected. I just wish I could say the same for you."

"Oh, don't you worry about me, dad. I'm plenty protected too."

With that, I drove out onto the street, honked once and drove to the nearest gas station to fuel up. And to see if they sold Twinkies.

13

Voodoo Woman

1. Monday 27th October, 1969 – Niceville, Florida

It sure felt good to be out on the open road with the wind in my hair and a fresh day ahead. Gran bopped to the radio as we drove from Pensacola over the border to Mobile, Alabama, and then crossed into Mississippi. All along the coast road, the damage from August's Hurricane Camille was still horribly evident – buildings smashed down to the foundations, lanes of the highway collapsed, trees snapped in half, power poles toppled, boats washed inland to rest in people's front yards.

Despite the detours and delays – and the almost ominous playing of Baby Please Don't Go and House of the Rising Sun on the radio – we entered Louisiana just before midday, crossed the Maestri bridge, and headed into New Orleans. I made my way to the French Quarter and parked down by the French Markets. First thing I did was found a pay phone, and called dad to let him know I'd arrived safely. Then I looked around for somewhere to grab some lunch. Nearby I found a street vendor selling po'boys near Jackson Square, and hungrily tucked in.

As I ate, I wandered amongst the historic buildings around the Square. Finally, I found myself back outside the French Markets. Lots of people bustled about, looking at the stalls. I bought a tourist map, and some strings of Mardi Gras beads as a gift for Karen, then stopped at a sidewalk café for a café au lait and beignets.

Despite the sense of urgency I felt about getting to L. A., I simply couldn't bear to hurry off. I returned to the caddy, but then stopped at New Orleans Cemetery Number One to see the tomb of the famous voodoo queen, Marie Laveau. Dark clouds gathered to the east as I wandered the neat rows of ornate marble above-ground tombs. It didn't take long to find the right one, surrounded as it was by a tour group led by someone dressed as Baron Samadhi.

Graffiti covered the walls, in particular, red crosses drawn in groups of three. It seemed plenty of people still believed Marie Laveau had the power to grant their wishes, even after being dead for so long.

"This place definitely has presence," I said with a shiver, brought on by the eerie atmosphere that fell after the tour group had moved on.

"Yes," Gran agreed. "Caused by all the people who've come here over the years asking Marie to help them and grant their wishes."

"But her spirit is still here."

"Oh no, her current incarnation has no idea of this other life. Right now, she's a legal secretary in Boston."

"So," I said, "all I'm picking up on is a great big goober of other people's psychic gunk?"

"'Fraid so," Gran said, chuckling.

237

"Yuck! So gross."

That kind of ruined it for me. I returned to the caddy, and Vaivea appeared as I settled into the driver's seat.

"You must move on," he said in a warning tone. "There is much danger about."

"Relax. It's early afternoon. What can possibly happen in broad daylight?"

"He's right," Gran said. "It *is* dangerous for you here, especially now."

"What, Halloween?"

"The veil is thinning. You never know what might come through."

"But Gran, wouldn't that be true no matter where I was?"

"Of course, my dear. But this city is full of mystery and magic – some of it very dark magic. There are things here that you've never encountered, terrifying things..."

"But I've got you two to guide and protect me. And I can always ask for more spirit protection, can't I? I just wanted to look around a bit before I leave. There's plenty of daylight left for that."

I examined my tourist map longingly, looking at all the interesting places marked on it. There were gardens and parks, cemeteries, the Spanish Fort, Pontchartrain Beach, rides on the street trams and paddle steamers... It sure did seem a shame to leave without experiencing a bit more of what New Orleans was famous for.

"Okay, how about we just swing by the old lady's place before I go?" I said. "Seeing as I'm supposed to be leaving my dear departed mother there."

"Yes, you need to do that," Gran said. "But be careful, my sparrow."

"I'm only going to drive past her house. It's not like I'm dropping in for afternoon tea."

I navigated to Ursulines Avenue, a quiet part of the French Quarter. It was full of historic Creole cottages and two-storey stucco townhouses in bright colours, with fancy ironwork on the balconies, shaded galleries, and shuttered windows and doors. I found the address on the envelope – a narrow, two-storey, pink-washed building with black cast-iron around balconies filled with pots of red-flowering geraniums. It was quite picturesque.

And something more. I felt an irresistible, tantalising pull towards the building.

"She's looking for you," Gran said.

"Who, Ms Moreau?"

"No, dear, your mother. She's in the spirit realm, but she's searching for you. Your father is having the house blessed to stop her hanging around."

"Yeah, like that'll work," I said with a laugh.

Then I sobered.

"Will it work? Will she really come looking for me if she can't stay there?"

"The blessing, no, that won't drive her away. But she *is* looking for her earthly remains, and we all know where those are."

"Great. That's all I need. A ghostly vampire on my trail. Maybe I should go back to the markets and buy some garlic, just in case."

"Oh, you won't need that," Gran said. "Your mother was fully infected for such a short time, I doubt it made any lasting impression on her soul."

"Fine, that's swell. Just the same, I'll be glad if I never meet another vampire for the rest of my life."

I felt an inexplicable urge to look at Ms Moreau's house again. Staring at the building, I tried to get a sense of the place and its occupant, but discerned nothing extraordinary. It puzzled me that I felt so drawn.

"Do whatever you need to do," Gran said softly. "We'll be right there with you."

Almost as though I was being guided by something outside of myself, I got out of the caddy and walked to the front door, Gran and Vaivea beside me. Something buzzed nearby. I stared at the intercom unit on the wall as a tinny voice issued from it.

"The door is open. Come on up. First door at the top of the stairs."

I felt compelled to do as instructed, despite my misgivings. I opened the door and stepped into a dim, narrow hallway containing a steep set of stairs up to the next level. I put my white wall of protection in place as I climbed. By the time I reached the next floor I wished I could just float places like Gran and Vaivea.

Then I remembered I could.

I stopped at the first door in the upstairs hallway, unsure of what to do next. There came a patter of feet on the other side, then the door creaked open a crack. A feminine face with bright black eyes peeked out at me, then suddenly the door swung wide open and I was attacked!

2.

"Whoa! Do you mind?" I gasped as I fought off the petite woman who had flown at me. "Please!"

The woman ceased her attempt to give me a bear hug, but she didn't back off.

"It's you!" she exclaimed. "Angela, it's really you! I can't believe you're here!"

"Er, it's Ange. Just Ange."

"Of course. Patsy told me you preferred your name shortened."

"Mama? Told you about me?"

"Oh yes. She told me all about you and Karen."

"But who are you?" I asked, perplexed. "I'm looking for Ms Moreau."

"I am Ms Moreau," the woman said with a sparkling smile.

"Er. I mean, the senior Ms Moreau."

"There is only one Ms Moreau here," she said with a nod, "and I'm it. Won't you please come in?"

I frowned as she stepped back into the room.

"I was under the impression that Ms Moreau was quite elderly."

"Oh, I'm much older than I look," she said brightly. "I guess I've done well for my age. Good skin, good hair, good eyes. Good teeth."

I suddenly felt nervous. Why would she mention something like teeth? I looked at her more closely. There was no way this woman was eighty. She looked about Karen's age, maybe in her late twenties. She noticed my hesitation, and smiled sweetly.

"It's alright. Please come in. I won't bite."

"Well, that's a relief," I said with a tight laugh.

Ms Moreau gestured through the door, and I entered a room right out of the Victorian era. It was cluttered – parquetry side-tables and porcelain knick-knacks on prim lace doilies, overstuffed chairs in heavy floral patterns, an upright piano, and great, ornamentally framed paintings loomed on the walls. My immediate reaction was to hope it wouldn't all cave in on us as we sat there.

"Coffee, my dear?"

"No thanks. I don't want to take up your time. I just want to know how you knew my mother."

Ms Moreau settled opposite me. She looked like a fragile doll in the embrace of the large chair.

"Would you mind telling me first how you found out about me?"

"I came across some letters," I answered truthfully.

Ms Moreau nodded, and sighed.

"So she's dead, then?"

My jaw dropped. How could she possibly know that? Was she another psychic like Amy, with a spirit guide to tell her things? I groped for something to say that wouldn't make me seem too stupid, but my mind didn't seem to work.

"My dear," Ms Moreau said, "there is obviously a lot you don't know. About your mother, as well as about me. I know what she was, and I think you do too."

I started. This was getting weirder and weirder.

"What do you mean, what she was?"

"Why, that she was a vampire, of course."

My stomach rose towards my mouth, and I could hardly breathe. How on earth did she know *that*?

"And for you to know that I exist means she must be dead," she continued. "I know she'd never have told you about me, or allowed you to see those letters. Are you sure you don't want a cup of coffee?"

To give myself some time to think, I nodded, and she got up

and went into the next room. A percolator gurgled, and the smell of coffee brewing kick-started my brain again. By the time Ms Moreau came back, I was composed.

"Thankyou," I said as she handed me a dainty cup on a saucer.

The coffee was black and smelt strong. I set it down on a little table beside my chair and turned to Ms Moreau.

"So how did you know my mother? You must've been close for her to tell you all about her family."

She smiled and sipped her coffee.

"Ah, yes. Patsy brought me photos of you and Karen every time she came to visit. I've got a drawer full of them in my bureau. Baby photos, school photos, college, visits home."

My mind boggled.

"But – you must have known each other for years!"

"Yes, my dear. She tracked me down while she was pregnant with you, and we only started to get to know each other properly after you were born."

My stomach lurched. Surely Ms Moreau would have been no more than a young child when Mama was pregnant with me.

"What do you mean, tracked you down?"

"My dear, I am Patsy's natural mother – her birth mother. Which also makes me yours and Karen's grandmother."

3.

I must have looked stunned. I sure felt stunned. I also felt confused at the obvious lie. She smiled gently and gestured towards my forgotten coffee cup. Obediently I picked it up and sipped, finding the strong brew settled my mind a little and grounded me.

"I gave Patsy up for adoption as a baby," Ms Moreau said. "When she found out she was adopted, she wanted to find me and build a relationship. It wasn't easy – we both had our issues to sort through. But we managed okay."

"Um, just one thing," I said. "My mother was fifty-four. You barely look thirty. How could you possibly be my grand-mother?"

"Oh, I've got a rare – condition," she said. "It keeps me from aging. Rest assured, I'm telling the truth."

Gran and Vaivea were somewhere behind me. '*Is this true?*' I thought, and felt affirmative replies. I breathed in deeply and focussed on my new-found relative. I was still in shock, but things had started to slide around in my brain, falling into place.

"So, how did you know my mother was a vampire?"

"Oh, I knew," she said, taking another sip of coffee. "When you've lived in a place like New Orleans all your life, you just know these things."

She didn't seem prepared to go into any more detail, so I tried a different tactic.

"Why didn't she tell us about you?"

"Ah," said Ms Moreau, putting her cup down. "I'm afraid I'm to blame for that. I asked her not to tell you or Karen. I'm pretty sure she didn't even tell your father, or any of her friends."

She laughed, a tinkly, jingly sound that hung in the air like bells chiming. I felt a warning from my two guardians, and inconspicuously softened my eyes to look at her aura. She was surrounded by the most pristine, sparkling white light imaginable. I was suspicious right away. No one's aura was that squeaky clean. Even Amy's hadn't been.

Which meant Ms Moreau had shielded herself. Which meant she had something to hide — something she was keen to keep secret. If I interpreted correctly, this old woman was something quite nasty herself.

"I really want to know how you knew Mama was a vampire," I insisted.

She looked at me quizzically, and I could feel her mind probing around. I strengthened the defensive wall I had around me, and she frowned.

"Very well," she said in a cold voice. "I knew Patsy was a vampire because I'm the one who infected her."

"You...?"

"Yes, Ange. A fitting end to a long, proud line. Well, not quite, I suppose. You and Karen will probably go on to have families. But they'll never know of their heritage. Why would I tell them? To have come from such crude stock, to have Voodoo witches and vampires in your family. No, I'm sure you wouldn't be too proud of that."

I did a double take.

"Voodoo witches?"

Ms Moreau narrowed her eyes on me.

"My great-grandmother was Marie Laveau, the so-called Witch Queen of New Orleans. I know you've been to her tomb. I can smell the grave on you."

My mind boggled again. So that was what Lou had meant by my French heritage. All along, he'd known things about me that I couldn't have begun to guess. I seethed as I realised how he had played on my ignorance. I felt Gran move beside me, put an arm around me, and I knew I needed to be more careful. I couldn't let my guard down in front of this woman.

As if she had picked up on my feelings, Ms Moreau rose abruptly from her chair. Petite as she was, she seemed to tower over me. I immediately started to gather my psychic resources. However, she didn't try to grab me or make any other move. She just stood very still, her deep black eyes resting on mine.

"Yes, my dear, witches and vampires. That's why I gave Patsy up for adoption – because of my 'rare condition' – and why I asked her not to tell anyone about me."

She sniffed.

"I'm a creature of the night, a harbinger of death. I could never love you properly or be a good grandmother. And I knew that if you started seeing me, sooner or later I would infect you. Perhaps both of you. I didn't want to infect Patsy, but the urge to feed and pro-create is so strong, so powerful – it cannot be overruled."

I sat stock still. I was afraid that if I moved, she would try to pin me down and infect me, too. However, she stepped graciously aside and gestured towards the door.

"Please don't tell Karen about me. If you do, make sure she doesn't come looking. This tragedy has to stop with me, now that Patsy is gone."

I quickly stood and walked to the door.

"Oh, and Ange?"

I turned, my heart beating a terrified tattoo in my chest. I was only a few steps from freedom, but the woman's voice was so compelling.

"Don't come here again if you know what's good for you. Leave New Orleans, today, or I may weaken and come looking for you."

4.

I walked out, got in my car, and drove off. I didn't know where I was going, just that I needed to get away from that woman as quickly as possible. And I had to stop and think. After taking a circuitous route, during which a song called Dracula's Daughter played on the radio, I found myself back on Decatur Street. So I parked, went into Jackson Square, and sat on the first bench I came to, trying furiously to shake the jitters Patrice Moreau had given me.

So, vampires virtually ran in the family. As if it wasn't shocking enough to find out my mother was adopted. Her side of the family hadn't even been family. No wonder I'd never liked them. And no wonder they never liked me – the small, dark intruder in their well-ordered, picture perfect, blue-eyed, fair-skinned and fair-haired world. Boy they made me sick.

But I wasn't about to grieve over them. I'd just met my true maternal grandmother, who turned out not only to be descended from Marie Laveau, but also the vampire who had infected my mother and now threatened to come after me as well. That was just *dandy*.

"Gran? Vaivea? I could really do with some advice about now."

Gran shimmered by my right shoulder.

"What do you want to know?"

"Well, I would've thought that was obvious," I said pee-vishly. "What the heck do I do now?"

"Do? Why, my sparrow, do exactly what you were planning to do. Keep going to L. A."

I frowned.

"Yeah, but I mean, what do I do about Ms Moreau? Should I really just leave and let her keep contaminating people? Shouldn't she be stopped?"

Vaivea cleared his throat.

"You have many skills, and methods of defending yourself against human adversaries. But you have never fought a vampire or anything else supernatural. It would be wise for you to leave those to the more experienced."

"Alright, so I'm not exactly Wonder Woman. But I've got to start somewhere. Maybe if I had a weapon of some kind, I'd be able to do some damage..."

"You don't just damage vampires," Gran said. "You must put them out of existence for good. Are you capable of killing?"

I gulped, then swallowed down the stab of fear her question produced. After all, it was only the second time in my life I'd even had to think about this subject.

"If it's for the greater good, yes."

She clucked sadly.

"So could we all, if we really had to. It's sometimes a necessary evil, to kill or be killed. But New Orleans isn't a good place to start out just learning. In case you hadn't noticed, it's absolutely crawling with people you don't want to tangle with."

I looked about. Jackson Square wasn't crowded, but a few families and couples strolled up and down enjoying the gardens. Some kids on roller-skates swept by, swerving to avoid pedestrians, whilst a group of young people in hippie clothes lazed on the grass under a tree, one of them strumming a guitar and singing I Love Everybody In My Heart.

Then I saw them. There were four, all grim-faced, pale-skinned youngsters in dark clothes and even darker sunnies, lounging on the next bench along. I nearly dismissed them as some sort of ultra-beatnik-noir-style Velvet Underground wannabes.

But I sensed something strange about them. Then I saw what it was. Their auras were very dark, mottled with grey and sickly colours. I probed a little with my mind, and withdrew quickly. Vampires! And they were all looking straight at me!

14

Keep On Running

1. Monday 27th October, 1969 – New Orleans – Shreveport, Louisiana

"Okay, point taken," I whispered to Gran.

I really didn't need any more vampires on my case. One was more than enough. I got up and strolled away, hoping they hadn't noticed me like I'd noticed them. My back itched, and I longed to look around.

"They follow," Vaivea said.

I groaned inwardly. This was exactly the sort of thing Amy had warned me to avoid, and I'd stupidly blundered right into it.

"Great. Just what I needed."

"Why do you run?" Vaivea asked.

"Are you serious?" I hissed back. "They don't exactly look like the welcome wagon. And didn't you guys just warn me not to tangle with their kind?"

I headed for the gates out onto Decatur Street, only to see two more of them standing there, waiting for me.

"Damn!" I swore, turning in the opposite direction. "I need help here! Any time now would be fine."

I picked up my pace, passing lawns and garden beds as I hurried towards the central statue of Andrew Jackson. I slowed down and pretended to gawk, just like any other visitor to the city. From its far side, I glanced back at the gates. A brilliant presence hovered there, surrounded by an unearthly white glow. He had an ethereal beauty that was to die for, with tumbling golden locks, flowing robes and the stature of a conquering gladiator.

I couldn't see his face, but I did see the spectacular wings folded down his back. Something long flashed in his hands, flames licking up and down its length. Archangel Michael, with his flaming Sword of Truth! I marvelled at his glory before turning away.

"Why can't it be him obsessing over me instead of Lou?" I asked Gran.

"Why, I'm sure you'd be a perfect match," she teased, chuckling heartily.

"Hah!" I said, continuing through the square. "Can't a girl dream?"

"Oh, he's an awesome angel," she agreed. "But then, your Osiris is a God."

I had no answer to that. I skirted a small fountain and reached the gates on the Saint Louis Cathedral side of Jackson Square. I didn't know which way to turn, as the vampires were now directly between me and the caddy. I wondered if I should hide out in the cathedral until the coast was clear.

"They would soon find you there," Vaivea said.

"You mean they can go in there? What about the Holy Water and stuff?"

"It may be consecrated ground to you, but to them it is just another building."

"What about Michael? Can't he stop them?"

"If the need exists."

"Well, I say the need exists! How else am I going to escape?"

"Go some place where they cannot go."

"That's what I'm trying to do. Otherwise I may as well stroll on over and invite them all to dinner. Main course, blood a la Ange..."

"Calm yourself. While you run in this manner, they can follow indefinitely. They have your scent."

"Great. Then I'll find cover and mingle — safety in numbers."

I glanced back to where I'd last seen Michael waiting for the vampires. My heart leapt into my throat as they skirted the statue of Andrew Jackson and headed straight towards me. Michael drifted above them, his luminous glow contrasting with the dark cloud shed by the vampire's auras. Why didn't he do something?

I turned and fled across Chartres Street, ducking and dodging tourists and strolling entertainers. A juggler leered at me as he casually flipped balls into the air. I gave him the look of death and joined the line of people outside the cathedral for the guided tour. As I waited, my last words nudged my memory. Numbers...

I recalled reading that vampires were hung up on counting stuff. I hooked a package out of my jacket pocket, tore the gift wrap off the Mardi Gras beads I'd bought, broke the strings, and let the beads slide off. They bounced all over the pavement, and I had to assure several bystanders that it was okay, I would just buy some more.

A moment later, I was inside. The Cathedral was full of light and movement, from the sun that poured in through the windows to the glow from the wispy chandeliers to the flags that hung at intervals down the nave.

The tour guide recounted the history of the site. A couple of people snapped photos, and no one else noticed as two of the vampires entered. I sidled past the font, a statue of a cherub holding a big seashell full of water, Gran and Vaivea at my side. I knew I wouldn't be able to stay there for long, but luckily, for the moment, I had the entire group of tourists between my pursuers and myself.

I peeped back through the tour group. Archangel Michael now hovered above the vampires, but he didn't seem very concerned. I wondered again why he didn't try to get rid of them. A couple of people looked up and around, clearly sensing something. The vampires stood at the outer edge of the group, glaring my way through their dark sunnies. I shivered. What was I going to do once the tour was over?

Then a man broke away from the group and circled around behind the vampires. They turned to watch him, and he stopped at the door. Lou! He crooked his finger at them, smiled his devastating smile, and they followed like lambs to the slaughter. I couldn't believe my eyes as they filed out after him, Michael hovering overhead. When they were gone I heaved a sigh of relief and sank onto the nearest pew.

"More of their kind gather," said Vaivea. "They sense the fallen one."

"What – Lou?"

"Rotten barrel of filth," Gran muttered.

"So, although he saved me from this lot, he's drawing more of them here?"

"Like a magnet," Gran said.

I was stumped. How was I going to get out of the Cathedral alive?

2.

The tour wound through the building. I hung at the back of the group, only half-listening as I tried to work out how to escape the vampires that I now imagined were clustered around each door, and possibly the windows too. I stretched my mind out, trying to sense how many there were, and collided with a wall of darkness that surrounded the cathedral.

"I wish Michael would just get me out of here," I said under my breath.

Then it hit me. I could get myself out of here. I'd forgotten how easy it had been to Wish myself home after that jaunt with Lou. The relief that washed over me mingled with feeling stupid that I hadn't thought of it earlier.

"Right. I'm Isis, a powerful Goddess. What am I doing hanging around here?"

"That's the spirit!" Gran said. "I was wondering how long it would take you to think of it."

"You could've hinted harder," I replied as I slipped back down the nave.

As I neared the doors, I checked to make sure no one was looking. Then I ducked behind a pillar and Wished myself into the front seat of my caddy. In the blink of an eye, I was behind the wheel, Gran and Vaivea in the back.

"Hold on," I said, turning the key in the ignition. "We're about to fly."

"Thought we just did," Gran said with a chuckle.

I drove up St Louis Street, looking for the western route out of town. With a bunch of vampires on my trail, I wasn't about to take any more chances. But I had just one itsy bitsy, teeny weenie problem. I didn't know how to get out of New Orleans to the west, so I pulled over to look at my road map.

"Ah, sense finally caught up with you, has it?"

"Ok, Gran, I just need to check the directions. It's not your blood they're going to suck if they catch up with us."

"You are not safe here," said Vaivea.

I glanced around and saw that I'd parked beside Cemetery Number One again.

"Right, I'm out of here," I said, tossing my map in the glove compartment.

Something suddenly landed on the bonnet with a thud. I jumped in my seat, eyes glued to the apparition that slowly unbent itself and stood in a swirl of black, ankle-length jacket. He had to be over six feet tall, with a long mop of black hair hanging almost to his shoulders, dark sunnies and a pair of serious knee-high black leather boots.

He grimaced at me in what might pass in undead circles for a smile, his lips twisted in a cruel leer. I knew I was in for deep, dark trouble.

"I guess this isn't a social call," I said, trying not to sound as frightened as I felt.

"Guess not," he rasped with a voice that sounded like it had endured centuries of heavy smoking.

"If you scratch the paintwork, you pay," I added.

The brave front must have worked, for he just stood there, eyeing me from behind his sunnies. I noticed several more vampires approaching from up ahead. Sweat trickled down my back.

"Don't you feel a just a little bit conspicuous, standing on the bonnet of my car? Or is it something you make a hobby of?"

"Do you ever shut up?"

"Well, we could stay here and chat all day, but I'm sure we both have better things to do."

"Hand it over."

"Huh?"

"Hand it over."

At my puzzled look, he nodded towards the back of the car. I glanced back out of the corner of one eye. Whatever he was referring to, it was lost on me.

"Hand what over?"

He sighed as if talking to a child who bored him greatly.

"You have the remains of one of our kind. We want her back."

Click! They wanted Mama's ashes. I was angry, and puzzled. What right did they have to demand I hand my mother over to them? She might be nothing more than a pile of white powder and soot, but she was still my mother. I took a deep breath, shifted the gearstick into reverse and gripped the steering wheel.

"Sorry, buddy, but she was one of my kind before she was one of your kind."

With that, I stepped hard on the pedal. The caddy lurched backwards and I steered her in reverse over three empty parking spaces before stopping to see what had become of my unwelcome caller.

He'd leapt into the air and now floated down before me, his jacket billowing around him. His boots hit the tarmac, and he cracked his knuckles.

"Oh dear," Gran said. "Perhaps you should've waited for him to move…"

"People who wait around die," I said grimly, putting the car back into drive.

I wasn't about to sit around and allow myself to be made into a human pincushion by this uncool cat. I punched my foot down on the pedal again, and the caddy flew towards him. He didn't have time to react. He went down under the car with a crunch of bones, and his followers scattered before I could mow them down as well.

"You definitely shouldn't have done that," Gran admonished. "They'll be after you now!"

"They were after me already!" I reminded her.

"They will continue to follow while you carry the ashes," Vaivea said.

"Then I'll find somewhere safe to leave them."

I continued around the block, back to Basin Street, thankful there was little traffic about to hold me up. Even the radio cheered me on, belting out 'We've Gotta Get Out Of This Place' as I turned at Poydras Street. When I saw the sign for the Lake Pontchartrain Causeway, I knew what to do.

"Hang on, we're taking a little detour."

I turned north onto the causeway, paid the toll, and laid down rubber, skimming the thin line of tarmac that stretched into the distance across the lake. After a few minutes I was completely surrounded by water, with nothing else to see but the parallel lanes carrying traffic to and from New Orleans. Heavy clouds had blown over, casting a soupy pall across the lake and the city behind me. I focussed straight ahead.

"I do admire your determination," Lou rhapsodised from the passenger seat, making me jump.

"Shit! Where'd you come from?"

"Do you know," he said, ignoring my outburst, "that you caused quite a stir in New Orleans, my dear?"

"Hey, they came looking for me, not the other way around!"

"True."

"And how was I to know they'd zero in on my mother's ashes?"

"Alas, they will be hard to deter. They feel they have a claim, you see…"

"Oh, they do, do they?"

I checked there were no cars behind me, then I pulled over and popped the boot.

"Let them claim this."

I got out and strode to the back of the car. The urn lay snuggled against my canvas bag to keep it from rolling around. I snatched it up, made sure the lid was on snugly, and hoisted it out over the water. As it fell, I Wished it encased in a block of solid concrete, just to make sure it never surfaced again. The cube of concrete disappeared beneath the brackish waters with a splash, and I got back in the caddy and continued on my way.

"One complication gone," I said with a smirk.

"Well, that's one way to take care of it," Lou said with a shrug. "However, that doesn't solve all your problems."

I glanced over at him.

"What do you mean?"

"Let's just say, those vampires aren't the only ones searching for you."

And with that, he vanished.

3.

I was pretty creeped out. For like the hundredth time that day. Shivers tap-danced up and down my back as I struggled to stay calm and focus on my driving.

"Filthy slime!" Gran said from the back seat.

"Okay, what did he mean? I have a feeling he didn't mean Mama. So who's looking for me?"

"Those with an interest in you," Vaivea said mysteriously.

"Can't you guys ever just tell me stuff straight?" I said. "I'm not a mind reader, you know!"

"You could be if you tried," Gran said.

I bit back a retort. Then I thought about what she'd said.

"Really?" I asked. "I can read people's minds? But should I? Would it even be... ethical?"

"Depends."

"Depends on what? Whether I'm about to be eaten or sucked dry of blood or something like that?"

"You already look at people's auras to check them out," Gran said. "You don't seem to have any ethical dilemmas with that."

"But auras are right out there. You can see them."

"Not everyone sees them. In fact, most people don't. Just like not everyone senses the presence of their guides and angels."

"Yeah, but mind-reading seems really invasive. And rude. I don't want to go barging into people's heads without permission."

Vaivea cleared his throat.

"You forget who you are."

"Oh yeah, that's right. I'm a Goddess. Sorry, I keep forgetting. But does that give me the right to invade people's minds and read their thoughts? Aren't thoughts supposed to be private?"

"Ordinary people are not your concern," Vaivea said, "although they're the reason for your mission. You must realise that you'll soon be dealing with others, which you've had a small taste of in New Orleans."

"You mean vampires and werewolves? Or other kinds of spirits? Angels? Demons? Gods... God?"

My mind boggled as I contemplated it all.

"Okay Gran, Vaivea. I just realised how much I don't know about what I'm heading into. I mean, I already knew I didn't know, but – you know what I mean."

"Of course, my sparrow. But it will all come to you in good time. Ask and you shall receive."

"Okay," I said with a sly smile, "I will ask! How about telling me about my spirit guide? Like, when will I get to meet them? And if it's not meant to be Amy, who is it? Just give me a hint – is it Archangel Michael?"

Fantasies of Michael drifted through my mind. After all, if Amy wasn't destined to be my guide, he'd certainly be the next best thing. I recalled the Led Zeppelin concert Gabe and I had gone to at the Jacksonville Coliseum back in August. Michael was the very image of their lead singer, Robert Plant (though I was quite sure from the way he moved and grooved his mojo on the stage that there was little angelic about him!) Mmmm – could I be that lucky?

I was still daydreaming of Archangel Michael when a lone figure appeared on the causeway ahead. I stomped on the brakes, but it was too late! In the split second before the caddy skidded into the person, details registered in my mind like I was in some sort of surreal nightmare. Female. Middle-aged. Average build. Blonde hair. Pink dress. I screamed as the car ploughed into her, through her...

That was weird. Her torso floated past me, her dress shimmering and her face turned towards me in a loving smile. My mind went haywire as the caddy screeched to a stop. I took a deep breath, my heart thumping crazily, then I turned to look. The woman still stood exactly where she was when I'd run her down. My blood ran cold.

4.

"Angela, darling."

"Mama?"

I felt nauseous. She was semi-transparent like Gran and Vaivea, having passed into their ghostly realm. She smiled and held out her hands as she floated closer, her pink nylon nightie shimmering hazily.

"Angela, I'm so glad to see you. I have no idea where I am. Please help me."

"Er, do you remember what happened?"

"Oh, we had some silly argument, didn't we? I'm so sorry, darling. I don't know what's happened. I feel so strange."

I didn't wonder. I saw the bloody gash across her neck where Lou's sword had separated her head from her body with a single blow. And she wasn't alone in feeling strange. My tummy did a weird jig just talking to her.

"Mama, we're on the Lake Pontchartrain Causeway, just outside New Orleans. I can't stay here, there's bound to be traffic. You can come with me if you like."

Mama looked up and down the causeway, bit her lip and frowned.

"Sweetheart, I've lost something. I've got to find it. I'm

not sure exactly what it is, or where it is, but I've got to keep looking. Can you help me?"

In an instant of startling clarity, I realised she was after her earthly remains. And I'd just put them at the bottom of Lake Pontchartrain.

"Er, look, Mama, I'd love to help you but I've got to keep going. I think what you're looking for is back that-a-way."

I pointed the way I'd come.

"Now, I'm going to visit Karen. I hope you find what you're after."

A truck approached, and I started the car.

"Oh. Tell Karen I love her, won't you? As soon as I've found it..."

I didn't hear the rest. I had to move or risk a crash. Besides, I still wasn't convinced I was far enough away from those vampires. I got the caddy up to speed, still swallowing down my nausea, and turned the radio up to distract myself. A powerful bassline boomed out and a heavily distorted guitar sizzled. I grimaced before the vocals even kicked in. Keep On Running by the Spencer Davis Group. Great song. Great *timing*.

Soon I saw the shoreline ahead, then I was back on dry land. But I didn't dare risk a stop yet. I wanted to put as much distance between myself and New Orleans as possible. I blazed along until I hit the next Interstate, and took the turn for Baton Rouge. The sun hung low in the sky by the time I got there, and I paused to decide what to do next. I still didn't want to stop, but my tummy had been rumbling for the last half hour, so I took a chance and hunted out a diner for a hurried meal.

While I ate, I scrutinised my road map. I saw with un-easiness that the direct route from New Orleans to Baton

Rouge was much shorter than the way I'd taken across Lake Pontchartrain. Anyone who really wanted to could track me down in half the time I'd taken to escape from them in the first place, and I didn't relish the thought of waking up to find a bunch of fangs in my flesh, relishing me.

So, it seemed best to keep going. I dug my thermos flask out of the car, got it filled with steaming hot coffee, and continued west into the sunset. My nerves twitched as darkness swallowed up the road, despite the high beams from the caddy's headlights. And despite the soothing voice of Roy Orbison. Of course, if it had been any song but Runnin' Scared...

An hour later I turned north at Opelousas, the night pressing in against the windows of my car. Finally I started to relax as I drove through Alexandria another hour on. I'd turned off the radio when Night of Fear came on. It was like someone out there was taunting me. I stopped at a garage and savoured the cool night air as I filled the tank, then continued driving. My thoughts kept going to Gabe while I ate up the miles, and I wondered if that meant I'd dream of him soon.

It was close to ten o'clock by the time I arrived at Shreveport. By then, my coffee was long gone and my eyelids were drooping. I stopped at the first motel I saw that had vacancies, and sweet-talked the night attendant into letting me have a room.

I was so completely clanked that I carried my bags up the stairs by sheer force of will alone, too tired to even think of using magic. All I wanted was to shut myself in safely, fall on the bed and sleep, hopefully with no interference from vampires or anything else. But when I entered my room with Gran, life took a different turn.

Candles burned on every surface. The floor was covered with luxurious cashmere rugs, and swags of silk in dark blues and rich purples hung at the windows. The bed was an exotic cavern swathed in blue silk curtains and covered with purple cushions and bolsters.

And laying back amongst it all, resplendent in a crimson silk robe, was Lou. My bag hit the floor with a thud as I surveyed the scene. Lou smiled seductively.

"Welcome, darling. Do you like?"

I gave him a look designed to turn boiling water into ice in less than a second, and shuffled over to the nearest chair to sit down. Gran floated at him, releasing a torrent of abuse.

"Why, you filth, you never give up! Go back to the crack in the earth you crawled out of, you slime, and take all your worthless frippery too. We decent folk don't want you here."

Lou sighed a little sigh, the way you would if someone caught you cheating at solitaire.

"My dear lady," he said, "you continue to be a vigilant chaperone, which is very commendable. I think you deserve a little vacation for all your devoted service."

"No!" I shouted.

But it was too late. Lou had clicked his fingers, and Gran was gone.

15

Time Is Tight

1. Monday 27th October, 1969 – Shreveport, Louisiana
I stormed over to the bed.

"Bring her back!"

"What's the magic word?"

"Bring her back!"

"Darling, she's the most crushing bore."

"Bring her back! Now!"

"But darling, why? She only ever thinks the worst of me. She's no fun at all."

"Do you blame her? You're the devil. What's she supposed to think of you?"

"Oh, that I'm a fun entity who enjoys his existence to the full... You know, I don't *care* what she thinks of me. If I obsessed about what every lowly human being – dead or alive – thought of me, I'd be less than a speck. She's not even in our league, darling."

"Stop calling me that," I snapped. "Just bring her back. Now."

Lou sighed again, sounding resigned, and waved his hand.

Gran floated at my side once more. I was so relieved to see her, I could have hugged her – if there was anything solid to hug. But something wasn't the same. She looked dazed.

"It was him," she said, looking at me in wonder. "After all these years. I can't believe it."

"Who, Gran?" I asked.

"John," she said reverently. "It was John, reborn in a new body."

I frowned. Grandpa's name had been John, and although I hadn't known him well – he'd died when I was just small – I felt that must be who she meant.

"You mean Grandpa? You saw him?"

"Yes," she said, nodding eagerly. "Oh, I knew he'd passed into a new life cycle, but now he's almost grown, and he's so much like he was – back then."

I understood. She and Grandpa had been childhood sweethearts who grew up next door to each other. If anyone knew Grandpa on sight, even in a new life, it was her.

"Well, that's fantastic, Gran," I said. "I hope he's doing well. But we have the here and now to deal with, and someone *here* isn't making it easy right *now*."

I stared pointedly at Lou, and he pouted.

"You just refuse to be impressed because you're stubborn," he said sulkily, and waved his hand.

All the lavish trimmings disappeared, leaving us in a normal motel room.

"There, happy now?" he said. "All that trouble for nothing."

"You probably whizzed it up in the blink of an eye, just like you took it away," I said, digging for my overnight bag.

"There you go, taking all the fun out of everything," he

lamented as I headed for the bathroom.

In the back of my mind I wondered if he might follow me, but I was left in peace to enjoy a warm shower. When I returned to the main room, I found Gran by the bed.

"Has Lou gone?" I asked, packing my overnight bag away.

"Hmmm," Gran answered vaguely.

"Still thinking about Grandpa?"

She smiled. I was about to throw myself on the bed, but then a delicious smell wafted my way. I sniffed – it smelt like roast chicken with all the trimmings. I examined the tiny kitchen alcove, which consisted of a fridge, a small bench top with a sink and some drawers, and an oven. I couldn't see anything out of order until I noticed that the oven was on at a low heat. I opened the door, and gasped. It was quail, surrounded by some sort of fancy potato arrangement, Julienne carrots, and mint peas.

"Gran, where did this come from?" I asked as I lifted the plate out.

"Huh? Oh, it must have been Lou. I saw him wave his hand in that direction before he disappeared. What is it?"

"Supper, by the looks of it."

I put the plate on the table, got a knife and fork out of the kitchen drawer, and sat down, suddenly feeling ravenous.

"You're not going to eat that, are you?" Gran asked in horror. "Food left by the devil – you can't!"

"Why not? It looks good, it smells good, and I'm hungry."

"But... it could be corrupted. It could be dirty, rotten, foul..."

"It is fowl," I said, trying the meat. "Quail. And there's nothing wrong with it."

"Oh Ange, my little sparrow. You can't trust the Devil. There could be any manner of contamination in that food."

"Gran, I understand your concern. But he wouldn't do that. He's trying to woe me, not kill me. He considers me an equal, which would make it really stupid to monkey with my food. If he'd wanted to, he could've done that ages ago."

"I know. But I still say you can't trust him. He's the devil, Lucifer, Satan – the most vile and evil thing on earth..."

"You rang?" purred Lou's voice from behind me.

I almost choked on my quail.

"Geez, do you have to do that?" I gasped, my eyes watering.

"I'm sorry, darling, but I heard my name being taken in vain."

I got myself a glass of water from the kitchenette. When I turned back to the table, Lou was seated on the chair next to mine. Gran looked unimpressed.

"Take a hike!" she said. "We don't want you here."

"Madam, I feel it fair to warn you that I can transport you elsewhere again, and next time it mightn't be so pleasant."

Gran pressed her lips together, scowling mutinously.

"That's better," Lou said, and turned to me. "So, how's the quail?"

"Very nice," I answered.

"Ovens aren't really my forte," he said blithely. "I prefer an open flame for cooking, so forgive me if it's a little – rare."

"Its fine," I assured him.

I speared some carrot on my fork, followed by the last delicious scraps of meat. When there was nothing left but a little pile of bones, I sat back and looked from Gran to Lou and back again.

"Well, are you happy now, Gran? I told you there was nothing wrong with it."

"Humph," Gran grunted.

"I'm very glad to hear it," Lou said.

He seemed anxious that I should like the meal, and I couldn't help but smile. He reminded me of a boy taking a girl on their first date.

"Okay," I said, "now for coffee. Allow me."

I hadn't been successful in Conjuring anything before, but for some reason, I felt supremely confident that I could now. I closed my eyes and imagined mugs, a milk jug, sugar bowl and coffee pot, all in vibrant purple, then silver spoons and sugar tongs, rich creamy milk, crystalline cubes of sugar, freshly roasted, aromatic coffee, and nodded my head. There it all was on the table before us. It had taken mere seconds.

"Oh Cheri," Lou said. "You are good!"

He poured and added several sugar cubes to his coffee, and I added milk to mine. We didn't speak again until we'd both taken a good, long sip. I wondered what else I could Conjure. If my coffee was this good, my chocolate would be divine!

"You excel," Lou said enthusiastically. "I couldn't have done better myself – well, not much better. Your powers are growing strong. God won't know what hit him!"

"If you must sit there and blaspheme," Gran said sulkily, "I'll go and visit Karen. Goodnight."

In a blink she was gone, but I knew Vaivea was nearby to protect me. I frowned in realisation. I was a Goddess. Did I really need protection?

"You are untutored and unskilled in many things," Vaivea said.

"I could teach you everything you need to know," Lou said softly, gazing at me.

His eyes were a dark, stormy grey just then, and they had a hypnotic effect.

269

"To be taught by only one teacher risks that the student may carry on the bias of that teacher," said Vaivea. "There are many lessons and many tutors to learn from."

"Ah, such wisdom," Lou said. "But too many cooks spoil the broth, you know. There would be no consistency in your lessons."

"I choose to learn as much as I can, and decide for myself what's important," I said. "If I choose wrong, I've only got myself to blame."

"Ooh, such a strong woman," Lou rhapsodised. "I like it!"

"Good, because now I choose to go to bed," I said, getting up from the table and Vanishing the coffee things.

"I wasn't finished yet!" Lou said, pouting.

I knew it was only an act. I felt tempted to throw something at him, but stopped myself just in time. Knowing him, he would probably consider it a come on. I didn't watch to see whether he disappeared or not. I brushed my teeth, then I switched the bedside lamp off and collapsed on the bed. As my eyes adjusted to the darkness, they were drawn to a faint shimmer at the foot of the bed. It was Vaivea.

"You must learn to be more careful," he said. "Danger lurks where you least expect it."

2.

As though to underline his words, some revellers down in the street whooped and hollered. Drunken laughter followed, then faded as they moved on. I yawned, snuggled down and closed my eyes.

I fell straight into a deep sleep, only to find myself back in the time of Isis.

I sat on a seashore. Behind me lay a large town, straddling the hills around a natural bay. Byblos, on the coast of Lebanon – only in ancient times it was called Gebal, a major port and trading centre in Canaan.

I felt intensely weary, which puzzled me. Surely Gods and Goddesses had unlimited energy? But then I realised that Isis had wandered much of the earth seeking the body of her beloved, even to the Far East, before hearing of the final destination of Set's box. And so she had trudged through the dust and dirt of many roads in her search. However, the sea breeze from the Mediterranean cooled my skin, and the sharp tang of the salt air also helped to restore me.

I seemed to go unnoticed amidst the hustle and bustle of merchants and livestock. Activity abounded everywhere I looked, people bartering and haggling over all manner of produce and animals in fast, unfamiliar tongues. I wet my hands in the lapping tide and splashed water on my face. The reflection that gazed back at me was that of an old woman, and I realised that Isis had disguised herself.

I now pondered my next move. I'd learned that Set's box had come to rest in a tamarisk bush, which then grew into a mighty tree on the Mediterranean shore. The tree exuded such a pleasing fragrance that King Malcander and Queen Astarte had ordered it to be cut down and fashioned into a pillar for their palace in Gebal.

So I needed to get inside the palace to find that pillar. But it was not the way of Isis to demand entrance because of who she was. I would have to find some subtle way to enter the royal household, a way that wouldn't arouse suspicion of my true identity.

A number of young women bathed in the cool waters

nearby. They chattered and laughed among themselves, and occasionally splashed each other playfully. One of them splashed me accidentally, wetting my bare arm. I smiled, indulgent of their light-hearted, girlish antics.

"Pardon me, good lady," said the splasher. "I meant not to wet you."

"You are pardoned," I replied. "No harm is done."

The girls were all very beautiful, and I wondered what their situation was.

"You are fortunate to be free of duties on this fine day," I continued. "It is perfect weather for bathing."

"We are indeed fortunate," another agreed. "None could be in happier circumstances than we of Queen Astarte's chambers."

My ears pricked up at that.

"You are the Queen's own handmaidens?"

"We are," replied a third. "She is the most kind, generous, and gracious of rulers."

"You are truly blessed, then," I said. "But how will you be presentable for the Queen after bathing, with your hair all wet and tangled? Allow me to braid it for you, if you will."

They looked at each other, puzzled.

"What do you mean?" asked one. "Are you skilled in the art of hairdressing?"

"I will show you," I answered.

I beckoned to the girl who'd splashed me, and turned her around so I could access her long, dark tresses. I combed them with my fingers and started braiding, a skill I certainly didn't know I possessed. As I worked, I breathed a glorious perfume into the hair, knowing it wouldn't go unnoticed once they returned to the palace. Thus I was sure I would soon be invited to enter that domain.

I braided the hair of all the young women in turn. They were in awe of my skill, and of the perfume I'd endowed them with, and thanked me profusely as they left. I sat and waited, and they soon returned, as I knew they would.

"Great lady," said the girl who had splashed me. "The Queen has asked for you, as she desires to know more of your skills and talents. Will you come to her now?"

"I will," I said, and got up.

I was sure Isis would have no qualms about meeting an earthly king and queen, but as we wound through the streets of Gebal, my heart thudded louder and louder with each step. Despite the glowing reports of Queen Astarte's attendants, I couldn't help but wonder if she'd really take so kindly to a stranger from another land coming into her royal apartments.

3.

I awoke suddenly, clutching my heaving chest. Panic subsided as I realised that I lay in my motel room. Light streamed through a chink in the curtains, unnaturally bright. Birds twittered from the balcony outside, and the little bit of sky I could see was startlingly blue. It was so perfect that I began to think something was bound to be up.

I looked around and saw Gran shimmering by my side.

"Your dreams are troubled," she said. "Was it your mother?"

"No, I regressed again," I said as I sat up and looked about for a clock. "Isis was about to find Osiris' body. But she had to go through King Malcander and Queen Astarte to do so. Heck – is that the time? I meant to get up at six-thirty."

It was quarter past seven. I hurried to get ready.

"You should take more time for rest," Gran admonished. "Especially when you've regressed in your dreams. That can take a lot of energy, you know."

"Yeah, I can tell," I said, yawning. "But I have to get to L.A., too. I have to be there to protect Karen, and to meet my spirit guide."

I rang dad to update him, then room service for a cooked breakfast of bacon, eggs and toast. After that I Conjured a large mug of coffee.

"You'll rot your insides, swilling that stuff," Gran said. "How many cups a day do you drink?"

"Not enough," I replied, and took a big sip.

"Pity Amy didn't warn you off it. Substances like that can block you from communicating with the spirit world effectively."

I considered that for perhaps half a second, but no – I couldn't possibly go without my coffee. As I brushed my hair and then packed, Gran floated from door to window, window to door, distracting me with her restless energy.

"So what's up?"

"Ah," she sighed. "Vaivea was right about there being undesirable sorts about, and the sooner we get moving, the better."

"What undesirable sorts?" I asked, suddenly worried. "Not more vampires?"

"Oh, one or two were on the prowl nearby," Gran answered. "And others. Troubled spirits, lost souls, that sort of thing."

"That's bad," I mumbled, now feeling distinctly jittery. "Look, is it just because it's coming up to Halloween, or is there something else I need to know?"

"Halloween's definitely drawing them out," Gran answered. "It always does, but there seem to be more than usual."

"Anything else?"

"I don't know, sweetheart. Could be the full moon. There's something in the air, something different, but your guess is as good as mine."

A knock on the door made me jump, but it was only the arrival of my breakfast. After eating, I paid my bill and loaded the caddy. Gran sat in the front passenger seat, I think to keep Lou from popping in again by virtue of its being occupied, and I filled my thermos with Conjured coffee, now that I knew how to.

I spied out the route west to Dallas on my map, then found a store and bought some snacks and a couple of chocolate bars – to help boost my energy levels, of course. I wondered as I drove away if I'd start to hallucinate as a result of all the caffeine. Vaivea looked grim as I sipped my coffee, and I noticed that he seemed dimmer than usual. That brought to mind Amy's warnings about what not to consume whilst working with spirit entities.

"Sorry but I need this to stay alert," I said, biting off some chocolate and letting it melt in my mouth. "I know you'll keep me out of danger. Mmmm..."

Crossing the state border, I cranked up the radio, and grimaced as it blared out Danger! Heartbreak Dead Ahead. Gran flickered dimly, then floated to the back seat of the caddy. I glanced in the rear view mirror. Vaivea was also very indistinct, and I almost wondered if I was losing my ability to see spirits. But no – I was a goddess, wasn't I? That couldn't happen.

Ahead of me in the distance, a long streak of lightning

flashed. I frowned. I really didn't like driving into a storm. But the soft top was up, so I gritted my teeth and kept going. It was half an hour before I reached wet tarmac, and soon after that the first spatters of rain hit my roof. It was dark and gloomy, and we drove along without talking while the radio played Raindrops Keep Fallin' On My Head.

As if to further blacken my mood – and it almost seemed deliberate in intent – I was next treated to the sickly-sweet, poppy tones of the Cowsills with The Rain, The Park & Other Things. I screwed up my face in disgust.

"Oh dear, why are we all so serious?" said a voice to my right.

"Filthy scum," said Gran.

"I knew it was too good to last," I said. "Run out of souls to torment, huh?"

"Cheri, where's the fun in that, I ask you? No, I just thought you all needed cheering up a bit. You look awfully dour, the lot of you."

I glanced at Lou. His eyes were a magnetic, glowing magenta, and he had all his charisma out in full force.

"Can it!" I snapped, glaring at the road ahead. "We don't need cheering up, by you or anyone else."

"Touchy, touchy," he said with a pout.

"Go play with some twisters," Gran muttered.

"What a good idea!" Lou said brightly. "I might just do that."

"Thanks Gran," I said, motioning to the empty seat beside me. "Now we'll probably have to dodge tornadoes as well as lightning."

"I doubt it," said Gran. "It's not you he'd aim them at, is it? Some poor, innocent farmer's family, maybe a church or two, other motorists. It's all the same to him."

"It wasn't me who suggested it in the first place."

Weirdly, the next song to play was Lightnin' Strikes. I shivered, wondering how safe we were on the open road. The rain increased steadily for the next half hour, and the wind gusted. I felt tempted to pull over and wait for the storm to ride itself out. But I knew the sooner I got to Dallas, the safer I would be. I could find a gas station to park at, grab some lunch, and have a leisurely drive to Oklahoma City in the afternoon. Then I'd set off on Route Sixty Six, fresh and well-rested, the next day.

The wind-shield wipers swiped back and forth rhythmically, the rain pounded on the soft top, and my heart leapt at every gust of wind that buffeted the caddy. The radio mysteriously stayed in keeping with the weather, blaring out Rain by the Beatles.

I reached Dallas just after eleven and pulled in at a large gas station and service centre. I left the car with a super-friendly attendant to fill up, check the oil and tyres, clean the windscreen, and park safely out of the weather, while I went into the café and ordered a burger and fries.

After I ate, I dragged a chair over to a pay phone in the corner and rang Karen to bring her up to date on my drive.

"Yeah, pretty uneventful," I lied through my teeth. "I left Mama in New Orleans – there's this old lady there she's friends with, so she's staying with her for a couple of days and flying back."

"I wondered about that," Karen said. "It seems strange she'd take off so soon after dad coming home, especially if he's not well. Is everything okay between them?"

"As far as I could see," I answered, my fingers crossed

behind my back. "Let's just say that he isn't sleeping in the spare room."

"Ange!"

"I was trying to be subtle."

"Give up. You've never been any good at it."

"You know me too well," I said.

"Maybe I should ring and catch up with him."

"Yeah, he'll appreciate that. But don't be surprised if he doesn't make much sense. He was still a bit woozy from the rabies shot when I left. And he's found God."

"Poor dad," Karen said. "I can't understand why Mama would leave like that."

"You know what a ditz she is."

"I wish you wouldn't call her that," Karen scolded. "She's had her share of problems, you know."

"Oh yeah, like the years of alcoholism I only just found out about. Seems I was the only one who didn't know."

"Ange, I'm so sorry. I really wanted to tell you – I could've done with your help. But dad thought it was better not to."

"He did, huh?"

"Don't take it personally. He felt it was ruining my life to be so caught up in looking after her and running the house, and he didn't want it to ruin yours too."

Something caught in my throat. That was just like dad. I'd always had the sneaking feeling that I was his favourite, though he'd never said so.

"Thanks sis. But you know, I really wish I'd been let in on the secret. It wouldn't have ruined my life to help – and it would've taken a burden off you."

"Don't worry about it, it's in the past. Let's just hope he can get her to seek help with her problem before it kills her."

"Sure. Have you seen any more of that creature in the mirror?"

"Once or twice. It freaks me out so much – it popped up in front of me in the bathroom mirror last night, and I screamed my head off. I didn't know what to tell Eric. I ended up saying I thought I'd seen a spider, but I could tell he thought I was nuts."

"I'll be there in a couple of days. Try and stay loose. Talk to you soon, okay?"

Next I rang dad, who was in the middle of hosting a meeting of his new men's group from church. I reassured him that I was safe and well, and then I rang Sagira.

"Ange, is that you? I'm so glad you rang, I've been so worried. It's terrible – we don't know what to do, we can't find him anywhere..."

"Whoa, slow down already," I said. "What's terrible? Who can't you find?"

"Adio! He disappeared two days ago and no one knows where he is!"

4.

"Adio?" I said. "You mean he just disappeared into thin air?"

"Yes!" Sagira answered. "I couldn't tell my parents, but I think he may be following you again."

A lump formed in my throat.

"But why? I've left Jacksonville. Surely he doesn't see me as a threat any more? And besides, how would he know where I'm going?"

"He's smart. He knows you have a sister in L. A. You're heading that way. And he has friends who might be able to track you down."

"But why?" I asked again. "What makes you think he's following me? What's the point?"

"He's still pretty ticked off at you, especially for leaving town where he can keep an eye on you. He told our parents he was going back to New York to deal with some business concerns, but I overheard him booking a motel room in New Orleans!"

That took me aback. I wondered if he had been there at the same time I was, and remembered the warnings that someone was looking for me.

"Does he have any contacts in Dallas?" I asked.

"Is that where you are now?"

"Yes. I got here an hour ago, and I'm just waiting out a storm before I keep going."

"Well, yes, he knows some people there. He might be able to use them to track you down. Please be careful, Ange. Adio always carries things to extremes. I keep telling Gabe you're safe and well so he doesn't worry, but I don't know how much he takes in."

Gabe. The soft spot in my heart ached at the sound of his name.

"Is there any improvement?" I asked.

"No, not yet. But the doctors say he's healing well, so we keep talking to him and reassuring him that he'll be okay."

"I miss him," I whispered.

"We all miss him," Sagira whispered back.

"I'm sorry, I didn't mean to get all heavy on you. Is there any other news?"

"No. What about you? Have you had any more regressions?"

"A couple."

I described my recent visits to Isis' world, including my run-in with Set and what had happened to Osiris.

"So much like our real lives," she said sadly. "I hope you don't run into Adio. He's so determined, it scares me to think he might find you. I don't know what he'd do then. Take care, Ange."

"You too, Sagira," I replied, and hung up. "Gran? Vaivea? I need to find out where Adio is and what he's planning."

Vaivea was a vague shadow by the wall, and I had trouble hearing his words.

"Adio is nearby. He attempts to locate you."

I shuddered, and had to force myself to breath deeply.

"Okay. Dallas is a big place. How does he think he'll find me here?"

"Mightn't be that hard," Gran said. "Think about it. You've never been to Dallas before, have you? So he's probably banking on you keeping to one of the main roads through town, so you don't get lost."

I swallowed nervously.

"Yeah, but he doesn't know that for sure. And even so, he'd have such a slim chance of finding me – it'd be pure luck. 'Cos I'm not going to stick around long. As soon as this storm's blown over, I'm outta here."

I jumped and spun around in my chair as someone entered the café. It was just a pot-bellied middle-aged man, with truck driver written all over him. I took another deep breath to calm myself, and forced my eyes away from the café's door. They fell on the sign pointing to the rest room.

"I'm going for a quick walk," I said. "Please, please, keep watch and let me know if Adio gets any nearer to finding me.

Okay?"

I almost ran to the rest room, shut the door behind me, and leaned back against it. Because I'd decided to get myself a little backup, and I didn't want anyone barging in until I was done.

"Archangel Michael?" I said. "I need your help. Please come."

A burst of radiance nearly blinded me. When I could peer through my lashes without my eyeballs burning, I saw that Michael hovered over near the wash basins, as glorious as ever.

"I hate to ask, but could you tone it down a bit? It's just that I like to look at whoever I'm talking to without doing my eyes permanent damage."

"As you wish," he said.

I was sure he wore a grin like the Cheshire Cat as his light faded to a muted glow, though his Sword of Truth still blazed with heavenly fire.

"Thanks. Someone who means me harm is trying to find me. I'd feel a lot safer if I knew you were keeping an eye out for him."

"What, like this?" Michael quipped, and raised a hand to his face.

I wasn't sure what he was up to until he held out his hand, complete with eyeball. The pupil was a brilliant blue, and appeared to focus on me. I recoiled.

"Ew, yuck, gross! Put it back!"

"Gets 'em every time," Michael said with a chuckle, and bounced it on the floor.

I noticed both his eyes were right where they belonged, in his head. He threw the extra one to me, and though the thought of touching it was repugnant, I automatically held out my hands to catch it.

It was just a rubber ball, made to look like an eye. I'd seen them countless times in Dime Stores. I didn't know whether to be angry or laugh at his silliness. In all honesty, I felt like flinging the ball at his head. Despite myself, laughter won.

"Okay, enough with the funnies. I don't know why Adio's after me, unless he has a bigger chip on his shoulder than I thought. But he's up to something, and I don't trust him. I don't want him delaying my journey. I don't even want to see him."

"Relax, he's miles away at the moment," Michael said casually, throwing his fiery sword from one hand to the other like a tennis player with a racket.

"Well, that's a relief," I said. "But what about the coming moments? He seems awfully determined."

"He is."

Michael threw his sword into the air one last time, where it arced in a perfect loop and landed smoothly in his right hand. Then he grinned at me as if he'd done something clever and expected to be praised, or given a Scooby snack or something. I sucked my cheek in and raised an eyebrow.

"Oh, lighten up. Yeah, he'll probably catch up with you somewhere, maybe even while you're still in Dallas, but you seem to keep forgetting who you are. You're more than equipped to deal with him. You did in that other lifetime, remember?"

And with that, he Disappeared.

"Fine, then!" I said, and chucked the ball after him.

A hand appeared out of thin air, plucked the ball from its course, and disappeared.

"Ooh, thanks," said Michael's disembodied voice.

"You're welcome," I grumbled back. "It's been real."

I slumped against the door, feeling dismal.

"Well, that was a disappointment," I said to no one in particular.

"What did you expect, dear?" Gran replied, floating through the wall next to me. "That the most powerful archangel would play bodyguard to a Goddess who has absolutely no need of him?"

"He did in New Orleans."

"Until you remembered that you could take care of things yourself."

"Oh. Yeah. So I did."

There didn't seem anything more to say, so I went back out to the café and had my thermos refilled with fresh, hot coffee. As I turned to leave, Vaivea appeared silently before me, making me jump.

"He has located you."

16

Windy

Adio! Gripping my thermos, I hurried out to the garage side of the service centre. The rain had stopped, and the wind was icy cold against my skin. But not as cold as I felt inside at the thought that Adio had managed to hunt me down. I saw the attendant who'd been so nice to me – he must have liked my smile, or my style, or something – standing over by the bowsers, watching for me. I hurried over to him, nearly slipping on the wet surface.

"Whoa there, ma'am, watch your step," he said, offering me his hand. "You'll do yourself an injury if you're not careful."

He flashed a warm smile at me. Poor guy, he looked so kind and decent, I hated to cut and run out on him. But I wanted to be well and truly gone before Adio had the chance to confront me.

"Er – thanks," I said, improvising shamelessly. "Sorry – gotta hurry – I have an appointment over town."

"I'll start her up for you," he said, fishing my car keys out

285

of his overall pocket.

I wanted to snatch them and run for the caddy, but I couldn't bear to be so rude. We hurried over to the open bay in the garage where the caddy was parked, my eyes flitting all around for signs of danger. The rain had only just stopped, judging by the wet tarmac and torrent of water in the gutters. I hoped the conditions would hold Adio up.

By the time we got to my car, I was so nervous I nearly dropped my thermos. The attendant unlocked the driver's side door and leaned in to slide the key into the ignition. The engine sprang to life, and he looked up with a grin.

"Mighty fine machine you've got here. Anything else I can do for you, ma'am?"

I froze before I could reply. A sleek black Mercury Cougar sedan had just pulled into the service centre, and came to a screeching stop right behind the caddy, blocking my exit. The passenger side door opened and Adio stepped out. His suit was crumpled, as if he had been in it all night, and I couldn't mistake the malicious gleam in his eyes when he removed his sunnies.

"Oh shit oh shit oh shit oh shit," I said under my breath, wondering how on earth to get out of this situation with the least damage.

Adio strode towards the caddy, followed by three other young men. They were all alike – clean shaven, close-cropped hair, late-twenties, dressed like they'd just come out of a Billy Graham crusade. I stuck my chin out defiantly as Adio neared.

"So, witch," he sneered. "Think you're gonna get away this time?"

"Hey, mister!" the attendant said.

I grabbed his arm to silence him.

"No go," I said quietly. "I'm not letting you get beaten up by these losers."

"What was that?" Adio asked belligerently.

"You heard," I said. "You and your little crowd of followers can go take a hike."

Then it hit me.

"In fact, that's a such a good idea, I think you will take a hike. Just the weather for it, too."

I nodded at the little group, and they Vanished. The attendant gasped.

"Did you see that?" he asked, pointing a shaky finger to where Adio and his companions had been. "They just – disappeared into thin air!"

"Who did?" I asked in an attempt to brazen it out.

He gaped at me, astonished.

"Those men – they were threatening you. They called you a witch and said you weren't going to escape."

He sure was sharp. But I couldn't let him hold me up any longer.

"Would you be a sweetie and move that car?" I said with a nod towards the black sedan. "Someone's blocked the driveway."

Confusion crossed his face, but then he sprang to attention. "Yes, ma'am. Right away."

I slid into the caddy as he hurried over to the sedan, got in and backed it out of the way. Then I drove out of the service centre, with a wave goodbye. I hoped I hadn't deranged him for life by Vanishing Adio and friends before his very eyes. I sighed as I headed north through the city, so flooded with relief that I felt like jelly.

"What did you do with them?" Gran asked.

I couldn't help but grin.

"Just what I said. I sent them hiking. I Wished them to the middle of some woods we passed on the way into Dallas. That should keep them busy."

"And your friend? What do you plan to do about him?"

I shrugged, almost giddy from my near-escape.

"Do I need to do something about him? He'll probably just chalk it up to a hectic day at work playing tricks on his eyes, go home and have a good sleep."

"Well, he's not on his way home yet, nor anything like sleeping," Gran said.

"What do you mean?" I asked, my elation fading.

My eyes flicked to my rear-view mirror. Right behind me was a black Mercury Cougar sedan, just like the car Adio and his cronies had been in. I swallowed nervously.

"You mean, he's following me? Why would he do that?"

"Looks like you made quite an impression," Gran said with a chuckle.

"Oh no," I groaned.

I kept an eye on the sedan as I wove through the traffic. I hadn't had time to research my route out of Dallas, and hoped I was on the right road for Oklahoma City. Much to my frustration, the black sedan stayed on my tail. Even more frustrating was the radio bursting into Jack the Ripper by Screaming Lord Sutch, followed by *that* song – the detested Angela Jones. I switched it off abruptly.

It rained again as I headed north, and I wondered if I should risk a stop to look at my map. I didn't want the attendant to catch up, although I was curious to know why he would tail me so closely. Passing through Carrollton, I lost sight of him behind a truck that cut in between us. I took a chance and turned at the next exit, pulled over and looked at my map. Good – I was on the right road for Oklahoma City.

"You have a visitor," Gran said as I put my map back in the glove compartment.

"Damn," I swore, and shoved the gear stick back into drive.

Not quickly enough. The passenger side door opened and the attendant threw himself in as the tyres spun, spraying mud and wet grass over the bonnet of the sedan parked behind. He slammed the door shut and turned to me, his face ashen.

2.

"I want to know what happened back there."

"Obviously," I said. "You wouldn't have chased me all the way across Dallas and beyond otherwise."

"Listen, I saw what happened. Those guys disappeared right before our eyes – they just vanished! Then you pretended like nothing happened. Well, I want to know what was going on, and I'm not getting out of this car until you tell me."

I considered my options as I turned back onto the north-bound highway. I could just wish him elsewhere, but alive, he would still have a tale to tell, which could cause me trouble. I wondered if I could erase myself from his memory, or just the bit where Adio and his friends had disappeared. I decided I probably could, but I was afraid to try, just in case I got it wrong and erased half his life memories, or all of them.

"Say, it'd be nice if you'd at least talk to me," he said. "I didn't come all this way for nothing. I want to know who you are and what exactly I saw back there."

"Alright," I answered, deciding to wing it and see what happened. "I'm a Goddess called Isis, incarnate in a human body, and those guys were my enemies. So I Wished them to be somewhere else, and they were magically sent there."

I glanced over to see what he made of my momentous announcement. He looked utterly gob-smacked, as I figured he would.

"Well, buddy, you asked," I said with a shrug.

I expected him to say I was crazy, and demand to be let out of the car, despite the rain, but he sat stock still and said nothing.

"You know, I could just let you out along here somewhere, and you could forget we ever met," I said. "Unless you'd like me to have a go at removing your memory of me, but I can't promise I'd do a good job. I haven't tried anything like that before."

"Tom."

"Huh?"

"My name. Tom McClintock."

"Oh. Ange. Just Ange."

"You know something, just Ange? This whole damned thing is doggone crazy. And the craziest thing about it is that I think I believe you."

"Even though you probably think I belong in an asylum by now?"

"Yeah," Tom said, cracking a wide grin. "In fact, this'll sound real weird, but I feel like you're totally different to everyone else somehow."

Gran chuckled softly from the back seat.

"Uh, yeah, I am," I said. "But in case you're wondering, I'm already taken."

"Um, I might have wondered that, too. But mostly I just want some answers."

I glanced across at him, and was reassured by the earnest expression in his eyes.

"Sorry, Tom. I guess I'm not used to people actually taking me seriously."

He took a deep breath, and nodded.

"But you are different. I know you are And you coming into the garage today was no accident, was it? It feels like we were fated to meet."

I couldn't think of another thing to say, so I didn't. The rain stopped, but the clouds still swirled above us, menacing in tones of steel blue and bruised grey. We cruised in silence for a while longer, skimming over Lewisville Lake, as dark and sultry as the sky it reflected. Then we reached Denton.

"Take the next off-ramp," Tom said.

I wasn't inclined to take orders from anyone, and gave him a look.

"I'm starving," he explained, "and I'm missing my lunch break. If you go off here, I'll direct you to the nearest burger joint."

I turned off at the next ramp, and Tom directed me a couple of blocks to a diner.

"Gee, thanks," he said as I parked the caddy. "Not the best weather to be out and about. These Texas Northers sure take it out of everyone."

A damp, cold gale blew as I followed Tom inside. I noticed his aura was full of cheerful colours, clean and healthy, and I also sensed a presence near him. Masculine. Closely related. He ordered, and I got a coffee, and we sat down.

"If you don't mind me asking, did you have a male relative pass away recently?"

A cloud passed over his face, and he nodded.

"Yeah," he said glumly. "My favourite uncle died a couple of weeks back. How did you know? Or shouldn't I ask?"

"I can sense his presence."

Tom's ears pricked up.

"Really? You mean, he's here with us right now?"

"Well, yeah. It's not unusual for people who have passed over to hang around the ones they loved in life. You were close?"

Tom smiled.

"Yeah, we were. Uncle Alan did all the kind of stuff with me my father never did. Dad took off when I was eleven, left me and my sister and mother and just disappeared. She tracked him down a couple of years later – he'd gone to Vegas and took up with a stripper or something. So we moved across Dallas to be closer to Uncle Alan and Aunt Minnie. They really helped us out a lot."

He blushed.

"Oh gee, you don't want to hear my life story! I kinda got carried away. Sorry."

"That's okay," I said. "Same thing happened to me. At least he waited until my sister and I were adults before he kicked up his heels."

"Oh, sorry to hear you've been through it too."

We both fell into silence as he munched his burger. I could tell Tom was a really nice guy, friendly and cheerful by nature despite the circumstances he'd just described. I could understand his curiosity over what had happened at the garage, and his need for answers. However, I needed to get back on the road as soon as possible, to get to Karen, and to find answers to questions of my own.

Besides, my heart was too full of Gabe to even consider

getting to know Tom better. I found the last mouthful of my coffee difficult to swallow as I wondered how Gabe was.

"You okay?" Tom asked.

"Yeah, just thinking about someone special back home."

"Your boyfriend?"

"Yeah."

I didn't want to talk about Gabe or what had happened to him, nor any of the other stuff I'd been through. I pushed my coffee cup away and straightened up.

"You in hurry to leave?" Tom asked, disappointed.

"Sorry, but I need to get to Oklahoma City. Can you tell me how long it takes to drive there?"

"Sure. It's about two and a half hours with no stops. So, is that where your 'appointment over town' is?"

"Oh. Sorry about that. I knew those guys were on their way and I had to get out of there quickly. I didn't like having to lie."

"That's okay. But who were they? What did they want with you?"

"It's a long story. I might write it all down one day – huh, it'd make quite a fantasy novel. If I do, I'll send a copy to you, okay?"

A warm, winsome smile crept across Tom's face.

"I'd like that, just Ange. I'd like that very much."

Tom finished his burger and fries, and sucked the last mouthful of his cola, and we went back outside.

"I could Wish you back to Dallas, if you like," I said. "I just don't know where you want to go, though."

Tom blinked and smiled.

"Really? Is it safe?"

"If you tell me somewhere I can visualise easily, I should be able to get you there okay."

"Sure! Just wish me back to the garage."

"Okay. But I can't do it here, in front of people."

"How about just over there?"

Tom pointed. In the next block over was a vacant lot with a grove of trees at the far end. We crossed the grassy lot and found a private spot amongst the trees. Tom gazed at me wistfully.

"You really can do it, can't you? Like you did to those other guys. Was he right when he called you a witch?"

I smiled.

"No. I told you, I'm a Goddess."

"Yeah, you sure are," said Tom, and I Wished him back to the garage in Dallas.

3.

Soon I was on my way to Oklahoma City. Gran didn't have much to say, probably because I'd cranked up the radio when I heard Spinning Wheel by Blood, Sweat and Tears come on . I got a shock when I looked in my rear view mirror and saw Lou, lounging on the back seat, ultra cool in his dark sunnies and bopping his head to each blast of the horns in the song.

A few minutes later we passed a bus full of old folk that attracted his interest, and he Disappeared. I groaned and wondered what mischief he was up to this time. A fresh outbreak of rain pelted down intermittently, the wind gusted, and the little traffic there was slowed to a snail's pace. I shivered as I recalled Gran telling Lou to go play with some twisters earlier that day. I tried not to think about it, and made myself sing along with the radio. Until Dizzy, by Tommy Roe, came on.

In Gainesville, lots of vehicles were pulled over to the side of the road to sit the weather out. I continued on, and the rain eased up just as I crossed Red River into Oklahoma.

"That's better," I said. "Now I can see again."

"Stay alert," Vaivea warned me.

"Alert is my middle name," I joked, and took a swig from my thermos. "Can't help it with all this coffee in my system."

"Ange, my sparrow," Gran said. "Do be careful..."

"Relax, I'm being careful," I replied. "Careful and alert. It's just a bit of wind and rain, you know. Unless there's something you're not telling me."

Right on cue, a new song came on the radio. I had to laugh. It was Windy by The Association.

"Oh boy, someone's having a joke with me!" I said. "I

wonder if Lou's telling them what to play?"

The wind blew stronger, and the caddy shuddered as we nosed into it. I had second thoughts about progressing as I remembered the damage left by Hurricane Camille along the Mississippi coast.

"Okay, maybe I'd better pull over and wait it out."

"There is no need," Vaivea said. "You can easily get past this."

I was sure I'd heard something similar recently, but I didn't stop to think about it as I needed all my wits to drive. I peered through the windshield, but all I could see were roiling grey clouds and damp countryside. The rain started again, and a dark line of trees near the road thrashed wildly in the wind.

"I have a bad feeling about this," I said. "Friggin' hell!"

From out of nowhere, a swirling grey tube of wind and dust skeined across the road, sucking everything in its path into its whirling vortex. And I was about to drive straight into it!

4.

I screamed as I stomped on the brakes. The caddy screeched to a stop about forty yards from the tornado, rocking in the wind, and The Association disappeared into a crackle of static. My eyes were glued to the funnel as it vacuumed a path through some shrubs on the other side of the road.

It was breath-taking in its raw natural power. A wide cloud of dust and debris rotated slowly around the lower vortex, from which the grey mass of the funnel widened into a solid bank of tumultuous cloud above. My insides clenched in horror as the funnel wobbled ponderously back and forth on its route towards us.

I felt my brain turn to mush with panic, until a little voice in the back of my head said 'remember who you are'. I remembered, and Wished the caddy a few miles down the road. In the blink of an eye we were past the tornado. It picked up speed as it skimmed away over the empty fields, and the wind dropped as more rain came down. The static cleared as the last jubilant chorus of the song wound itself out. I snapped the radio off and slumped, sick to the stomach.

"You must move," Vaivea said. "There are more of them."

If there was one thing I didn't feel like doing, it was moving. But I felt even less like encountering another twister. Nausea gripped my insides, and I fought it down. Rain hammered at the soft-top as I pulled back onto the road and crept along, peering hard out the windshield.

Despite my shakiness, we got to the next town without further incident. I turned off the highway and approached the first roadhouse I saw, parked close to the building and ran for the entrance. The eerie drone of the tornado siren sent shivers down my spine. The door banged shut behind me, and a couple of guys huddled at the counter turned to look as a radio blared the latest weather service report.

"Do you serve chamomile tea?" I blurted, and sank onto the nearest chair.

The bearded man on my side of the counter hurried to me,

whilst the other one disappeared out back.

"Are you alright, Miss?"

"Uh huh. Just dodged a twister coming into town. My nerves of steel are in slight need of reinforcement."

"Close call, huh? You need something stronger than tea by the sounds of it."

"Nah, gotta keep driving as soon as I'm up to it."

The man shook his head.

"Well, you got more guts than most folk. Say, you're not one of those crazy storm chasers are you?"

"No way. I never want to see another twister that close again, ever."

The other man came out with a steaming mug.

"Here you are, Ma'am. 'Fraid it's just normal tea. Ain't got no other kind."

I thanked him, took it, and inhaled the fragrant steam.

"She was just about run down by one," Beard Man said.

"Really? No wonder you look so shaky there, little Miss. Hope the tea helps."

"Yeah," I said, "me too. I might have something a bit stronger when I get to Oklahoma City."

The men turned back to the radio as a new report was posted.

"And we've just received two confirmed sightings of tornadoes heading south east from the Marietta area, whilst a third has been confirmed travelling due south down the Interstate 35..."

"That one," I said with a shudder. "It was huge!"

"You were lucky to get out of it with no damage," said Tea Man.

The door opened and two fresh-faced young men came in, grinning broadly.

"...a real roof-lifter!" one was saying excitedly. "Nearly took down our barn!"

"Absolutely flattened the Smith's place," said the other. "Not a thing left standing."

"Which one's that, son?" asked Tea Man.

"One heading south," the young man replied. "It was enormous, too. Couldn't see touchdown for dust – there was some wild stuff flying around in there!"

"Well, this little Missy here nearly drove straight into it," said Beard Man, sounding impressed that I was still around to tell the tale.

And then he asked me to tell it. I conveyed it in under a minute, minus any mention of Goddess powers, but it took a good half hour of excited discussion from the men before I could extract myself politely and drive on.

By then the immediate threat was over, and I couldn't wait to get back on the road. Thankfully, the wind had dropped to a strong breeze, and I relaxed a bit. I hoped like mad we'd left behind both vampires and tornados, and although the sky was still cloudy, I cruised along with less worries than I'd had since leaving New Orleans.

"Well, Cheri, you can't say it wasn't exciting."

I groaned. Lou was the last person – er, entity – I wanted to deal with just then.

"Can't I get just a moment's peace?"

"Dull, dull, dull. I thought you'd enjoy seeing nature in all its might."

"If you sent that twister after me," I started, but couldn't think how to finish.

"Oh darling, don't you think I have better things to do than menace you with a whirlwind or two?"

"I can never tell with you," I replied. "So do you have some reason to menace me now? 'Cause if you don't, I'd like a little quiet time."

"Ooh, you brutalise me," Lou complained, but continued to smile.

"I'm beginning to think you like it."

"I'm beginning to think you like doing it."

"Filthy predator," Gran muttered from the back. "You're lower than a skunk's sprayer."

Lou looked proud.

"That's pretty low, I grant you. But I can be much, much lower than that."

"Look, what do you want this time?" I said. "I've already given you my answer about us working together. Not happening. So what else is there?"

Lou removed his sunnies and gazed at me intensely. I knew I shouldn't look, but I just couldn't help it. I glanced over, then set my attention firmly on the road. Silver. His eyes were silver. Well, a soft, lustrous grey with a silver sheen, like a cats eye gem. And he'd never looked more dashing or – dare I say – devilish. I wondered briefly if he was using his powers to entrance me after all.

"What would be the point?" he said softly. "I already have you."

I remembered too late to put up my protective shield. Damn! I wondered if there was really any point, considering who he was.

"You forget," Lou said in a low tone. "I'm not a God or Goddess like you. I'm an angel, a fallen angel, yes, but an angel all the same. You're far more powerful – it is I who needs protection from you."

"That's ridiculous," I said with a frown. "You're the devil, Satan, Lucifer, Beelzebub, evil incarnate. What do you have to fear from me?"

Lou smirked condescendingly.

"I, like you, have many names. But we need to get something straight. I am not Beelzebub. He is a Prince of Hell, and also my Lieutenant, and Lord of the Flies. I am known as The Devil, but there are many entities known as devils, or demons, under my control. Belial and Mastema are names I had early on, and I was later labelled with Lucifer through human mistranslations. Or, if you like, call me Satan, though it more properly meant an adversary or accuser. Let's see, what else?"

"Whoa! That'll do, okay? Didn't ask for your life story."

"Really? But it's so fascinating."

I shot him an exasperated look.

"You don't know what you're missing, Cheri."

"I told you not to call me that."

"Oh. And I do so like it. It suits your French heritage..."

I shot him another look, one designed to wither the strongest oak tree.

"You're no fun today," Lou said with a pout. "Maybe I should just pop on ahead and organise your welcome party in Oklahoma City, hmmm?"

He Vanished before I could say another word. Probably a good thing, because it wouldn't have been a nice one.

5.

Much to my relief, nothing else menaced or otherwise held me up on the rest of that leg, and I got to Oklahoma City in the late afternoon, tired but safe. I stopped at a diner, and plotted my route to New Mexico on my road map over yet another dinner of burger and fries, excited that at last I'd be driving on the famous Route 66.

It was dark when I got back to the caddy, and I headed down the main strip looking for a motel for the night. I kept expecting to see evidence of the welcome party Lou had threatened to organise, but the only indication I saw of his presence in Oklahoma City was that every Jack-O-Lantern I passed winked at me.

I found a motel, had a hot shower, and made myself comfortable in front of the TV. I didn't hold out much hope of finding anything I'd enjoy watching as I flicked through game shows, variety shows, and other programs designed to sedate the masses, and was about to give up when a familiar scene caught my eye. A long, sweeping view of rocky islands in a peacock blue lake, sun-baked colonnades as the camera moved through half-submerged ruins to focus on the upper ramparts of a great granite temple...

"Philae?" I murmured. "Philae! But... It wasn't under water last time I saw it!"

I watched on in horror, and learned that Philae – home to my beautiful temple – had been at least partially under water since the early nineteen hundreds, due to the building of the Aswan Low Dam. Now that the Aswan High Dam was to be built, a huge project launched by UNESCO was underway to deconstruct all the ruins and monuments in the area to be flooded, so they could be rebuilt on higher land.

"But they can't move my temple," I said. "This is a desecration!"

"They must," Gran said. "Otherwise it – and all the other buildings on the island – may be destroyed."

"They shouldn't have flooded it in the first place!"

"They must have had their reasons for building the dam where they did..."

"Gran, they can't do this! That island is sacred! I have to go there – I have to stop them!"

"You must learn to accept temporal matters as they are," said Vaivea sternly. "What has been done cannot be undone..."

"You wanna bet?" I cried, getting to my feet. "I'll *make* them stop! I'll Magic their asses to Timbuktu! I'll rip those dams down with my bare hands, if I have to!"

"It is not the way of Isis to resort to childish threats of violence."

"And nor should Angela Jones," said a husky female voice behind me.

I spun around, the scent of patchouli wafting over me.

"Amy! You're here!"

Amy smiled and held a finger to her lips.

"Hush now, honey. I understand why you're upset. But trust me, this is a small matter compared to what you're really here for."

"It is?"

"Are you forgetting your mission?" Amy asked.

"She's always forgetting her mission," Gran said with a sigh.

"Well, I told you that you were here for greater things, and it's true. You should listen to your spirit helpers, and let them guide you."

"I try," I said, feeling abashed. "But I don't always find them very helpful."

A sudden thought lit hope in me.

"Have you come to be my spirit guide?"

Amy just smiled, and faded softly away.

"No! Don't go... Amy?"

Not a trace of her remained, not even a whiff of patchouli. I sighed, feeling about as deflated as I could be.

"Great! So I don't know if Amy is my guide. I'm not sure what my mission is. I'm not even allowed to go and save Philae. My mother's a dead, alcoholic vampire. My dad's got religion. Gabe could still die. The devil's trying to seduce me. And I'm being stalked by a psycho with two lifetimes of grudges. Could things get any crumbier?"

"Sure they could," Gran said. "But that's up to you, isn't it?"

I shrugged.

"I don't know. I feel so helpless..."

"The Philae that you knew is still there, where it has always been," Vaivea said.

"What, ten foot under water?"

"No. It's past is still available to you, and to all mythic beings. You can still go to it, as it was at any point in history."

I kind of gawped at him, then turned back to Gran.

"What, time travel? How am I supposed – oh, that's right."

I'd again forgotten that I was more than a mere human. I could just twitch my nose like Samantha in Bewitched, and I'd be there. After all, I'd already been there, thanks to Lou.

"Okay, so is there some actual reason I need to go back there in ancient times?"

"That is not for me to reveal," Vaivea said, and Vanished.

"Well, how dramatic," I said. "Did he have to split just as it got interesting?"

"You've heard all you need to for the moment."

"Aw, come on Gran. What's going to happen at Philae?"

"You'll figure it out in time. Then you'll see how serious this all is."

I sighed. Nothing was ever straightforward. I had a whole lot to think about as I curled up in bed, and I mulled over it all for ages before I fell asleep.

Some time later I drifted back to consciousness, then awoke fully with a shock. I seemed to be spinning around and around a bright light. My heart raced, and my body felt strangely contorted.

Panic hit me as I thrashed my limbs about in a desperate attempt to control them. But it was no use. My arms pumped the air at my sides, fanning a fire. I could feel its heat rolling at me in waves, smell the scent of fragrant wood and sweet incense. It was too dark outside the range of the flames to see where I was.

A fresh terror gripped me as a large creature ran my way, screaming. I thought I was about to die.

17

(Get Your Kicks On) Route 66

1. Tuesday 28th October, 1969 – Oklahoma City, Oklahoma

"My baby!"

As the words registered, I saw that the creature was Queen Astarte. I couldn't understand why she looked so big, and why I was looking down at her from a height. But she wasn't the least bit interested in me. Instead, she reached straight into the fire and pulled out a bundle of cloth.

I was too caught up in my own drama to notice anything else. I found myself swooping at the floor, fast. Then, all of a sudden, I stood before Queen Astarte, back to my normal size and appearance. The queen was startled, but stood her ground, hugging the bundle to herself.

"Who are you, that you can take the shape of a swallow and then return to human form? Speak!"

I was a little flustered to hear that I'd turned into a bird without knowing it. But I didn't have time to think about it.

"I am Isis, and by your actions, you have now deprived you beloved son of the immortality I wished to bestow upon him."

The queen's face was a mask of shock as she sank to her knees before me, still clutching her baby.

"Oh, my Lady," she whispered, and bowed her head.

At that moment King Malcander rushed into the nursery room, followed by a number of guards. At the sight of his Queen kneeling before me, he frowned.

"What is this? Is royalty to bow before their servants now?"

He made to help the queen to her feet, but she shook him off.

"We are in the presence of a power far greater than our own," she said in a low voice. "Be humbled before the mighty Lady Isis."

King Malcander stared at me, then silently joined the queen. The guards likewise sank to their knees, followed by two of the queen's handmaidens who had come at her scream. Another moment, I thought, and the whole palace will be here. No wonder Isis wanted to hide her identity. That sort of fame brought a heavy price to pay.

But at least now I understood what was going on. Isis had become a trusted presence in the Royal Palace, and had healed little Prince Dictys, who had been ill. She had become fond of the baby, and decided to make him immortal. She hadn't counted on Queen Astarte's interruption.

"Rise," I instructed. "I have a boon to ask of you."

"Anything you desire, my Lady," the King said, helping the Queen to her feet..

"It is but a small thing to you, but a great one to me. Have you a pillar in your palace which was once the trunk of a mighty tamarisk tree?"

The king and queen glanced at each other in surprise.

"Certainly there is such a pillar here," the Queen replied.

"Take me to it."

They exchanged confused looks, then the king and queen and their retinue escorted me through the palace to the throne room. Central in the room stood a great tree trunk, straight and tall and exuding a sweet, spicy scent. I went to it and ran my hands over the bark, briefly wondering how to get the box containing Osiris' body out of the trunk. But Isis knew what to do.

I laid my cheek against the rough bark, and a string of words I didn't understand slithered off my tongue. Before I knew it, the trunk had split neatly down the centre and moved apart, leaving Set's ornate box suspended in the air between the two halves. I commanded the box to float to the floor, and the tree trunk sealed up again, leaving no indication of ever having been sundered.

All those around me exclaimed in surprise, but I barely heard them. I knelt by the box – the coffin of Osiris – and slumped onto it, sobbing, my tears falling on the inlaid ivory and gems on the lid. My mind grew hazy, dark clouds swirled around me, and I woke up hugging my soggy pillow and sniffling.

The room was dark, although it was near seven in the morning. I rose and dressed silently, feeling too solemn to talk to Gran. I stopped at a diner for breakfast, then made tracks through Oklahoma City. Finally, I was on Route Sixty Six. With the soft top down, the wind in my hair, and the radio on, my spirits started to lift. Even if I did have to endure some dreadful Halloween-themed songs like I Was a Teenage Creature, and House of Horrors...

I thought about going to my temple on Philae by travelling back in time. The images from the documentary were still fresh in my mind, and so were my memories from when Lou took me there. Sparkling blue water, picturesque views, stately structures covered in vivid paintwork. I remembered the chanting of my priests and priestesses, and a feeling of excitement grew in me.

El Reno came and went in a flash, and then we crossed the Canadian River Bridge, with its panoramic view. Small Route Sixty Six towns flashed by – Sayre, Erick, Texola. The landscape stretched barren and desolate in all directions – mile after mile of prairies with few distinguishing features. Keeping in suite, the radio station came up with way out old tunes like The Graveyard by The Phantom Five, and Dead by The Poets.

Just after Texola, we crossed back into the Texas panhandle. The caddy ate up the miles as the highway ran in a nearly straight line over the endless prairies. I stopped for lunch in Amarillo, then continued on through the open country.

Small communities and isolated farm houses whizzed by as I burned up the road in a blur of tarmac and wide blue skies. Over the border in New Mexico, I stopped at Cline's Corners to use the facilities and check my map. A bit further on, I noticed that we'd left the plains behind. Cuttings rose on each side of the highway, and I soon felt the rise in elevation as I wound through the hilly country.

Soon I found myself driving into the blazing late afternoon sun. Lucky my sunnies are dark. Real dark. At Albuquerque, I grabbed some takeout and found a picnic spot alongside the Rio Grande to sit and eat, and watch the sunset. Shades of pink and orange spilled across the pale western sky, and a fiery glow stained the dusky horizon, though a large, glowing moon was already visible.

I checked into a motel, made my room as dark as possible, and slipped into bed. Gran settled nearby and Vaivea disappeared for the time being. Although it had been a long drive and I was tired, my mind was too active to go to sleep right away, so I decided to do a regression.

I closed my eyes and focussed on the Temple of Philae. I hoped that would ensure a regression as Isis to that place, but I was wrong. When I became aware of being in her world, she wasn't in the stately, peaceful temple with the soothing chants of her priests and priestesses in her ears.

Instead, Isis struggled through a dark marsh in a delirious panic. Tall papyrus plants swayed around her on the evening breeze, stars twinkled in the velvet sky above. She seemed unfocused and blind to her surroundings. All that mattered was that she return to her hiding place. Her thoughts were so scattered that I wondered if she was being chased by something so terrible that even the mighty Isis couldn't overcome it.

"Sister! Stop, please..."

A shadowy figure appeared just ahead, limned by the moonlight. I gasped as I recognised her, though how, I don't know. In this life, Karen looked like an ancient Egyptian woman – long black hair with bangs, honeyed skin, and dark, almond-shaped eyes. She also appeared to be distressed, just as Isis was.

"Where is he?" Isis gasped, skidding to a stop.

"I... I'm sorry," Nephthys faltered, tears rolling down her face. "Sutekh tricked me, I swear it..."

Isis cried out and leapt forward. She burst into a small clearing surrounded by date palms and thorny shrubs. Set's ornate box sat squarely in the centre, although she'd left it hidden in the bushes, with her sister to guard it. The lid lay to one side. Isis stumbled as she reached the box, sensing what she already feared was true.

The box was empty. Osiris' body was gone.

2.

"No!" Isis screamed.

She collapsed by the coffin, sobbing. A night breeze turned the tears icy on her face. Isis was too sunk in her misery to notice. Her love was gone once again, taken from her before she had a chance to return him to life. Engulfed by the racking sobs, I didn't notice my return to the motel room in Albuquerque. When I finally became aware of my change in location, I nearly jumped out of my skin.

"Jeez, I didn't expect that!" I said as I looked for Gran's comforting glow. "I'll never get used to all this zapping about."

"Yes you will," she said, gliding to my side. "Why don't you practice doing it intentionally? Then when it happens by accident you'll be more attuned to it."

"Of course," I said. "I should've thought of that. But where will I go?"

Gran smiled and shook her head.

"How can you even wonder that when you left your heart back in Jacksonville?"

"Gabe!" I said. " I'll visit Gabe!"

I closed my eyes and Wished myself to Gabe's hospital room. Seconds later I stood right next to his bed. Light from the corridor lit the room faintly, and I saw his chest rise and fall evenly in the semi-darkness. But his eyes were still shut, all his facial muscles relaxed in sleep.

"Gabe," I said softly. "I'm here. I've worked out how I can come and visit you whenever I want to, just by Wishing myself here. I love you so much."

I sat on the edge of the bed, held his hand, stroked his face, whispered my love, for half an hour or more. I also wondered when I was going to learn how to heal him, and hoped it would be soon. Then I kissed his forehead, wished him sweet dreams, and returned to my motel room.

I got into bed, but I still didn't feel like sleeping. With a sigh, I reached down for the bag of books where I'd stashed them beside the bed, and looked for one that might lull me off to sleep.

I was immersed in a volume of world myths, trying to get my head around the complex relationships between the deities of the ancient Greeks, when a warning tingle told me I was being watched. I rolled over to look around – straight into a pair of fiery red eyes. I squealed in terror.

"Darling, must you make such a dreadful noise? I've heard wild boars in the Australian outback make more appetising sounds."

"Fiend!" I hissed. "How did you think I'd react to those awful, flaming red eyes? Change them! Now! Or I won't ever talk to you again!"

My boldness took my own breath away, but I guess by then my goddess status must've sunk in. Lou obediently toned down his eye colour to amber, then hazel, which suited him curiously well. It served to make him look even more mischievous than usual as he lounged on the other side of the bed.

"Is this more to your liking?" he asked.

I frowned. Every word he uttered dripped with innuendo.

"It's better," I replied sulkily.

I really hoped he'd go away. Gran hovered nearby, glowing a faint red, but silent. I could pretty much imagine what she would have liked to say. Mostly because I felt like saying it too.

"What, no quick wit?" Lou asked. "No stinging retorts? No savoir faire?"

"No ma cheri, no sauvignon blanc, no caviar, no pâté de fois gras?"

I couldn't help but bite back. I only wished I had managed to pick up some real French on my way through New Orleans.

"Ooh la la," Lou chuckled, apparently delighted. "For you, my dear, anything."

A gleaming silver platter Appeared on the bed between us, upon which rested a small crystal bowl of black caviar, a slab of pâté, delicately thin water crackers and two glasses of a golden white liquid. I sighed.

"Is it really made from goose livers?"

"The pâté? Only the finest livers from the fattest geese."

"Gross. I think I'll pass."

He waved his hand and the pate Disappeared.

"I didn't much feel like it anyway," he said, handing me one of the wine glasses. "Far too rich to eat just before bed."

I sipped, then sipped again. It was a mellow, fruity wine, and I enjoyed the sweetness of it.

"Of course, ambrosia would be more fitting," Lou said.

He smiled indulgently and flicked his tongue over his lips in an unmistakable gesture. I stared, not because I wanted to, but because I had for some reason entertained the notion that the devil had a forked tongue. It seemed rather odd that he didn't. He mistook my interest, and arched his eyebrows even more.

"Darling, why not stop all this silly pretence and just do what comes naturally?"

My gaze moved from his sensuous, full lips to his twinkling eyes. I knew what he meant, but for some reason I just didn't have it in me to argue.

"Not tonight," I replied dryly. "I have a headache."

I tossed back the rest of the wine, threw the glass over my shoulder and rolled onto my side, putting my back to him. I also used my powers to switch off the bedside lamp. I don't know what became of the wine glass. I didn't hear it smash, so I assumed Lou had Vanished it.

The weight on the bed behind me lightened, and I hoped that he'd Vanished, too, but it was just the tray of goodies Disappearing. There was another adjustment of weight as Lou settled in right behind me. I heard his quiet breathing, felt his longing for me. I'd never get any sleep while he was there.

So I Wished myself to Karen and Eric's apartment in L. A., thinking I could just hide out there until Lou had gone. I'd visited Karen and Eric only once since they were married, and hoped I remembered the layout of their apartment well enough to Wish myself to a spot where I wouldn't be seen.

It worked, because I found myself laying on the floor of the walk-in wardrobe connected to their bedroom. I heard raised voices, and quickly Wished myself Invisible in case one of them opened the door.

"You must have known!" said Eric. "How could you not know?"

"Honey, you have to believe me," Karen said. "I had no

idea."

I could hear the tears in her voice, and my heart squeezed. I hoped little Newton was fast asleep and couldn't hear his parents arguing.

"Do you have any idea how big a shock this is for me?" Eric said. "To find out like this – this way – and now. What were you thinking?"

"Darling, I'm so, so sorry," Karen said, her voice trembling. "If I could take it back and undo it, I would. I had no idea this would happen. Honestly."

I seemed to have stumbled in at a very bad time. My curiosity was madly aroused, and resentment at Eric's manner prickled me unbearably, but I knew I had no business hearing this argument, that whatever it was, I had to hear it from Karen's lips and not by listening in on a private conversation. Though my heart bled for my sister, I closed my eyes and Wished myself back to my motel room.

To my surprise, Lou still lay exactly where he'd been when I left. I wondered if angels (or demons) actually slept and if I should just park myself on the sofa to avoid unwanted contact with him. I didn't know where Gran was, and Vaivea didn't seem to be around either.

Lou snored softly, and indignation swept through me. How dare he! Well, I wasn't going to let him chase me from my own bed. I didn't care if he was faking sleep – all the better if he was. I'd so catch him out if he tried any monkey business, and he wouldn't get away unscathed! I moved as close to my edge of the bed as possible, and fell asleep thinking of suitable punishments should Lou even dream of misbehaving.

3.

Early morning light moved gently through a gap in the curtains. It flashed across my face and brought me back to consciousness. I blinked, too full of hazy, sleepy warmth to want to move. And the arm draped heavily around me felt so comforting. I wondered briefly if I was dreaming of the time Gabe and I had gone to New York City together, to meet his folks.

Then my memory kicked in, and my stomach clenched. Had I just spent the night in bed with the devil? I felt his warm, soft breath on my neck, the tickle of his goatee on my shoulder, the weight of his body pressing against my back. I lay for a while almost paralysed, wondering how to get out of it with the least damage, and if I would ever be able to look Gabe in the face again.

A faint shimmer near the foot of the bed caught my eye. Vaivea stood there, still, impassive. I groaned inwardly as I remembered his admonishments about my weakness for the temptation Lou offered. I hadn't believed him at the time, but now I saw how very naive I'd been. I'd softened my attitude towards Lou, and he'd wedged open the chink in my armour with expert skill.

Still, I never had been one for self-pity or backing down, so I decided to brazen it out. I took a deep breath and abruptly sat up.

"Well, that was interesting," I said as I stood and stretched.

"What was, my dear?"

I turned and looked down at Lou. He'd tucked his arm back against his chest, but otherwise hadn't moved. He gazed languidly up at me, a gentle smile on his face. The effect was almost touching – until I noticed his eyes.

"Eww, that's just wrong," I said.

"What is, my dear?"

I screwed my face up in distaste.

"That. Your eyes. Pink. So gross."

"A reflection of my feelings for you, ma cheri."

"Rubbish. Change them or I'll chunder right on you."

Lou sighed and changed his eyes back to hazel. I had to admit, it suited him.

"So what was so 'interesting', darling?"

"That you behaved yourself," I said dryly as I grabbed out clean clothes for the day and went to the bathroom to change.

I don't know what made me think Lou would respect my privacy – he obviously wouldn't need to maintain a physical presence to spy on me if he wished – but even so, I felt it important to keep up my standards, especially after my slip-up. When I came out, Lou had a simple breakfast of hot ham steaks, a leafy salad, crusty bread, and cheese spread on the table. I didn't think twice about tucking in. I was ravenous.

"Don't you think you should be more careful?" Gran said from behind me.

"Yeah," I said around a mouthful of food. "This bread is so fresh! Mmmm!"

I looked around for something to drink, and a steaming mug of coffee Appeared.

"I've tried yours, now you try mine," Lou said from his side of the table.

"For Pete's sake!" Gran huffed, and disappeared.

"Oh dear," Lou said. "What can the matter be, do you think?"

I wagged my knife at him.

"She has a point, you know."

Lou eyed the utensil.

"So have you, my dear."

"Sorry. But she's right. Here I am, sitting down to eat with the devil. Most people would be mortified."

"Well, thankfully you're not most people. Actually, you're not even people. You're better."

I cleaned up everything on my plate, and sank back in my chair with the mug of coffee. Lou had sampled various parts of his own meal, but hadn't consumed a great deal. I suddenly felt self-conscious about stuffing myself so heartily.

"Thanks for the chow," I said, striving to stay flippant.

"You're welcome," Lou said, and Vanished everything from the table with a sweep of his hand. "It's a pity you want to rush off, my dear. You do realise that you can simply Wish yourself and your belongings to L. A.?"

"Sure I do. But how am I going to explain to Karen why I got there so fast? I think I'd better stick to driving. Besides, I promised dad I'd scope out Route Sixty Six for him."

"In that case, I'd better not hold you up any further. Au revoir, ma cheri."

Suddenly he was gone. I blinked and looked about. Something stirred inside me, and I clenched my teeth and swallowed it down.

"For goodness sake, get a grip," I told myself. "He's the devil!"

It was cool and gusty outside, and I forgot about Lou as I settled into the car and drove out onto the road. Gran Appeared next to me, and I jumped.

"Thanks for the warning," I said. "Have a nice trip?"

"I've just been visiting with Karen," she said.

"How is she?" I asked, suddenly worried for my sister.

"Things are difficult in her life at the moment."

"Difficult how?" I asked as we turned back onto Route Sixty Six.

"Her situation is causing her great emotional distress."

"Eric?" I asked, wishing Gran would just get right to the point.

"Partially."

"Can you tell me what's wrong? If he's not treating her right, I'll kill him!"

"The problem is their private business, and you know very well that Karen will tell you if you ask her."

"I know. Is there anything I can do to help?"

"Just be there for her when she does decide to tell you," Gran answered.

I took some deep breaths. My body seemed weighed down with all the worry I felt for my sister, and I tried to let it go for the time being. So I turned up the radio and lay down some serious rubber on the Rio Grande bridge and beyond. Steppenwolf blared all around me, the soft-top was down and my hair whipped back in the wind. Yes! I was born to be wild!

Gran and Vaivea were quiet, although, to be fair, they would've needed a big-ass megaphone to be heard over the radio. But the music helped take my mind off Gabe, and Karen, and the rest of the mess I had to deal with.

After Albuquerque, all was a vast nothingness of flat, reddish plains, punctuated at intervals by sharp-pinnacled hills and flat-topped mesa. The country became mountainous as I crossed the dark lava flows before Grants, then more plains surrounded by sagebrush, great red bluffs and towering mesa approaching Gallup.

Just over the border in Arizona stretched a string of stores and Native American trading posts. I wondered if I should stop for a look. I'd heard that some trading posts sold cheap imported goods, and tourists often didn't know the difference. On a whim, I pulled over.

"Vaivea, I want some real Indian beads for Karen, seeing as I lost those beads I got in New Orleans. Can you please tell me what's authentic in here?"

"As you wish."

I entered one of the stores, my ghostly entourage behind me. An elderly Native American woman and middle-aged man behind the counter greeted me. Then the woman did the best double take I'd ever seen. But it wasn't me she stared at. It was Vaivea and Gran. Judging by her expression, I figured she could see them plain as day.

"It's okay," I said nonchalantly. "They're with me."

If possible, she looked even more dumbfounded. She whispered to the man as I turned to the nearest jewellery stand to examine the squash blossom necklaces and beaded bracelets there. I soon found something I knew Karen would like – a delicate turquoise beaded bracelet with sterling silver feather charms. Vaivea verified that it was authentically Indian made, and I took it to the counter.

The man served me. He took the bracelet with trembling hands, and glanced behind me again and again as he gift-wrapped it and took my money. The woman hung back, and spoke as the man handed me my purchase.

"You walk with the spirits, little one."

"My mother still believes in the old Navajo ways," the man said with a nervous smile. "She says a Ghost walks with you."

"Two," she corrected. "One is Indian. He does not rest in the Happy Hunting Ground, but is attached to the living. And the other is a blood relative. Please, be gone from here before you attract more of these spirits to haunt us!"

"These are my companions," I said. "My spirit guides. They go where I go."

She leaned back a little and stared at me.

"You attract all kinds of evil things. Spirits of the dead seek your company. Soon the coyote will cross your path and the owl will call your name, and worse again. Leave this place!"

4.

I hurried from the store, got in the caddy and roared away down the highway.

"What did you have to go and rile her up for?" Gran said.

"I happen to think a little mutual respect might have gone a long way. It doesn't matter, nothing happened to get bent out of shape about. Anyway, do I really need to worry about coyotes and owls?"

The afternoon sun glared on the Little Colorado River as I drove. The rolling prairies offered little to look at, except more prairies. And sky. Famous Route Sixty Six trading posts flashed by – Geronimo Trading Post, Jack Rabbit Trading Post, where I stopped to snap a photo of the giant jack rabbit for dad. The radio kept up the Halloween theme, this time with Ghost Guitars, Werewolf, and on the same theme, Mr Were-Wolf.

The smell of rain preceded the clouds that built heavily on the horizon. I stopped at Winslow and put the soft top up, then headed into the approaching storm. The sky darkened rapidly, the wind gusted, and it started to rain as I passed Winona. Trees, shrubs and boulders flitted by outside my windows. I felt tired, and concentrated harder on my driving as we continued through intermittent showers.

I'd forgotten the Navajo woman's words from earlier. The only thing on my mind was the road ahead. Then trouble hit unexpectedly. The front driver's side tyre blew out, forcing me to pull over.

"Far out!" I said, examining the damage by torchlight as rain pelted the waterproof poncho I held over my head. "I wonder if there's a mechanic in Flagstaff..."

"Do we have to keep reminding you who you are?"

Gran sounded exasperated, and I couldn't say I blamed her.

"Of course. I'll just wriggle my nose and it will be all fixed. Brrrr!"

I straightened and looked around. There was little to see. Patches of dead grass, bushes and trees swaying in the wind. It registered that I felt nervous. I turned back to the car, but had the irresistible urge to look around again. That's when I worked out that I was being watched.

"Okay, who's out there?" I asked my guides as I swung my torch around in an arc over the landscape.

"Nothing of consequence," Vaivea said.

I huffed in annoyance.

"Don't shine me on, man. It feels pretty darned creepy and I want to know who or what the hell it is."

At that moment, an abrupt thrashing of wings drew my attention to some bushes a bit further back from the road. I swung the torch that way, and two yellow, disk-like eyes glared back at me.

"Whhooo whhooo! Whhooo whhooo!"

"Not me," I answered sarcastically. "No points until you know my name."

Then an eerie moan became audible. I jumped, pointing my torch this way and that as it increased in intensity to a full blooded howl.

"For crying out loud," I said, rolling my eyes. "That Navaho women jinxed me! Hey Gran, coyotes don't usually go near people, do they?"

The howls became louder, more mournful, then suddenly cut off. I swung the torch around again, but I already sensed that the coyote was moving away. Even so, I sure didn't want to stick around to find out. I Wished the blown out tyre repaired and got back in the caddy.

"Stay alert," Gran advised me, a warning note in her voice. "Why?"

"Just trust me."

"Gran, is there something I need to know about up ahead?"

"Just stay alert and be careful."

I sighed and rubbed my forehead. Spirits sure could be frustrating.

"Why? Is the talking owl going to guess my name? Or do you think that coyote will come back and perhaps pee on the tyres?"

Thunder rumbled and lightning arced across the sky with an electric sizzle as the rain became heavier. It thundered down on the soft top and cut vision significantly. I decided to wait until it eased, and put my headlights on high beam, staring ahead intently through the back and forth slash of the windshield wipers. Shadows leapt and swayed in the darkness outside, misted by the downpour of rain. An eerie prickle crept up my spine.

Then I heard a new noise over all the others. I listened hard, barely breathing. Grunts? Whines? Someone shouting? I reached out with my mind and immediately picked up on fear. Someone nearby was terrified. And coming my way fast.

18

The Burning of the Midnight Lamp

1. Thursday 30th October 1969 – Flagstaff, Arizona

Seconds later, a man ran onto the road. He was dark-skinned and wore an old parka, jeans, and hiking boots. He scrambled to the passenger side door and yanked it open.

"Hey!" I exclaimed in alarm.

"Back up!" he cried as he thrust himself into the seat and slammed the door.

"I'd like to know what's going on first," I said, too curious to be annoyed.

His eyes bulged as he stared through the windshield. He barely spared me a glance as I spoke. I could smell his terror, a sweaty, feral stench.

I reached out with my mind once more, and came across another presence. It was some species of animal, though what, I couldn't tell. The overwhelming impression was of curiosity, though there was fear and rage mingled in with it.

"Are you gonna back up or what? It'll rip your soft-top open like the lid of a sardine tin if you don't move!"

"What's out there?"

"Are you a goddam crazy woman or something? It's enormous and it stinks and its gonna kill us if we stay here! Let's get going!"

Suddenly he froze, the whites of his eyes showing. I followed his terrified gaze, and my breath caught. At the edge of the pool of light from my headlights, something very large shambled onto the road. It stood erect like a human, a good eight feet tall, and was covered in dark brown hair. I could just make out beady eyes beneath a prominent brow ridge, shining eerily red in the glare of the headlights.

It turned and disappeared into the shrubs, long arms swinging. I turned back to the man, who was just about hyperventilating.

"Bigfoot," I said casually, though I was kind of excited. "Doesn't like confrontations, from what I've heard. Vegetarian, too. Relax, it's gone."

The man sat stiff as a ramrod, as far back into the seat as he could get. Only his eyes moved, flicking my way before returning to the scene of his terror. He took a deep breath and finally relaxed.

"Bigfoot, huh? That's amazing. All these years of hiking in the wilderness, and I've never seen one before. You sure it's gone?"

I reached out with my mind, but traces of the creature had faded.

"It's moving away to the northeast," I said.

The man ran a trembling hand over his lower face, then turned to me with a strange expression.

"How you know where that thing's heading? You psychic or something?"

I shrugged as I pulled back out onto the road and drove on.

"Yep. Good thing I was here, or it might still be on your trail. You never know what might happen with wild creatures."

"Yeah, well it sounded pretty mean. It started chasing me a couple of miles back, an' I wasn't inclined to hang about an' see what it wanted."

The man sat silent for a moment, then shook himself back to the present.

"Sorry, I should be thanking you. I'm glad you turned up when you did, even if that thing wasn't dangerous."

"Hey, that's okay. If I hadn't stopped for a flat tyre, I would've been long gone before you even got there. Call it a twist of fate."

The man snorted softly.

"Yeah, guess I know all about that."

Something about him bothered me.

"So, what were you doing all alone in the middle nowhere, in this weather?"

"I could ask the same of you."

"Just heading to L.A. to visit my sister," I said truthfully.

There was a pause before he continued.

"Oh. Well, I just like hiking. I was checking out Walnut Canyon over there, the Indian dwellings and stuff. It started raining, and then that thing came after me."

"Did you drive here? I could take you back to your car."

"Er, no, I've just been hitching rides along the way."

Something wasn't right. I tried to see his aura out of the corner of my eye. It wasn't very bright. I slowed the car and glanced over. Lots of darkness, patches of grey and brown.

"Um – is there anywhere you want to be dropped off?"

"You heading into Flagstaff?"

I nodded. I didn't want to keep his company any longer than necessary.

"Yeah. I can drop you there."

"That'll do. Long as I can get back on the highway tomorrow and hitch a ride."

"Where are you heading?"

"Not sure. East. That's all I know."

"Just following the sun?" I asked.

"Huh, yeah," he said with a sudden laugh. "Or the maybe the moon..."

Uh oh. Crazy as. Like, straight from the cuckoo's nest. I glanced at him again. His eyes glinted in the darkness and my heart thudded even harder. I didn't dare drive any faster with the rain pouring down, so I put up my psychic shield, just in case.

And not a moment too soon. The guy groaned and rubbed his temples, then he started to breath heavily again. I didn't know what was going on with him, but it freaked me out big time. He looked over at me with a pained expression.

"Blasted full moon," he croaked as his body went into convulsions.

"What's happening?" I asked, trying not to panic.

"Sorry – that – time of – the month..."

He attempted to laugh, but the sound turned into a serious of yelps. I looked his way again, and saw that his teeth had lengthened into fangs and fur had sprouted wherever his skin showed.

I was paralysed with fear. I'd picked up a werewolf, and he was changing right in my car!

2.

I pulled the caddy up on the side of the road. I had to decide super-quickly whether I should get out and run, or pray for help and take my chances. The guy stopped convulsing, and leaned back in the seat, breathing heavily.

"Not – funny, huh?"

"Um," I said, wishing my brain would work.

It didn't help in any way, shape, or form that the next tune the radio played was I'm The Wolfman by Round Robin.

"Yeah – guess not," he groaned.

I couldn't think what to say, so I attempted to calm my feverish thoughts and decide on a course of action. The first thing that popped into my head was the irrational idea that I should Wish him to the moon – only that could make it rather dangerous for any future astronauts who went up there. The second was a voice – Gran's voice.

"Remember who you are, my sparrow. Remember!"

Isis. So, what would Isis do? Isis was a healer... I looked over at the guy in the passenger seat. The transformation was still in progress, slowly changing him from human to werewolf. His nose had lengthened, morphed into a snout, and his ears had grown long and pointed.

"Are you kidding?" I thought. "How on earth can I heal THAT?"

But my brain finally ticked over. Lycanthropy was an infection, and an infection was simply a type of negative energy. Energy could be cleansed and purified until it was balanced again. That was what all spirit-based healers did – manipulate energy. And Isis was considered a great healer. So...

"Er, I know this might sound strange, but I'd like to try and heal you."

The form in the other seat yelped painfully in laughter, which sent his body into spasms again.

"Okay, try to stay calm and I'll do what I can."

I closed my eyes and retreated into my mind. My third eye, centred between my physical eyes, opened, and I saw the man's energetic form. Being a werewolf, he had adopted many animal instincts, but I sensed that he'd struggled to retain his human qualities and to come to terms with his condition. I felt great pity and sorrow for all he'd been through, and called on my inner resources with true intent.

"I am Isis, and I have the power to heal," I said inwardly. "I wish to heal this man, who was infected through no fault of his own. For the highest good, let me find the way to help him."

A tingly feeling welled inside me, and travelled from the root of my spine up through my body until it reached the crown of my head. My inner vision saw my chakras spinning, all with clean, clear colours, perfectly balanced and giving off powerful energy. The energy gathered, then moved down my arms and out my fingertips, into the man's body.

The rainbow colours travelled through his being, activating his diseased chakras. They turned slowly at first, sluggish from the infection, then rotated faster and faster, until they spun like pinwheels in a wind. As they spun, the darkness in his aura faded, dissipating until only clean, bright light surrounded him. It was done. I withdrew my powers, cleared and grounded my mind and body, and opened my eyes.

The metamorphosis had reversed, leaving the man as he'd been before it started. He stared at his hands, then felt his face. Finally he turned to me, his eyes nearly bugging out.

"Friggin' hell," he whispered. "It's gone. It's really gone."

I was elated for him, for the success of my daring venture. I was also exhausted from doing such intense energy work. I raised a faint smile and breathed deeply.

"So, how do you feel now?"

He shook his head and stared at me, then at his hands again. "I..."

He lapsed into silence as he examined his arms, his chest, his upper legs. Finally he pulled himself together.

"I feel – fine. I – you... I should be a slavering beast by now, I should be ripping you apart... What happened?"

I laughed softly, which was all I had the energy to do.

"You wouldn't believe me if I told you. But you are cured."

"Cured? You cured me? I've had this for years. I thought there was no cure."

"Believe me, you are cured."

"Really cured? How? Who – what are you?"

I didn't know how to answer that and not sound certifiably insane, so I just smiled at him. It didn't help.

"Lady, you're really starting to freak me out. You're almost scarier than that Bigfoot. I don't even know your name!"

"Sorry. I'm Ange."

I extended my right hand and waited. He hesitated, then shook it.

"Lester."

"Of course you are," I said, and laughed again. "I should've guessed."

"Huh? Now you're getting really freaky. Maybe I should've taken my chances out there with that other thing after all."

"You're looking for Amy," I stated.

He stiffened, staring at me hard.

"I'm psychic," I said with a shrug.

"Yeah, okay, that's cool. I got no problem with that. Can you tell me anything about her – like how she is, where she is?"

"Yes. But I'm afraid it's not good news."

His face fell.

"Amy?"

"I'm sorry," I said softly. "Lester, she's gone."

Lester sagged into his seat and sighed deeply. Tears gathered in his dark eyes, but he no longer questioned my mysterious knowledge.

"Do you know how?"

"Her house burned down."

"Oh shit," he said, and sobbed noiselessly for several minutes.

I sat in silence while he grieved, wishing I had better news. While we sat there, I sensed another presence in the car with us. It seemed familiar, especially when I caught a whiff of spicy scent.

"Lester, I think we have a visitor."

He looked up in surprise, and glanced out the windshield and windows.

"Not out there. In here."

He frowned at me, tears still trickling down his cheeks. Then he smelt the patchouli.

"Amy! Amy, love! Of course – you're in spirit now!"

"Yes, honey," came Amy's voice, wavery through the ether. "I'm sorry I couldn't come before now. But we'll never be apart again, I promise."

He sobbed again, whether from joy or sadness I couldn't tell. He finally pulled himself together enough to talk.

"I'm still tracking Jesse, after all these years. More slippery than an eel, that one. I was right on his heels until we headed into the desert country a few weeks ago. It took me ages to pick up his scent again..."

"He found me," Amy said, and Lester gasped. "He tracked me down where I was living in Florida. That's when the house burnt down. You won't have to track him any more, honey. He's dead."

Lester nodded as her words sank in.

"I'm just sorry it came at such a cost," he said with a heavy sigh.

"So, shall we keep going to Flagstaff?" I asked.

"Sure," Lester answered. "As good a place as any to start a new life, I guess. Thankyou for healing me, Ange. You've given me my life back. I owe you big time."

"Thankyou from me as well, honey," said Amy. "Bless you."

"My pleasure," I said, pulling back out on the road. "What will you do now?"

"I don't rightly know," Lester answered. "I'm supposed to have been dead for years. I don't officially exist. But I still got a bit of money that I saved, and I guess I'll work something out."

"I hope so, Lester," I said. "And Amy, I've wanted to speak to you so badly..."

"Honey, I know you have lots of questions and want some answers. But I can't interfere in the course of your journey. I'll just tell you this – you have all the help you need for the moment."

"I so want you to be my guide," I said hopefully.

"That would be a great honour. Please, just trust for a little longer that things are happening the way they are for the best outcome."

I sensed that I'd exhausted that topic. A few minutes later, we cruised into Flagstaff. The rain had eased, and I pulled up at the first gas station I saw. Lester got out and walked around to the driver's side window to say goodbye.

"Take care of yourself, Lester," I said. "And good luck."

"Thanks. I'll probably need it. I have no idea where I'm going. But I'll be okay, as long as Amy and I are together, even in this way. Bye for now."

"For now," I echoed, as he walked off.

"For now, honey," I heard Amy's voice in my head.

I glanced after Lester as I pulled out onto the road again. I just made out a shimmery presence walking by his side, arm about his shoulders, a wild tumble of hair swaying down its back.

3.

As I drove on, I couldn't stop thinking about what I'd just done. I'd used the power of Isis to heal someone. And not just any sort of healing – I cured a werewolf, for goodness sake! I couldn't help but think that it was time to try my powers out on Gabe, to heal him. I only wished I'd known how to do it in time to save my mother.

I checked into a motel room in central Flagstaff, carrying my bags and a burger and fries. I buzzed with so much excitement, I could barely swallow the food. I brushed my teeth thoroughly, anticipating lots of kisses after I healed Gabe, and took some time to freshen up, as I didn't want to go too early and find his family still there.

Finally I took a deep breath and Wished myself to Gabe's

hospital room. I found it dark and quiet, but still Wished myself Invisible, just in case. The sound of the ventilator and other hospital equipment seemed unnaturally loud, and I heard the low murmur of voices from the corridor as doctors and nurses went about their business.

I moved to Gabe's bed and gazed down on him. He didn't look any different to the last time I'd seen him, except his aura seemed a little duller than before. I prepared mentally, calmed myself as best I could – although the prospect of soon having Gabe restored to good health made my heart thrum crazily, like Keith Moon's drumming – and I got started.

Just as I had with Lester, I asked to be a conduit for healing, and soon my energy was on the move, flowing down through my hands into Gabe's body. My third eye saw the energy moving over him, flowing throughout his own auric field.

But it was different this time. The healing energy didn't merge into Gabe's energy field as it had with Lester, and therefore didn't affect his chakras. It was as though there was a force field around him, keeping other energies out. I moved my hands to different parts of his body, trying to find an access point, but there wasn't one.

After a few minutes of trying to pour healing into Gabe, without success, I started to feel light-headed. I realised that I was depleting myself of energy in the attempt to heal Gabe, and reluctantly withdrew. Tears welled up in my eyes. What on earth had gone wrong? I'd healed a werewolf, so surely I could heal Gabe?

"I'm sorry," I whispered. "I tried. And I'll keep trying until I do heal you, okay? I won't give up, I promise."

I kissed him on the forehead and Wished myself back to the motel in Flagstaff. I was so tired, I barely stopped to take my boots off before I crawled into bed still dressed, sank into the soft pillow, and fell asleep. Only seconds later I found myself blinded by blazing sunlight. My hands flew to shield my eyes, and in the moment it took for them to adjust, I cast my senses out. But I was utterly alone.

I felt hot sand burn under my feet. The high dunes around me funnelled the heat and glare of the overhead sun straight into the valley through which I walked. The wind gusted, a harsh, dry wind that whipped up wisps of sand and flung them across my path in feathery curtains. My eyes felt gritty, and I realised that Isis had walked this lonely path for some time.

But the discomfort I felt on the outside was nothing compared to what I felt inside. A horribly hollow sensation in my heart and stomach dominated my senses. It was as if someone had ripped my insides out. Once again, Isis had lost her beloved. Set's voice had rung out across Kemet, boasting of his latest despicable act. And every ear that heard his voice regretted the hearing, and every eye bore a sea of tears, Isis more than any other.

"It is not possible to destroy the body of a god! Yet I have done it – for I have destroyed Usir!"

His laughter had echoed through the land, and all who heard it trembled and hid. All but Isis, consumed by grief, and her sister Nephthys, riddled with guilt for allowing Set to trick her into revealing the location of Osiris' body. Together, the sisters went forth to search, as jealous Set, Lord of the Desert, Lord of Chaos and all that was evil, had torn the perfect body of Osiris in to fourteen pieces and scattered them across Kemet, to prevent Isis from ever returning him to life.

I awoke immediately, in shock. I'd read the myths of Isis and Osiris and knew that this would happen, but that didn't take away the horror of living through it in the regression. Especially after what had happened in Gabe's hospital room. Or rather, what hadn't happened. I tried to go back to sleep, but it was futile. I tossed and turned until after midnight, then decided to pack myself up and leave.

"It's not wise to skip your sleep," Gran said, shimmering softly beside me as I pulled out of the motel parking lot. "You'll regret it."

"Look, there's no way I could sleep now. I'll be careful, I promise."

I Wished my thermos refilled with strong, hot coffee, and kept driving. Wilson Pickett kept me company at first, singing In The Midnight Hour. In the dark I passed through Seligman and Kingman, then the highway turned south. The rain had stopped, and pale moonlight struggled through the tattered clouds, casting a watery sheen over the empty plains.

The Black Mountains rose and fell in the distance, an inky, jagged outline on the eastern horizon as I crept nearer to California. I turned the radio up a little more to distract myself, hoping that Wolfman Jack would cheer me up with his banter.

"Oh yeah, baby, this year is gonna be the ookiest, the kookiest, the spookiest Halloween ever!" came his gravelly voice. "And these cats from England are as spooky as they come! Let me ask you, baby – are you feeling *pink*? Ooooh, I can tell you, I'm sure feeling pink! Like Pink Floyd – and Lucifer Sam!"

And right on cue, as the song started, Lou Appeared in the passenger seat.

"Are you enjoying your dreary trip, ma cheri?"

"I was."

"Just for once, couldn't you greet me in a civil manner?"

"Just for once, couldn't you just take a hint and leave me alone?"

Lou sighed deeply.

"My darling, we've been through so much together and still you treat me with disdain. I do wish you'd accept my help and my presence in your life. I'm not going away just because you hurl offensive remarks at me at every opportunity."

"You're not, huh?"

"No."

Lou bopped with the music until the song ended, then cleared his throat dramatically.

"You can't ignore me forever."

"Yes I can."

"Forever's too long a time."

"Wanna bet?"

"Fine. We will continue this conversation later."

"You're going?" I asked hopefully.

"For now. But it is strictly au revior, my dear, not adieu!"

Lou touched his fingers to his lips and blew me a kiss, then Disappeared. Too late, I flipped him the bird, and cursed under my breath as I returned my attention to the road. We continued around the end of the Black Mountains, whose rocky escarpments frowned darkly under the moonlight. Finally we crossed the Colorado River, which was also the California state line, continued to the north, and arrived at Needles. I breathed a sigh of relief on my return to civilisation.

Civilisation it might have been, but at three o'clock in the morning, the place was dead. My lack of sleep was starting to catch up with me, so I parked in the first car park I came to and snuggled under a picnic blanket on the back seat. I don't know how I got to sleep under such uncomfortable circumstances, but I must've done so because waking up occurred abruptly some time later, as the first rays of the dawning sun forced their way in through the windows of the caddy.

I groaned as I stretched all my joints. It was then that I noticed my picnic blanket had been augmented by the addition of a soft, black woollen blanket with a large silver 'L' embroidered in the centre.

"Lou been here, huh?"

"'Fraid so," Gran muttered.

I left it at that and got out of the car. The air was crisp, and I breathed deeply as I looked around. I found an eatery that opened early, breakfasted, and had my thermos filled with coffee. Finally, I found a payphone and rang Karen to let her know my progress, only to be greeted by her scared, breathless voice.

"Ange, is that you? Thank goodness you rang – I'm so scared I don't know what to do..."

4.

"Why? What's going on?"

"That – *thing* – I told you about? It's getting worse! It keeps looking at me out of mirrors, not just Gran's but the one in the bathroom and my hand mirror and the windows and the television and anything else shiny..."

"Whoa – what? You mean you're seeing it everywhere?"

"Yes! Anything that casts a reflection – I even saw it spying on me from my saucepans last night! And from the faucets, and... and *spoons*! Eric thinks I've gone crazy, because I keep jumping and dropping things. I just want to pack Newt up and get out of here until you arrive, but I can't because I'm expecting the plumber..."

"Okay, you just stay put and I'll be right there..."

"Really? Are you in L.A. already?"

"Not quite. I've just crossed into California and I'm ringing from Needles. But look, I promise I'll be there very soon."

"It'll take you at least five hours to drive all that way – you won't get here until after lunch time..."

"Er, I know a shortcut. Just trust me, I'll be there much quicker than that. See you soon, okay?"

"If you say so. Please drive safely, Ange – I don't know how I'll manage if anything happens to you!"

My heart clenched painfully at her words. I wanted to tell her everything would be alright, but I'd have no time to explain why until I got there. Back in the caddy, I started towards Barstow at a leisurely pace, California Sun blaring from the speakers. All around stretched desert plains of parched grass and low shrub. Rocky brown hills rose abruptly at intervals, only to subside again. Mountains in the far distance appeared like smoky bumps on the horizon, blue light playing on blue shadow.

Despite my worries, I found myself enjoying the drive. With the soft-top down, my hair whipped back in the wind, and I felt at peace. My failure to heal Gabe still haunted me, but I figured that I must've used up so much energy healing Lester that I didn't have enough to heal Gabe at the time I went. So, I'd just try again later, when I was well rested.

I drove until I thought Eric would have left for work, then I Wished the caddy to the parking bays underneath Karen and Eric's marina apartment. I sat there quietly for a while, trying to work out what to say to Karen, how to explain my ability to get from one side of California to the other in such a short time. And the rest of it. I knew I had to tell her the whole truth, from beginning to end, but I felt sure she'd ring for the men in the white coats to come and take me away before I was even halfway through my story.

I gathered my luggage and found my way up to the building's foyer. It was a bright and breezy morning at the marina, but the crisp tang of salty ocean air did little to help me think. I stared at the payphone for another few minutes before picking up the handset and dialling.

"Karen?"

"Is that you, Ange? Where are you calling from? Has something happened?"

"No, it's okay. Can you come down to the foyer?"

"Why? You can't possibly be here yet – it's less than an hour since you rang from Needles…"

"Look, I'll explain everything once I'm there. I just need you to come down to the foyer because I'm dead tired and I can't remember what number your apartment is."

"Okay, Newt and I will be right down."

As I replaced the handset, I looked for Gran and Vaivea. They both shimmered beside me.

"Look, I'm not sure what I'm going to say to Karen yet, so please help me out if you can, okay? She's already not going to believe half of this…"

I watched as the display above the nearby elevator lit up with the number three.

"And this 'thing' Karen keeps seeing? If she's really in some sort of danger, I'd appreciate as much advice as you can give me…"

The elevator pinged as it reached the ground floor, and the doors slid open. I couldn't help but grin as Karen and Newt appeared before me. Newt wriggled in his mother's arms.

"Put me down, Mama! I wanna see Auntie Ange!"

Karen lowered him to the floor with a smile. The child ran at me full pelt, and I laughed as he threw his chubby little arms around my legs.

"Hey Auntie Ange! Mama told me all about you. Are you coming to stay?"

"I sure am," I said as I knelt and hugged him back. "And your Mama's told me all about you, too. I bet we'll be best friends."

I drank in Newt's appearance. I'd seen photos, of course, but that wasn't the same. He'd inherited most of Karen's facial features, but with darker colouring. His skin was a rich, honeyed tone, his thick, wavy hair so dark it was almost black, and he had big, melting brown eyes. In fact, he looked almost the complete opposite of Eric in every way. Something else about him seemed familiar, but I couldn't think why.

"Sis," Karen said as I stood up.

She hugged me fiercely, wiping tears from her eyes.

"Whoa, I'll have to visit more often," I said, laughing as I hugged her back.

"Ange, I've missed you so much! Let me look at you!"

She held me at arm's length and we gazed at each other. I took in her soft, rounded face, warm brown eyes, perfect nose, shoulder-length chestnut hair, luxuriant and wavy, and marvelled that two such different individuals could be so closely related.

"You don't look as scrawny as usual," she said with a wicked grin.

"Really? Gee, after all those days of driving and eating and sleeping..."

"You haven't changed," she said with a smile. "Come on, let's go up."

I shouldered my bags as Karen swung Newt up to her hip, and we entered the elevator. I quickly told them the cleaned up, tourist-friendly version of my road trip without any mention of vampires, werewolves, ghostly spirits, angels, Isis, and especially Lou. The elevator pinged as we stopped at the third floor, where we continued on around the corner and down a long corridor. Karen unlocked a door near the end and led me into the apartment.

"Sorry to put you in with Newt, but I thought it would be more comfortable than sleeping on the sofa. He does sleep through the night."

"That's okay. I doubt he could wake me tonight if he threw all his toys on me and set them on fire."

"Ange! Don't give him ideas!"

She led me into Newt's room, where she'd set up a mattress on the floor with blankets and a pillow. I dumped my bags and we went back out to the kitchen, where Karen made us mugs of coffee. I noticed a transistor radio on the counter, and switched it on, catching Spooky by the Classics IV. Newt had scrambled onto a chair at the dining table, where he was busy drawing with crayons in a large sketch book.

"He's always busy creating," Karen said proudly. "Either he's drawing and colouring in, or making things with his building blocks. We were thinking of buying him a Meccano set for Christmas."

"Sounds like he really takes after his father," I commented.

At that, Karen's face clouded. I drew her into the kitchen, away from Newt.

"Hey, what's wrong?" I asked. "Are you and Eric going to

be okay?"

"I don't know. Thing's were already rocky, and now this... this 'thing' I've been seeing... I tried to ignore it, but it appears so suddenly that I nearly always scream or gasp or drop something. Eric thinks I'm going crazy, which is making everything a hundred times worse."

"And he hasn't seen anything strange himself? No? What about Newt?"

"I'm not sure. I've seen him looking at the television set when it wasn't even switched on, looking really hard as if he was trying to work out what he was seeing. This morning I heard him talking to it, but it was switched off. I can't tell if he's just playing pretend, or if he's seen this thing himself."

"I sure hope it pops its ugly mug up for me to get a look at," I said. "If I can work out what it is, I might be able to work out how to get rid of it."

"But what if it's dangerous? I'm scared to go too close to any of the mirrors or the TV or anything, just in case."

"I don't imagine it really is," I said. "It hasn't tried to hurt anyone, has it? I'm surprised anything like that would even know you were there, after what Amy told me."

"Your psychic friend? What did she say?"

"That there's a very good reason why you've never seen anything weird..."

Karen's eyebrows arched upwards.

"Please listen, sis," I begged. "You have a charmed life. Dark things don't come near you because they don't know you're there. You don't know how lucky you are."

Karen sniffed.

"I wouldn't call myself so lucky, or charmed, or anything like it. If you knew the mess my marriage is in, you wouldn't either."

"Tell me," I said. "Please tell me."

"Okay. Well, basically, we've just found out that Eric isn't Newt's father."

19

Bad Moon Rising

1. Friday, 31st October, 1969 – Los Angeles, California

I was stunned. I'd had no idea what I would hear, but I hadn't thought it would be anything like that.

"When Newt was so ill a month back, and the doctors thought he might need a blood transfusion, Eric was the first to put up his hand. Then when they tested his blood, they found he wasn't a match. So he's not Newt's biological father, and now he's angry at me and it's all a mess..."

Tears poured down Karen's cheeks, and she wiped them away. I was still in shock, wondering how on earth it had happened. Karen would never sleep around. But at least I now understood what they'd been arguing about when I'd Wished myself to their apartment.

"Sis, I'm so sorry. I don't know what to say."

Karen nodded as she struggled to control her emotions. She blinked away her tears and composed herself.

"You know," she said, "I've thought and thought, trying to work it all out. And there's only one explanation that fits. You remember my bridal shower?"

"Yeah, I wish. I couldn't even go. I was so sick from the flight over that I spent two days in bed while my guts danced the twist inside of me."

The memory still rankled.

"Well, remember how I told you I went to a discotheque with some of the girls from work that night, and saw this really cute guy?"

"Yeah."

"I – I didn't tell you all of it at the time," Karen said quietly, and looked down at her clasped hands. "I did a bit more than just have a drink with him."

"Oh Karen," I said, and reached for her hands.

"I didn't mean to be unfaithful, exactly," she continued, her voice trembling. "But he was such a hunk, and I thought what the heck, it'll be the last time I get to do something fun and dangerous and impulsive before settling down."

I swallowed down the heaviness I felt around my heart. I didn't want to cry and make Karen feel even worse. Besides, we'd have to think of something to tell Newt if we fell about the kitchen bawling.

"Didn't you use a rubber?" I asked.

"Yes, but – it broke. I cleaned myself up straight away, but I guess it was too late. And it's funny, you think, 'that won't happen to me', but it can, and it does, and then what? A marriage falling apart because of one stupid slip-up…"

Fresh tears sprang to her eyes, and she let them fall. I put my arms around her, and looked over to check on Newt. He stared back at us with wide eyes.

"It's okay, Newt," I said, a little wavery myself. "Your mother and I are having a good old heart to heart."

"Is Mama crying?"

"A little, but she's okay now."

Karen somehow manifested a radiant smile that reassured the little boy, before turning back to me.

"Look," she said, "it's a bad situation, but I'm trying to win Eric around."

"Right."

Personally, I didn't hold out much hope. Eric didn't strike me as having the generosity of spirit to forgive and forget, and happily settle into being a father to someone else's child.

"Well, he's been Newt's daddy for three and a half years," she continued. "Being a father is about more than just the biological side of it."

"It does explain why Newt doesn't look anything like Eric."

"I know. Before the blood test, I'd just put his colouring down to dad's Egyptian and Welsh blood."

"So this guy?"

"He looked kind of Middle Eastern. I never got around to asking. But he'd obviously been raised in America."

"Do you remember his name?"

"Oh, Abraham or something biblical sounding. It was pretty noisy. And I didn't want to ask again in case I sounded stupid. I didn't think it would matter anyway, after that night."

Karen wiped her eyes, and I rubbed her shoulder gently. Gran hovered at her other side, giving what comfort she could. I hated seeing my sister in such misery, and tried to think of something to cheer her up.

"Hey, just give me a moment," I said. "I've got something for you."

I went to Newt's room and dug Karen's gifts out of my bag. When I returned, I held one in each hand, inviting her to choose. She took the blue velveteen pouch that contained the unicorn necklace, opened it and slid the pendant out on her hand.

"Ange, it's beautiful," she cried, her face radiant.

She held the chain up to her neck and I clasped it for her. Then she opened the parcel with the Navaho beads.

"Oh my, real Indian beads," she said, delighted. "Turquoise, too."

She put the bracelet on and hugged me again.

"Thanks for thinking of me. I wish I had something nice for you."

"No, it's my pleasure," I said with a laugh. "They're gifts to thank you for having me here. Especially considering the circumstances. And I also got you some Mardi Gras beads in New Orleans, but they kind of got commandeered for other uses."

"I don't think I'll ask," Karen said with a laugh. "Thanks – I love them. You know, let's go and get some fresh air. We could walk down to the Mother's Beach..."

"I thought you were expecting the plumber."

"I rang the company and they said he'd come tomorrow or the day after. So we're free to go out, if you want to."

"Sure, sounds good."

Karen packed Newton into his stroller, we took the elevator to the ground floor, and then walked to the road that ran through the complex. The signs of recent construction were still evident – ground bare of plants, the smell of fresh paint and sawdust, the sound of heavy machinery on the other side of the marina. Some of the land was still open and unbuilt on, though nearly all the marina basins were crowded with small boats and yachts in the slips.

"This will be nice when it's finished," I said hopefully. "Though I still don't know why you wanted to live here."

"Oh, it wasn't my choice, exactly," Karen said. "I would've been happy anywhere, but Eric really wanted to live by the sea and he fell in love with this area."

"It must cost a fortune."

"Yeah, it's not cheap."

Karen didn't sound happy.

"But he can afford it, right? Being an architect and all."

"Only just. He's still only a junior in his firm. We have to go without a lot of things to afford that place. But it's worth it, I suppose."

I uncharitably wondered if Eric was more in love with the bragging rights that accompanied such a property. A seagull swooped and landed on the ground ahead, eyeing us boldly. It reminded me of my trip to Destin with dad.

"You should visit home sometime. Dad would love to see you and Newt."

"Maybe. And what about you? Where are you off to next?"

That caught me by surprise. I'd deliberately put off thinking about it, because I didn't have a clue what to do once I got to L.A., apart from protecting Karen from her mysterious threat, and telling her the whole story about – well, everything.

"I didn't really make plans."

Karen frowned.

"That's not like you."

"Maybe I'm mellowing in my old age."

"No way. What about Gabe? If something like that had happened to Eric, I would never have gone and left him there in hospital to travel across the country. I don't understand why you did that."

"Look, I didn't want to go. But I just had to."

"What do you mean?"

"It's kind of hard to explain."

"You're not just running away?"

I stopped dead, and Karen stopped the stroller beside me.

"Running away from what?"

"Well, Gabe being shot in front of you must've been horrific. You could still be in shock. And then not knowing if he'll be okay, and then his family saying you couldn't see him any more. Maybe, deep down inside, you couldn't cope with being in Jacksonville any more, and you felt you just had to get away."

I blinked. It sounded reasonable, but I knew better.

"Look, Karen, there's heaps I've still got to tell you – stuff you're barely going to believe. What happened to Gabe *was* horrible, but so much has happened since then, and most of it not very good... Did I tell you that my friend Amy was killed when her house burnt down? Or that I've had creepy things stalking me all the way here? And you know what? That's just scratching the surface!"

2.

Karen gasped in shock, and I forced myself to calm down.

"Ange... Why didn't you tell me these things were happening?"

"I couldn't. Not over the phone. I had to wait until we were face to face because honestly, I'm still trying to deal with it all. Just give me a chance to catch up to myself, and I'll tell you everything, okay? I know I'm asking you to trust me big time, but you have to. I promise everything will turn out for the best!"

Karen frowned, confused. I started walking again, and she pushed the stroller after me. The road curved and ran towards a small, protected beach. The sea breeze was fresh and made my skin tingle, and I breathed deeply. We passed a line of change rooms and then walked onto the beach itself. Karen let Newt out of the stroller.

"Don't go too far," she called as he pattered off.

We watched as he made patterns with his hands and feet in the sand, picked up shells and pebbles and brought them back to show us.

"So," Karen said. "What *are* you going to do now? I thought you were coming to stay for a short holiday, and I had enough trouble just getting Eric to agree to that."

"I really don't know. I'm kind of just waiting for inspiration to hit me."

"We still don't get why you drove all that way. He thinks you're mad for not flying."

"He probably thinks I should've ridden my broom, too," I said.

Karen sighed.

"I'm sorry you don't like him. I wish you'd given him a chance at the beginning instead of just declaring war."

"Hold on a minute – I declared war? I gave him every chance, even after I realised I didn't like him. It was *him* that didn't like *me* at first glare."

"See? You've always got to be right."

"And he hasn't?"

Karen bit her lip. Newt ran up with a shell, which we dutifully examined and exclaimed over, then he scampered off to look for more.

"Hey, I'm sorry," I said. "I'm trying to learn not to be so judgemental of people. But it does help if they're trying too."

"I know. He can be very – straightforward at times. I hate to admit this, but a lot of my friends can't stand him. In fact, a couple of them won't see me any more because of him. He's not easy to be with."

My heart overflowed as I hugged her. She hugged me back fiercely, tears sparkling in her eyes.

"We'll just have to stick together, sis," I said, patting her shoulder.

Newt approached again, this time with a long strand of brown seaweed.

"Yuck," Karen said. "Please don't bring that any closer. I can smell it from here."

He giggled wickedly and dropped it on the sand, then dashed off again. I couldn't help but laugh, and Karen joined in. We continued along the beach slowly, the striking blue of the marina off to our right. Newt ran up with a fistful of small pebbles he'd collected, all washed smooth by the sea.

"Lovely, darling," Karen said sincerely. "Much nicer than seaweed."

He left the little pile on the sand and went off on a new adventure. Karen gazed off into the distance, a dreamy, faraway look on her face.

"Remember when we were at New Egypt?"

That threw me momentarily, but then my brain kicked in. New Egypt, New Jersey, was where we'd lived when dad was stationed at McGuire Air Force Base. We were only there for a couple of years, and I'd just turned six when dad got transferred on, so I didn't remember a lot about it.

"Just. Why?"

"Remember our holidays at Point Pleasant those two summers? How we'd go down to the beach, and dad'd help us build sand castles, and Mama would sit under that huge umbrella so she wouldn't get burned? I think that's why I love the sea."

The memories awakened and I smiled. As far as I could recall, it had been a happy life in New Jersey. And I could understand Karen's sentiments about living by the sea – after all, I did myself. Then, like a thunderclap, the names clicked in.

"Hey, New Egypt!"

"Yeah?"

"Well, don't you think that's a bit more than coincidence? With dad's heritage? We should've lived in New Hanover – that was closer to McGuire – but we didn't."

"Yeah, dad always said he couldn't resist. He thought it was a great joke."

Karen smiled, then took a deep breath and turned back to me.

"Can you at least tell me what's going on with Mama and dad?" she asked. "What's really been happening at home?"

"Okay. When I turned up, dad was back and it looked like they'd made up."

Karen frowned.

"There's more to it than that, isn't there? I know you – I know when you're not telling the whole story. And I rang dad, and he kind of glossed the whole thing over."

"Well, what do you expect? He was embarrassed about having made such a goat out of himself over that girl. He just wanted to settle down and put it behind him."

"Sure. But what about the dog attack? What really happened? I've never heard of dogs biting anyone on the chest –

let alone a full grown man!"

"Yeah, I know. It was weird, and there is more to it. And I don't really know where to start…"

"Just start at the beginning," she said.

"I wish it was that easy. I'm not even sure what the beginning was – whether it was Gabe getting shot, or the weird stuff back when I was a kid, or if it was thousands of years ago, when the Ennead first walked the earth…"

"Ange, you're making no sense. What are you talking about?"

Newt toddled up with a pretty piece of driftwood, bleached to a creamy white.

"This is for you, Aunty Ange," he said solemnly as he held it out.

"Why, thankyou sweetie," I said as I took it.

I watched him scamper across the sand, then turned back to Karen, who looked as confused as all hell.

"Er – do you want to sit down somewhere?" I asked.

Karen took a deep breath and shook her head.

"No, we'd better go home. It's nearly lunch time. Newt – time to go!"

Newt's face fell. He begged for more time, but Karen was firm. She strapped him into his stroller, and he threw a little tantrum and cried for a couple of minutes. Karen picked up the pace going back, leaving us too out of breath for small talk. When we reached the apartment, Karen launched straight into making sandwiches for lunch, whilst I made us mugs of coffee.

We kept the talk light-hearted while we ate. Newt asked lots of questions about where I lived and what I did at work, and I told him about the happier aspects of dealing with animals at the clinic. Finally Karen bundled him off for his afternoon nap, and I piled our lunch things in the sink and started washing them.

"Thanks," she said when she returned, and grabbed a towel to do the drying. "It's such a struggle to get him to take naps now. He thinks he's too big for them."

We finished the washing and drying in silence while the radio hurled more Halloween songs at us — I Dig You Baby by Bob McFadden, and Beware by Bill Buchanan. After Karen had put everything away, she turned to face me with an expectant, inquiring look.

"So, is now a good time?" she asked. "I need to know what's been going on. So, come on, sock it to me."

I felt suddenly awkward and tongue-tied. I had hoped this moment would come later. Much later.

3.

"Er... Okay. Just let me grab something that'll help me explain."

I figured if I had to tell Karen about everything, I might as well have a little help from my collection of books. But on reaching Newt's room, I found him sitting by my things, having pulled most of the books out to look at. I watched him for a moment, amazed that he was so gentle, almost reverential, with them. Most three year olds, I thought, would be ravening to tear the pages out and drawn on them with crayons. He must've felt my gaze on him, and looked up at me brightly.

"Horsy!" he said, and pointed at the pages before him.

I knelt beside him. He had the book on mythical creatures

open, right on the pages about unicorns. I couldn't help but grin.

"That's a unicorn. Did you know your Mama likes unicorns too?"

He looked up at me with eyes older than time. It made my heart ache.

"Who's that lady, Auntie Ange?"

I blinked and looked around. No one else was in the room, just us and Gran.

"Which lady do you mean?"

"That lady there."

I knew then that he could see her. I didn't quite know how to explain.

"That's your great grandmother Jones. Have you seen her before?"

He nodded emphatically.

"Yes!" he said. "She comes here lots, but she never says anything."

"That's because she hasn't got a body, like us," I said, hoping not to freak him out. "She went to heaven a long time ago, but she visits whenever she can."

"Don't sugar-coat it for him," said her crackly voice. "He's an old soul, as if you couldn't tell. He understands more than you think."

"Wow, she talked!" Newt cried. "Say something else, Gran'ma!"

"Indeed I shall," Gran said. "I've often wanted to, but I didn't know how Karen would take it having me hanging around, let alone hearing me talk."

"Probably freak her," I said. "She's never been into anything spooky."

"Speak for yourself!" Gran said with a chuckle. "Nothing spooky about me!"

"You're not spooky Gran'ma," Newt said. "I like you."

"And I like you. In fact, I love you very much."

The door creaked open a crack, and Karen peered in.

"I heard talking," she said. "Newt, aren't you supposed to be taking a nap?"

Before I could say anything, Newt jumped right in.

"Mama, Gran'ma's here. She talked to me!"

Karen smiled and came into the room.

"That's nice, Newt. But isn't your grandma back in Florida?"

"No, she's here. She's right beside you, Mama."

Karen turned slowly, and her eyes searched the room. I could tell she was unsettled by Newt's words.

"He means our Gran, Karen. Grandma Jones."

Her face cleared, and she smiled.

"Do you know, there've been so many times when I'd swear I felt her presence. Do you think she really comes to watch over us sometimes?"

"Yes, she does," I answered. "She watches over me, too."

"Wow," Karen breathed as tears sprang to her eyes. "No wonder I've always felt her love so strongly."

Gran put her arms around Karen and Newt clapped his hands gleefully.

"She's hugging you, Mama! Like this."

He threw his arms around me and squeezed tight. I was so tickled pink by his childish exuberance that I laughed from right down deep inside, somewhere that hadn't been touched like this in a long time. I should've known it was too good to last.

"An' who's the other lady, Auntie Ange?"

I stiffened and looked around.

"Mama! What are you doing here?"

Karen looked at me like I'd suddenly grown another head. I stared back, desperate to Wish myself to a deserted tropical island where there was nothing I had to explain to anyone anytime. But I couldn't run out on my sister and leave her hanging.

"Okay, let's get Newt settled back down, and I'll tell you everything."

Karen looked at me hard, then she got Newt back to bed as I gathered up my books. As I stood and shouldered the carry-all, Newt grinned at Mama, and she made cute faces back at him. I could've puked. I'm sure she never did the 'aren't-you-a-cute-baby' routine with me when I was small. I just hoped like hell he wouldn't ask about the red scar across her neck.

As if things weren't crazy enough already, I heard the chorus of They're Coming To Take Me Away issuing from the radio in the kitchen. I grimaced, and used my powers to turn the volume down lower. Karen led the way out of Newt's room and closed the door. I dumped the bag of books on the dining table, and we sat side by side.

"Now, are you going to tell me what's going on?" she asked. "What really happened with Mama? Why can't I even contact her? And what was going on in Newt's bedroom just then?"

Damn, I wished I had got in first. But I didn't, and knowing I had a lot to explain, I proceeded.

"Okay, the thing with Mama was, I found out she was adopted."

Karen stared at me in disbelief.

"Adopted? You mean Nan and Pop Urkhart aren't our real

grandparents?"

"Looks like it," I said.

"She never told me!"

Karen's eyes filled with tears, and I grabbed her hand.

"Hey, she never told me either. She never even told dad. But at least that means we're not really related to the Urkharts, which is fine by me."

"I like them," Karen said with a sniff.

"Well, you can stay friends with them if you like. But I can't stand them. Stuffy, prim and proper – they should've all been funeral directors."

"They're not that bad," she said, giving me a look. "So did you find out anything about Mama's birth family?"

I'd dreaded this question. The words of Patrice Moreau echoed through my head, and I shuddered.

"Well, her mother lived in New Orleans all her life. Mama tracked her down not long after I was born and visited her from time to time."

"So that's why she went away every now and then," Karen said. "I wish she'd taken us! So what else do you know?"

Karen's tone became hungry, urgent. I weighed up carefully what to reveal.

"Her name was Patrice Moreau, and she had French and Creole heritage."

"And?"

"Sorry, sis. That's it. I was told there might've been a connection to Marie Laveau, the famous witch queen of New Orleans, but probably lots of people living there say that, just because she was someone famous. Or infamous."

"That's it? That's all you found out?"

I smiled half-heartedly. Karen leaned back in her chair, her face sad.

"Poor Mama. I wish she'd told us. I wonder why she never said anything."

I shrugged, and hoped that would do. But then Mama floated forward.

"I couldn't tell you, honey! Patrice Moreau was a very evil woman, and I had to protect you both from her!"

I sat stock still as Karen turned to look at me quizzically.

"Did you say something?"

"When?"

"Just then. I'm sure I heard a voice."

"Really? What did it say?"

"I don't know. It was just a whisper. Maybe I imagined it."

But Mama, heaven forbid, couldn't leave it at that. She gathered her energy and put on a full-fledged manifestation, speaking loudly and clearly right at Karen's face.

"I said, Patrice-Moreau-was-a-very-evil-woman-and-I-had-to-protect-you-both-from-her!"

4.

Karen gasped and her face drained of colour.

"Mama? How did you get here – why can I see through you? What's that scar?"

She reached to touch Mama's arm, and her hand passed right through it. Mama, perhaps running low on energy, faded away. I bit my lip as Karen turned to me in shock.

"Mama's a ghost? But that means she's..."

"Sis – I'm so sorry. She had a – sort of – accident... I was just about to tell you."

I comforted Karen as best I could for the next half hour as

she cried quietly into her hands. I'd hoped to get away with an edited version of the whole tale, but clearly, I was mistaken. I could barely meet Karen's tear-filled eyes as I wondered how best to explain the rest of it. So I decided, once she'd finished crying, to tell her the plain, blunt truth and get it all out of the way.

"Karen, Mama passed away. She and our grandmother, Patrice Moreau, were..."

I stopped myself just in time as I spied Newt peering out of his bedroom door. I tried a more creative approach.

"Er, you remember Grandpa on The Munsters?"

Karen looked bewildered.

"Grandpa? Yes, but he was a..."

"Yeah, I know," I interrupted before she could say the 'V' word. "Well, let's just say that Grandma Moreau is one too."

Karen looked even more baffled.

"You mean... but that's impossible! They don't even exist – do they?"

"Yes, they do."

"But how? I thought they were just myth."

"Believe me, they're real. I had a swarm of them on my tail out of New Orleans. I thought I was dead meat for a while there."

"And she was one of them?"

"Yes. Well, not the ones that were chasing me, but she's one of their kind."

Karen raised a sceptical eyebrow.

"Look," I said, "there are lots of supernatural things out there that we can't prove exist. This is one of them. These creatures are real. I've seen them. I've talked to them. They came after me. One of them stood right on the bonnet of the caddy. I wouldn't make this up, Karen."

She nodded, the hint of a frown on her forehead.

"I guess people have believed in them for a long time," she said shakily, "and there's usually no smoke without a fire."

"I'm sorry. I know this is hard for you to believe. But it's true – Grandma Moreau is one of them, which is why she gave up our mother as a baby, because she didn't want her to be infected with it."

"Did you actually – meet her?" Karen asked.

I hadn't wanted to even admit that our newly discovered relative was still alive and kicking – or pricking, considering her fangs. The last thing I wanted was for Karen to get all het up and want to go meet said relative for herself.

"Yes, but it wasn't pleasant. She warned me to leave and never come back, and to tell you not to try and track her down. She's dangerous – she said so herself – and she doesn't want to infect any more family members."

Karen stiffened.

"Any more? You mean..."

"Look, she made the mistake of letting Mama get close, and the temptation was too much in the end. She said the urge to feed and spread the infection was too strong."

Karen's face twisted in horror, although I also saw fascination in her eyes.

"Our mother? She turned our mother into one? Oh Ange."

She fell into silence, sitting so still I started to wonder if she was quietly having her own private nervous breakdown. Or maybe nineteen of them... I kept talking to fill up the space.

"It was Mama who attacked dad. Once she was fully converted, she could take on the form of a wolf, and that's what bit him. So..."

"Stop. Just stop."

Karen's voice was calm, but her eyes were so turbulent I could only guess at the storms brewing inside her.

"I'm sorry. I know it's a lot to take in."

"Ange, this is all too weird. It's the stuff of fantasy. But you say it's real. I've never seen anything to suggest they even exist. I don't know what to think. If you're telling the truth, we're all in big trouble. And if you're not – well, you've been through a lot lately, and maybe there's some kind of treatment that could help you..."

"Whoa, just a minute! Okay, seeing Gabe shot was bad, and being thrown out by his family. And losing Amy, and then Mama – you know what? I was faced with having to kill my own mother because of what she was. She would've infected dad too if she wasn't stopped. And I've been chased and terrorised by all kinds of creatures you can't even begin to imagine. Who'll I tell all that to without being locked up, huh? Who?"

Karen seemed to be in a state of shock. I glanced over at Newt's bedroom door, hoping he wasn't distressed by my tone, but by then, he'd sat himself quietly down with his building blocks in the loungeroom, and appeared not to be interested in our conversation. I inhaled deeply and faced Karen again.

"Look, you're right – it has been difficult. But what you're talking about won't help me. No one trained in any institution you can name will take any of this seriously. I had a hard enough time getting you to. And there's still heaps you don't know."

I knew Karen was horrified by what I'd said, but she was going to have to hear it sooner or later.

"What do you mean, kill your own mother?" she said, incredulous. "Are you completely demented?"

5.

"Look, most – of them – have no conscience about who they feed off or infect. Patrice Moreau did, and she only caved in after years of contact with Mama. She said she didn't want to, but it was too strong to fight. Mama didn't have a second thought about biting dad when she came home from New Orleans. That's what I was facing."

"You would've killed our Mama? Oh Ange – that's murder!"

"It wasn't Mama any more! Mama as we knew her was gone, leaving a wild, bloodthirsty monster in her place. And dad would've been her first victim. And then who? Me? You? Newt?"

Karen shuddered as she glanced over to where Newt was playing in the loungeroom.

"So what happened? You never said what happened to her."

"Let's just say a guardian angel stepped in and stopped her."

"A guardian angel? Like, with wings and a halo and heavenly choirs?"

"Er, no. I mean, he is an angel, but he doesn't go in for all the trappings."

"So," Karen said, "you're telling me an angel of the Lord came down into our parent's house and – and – killed our mother because she was a you-know-what?"

I had to admit, it would sound ridiculous to most people. But as Lou had so astutely pointed out, I'd never been most people.

"He's a very special – angel. He's been helping me out for quite a while now."

I realised that despite all the times I'd rejected him, insulted him, and otherwise told him to buzz off, Lou had often been there when I was in need, helped me learn, and even saved my skin once or twice. That didn't sit well. I suddenly felt awkward, like I should thank him or something. *Thank the devil?* No way, not for all the tea in China!

"Ange, this is all too horrible, and too weird. I honestly don't know what to believe any more."

"I know, sis. A month back, I wouldn't have believed half of it either. But it's all real. I've had to get used to it very quickly. Which mightn't have been so difficult if I still had Amy to help protect and teach me."

"So how do you know it's real and not just in your head?" Karen asked, giving me a searching look. "How are you so sure you haven't just dreamed all of it up..."

"It's not a dream. Huh, sometimes I wish it was, but believe me, it's not. Listen, why don't you try ringing dad? Ask him what really happened with Mama, and how he was saved from her, and how he was healed. I'm not sure how much sense he'll make, but just try it."

Karen sighed, and slowly, like she was moving in a dream, got up and walked to the telephone in the hallway. I heard her voice as she greeted dad, followed by a long period of conversation where she spoke intermittently in a low voice. Finally, she hung up and came back to sit by me at the dining table.

"Well?" I asked.

"Yeah. His version tallies with yours, even with all his talk of God and avenging angels and stuff."

"Now do you understand why I waited to tell you about it? I couldn't have told you over the phone, and I couldn't just blurt it all out once I got here. And I would've done anything I could to save you all this pain and heartache, but you had to know all of it, the honest truth of it, for your own – and Newt's – protection. As it is, I've still only told you the half of it..."

Karen's face froze in a horrified grimace.

"Only half? Ange, I don't know if I can bear to hear any more of this!"

"Alright... How long until Eric gets home from work?"

Karen checked the wall clock in the lounge area.

"About an hour, if he gets away on time. Surely it won't take that long to tell me the rest of – whatever it is?"

"It might. If I keep going now and tell you everything, I want you to hear it all without any interruptions."

"That's a nice way of saying you don't want Eric walking in on it."

"Yeah, okay. I don't want Eric to hear 'cos he won't believe a word, and frankly, I don't have the patience to deal with him. If you make me, I may end up tying his arms and legs like a pretzel and stuffing a pineapple in his mouth to shut him up."

Karen's face clouded.

"I guess you're right. His level of tolerance is pretty low at the best of times, but with the way things are at the moment, they'd be practically non-existent."

"Because of the thing with Newt?"

"Yeah. It's made him really raw. And don't call Newton 'Newt' in front of Eric. He hates it."

"Look, why don't we take a break and see if we can tempt this thing in the mirror to show itself to me?" I asked. "Who knows, I might be able to do something about it."

Karen set Newt in front of the children's shows on the television, and reluctantly led me to her bedroom.

"I covered it over so I couldn't see that thing looking at me," she said as she crossed the room and swept a bedsheet from an antique floor mirror. "Of course, Eric thinks I'm insane – I told him that the full moon shines on it through the window at night and keeps me awake. He said to just move it, but..."

I walked up to the mirror. Its elegant mahogany frame shone with polish, the bevelled cut glass etched with a simple floral design top and bottom. I remembered it standing in Gran's bedroom when I was a child, and I was glad she'd left it to Karen. I sat on the edge of the bed, peering intently into its reflective surface.

"Nothing nasty there now. Just a beautiful old mirror."

"I know," she said. "But do be careful. I haven't been able to work out if there's any pattern in when that thing shows up..."

I'd allowed my eyes to wander around the room, but was jerked back to attention at Karen's scream. There, in the mirror's surface, loomed a dark figure. Its lips curled back in a silent sneer as it swiftly reached through the glass and grabbed hold of Karen's arm!

20

She Said She Said

1. Friday 31st October 1969 – Los Angeles, California

I leapt up and grabbed Karen's free arm, just as the figure pulled her towards the mirror. She screamed again as she was tugged one way, then the other. I stared at the form in the glass. There was no mistaking the elongated snout, squared-off ears, and vivid red hair.

"Let go, Set!" I growled through my teeth, giving him a death glare.

"She is mine by right of marriage," he snarled back, tightening his grip.

Karen blanched in pain and started to cry.

"She doesn't know about Nephthys yet!" I said. "Give her time to understand..."

"I have wasted too much time already," Set said, his voice as steely as his gaze. "She is my wife, and I will have her!"

I struggled to haul Karen away from him, but my sneakers started to slide on the carpet as Set slowly pulled us towards the mirror. I realised that he was stronger than both of us, and wondered what else I could do to save my sister.

"Smash the mirror," came Vaivea's voice in my head.

I looked around for something to use, and saw a chair in front of Karen's dressing table. I Levitated it over to us, and then flung it as hard as I could. It struck the mirror near the bottom, where the glass was still solid, the sharp crack and smash reverberating through our ears. Karen and I fell backwards as Set released his grip. Shards and fragments of glass tinkled down as we landed on the floor.

"Karen!" I cried, scrambling to my feet. "Are you okay?"

She lay completely still, barely breathing, her eyes squeezed shut.

"Is it gone?" she whispered.

"Yes, it's gone. Come on, get up before Newt comes to see what happened."

At mention of her son, she opened her eyes and got to her feet. I helped her over to the bed, where she sat, gazing sadly at the empty frame.

"Gran's lovely old mirror," she said with a shaky sigh. "I'm sorry. It was the only way I could get you free from him."

"From *him*? Do you know who that was, that... fiend that grabbed me?"

I hesitated to answer. I knew that once I started to explain about us being ancient deities who'd incarnated, I'd have to tell her everything else. And that thought sure was daunting. However, fate intervened.

"Mama?"

The small, scared voice from the doorway motivated Karen far more than anything I could say. She leapt up and hurried over to Newt, hugging him close.

"It's alright, darling," she crooned. "Mama just had a little accident, that's all. I'm okay now. Everything's alright."

I joined her by the door.

"How about I clean up this mess while you go and sit with Newt for a bit?"

"Okay. There's newspaper on the kitchen counter, and the vacuum cleaner is in the broom closet in the main bathroom."

Karen carried Newt back to the loungeroom, and I set about getting rid of the broken glass. I laid the newspaper down by the mirror, and carefully picked up the largest piece. Set's image formed in the fragments, his snout drawn back in a snarl.

"This isn't over, sister. I will have her, and you can't stop me!"

Before I could respond, he Disappeared. I continued picking up the pieces of glass, hoping he would back off for a while. Things were crazy enough for Karen without Set adding to her problems. I wrapped all the fragments in newspaper and put them in the bin, then vacuumed the bedroom thoroughly. With the chair returned to its place, and the bedsheet draped back over the empty mirror frame, the room looked just as it had when I first walked in.

Finally, I went to find my sister and nephew. Karen sat on one of the sofas in the lounge area, dabbing ointment on a number of scratches on her legs and arms whilst Newt snuggled against her.

"Thankfully, none of these are very deep," she said, finishing up. "I really don't know how I'm going to explain all of this to Eric..."

Her voice broke as she said her husband's name, and I put an arm around her.

"Let's not worry about that just yet," I said. "How about I

go and clean up, and then I'll give you a hand with dinner?"

"Sure. Take your time. I'm doing a casserole."

I did take my time, having a soak in the bathtub and then getting ready for dinner. By the time I returned to the kitchen, good smells were already wafting through the apartment. I helped Karen whiz up a packet of chocolate cake mix for dessert, and grinned as I watched Newt eagerly scrape the mixing bowl clean.

"It'll taste even better once it's baked," I told him, as he licked the mixture off his fingers.

A noise at the front door made us turn. Eric, tall, angular, and fair in a raw, reddish sort of way, stood awkwardly by the entrance to the kitchen.

"Honey," Karen said brightly. "You remember my sister, Ange?"

"Er, yes, I do," he replied in a tone that implied he'd rather not. "Ange – I expect Karen has made you comfortable."

It sounded more like an accusation than a question.

"Sure," I replied. "Thankyou both for having me."

Eric pursed his thin lips, gave a curt nod, and turned for the main bedroom. Karen finished up in the kitchen whilst I set the table for dinner, and after Eric had showered and changed, we sat down to eat.

Eric barely said a word during dinner, a thick lamb casserole that had been one of Gran's recipes. Newt also devoured a small bowl of the stew – even the vegetables – and pronounced it to be 'very yum'.

Karen and I tried to make small talk, though it was difficult to ignore Eric's thinly disguised hatred. I wondered exactly what I'd said or done to deserve this attitude, and thought back over the few times we'd met or spoken. Sure, I'd never thought much of him, and I believed Karen could have done so much better than this blunt, humourless fellow. But he could've tried to be more likeable.

After dinner, Karen washed up and I dried. Once Newt had been bathed and put to bed, I brushed my teeth and hit the sack myself, ready for an early night. I hoped I wouldn't wake up from a regression screaming or crying in the middle of the night and scare the poor child to death, but morning came and the peace hadn't been shattered. I allowed myself the luxury of sleeping in until Eric had gone to work, then I freshened up and dressed before stumbling to the kitchen looking for coffee.

"Wake up, sleepyhead!" Karen said, pushing a freshly made mug in front of me.

"Wanna hand with breakfast?" I mumbled through a yawn.

"No, its nearly done. Eric's had his and gone to work, but I've got something special for us."

Karen had grilled croissants with ham and cheese, put out freshly baked banana bread, some strawberries and cream, and more freshly brewed coffee. These treats went a long way towards lifting our spirits. Afterwards, Karen set Newt at the dining table with a sketch book and crayons. She turned to me with a resigned look on her face.

"So, you've got more to tell me," she said, nodding towards the loungeroom. "Better get on with it, I guess."

Before we could move, a knock sounded at the apartment door. Karen went to answer it. I heard muted voices, and she returned, followed by Lou.

"You!" I cried, nearly jumping out of my skin.

I frowned as I saw his tradesmen's overalls, toolbox, and the I.D. badge on his chest. Gran glowered, Karen looked puzzled, and Newt craned to see who it was.

"The plumbing is faulty," Karen said. "We've been on the waiting list for ages."

"At your service, ma'am," said Lou, and turned towards the kitchen sink.

"Whoa, you can't just walk in here pretending to be a plumber," I said, planting myself between him and the sink with my hands firmly on my hips. "I don't want you here. You leave us alone. Or else!"

"Ange!" Karen cried. "I don't know who you think that is, but he's here to fix the pipes and he's not going until he's done it!"

"Look, I know this – person," I explained. "He's not who he says he is. Trust me, you don't want him in your home."

Karen blanched. She picked Newt up and held him close, as much to comfort herself as him. Mama and Gran floated either side of her, as though to protect them.

"I'm sorry, Mr Cypher," Karen said. "I honestly don't know what to think."

I turned on him and peered at his I.D. badge. It said 'Lou Cypher'.

"For crying out loud, you didn't even bother to give a fake name!"

"This is the name I'm known by," he answered, wearing his best poker face.

"Right!" I hissed back. "That's it!"

I Wished us to the top of the nearest skyscraper. An icy wind gusted around us, and I shivered. Lou didn't. For someone from hell, he sure didn't seem to mind the cold.

"Bracing, isn't it?" he stated, and breathed in deeply.

"Cut the crap. What were you doing at Karen's?"

"Oh darling, what have I got to do to see you these days?"

"Rot. You've never had any trouble intruding on my life before."

"Intruding? Am I not welcome?"

"You know you're not. Especially around Karen and Newt."

"Not that I'd call that tiny apartment ideal, ma cheri. There was a veritable crowd in there."

I counted in my mind, and realised that − with the dead as well as the living − there were Gran, Vaivea, Patsy, Karen, and Newt, besides myself and Lou. And next to Set, Lou was the last entity I wanted anywhere near my sister and nephew. Then I realised something else.

"Oh no!" I cried. "They'll be wondering what the heck happened to us!"

2.

"Allow me," Lou said.

Instantly we were back in the apartment. Karen hadn't moved, but her face was ashen and she shook like a leaf. Newt ran around, excitedly poking into all sorts of unlikely places. Looking for us, I realised.

"Karen, I'm so sorry," I said, and moved forward to put my arms around her.

She stepped back and stared at me hard.

"Who are you?" she asked, her voice a whisper.

My heart squeezed painfully.

"It's me. Ange. I didn't mean to scare you or Newt."

"Oh, Newt's okay. He thought it was a neat trick. Wish I knew what to think!"

Her eyes then sought out Lou.

"And you. I don't know who or what you are either, Mister, but I don't feel like having strangers in my home just now."

"As you wish."

Lou bobbed his head, then turned and nodded at the sink.

"Oh, and your little plumbing problem is fixed. My gift to you."

He slowly faded away before our eyes.

"Wow!" exclaimed Newt. "How'd he do that?"

"Er, magic," I said. "Do you like magic?"

"Yes! Yes!" he replied, and clapped his hands. "I *love* magic!"

"Do you want to do some more drawing, sweetheart?" Karen said shakily.

Newt grinned and went to his sketch book. Karen took my arm and dragged me down the corridor to her bedroom again. Once there, she rounded on me.

"What kind of trick was that? How'd you do it? And who was that man if he wasn't the plumber?"

"Whoa, sis, please! I didn't mean to do it. I was so angry at him turning up here, I wasn't thinking straight. Just trust me, he's someone you don't want to know."

"But what happened? It's like you've turned into some kind of witch all of a sudden, and it's freaking me out!"

"It's not like that," I said, shuddering at her use of Adio's favourite derogatory name for me. "I'm not a witch."

"You studied paganism," Karen said. "And other witchy sort of stuff."

"Yeah, but I could never do magic their way."

"Their way? What do you mean?"

"Look, I only learned how to really do magic since Gabe's accident."

"But how? If you're not a witch, what the heck are you?"

The last thing I wanted to do was to tell her, and risk losing my sister forever. I had to prove it. So I took a deep breath, grabbed her hands, and Wished. Karen squealed in fright as we re-Appeared inside Newt's bedroom.

"What happened? How did we get here? Did you do that?"

Karen seemed petrified, although her mouth worked just fine.

"Yeah, I know it's a big shock," I said. "I was the same the first time I got Wished somewhere."

"You *got* Wished? You mean, there are others out there who can just Wish people all over the place?"

I couldn't help but smile, despite her obvious discomfort with the idea.

"It's not like that. Well, I don't think it is. At least..."

I realised I still didn't know didley about what I was doing. I sighed.

"Karen, I know it's a big ask, but you have to trust me on this. We may have been born mortal, but we have a special gift that I've only just started learning about."

"We?" Karen squeaked.

I started to worry that she would faint, or have a heart attack, or otherwise flake out on me. I Wished us back to her bedroom, and she jumped again as she saw where we were.

"Oh my God, would you please stop it? This is the freakiest thing that's ever happened to me!"

"Sorry. You looked like you needed to sit down."

"Sit down? I think I need a Valium!"

"Okay. I'll talk. You listen. And please, don't judge. All this is really true. I can prove it... Okay?"

She took a deep breath and nodded.

"Okay," I said. "Once upon a time in Egypt..."

"Egypt?"

"Sshhh. Once upon a time in Egypt, there were a God and Goddess called Geb and Nut, who had four children – Isis, Osiris, Nephthys, and Set. When they grew up, Isis and Osiris married, and Nephthys and Set married."

Karen looked sceptical, but at least she'd stopped interrupting me.

"Set hated Isis and Osiris with a passion. He murdered Osiris and tried to take the throne of Egypt, but had to battle Horus, the son of his brother and sister, for it. You follow me so far?"

"Yup."

"Right. Well, eventually Horus won and he ruled Egypt. And Isis forgave Set all his evil, and became a great icon of compassion and the ultimate feminine virtues. Osiris ruled the underworld, along with Anubis, who was the son of Nephthys and..."

Here I stopped. Not because I didn't know what came next, but because I did. And it disturbed me big time.

3.

"Set?" Karen guessed.

"No," I said slowly. "Set never fathered any children."

I wished I could stop thinking. I didn't at all like what was going on in my head. I looked into Karen's eyes, and saw only more questions.

"Well, the long and the short of it is that they were all real, and that they've reincarnated in human form. And we're them."

Karen blinked.

"What do you mean?"

"Just what I said. I did a past life regression with Amy, and found out I'm Isis."

"You really believe that?"

"How else do you explain my powers? I can do lots more, too. Wanna see?"

I Wished a mug into my hand, and it appeared. Karen recoiled, still frightened and unsure.

"Take it, its chamomile tea. Like Gran used to make."

Gingerly, she reached for the mug, and I gave it to her. She sipped cautiously.

"Karen, it's okay. I'd never put you in any danger. Part of the reason I came here was to protect you. We can even pop out for just a moment while Newt's busy drawing. He'll never know we were gone."

"No way – I can't leave my baby! Anything could happen to him."

"Look, we'll only be gone for a few minutes, if that. Gran and Mama can keep an eye on him. I really need you to see something."

She eyed me suspiciously, and I despaired of ever convincing her.

"You promise?" she said. "Nothing bad will happen to him?"

"I promise."

She sipped the tea again, deep in thought.

"Where do you want to take me?"

"There's someone I think you should meet. Ready?"

She put the mug on the dressing table and placed her hands in mine. She still shook, and I realised she was terrified. But she put her bravest face on and waited for me to do it. So I did.

We Appeared in the blink of an eye, although Karen chose not to look. I also took the precaution of Wishing the door locked, as it was broad daylight, and I wasn't sure Karen could cope with Invisibility on top of everything else.

"Hey, we're here," I said.

Karen opened her eyes, and they widened in surprise as she looked about.

"It's a hospital room," she said in wonder.

Then she saw the figure on the bed.

"Yeah," I said. "Welcome to Jacksonville, Florida. And say hello to Gabe."

She approached the bed slowly, cautiously, as if afraid she'd wake him.

"He's still in a coma," I said sadly.

I moved to the head of the bed and stroked Gabe's face. Most of the bandages were gone now, and his shaved hair had grown out. But his eyes were still closed, his chest still rose and fell with the pumping of the ventilator, and his aura seemed just that little bit dimmer than it had been the last time I saw him.

"Gabe, I'm here," I said. "I love you."

The words came automatically, well-worn and comfortable. But with the suspicions I now harboured, I wondered if that might change. I looked over at Karen. Her eyes were locked on Gabe's face, and an unreadable emotion had swept over her.

"Gabe, I've brought Karen to meet you. Karen, this is Gabe. And also Osiris."

She glanced at me, then back at Gabe.

"And Gabe, Karen is our sister Nephthys."

I heard her sharp intake of breath, but her expression remained unchanged. I wondered what was going on in her head.

"But maybe introductions aren't necessary?"

I think it was the scariest question I'd ever asked in my life, and I dreaded the answer. The silence stretched on as Karen stared at Gabe. I tried to keep one eye on each of them, as the clock on the wall ticked unnaturally loudly. At last Karen gave a little sigh and looked at me regretfully. A tear crept down one cheek.

"Oh Ange, I'm so, so sorry."

I waited, barely breathing at all. I knew what she was going to say. I knew the truth, and I desperately wished not to hear it. I tried to stretch out time, as though it wasn't at breaking point already. But the silence couldn't last forever, and with a strangled sob, Karen broke that silence and my heart with her next words.

"It's him, Ange. The guy I slept with on the night of my bridal shower. Gabe is Newton's father."

4.

In the minutes after we'd returned to the apartment, silence engulfed us. Neither of us could think of anything to say, and I'm not entirely sure either of us could've forced out a word without cracking the fragile air around us just like Gran's mirror. For once shattered, it could never be put back together again.

To give us both some space, I went and tidied my belongings in Newt's room. Karen occupied herself in the kitchen whilst Newt kept colouring with his crayons on the dining room table. When I was done, I wandered over and looked at his work.

"Gee, you're doing great," I said. "You've hardly gone

outside the lines at all."

"Must get it from his father," Karen said. "Oh..."

Her words had been automatic, just as my words of love to Gabe had been. What made it so much worse was her sadness when she realised what she'd said. While Newt's paternity was still anonymous, it was easy to think of Eric in that role, as he'd been there all along. But now that we knew who the father was, accepted ideas would have to change to reflect the new reality. And that would take time.

"Karen?" I said, and went to her. "It's okay. I'm not mad at you or Newt. It's just one of those things."

"Ange... I don't know what to think. Or say. Or do. I never meant to hurt you."

"I know. It's no one's fault. It happened years before I even met Gabe. How could any of us have known?"

"Yeah, but all the same, you must feel pretty torn up."

I didn't need to think twice about her words to know that she was right. I felt like all the air was knocked out of me, that I was doomed to walk around as a two-dimensional person for the rest of my life. My brain just couldn't cope with the emotion of it all, and I knew that once the shock wore off, I'd be the biggest mess around. But I'd cross that bridge when I came to it.

"Look, I don't want to fall into the trap of blaming, or begrudging, or feeling sorry for myself. I do feel bad, but what's done can't be undone, so I guess we'll all just have to get over ourselves and make the best of it. After all, we've still got each other."

"You still want to be my sister?" Karen asked.

"You still want to be mine?"

Karen's lips twitched, and her irrepressible smile broke

forth.

"Donkey."

"That's the spirit," I said, and we held each other tightly for the longest time.

Finally Newt came and pulled at Karen's arm.

"Are you okay, Mama?"

"Yes, darling," Karen answered.

She sank onto the nearest chair and pulled him close. After a moment, he giggled and pulled free. Gran and Mama floated nearby, and Newt waved at them.

"I wish you wouldn't do that, darling," Karen said, her eyes darting about.

"It's alright, Mama. They want to be friends."

She looked at me, clearly disturbed.

"Who – Gran Jones and Mama? You can see them, right?"

"Yep. Clear as day. Right over there by the window."

"Okay, if you say so."

Newt returned to his colouring in, so Karen made us mugs of coffee and we sat out on the patio. A lazy breeze stirred the distant palm trees, and a variety of yachts and pleasure cruisers bobbed gently in the marina below. It was almost a shame to spoil the tranquillity with talk.

"So you see and hear Gran all the time?" Karen asked.

"Yes."

"Where is she now?"

"Right beside you. Do you see the air shimmering?"

Karen turned to look.

"I don't think I see anything."

"It helps if you soften your eyes a bit, like they're slightly out of focus."

She tried again, and a strange look crossed her face. I knew she had picked it up.

"And Mama?"

"She's not here right now. She might be hanging around dad, but apparently he had the house blessed to try and keep her from bugging him."

"Oh my Lord."

"My guide's here too," I said, as I sensed Vaivea's presence. "He's a Cheyenne Indian shaman called Vaiveahtoish."

"Ahem."

"Got some ectoplasm stuck in your throat?" I asked.

"You know I am not your personal guide. I am only here until your true guide is ready to be revealed."

"Sorry, forgot," I said. "Anyway, if Karen can see Gran, can't she see you too?"

"Perception of entities and energies depends on what each spirit presence desires the individual to see," he said. "Becoming visual on your plain requires much energy, which is not an efficient way of communicating."

"Boy, you sure are stuffy today. Why the big lecture? I can see you both whenever you're with me."

"You have the powers of a great Goddess. We need not make any special effort for you to visualise us. A skill your sister is yet to learn."

"Oh."

"Your guide is now ready to become known to you."

"Oh, good! It's about time – is it Amy? Or Michael?"

"You have no further need of me, so I have been assigned new duties. Goodbye, My Lady."

I felt a pang of sadness. Vaivea had taught me a lot, for which I was grateful.

"Goodbye, Vaivea. Thankyou, thanks for everything."

His presence faded away, and I blinked back sudden tears.

"Now that's no way to greet your guide."

I didn't bother to turn. I'd know that voice anywhere. And my heart sank like a tonne of bricks.

"Heaven help me," I said.

Lou lounged against the balcony rail, suave in black leather and dark sunnies. Karen could see him, and got the shock of her life.

"You! The plumber! Ange, what on earth's going on?"

I sighed and took a long sip of coffee. It didn't help me think of an easy way to explain, but it gave me a few seconds to get myself under control.

"So this is what it all boils down to? You can't get me one way, so you just find another."

"Oh ma cheri, you must have known I'd get you in the end."

"You planned it all..."

"Oh contraire! This wasn't my doing – it was pre-ordained."

I felt like laughing, only it wasn't funny. Karen looked completely baffled.

"How can you have a plumber for a spirit guide? He's not even a spirit... is he?"

"Well, he's certainly not a plumber," I said. "Karen, this is Lou. His annoying presence has bugged me since I visited Amy. He's not a spirit, he's... an angel."

Karen switched from baffled to stunned. She looked him up and down, and I could tell she liked what she saw.

"Oh. But why do you say he's annoying? I thought angels were full of love and light and were there to help us."

Lou waggled his eyebrows up and down and smiled seduc-tively. I would've puked if I'd had the energy. Instead, I sighed.

"Karen, that's most angels. This angel is not most angels. Take it from me, he's got annoying down to a fine art."

"Darling, I have most things down to a fine art," Lou said with a sleazy smile. "Especially the things that most of my brethren are not noted for."

Karen switched back from stunned to baffled. I heartily wished I could blast Lou into nothingness, leaving only a puff of smoke and a singed smell. However, I kind of knew that it wasn't good etiquette to Disintegrate one's spirit guide, no matter how much one disliked him. The look on my face must've said all of that and more, because Lou was suddenly keen to leave.

"I've just got one thing to say to you, ma cheri," he said in a low voice. "I, Lucifer, am your spirit guide whether you like it or not. This was decided by a power higher than I, and higher, believe it or not, than your own sweet self. It is non-negotiable, so I suggest you get used to the idea and deal with it so we can work together for your good and mine."

I raised an eyebrow. I really wanted to react in a grander way, and I certainly wanted to say something about it, but in the end, I just couldn't summon the enthusiasm. At least Karen looked shocked at learning Lou's true identity.

Then, he Disappeared.

Afterword

Thankyou for taking the first part of the journey with Ange. I very much hope that you have enjoyed the story so far. I have a couple of things to add that might be of interest – a glossary of terms relevant to Ancient Egypt and it's religion, and also a glossary of the wonderful music of the 1960's (and 1950's) that has appeared in this book.

Ancient Egypt Glossary:

Isis: (Eeset, Ahset, Eesay) Regarded as the great mother goddess of ancient Egypt, Isis was the sister and wife of the god Osiris. Together they played a major role in many stories in Egyptian mythology, particularly in myths about rebirth and resurrection. The cult of Isis became very popular in Egypt and eventually spread to other parts of the Mediterranean world, including ancient Greece and Rome.

Osiris: (Asar, Wesir, Ausar, Unnefer, Usir) Osiris, god of the dead and the underworld Duat, was one of the most important deities in ancient Egypt. A fertility god in the Pre-Dynastic Period, he had by about 2400 BCE become also a funerary god and the personification of dead pharaohs. With his sister-consort Isis and their son Horus, he formed the great triad of Abydos (about 520 km south of Cairo). He was credited with teaching the skills of agriculture to the Egyptians.

Nephthys: (Nebthet, Neber-Het, Nebet-het) Nephthys was typically paired with her sister Isis in funerary rites because of their role as protectors of the mummy and the god Osiris and as the sister-wife of Set.

Set: (Seth, Setesh, Sutekh, Setekh, Suty) a god of the desert, storms, and foreigners. In later myths he is also the god of darkness and chaos.

Anubis: (Anoup, Anpu) The son of Nephthys and either Set or Osiris, who is depicted with the head of a jackal. Depicted as a protector of graves as early as the First Dynasty, Anubis was also an embalmer. One of his prominent roles was to usher the souls of the dead into the afterlife. He attended the weighing scale during The Weighing of the Heart.

Ennead of Heliopolis: Group of twelve deities who were worshipped at Heliopolis, located near where Cairo is today.

Kemet: The ancient Egyptian name for the land of Egypt.

Ka: A principal aspect of the soul of a human being or of a god, similar to 'life force' or 'essence'.

Was Sceptre: A symbol of power or dominion, associated with ancient Egyptian deities such as Set or Anubis as well as with the pharaoh.

(Various sources; attributions available on request)

Music Glossary:

Chapter 1.
   Something In The Air – Buffalo Springfield (1969)
   Give Peace A Chance – Plastic Ono Band (1969)
   Get Together – The Youngbloods (1967; re-released 1969)
   People Gotta Be Free – The Rascals (1960)
   The Girl From Ipanema – Sergio Mendes (1964)
   Crosstown Traffic – Jimi Hendrix (1968)
   Angela Jones – Johnny Ferguson (1960)

Chapter 2.
   She's A Rainbow – The Rolling Stones (1967)
   Incense & Peppermints – Strawberry Alarm Clock (1967)

Chapter 3.
   Season Of The Witch – Donovan (1966)

Chapter 4.
   Good Morning Starshine – Oliver (1969)
   Rhythm Of The Falling Rain – The Cascades (1963)
   Spooksville – The Nu-Trends (1963)

Chapter 5.
   Everybody's Been Burned – The Byrds (1967)
   Monster Mash – Bobby 'Boris' Pickett & The Crypt-Kickers (1962)

Chapter 6.
   Over, Under, Sideways, Down – The Yardbirds (1966)
   The Purple People Eater – Sheb Wooley (1958)

Chapter 7.
    Goin' Up The Country – Canned Heat (1968)
    Get Back – The Beatles (1969)
    My Cherie Amour – Stevie Wonder (1969)
    My Generation – The Who (1965)
    Sympathy For The Devil – The Rolling Stones (1968)
    The Blob – The Five Blobs (1958)
    Rockin' In The Graveyard – Jackie Morningstar (1959)
    I'll Do My Crying In The Rain – Everly Brothers (1962)

Chapter 8.
    King Midas In Reverse – The Hollies (1967)

Chapter 9.
    Strange Days – The Doors (1967)
    Delilah – Tom Jones (1968)
    Que Sera Sera – Doris Day (1956)

Chapter 10.
    Suspicious Minds – Elvis Presley (1968)

Chapter 11.
    Magic Carpet Ride – Steppenwolf (1968)
    The Witchdoctor – David Seville (1958)
    He's A Vampire – Archie King (1959)
    Strange Brew – Cream (1967)

Chapter 12.
    Wild Thing – The Troggs (1966)

Chapter 13.

Voodoo Woman – Simon Stokes & The Nighthawks (1969)
Baby Please Don't Go – Them (1964)
House Of The Rising Sun – The Animals (1964)
Dracula's Daughter – Screaming Lord Sutch (1964)

Chapter 14.
Keep On Running – The Spencer Davis Group (1965)
We've Got To Get Out Of This Place – The Animals (1965)
Running Scared – Roy Orbison (1961)
Night Of Fear – The Move (1968)

Chapter 15.
Time Is Tight – Booker T And The MG's (1969)
Danger! Heartbreak Dead Ahead – The Marvelettes (1965)
Raindrops Keep Fallin' On My Head – BJ Thomas (1969)
The Rain, The Park And Other Things – The Cowsills (1967)
Lightnin' Strikes – Lou Christie (1966)
Rain – The Beatles (1966)

Chapter 16.
Windy – The Association (1967)
Jack The Ripper – Screaming Lord Sutch (1963)
Spinning Wheel – Blood, Sweat & Tears (1969)
Dizzy – Tommy Roe (1968)

Chapter 17.
(Get Your Kicks On) Route 66 – The Rolling Stones (1964)
I Was A Teenage Creature – Lord Luthor (1958)
House Of Horrors – Merv Griffin (1962)
The Graveyard – The Phantom Five (1964)
Dead – The Poets (1958)

Born To Be Wild – Steppenwolf (1968)

Ghost Guitars – Baron Daemon & The Vampires (1963)

Werewolf – The Frantics (1960)

Mr Werewolf – The Kact-Ties (1963)

Chapter 18.

The Burning Of The Midnight Lamp – Jimi Hendrix (1968)

I'm The Wolfman – Round Robin (1965)

In The Midnight Hour – Wilson Pickett (1965)

Lucifer Sam – Pink Floyd (1967)

California Sun – The Rivieras (1964)

Chapter 19.

Bad Moon Rising – Credence Clearwater Revival (1969)

Spooky – The Classics IV (1968)

I Dig You Baby – Bob McFadden (1959)

Beware – Bill Buchanan (1962)

They're Coming To Take Me Away – (1966)

Chapter 20.

She Said She Said – The Beatles (1966)

About the Author

Lana Lea is a poet, artist, designer, short story writer, and author of retro-fantasy and high-fantasy novels.

Drawing on a lifetime of studying history and mythology, Lana writes fantasy that artfully weaves character-driven storylines with fascinating and fantastical motifs in past eras.

Lana freelances as an editor and proof-reader, participates in National Novel Writing Month every November, hosts creative writing and poetry workshops, and runs the Generation XYZ Writing Group.

Lana lives and works in Rockhampton, Queensland, and loves nothing more a good coffee, a good book, and spending time with her cats.

And with her ever-patient and supportive husband.

You can connect with me on:
🌐 https://www.lanaleaauthor.com
📘 https://www.facebook.com/lanaleaauthor

CPSIA information can be obtained
at www.ICGtesting.com
Printed in the USA
BVHW081128040321
601713BV00001B/40